ALSEA RISING

THE SEVENTH STAR

FLETCHER DELANCEY

HEARTSOME PUBLISHING

For all those who love.
You bear within you a spark of the divine.

When our sea-dwelling ancestors forgot the importance of family and lost their future children, they cried out to Fahla to save them. Our Goddess wept, for she could not repair the damage they had done themselves. Instead, she offered a second chance. She gave them new bodies to bear the next generation, imbued them with her divine spark, and bid them leave their cities in the sea to build new lives on land.

We are those children. Yet we did not learn from the mistakes of our parents. We made similar foolish choices, chasing status and limiting love to the forms which met our approval. We forgot that love is divine. As our ancestors lost their children, so we lost our divine tyrees.

Once again, Fahla could not heal our self-inflicted wounds. Instead, she brought us children of the stars, who carried seeds that replanted our divine tyrees. But with those seeds came great danger. With them came other star-children, who envied Fahla's gifts and sought to abuse them.

Even our Goddess cannot save us from our mistakes. But she can give us the means to save ourselves, if we will but remember her lessons: Family is paramount, and love is divine.

Lanaril Satran
The Book of Verity

CONTENTS

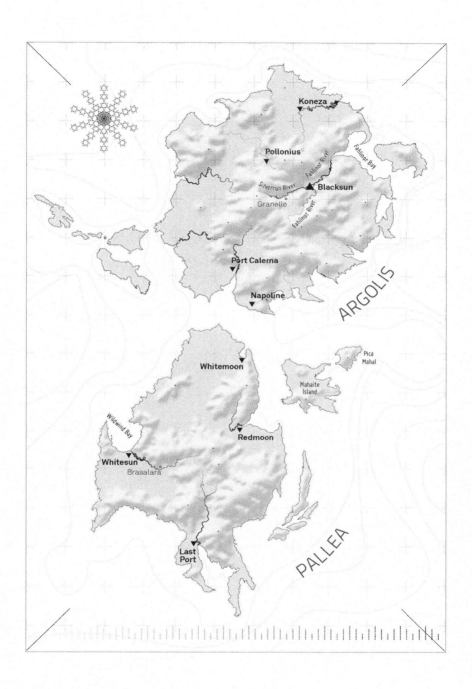

1

LAUNCH

Commander Cox didn't speak a word as he led Rahel into the lift. She stepped in and turned, keeping her eyes forward.

"Sedated, eh? Not what I thought you'd do."

She relaxed her rigid stance. From the moment he entered the bridge, she had sensed his admiration, colored with concern and a thread of envy.

"What did you think I'd do?"

"One quick swing with that stave would have put the captain in charge."

"It would have been more satisfying," she admitted. "But worse in the long term."

"That's for damned sure. Shuttle bay."

Her head snapped around. "I thought we were going to the brig."

"Captain Serrado didn't order me to put you in the brig. She ordered me to take you off her bridge, which I have done. She also wanted you deported at the first opportunity. I'm doing that now."

Candini's fighter was in the shuttle bay.

Her first, joyous thought was that she would still fight this battle. Her second was a staggering realization.

Despite being taken by surprise, despite having less than a minute to come up with a plan, Captain Serrado had gotten her off the ship. Legally, safely, and without repercussions for anyone on her staff. No one could fault Cox for his interpretation of the orders. After all, they were on the cusp of battle. Candini's alternate gunner was on Alsea; there was no time to go back for him. Without a gunner, her effectiveness would be significantly reduced.

When the battle was over, Candini would return to base and Rahel would step onto Alsean soil a free woman. The politics would no doubt rage over her head as the Protectorate officially protested the lack of internal justice, but Lancer Tal would defend her—especially once she learned what Admiral Greve had tried to do.

She could still feel the oily weight of his anticipation. He had relished the moment as he set the trap, knowing Serrado would disobey an order that endangered two ships and their crews. He had used her honor against her.

The lift doors opened, revealing a hive of activity.

"Finally!" Candini shouted. She was already in her flight suit, jogging across the bay and pointing toward the locker room. "Get your ass in there and get suited up!"

"May your goddess fly with you," Cox said.

She wished she had more time. "And with all of you. Thank you, Commander."

In the locker room, she stripped down and yanked her suit off the hanger, thinking wistfully of the friends she was leaving behind. They deserved a better farewell than her sudden disappearance. Quantum com calls could not hold a candle to the warmrons that Gaians gave so freely.

Her change surely set a new speed record, yet when she raced up the ladder and landed in her seat, Candini gave an impatient huff.

"It's about time," she grumbled, tapping the controls to stow the ladder and seal the cockpit.

"Unavoidable delay." Rahel opened the storage beneath her seat and squeezed in her rolled-up Bondlancer's Guard uniform.

"Doing what, picking your ass? This is the real thing, Red." She pulled back on the control stick, guiding the fighter off the deck and toward the exit tunnel. "And since when do you bring that uniform with you? Is it some sort of good luck charm?"

Rahel snapped her harness in place and settled back to watch the green guidance lights. "You won't believe it when I tell you."

2

CALM BEFORE THE STORM

"Slow down, tyrina. They won't be here in the next five ticks."

Salomen tripped trying to shove a leg into her trousers and needed two hops to regain her balance. "They're a day early! I'm not ready! How are you so shekking calm about it?"

Even if they didn't share emotions, the use of profanity was a waving flag. Salomen rarely swore.

Tal crossed the room and held her by the shoulders. "Tyrina. Stop."

"There's no time—"

"There *is* time. You're allowing fear to override your logic." She pushed Salomen backward.

"What are you—stop this, I need to get my shirt on."

"You're lovely without it." Two more steps.

"There are no words to express how *not* in the mood I am for that."

She reached her goal and turned them in place. "Look."

Frowning, Salomen looked past Tal's shoulder. "At what?"

"The base. The trees. The Blacksun skyline. Look at the sunlight reflecting off the buildings. It's all still there."

"It might not be if we don't—"

"Salomen. Look at it. Breathe." She fumbled behind her back and threw open the window. Crisp morning air flowed in, carrying birdsong, warriors' voices, and the sound of rustling leaves. In another hantick, the morning breeze would die down and the still air of summer would begin heating up the day.

She looked into Salomen's eyes and inhaled deeply, then exhaled.

After a charged moment of resistance, Salomen followed suit. Her eyes slipped shut. "I'm afraid," she whispered.

"I know. It's all right."

"Everything depends on me." Her voice caught. "How can it be all right? The entire plan rests on my shoulders and I'm shekking terrified. It should have been you!"

"No." Tal brought their foreheads together. "It has always been you. Fahla chose you for a reason. I trust her wisdom, and I trust you."

Salomen collapsed against her, wrapping her in a desperate warmron. "What if I fail?"

"Then I will help you pick yourself up and we'll try again. You're not the missile, Salomen. You're the launcher. If you miss, we launch again. And again, until we succeed. It rests on *our* shoulders, not just yours."

She willed determination into the trembling body in her arms. Salomen had faced every aspect of this plan with unflinching courage, but until this morning, it had all been theoretical. Ekatya's quantum com call made it real. Her news that the Voloth had upended their battle plan made it terrifying.

"We're already at a disadvantage." Salomen straightened, wiping her eyes. "All those ninedays of preparation—"

"Ekatya will handle it. Trust her to be the warship captain she is. Everyone has their roles. Our fighters will work harder to defend the space elevator, Ekatya will take down as many ships as she can—none of that changes what *we* do. Our plan is exactly the same."

"Goddess above, I envy your battle experience."

"No, you don't." Tal could not imagine her peaceful bondmate drawing blood. This was the woman who cupped hairy watchers in her hands and carried them off the trail to safety. Tal wouldn't touch the things, but Salomen saw value in even the lowest forms of life.

"Perhaps not the experience," Salomen conceded, pulling the shirt over her head. "But the calm that comes with it."

Tal walked to the closet and retrieved their combat vests. Back at the windows, she dropped hers to the floor, then opened the other and held it up. "Fear is strongest when it has no competition. Once you make that jump, once you begin what you've trained for, you'll have a focus other than your fear. You'll still feel it, but it won't control you."

Salomen slipped her arms through and settled the vest in place. "So I can look forward to gibbering panic for another hantick or so?"

"Look at that." Smiling, she sealed the front and gave it a pat. "You're already halfway there. Making jokes is an excellent sign."

"It's not much of a joke," Salomen grumbled, but she moved with more of her usual fluidity as she picked up Tal's vest to return the favor. "Did we formally thank the Protectorate for sharing their flexible light armor technology?"

"Not exactly, since it wasn't the Protectorate that did the sharing. I did thank Lhyn."

"So did I." A quick smile crossed her face as she closed the seal. It was small but significant, and her emotions reflected the change. "These are certainly more comfortable than a cuirass."

"More practical, too. A little lacking in style." Tal caught her hands. "If you remember nothing else when things get tricky, remember this. A battle never goes exactly the way we expect. Plans are guaranteed to fall apart. What separates the victors from the rest is their ability to adapt."

"I've been practicing the same plan for a moon and a half and *now* you tell me to adapt?"

"I'm telling you that I'll be right there with you, helping you do it."

Salomen took in a deep breath and let it out slowly. "All right. Let's go meet the divine tyrees. You know you'll be repeating this speech to them."

"Without the hand holding, I hope."

They activated their earcuffs, officially ending their bubble of calm.

"Colonel Razine, Salomen and I are prepped and moving to the quad. Any updates from the *Phoenix*?"

"*Captain Serrado has engaged the enemy,*" Razine said. "*There are five destroyers and two heavy cruisers.*"

"More than two-to-one odds!" Salomen's fear rose once more.

"*I wouldn't worry, Bondlancer. It started at three-to-one. Captain Serrado has already vaporized a heavy cruiser, and the* Victory *and* Thea *worked together to take down a destroyer.*" Satisfaction rang through Razine's voice. "*We have the Savior on our side, and she's not fighting alone.*"

"Neither are we," Tal said.

3

RACING THE STARS

The *Phoenix's* fighters launched with them, just as they had in the last several war games, but the familiarity ended there. In their games, they had all flown to Alsea together. Sixty-one fighters traversing the distance meant that any missiles slipping past the *Phoenix* were easy pickings. Rahel had complained about having too few opportunities to take a shot.

Now she had none.

With the *Phoenix* moving up to support the *Victory* and *Thea*, Captain Serrado had ordered her fighters to take the ship's place. All sixty were arrayed in a defensive net, prepared to neutralize any missiles that came their way. Alone, Rahel and Candini sped toward Alsea.

"Not a single missile yet," Rahel observed. "The Voloth are picking their asses, as you would say. Why aren't they targeting the elevator?"

"They haven't done a damned thing we expected." Candini glanced at the battle grid display. "I don't like it. At all."

"Captain Serrado said they would study her tactics. That they'd be developing strategies to neutralize her. This has to be part of that, but I don't understand how."

"Or it's not part of their strategy and they don't have time to fire missiles our way because they're busy trying not to get blown to atoms. I bet they were expecting her to be closer to Alsea. They didn't think she'd be waiting for them."

"She wouldn't if Greve had his way." Rahel had known it was the right thing to do when she did it, but she hadn't expected such swift confirmation. Watching nine ships come out of base space—including three heavy cruisers that rivaled the *Phoenix* for size—had eradicated any tendrils of concern.

"Best thing you ever did," Candini growled. "I'd have shot him."

"No, you wouldn't."

"Fine, then I'd have introduced my fist to his face. Several times. And none of this dokshin about laying him gently on the deck. You should have dropped him to see how far his head bounced."

"I was advised against that."

"By the same person who got you that sedative? It was Lancer Tal, wasn't it?"

Rahel passed a finger over her lips, miming the movement of sealing an Alsean shirt.

"Asshead."

"It's cute that you still swear in Common. If it were just me, I'd tell you. I can't risk my, um, advisor."

"Yeah, I know. At least I can get a copy of the security logs. That footage will be on the black market by the end of the day." Her glee faded as soon as it had appeared. "Shek, are you seeing this? They're practically ignoring the *Victory* and *Thea* and going after the *Phoenix*. Maybe that's why they haven't targeted the elevator. Maybe their orders were to take out Serrado first, then focus on Alsea. It would explain the huge number of ships."

"Three-to-one odds." Rahel shook her head. "What a testament to her reputation. She must be greatly feared in the Voloth Empire."

"Hated, feared, same thing. She's the best and they know it."

Their quantum com activated in a voice-only call from the Fleet wing commander. *"New orders, Nightwing. We're joining you at the space elevator, both squadrons. Serrado's worried about the Voloth overleaping us if the battle breaks at the minefield."*

"Well, they haven't been doing anything else we expected," Candini said. "Come on over, the weather's fine."

4

LEFT BEHIND

Lanaril had lit six rows of oil bowls when someone walked to the rack nearest hers and began lighting their own.

She kept her head down, hiding her scowl. The temple was quiet at this hantick. With so few worshipers using the space, it was rude beyond belief to crowd her as this unknown person was doing.

They had probably recognized her, though she was not wearing her templar's tunic. If they were hoping for aid or wisdom from the Lead Templar, they would be sadly disappointed. She had none to spare.

She lit the seventh and eighth rows with increasing anger. The one time she needed her own respite in this holy place, and this dokker's backside couldn't respect it?

The ninth row went by in a silent litany of curses. By the time she finished the tenth, she was irate enough to show it. She slammed her wand of eternal flame back in its holder and turned, hands on her hips as she prepared to give a lesson in courtesy.

Lhyn Rivers looked up, startled. "Are you all right?"

"Great Mother." She had a chest full of anger and nowhere to direct it. "I didn't realize it was you. I was about to tell a rude blindworm where she could put her eternal flame."

"How could—oh. You have your blocks up." Lhyn replaced her wand with far more grace. "I'm sorry. I assumed you'd know it was me. I should have realized you'd be blocking everyone out."

"Why are you here?" Not until she saw Lhyn's flinch did she realize how that had sounded. "No, you have every right to find comfort in the temple. I only—" She stopped, trying to center herself. "Please ignore me. I'm not at my best this morning."

"Of course you're not. I'm not either. That's why I came, to ask if you'd like to wait with me." Lhyn stepped closer and held up her hands. "I know how it feels to be the one left behind."

Yes, Lanaril thought as their palms met. She knew exactly how it felt.

"We said our goodbyes when she flew down to Whitemoon Base." The words came unbidden, four days of stoic strength undone by a touch. "I thought I was doing well. No tears and no fear that she wouldn't come back. We had a Shared joining that morning, and I was . . ." She swallowed, a sudden tightness in her throat making her voice hoarse. "I was proud of myself for sending her away with a smile. I cannot smile now."

Lhyn interlaced their fingers and brought their hands down, turning a palm touch into a more intimate gesture of friendship. "She doesn't need you to smile now. She needs you to be there when she gets back. So we wait."

"I had no idea it would be so difficult. The waiting."

"It's the hardest thing in the universe. Ekatya is fighting right now, and she can't spare a piptick to reassure me or give me an update. I don't know what's happening. I can only imagine, and I have a vivid imagination."

"So do I, it seems."

"Come with me to Blacksun Base. It's where I waited during the Battle of Alsea. I thought it would be apropos."

Her shrug was unconvincing, but Lanaril appreciated the effort. "Ah, then it's only coincidence that Andira and Salomen are there."

"If I have to wait, I'd rather do it where I can see some of the action. And where I can be with the people I love." She saw Lanaril's hesitation and added, "If you're worried about Alsea Ascendant, Micah says he prefers to have you on the base anyway. He'll cancel your escort to the *Caphenon*."

Micah had made it clear that he considered her a high-priority contributor to Alsea Ascendant and should be housed with the Primes. She had insisted she could do more good with the greater numbers of evacuees being sent to the ship. Now, with the battle upon them, she was reconsidering.

"Please," Lhyn said quietly. "You should be in the safest place. And I need my friend."

She glanced at her oil rack, one hundred flames dancing in the air currents that drifted through the open temple doors, and realized that Lhyn's presence was no coincidence.

"I asked Fahla to guide those defending us today," she said. "And to guide me in knowing how I can best serve. Perhaps the key is not how many need me, but who needs me the most." She squeezed Lhyn's hands. "Shall we? Then I can be with the people I love, too."

Relief flowed through their touch. "All but one," Lhyn said.

"There are a few more scattered around Alsea. But in terms of those doing the fighting? All but one."

5

TAKING ODDS

Ekatya swiveled her command chair to the left, then to the right, then flipped it straight back in an effort to keep the battle in view. Lieutenant Scarp was putting her ship through its paces, spinning them away from the astonishing number of shield breakers that filled her display. She had given up trying to direct him. The battle was changing too rapidly; the delay between her order and his response could easily leave them vulnerable.

When this was over, she vowed, she would promote him to lieutenant commander. He had come a long way from the blushing pilot who took her brand-new ship out of space dock for its maiden voyage. His calm competence under a level of fire most pilots would never see was already a good enough reason. The fact that he had so far saved their asses twice was another.

As it turned out, she was not the only captain who had been drilling her crew in the Serrado Spin. The Voloth had copied the tactic and were performing it extremely well. She had never before been on the receiving end of it and was not enjoying the experience.

Fighting defensively was neither her preference nor her best skill, but there had been little choice once the Voloth recovered from their exit transition. Killing two ships in those precious few seconds had improved the odds, but not enough. Still, it could have been much worse. Had she left the *Thea* and *Victory* on their own, they would already be space dust. There was no doubt that the battle record would vindicate her decision and prove Greve's incompetence.

That didn't help, she thought grimly as the *Phoenix*'s automated defenses took out a swarm of shield breakers on their tail. Assuming she survived this battle, she would be sent back to Command Dome for yet another set of drawn-out proceedings in which personal and political agendas carried the same weight as the truth.

Merely imagining it made her furious. But fury kept her mind sharp, and she needed that now.

The *Victory* and *Thea* had diverted the attention of a heavy cruiser, swooping around it like small birds attacking a raptor and forcing it to defend itself. Two months of war games had molded Captains Kabbai and Teriyong into a formidable team, well used to working together against a larger opponent. Their tactics were successful enough that the cruiser's supporting destroyers had abandoned their harassment of the *Phoenix* and were now attempting to corner their Fleet counterparts.

Ekatya could not breathe easy, given the heavy cruiser and three destroyers she still faced. They desperately needed to reduce these odds.

"Incoming Delfin torpedoes, gamma-one-eight through ten!"

She spun her chair forward. On the battle grid overlaying her displays, four glaring yellow markers were curving in toward her bow, the size and vivid color representing their high threat.

The Voloth ships were working in concert, destroyers harassing her flanks while the heavy cruiser tried to break her bow shields. Yet Delfins at this point made little sense. Her shields were still intact; most of the explosive yield would be wasted.

But not all. With a start, she realized that the cruiser's captain was using Delfins in place of shield breakers.

Great galaxies, had the Voloth Empire discovered an asteroid made of teracite? She commanded one of the largest warships in Fleet, and even she had a limited number of Delfins in her armory. The necessary mineral for their construction was rare and difficult to refine, making each torpedo as expensive as a small shuttle. No one launched Delfins except as a ship-killing final assault. For the Voloth to fire them this early in the battle meant they carried unprecedented firepower designed for one thing: to get the *Phoenix* out of their way.

"Helm, hard to port," she ordered. "Team One, both tubes on incoming Delfin torpedoes. Starboard weapons, one tube on the Delfins and keep that destroyer occupied."

Her best weapons team was on the starboard side. If anyone could neutralize this threat, it would be Warrant Officer Roris and her team, but even they couldn't take out four at once. Each weapons room was equipped with two missile launch tubes; Roris's team didn't have enough time to reload and fire a second set. By diverting half her starboard weapons, Ekatya was giving an opening to the destroyer on that side.

She saw no other option.

Her automated defenses were already firing the rail guns, attempting to shoot down the torpedoes. It was pointless. Rail gun projectiles were ineffective against the heavily shielded Delfins. Only a missile could neutralize them.

A broadside of shield breakers and missiles appeared on the battle grid, the former targeting the destroyer and the latter tracking toward the Delfins. Two missiles were well in front of the rest.

Roris may as well have put her signature on them. Only her team would fire that quickly—and that accurately, Ekatya thought as two Delfins winked out of existence.

A second and a half later, the other two were hit.

Vibrations through her seat told of the impact on her own shields: the destroyer had taken its opening. A quick glance at her console showed the negligible result, thanks to her rail guns and the fact that the window of opportunity had been so limited.

"Show them our port side," she ordered. "Keep them busy."

She needed a little breathing room to flesh out an idea. If the Voloth wanted her that badly, she would oblige.

Two minutes later, she issued instructions to her weapons teams, navigation, and helm. It was another ten minutes before she saw the necessary configuration. A few taps to her console marked the bridge display with her intent.

"Helm, drop us in."

Lieutenant Scarp obeyed without question, despite her order putting them in a narrow space between the heavy cruiser and a destroyer. Where before her ship had been in constant motion, making itself a difficult target, it now appeared that she was gambling on a close bombardment.

Both the heavy cruiser and destroyer were at risk unless they moved away, but they had little incentive to do so when her ship was taking a far greater risk. As long as the *Phoenix* held position, it was easily targeted by the two nearest ships and the other two destroyers, which were swooping in to take advantage.

She would never have considered this had the *Victory* and *Thea* not kept the second heavy cruiser and its support ships occupied. Even so, the *Phoenix* was under assault on all sides. And they were ridiculously close to the destroyer, making it impossible to defend against its broadside. Her port shields were taking a beating.

But so were the shields of the destroyer.

She watched the display as a blizzard of weaponry flew between all five ships, though with a difference the Voloth captains should notice: her starboard weapons were not firing at the same rate as port.

"Come on, you asshead," she murmured. "I'm taking hits and something's wrong. Finish me off."

As if the heavy cruiser captain had heard, four more Delfins appeared on her display.

"There you are. Helm, prepare to jump. All hands, brace, brace, brace!"

"Ready," Scarp said.

The subtle hum of surf engines vibrated through her feet. Scarp was ramping up the engine power while keeping it disengaged from the drive.

"On my mark."

The Delfins screamed across space, certain death packed into metal cylinders and waiting only for release.

"Steady." Ekatya's eyes were locked to the battle grid as four yellow trails lengthened, growing ever nearer. "Steady . . . steady . . . mark!"

The battle grid blurred as the *Phoenix* accelerated abruptly, overwhelming the inertial dampeners. Ekatya was slammed into the back of her seat, then hurled forward against her battle harness when Scarp threw the engines into reverse. As he used their stopping power to slew the ship around, she sucked air into sluggish lungs and hoped her crew had taken the brace warning seriously.

Though warships were built for rapid jumps, this went well beyond normal operations. Command Dome would probably put a warning in her file for such a reckless move.

But it worked. One second after their jump, the Delfins passed through the space the *Phoenix* had previously occupied. Three seconds after that, they impacted the destroyer through its weakened shields.

Ekatya did not have the opportunity to see its destruction. Scarp had come about and executed the second jump, putting them back where they started but on the other side of the heavy cruiser. Had the calculations of her navigation officer been anything less than perfect, both ships would now be battle trash.

The heavy cruiser's automated defenses remained silent, confused by the massive target so near rather than the smaller and more distant targets it was programmed for. The other two destroyers also seemed baffled by the sudden disappearance of their target and its reappearance in the wrong place, as well as the ongoing disintegration of their sister ship. They had no clear shots until they could swing around.

With fierce pride in her crew, Ekatya called out the order.

"Fire!"

A broadside of shield breakers exploded against the cruiser's shields almost as soon as they were launched, so close were the two ships.

"Rotate!"

Lieutenant Scarp smoothly flipped the *Phoenix*, bringing their port weapons to bear.

"Shields soft," her weapons officer called.

Had that been a destroyer, the shields would already be gone. The much larger cruiser was harder to break.

"Port weapons, fire!"

A few lonely laser cannon bolts sizzled across the space. On the bridge of the heavy cruiser, the weapons officer must have turned to the one defense immediately at hand. Scattered shield breakers spat from individual weapons rooms, the efforts of desperate crew operating without orders.

Only four of her shield breakers were neutralized. The other forty-six slammed into their target.

"Rotate!"

"Shields redlined. Nose to tail," came the triumphant announcement.

The heavy cruiser's rail guns lit up, switched to manual control at last. A broadside of shield breakers—and two Delfin torpedoes—flew toward them at the same time.

That captain had made a fatal mistake.

With no shields remaining and the bridge officers rattled after blowing up their own destroyer, the only sane choice was to flee. But the Voloth wanted the *Phoenix*, and here she was, a target that couldn't be missed. Not only that, she had completed a Serrado Spin. The captain had made a reasonable assumption that her tubes were empty and she was momentarily open to attack.

They didn't know she had drilled her crew in a double spin.

"Starboard weapons, fire!"

Forty-two missiles streaked toward the heavy cruiser. Eight more converged on the more imminent threat, fired by the best teams on her starboard side. She had told them to expect the Delfins on this rotation, and they did her proud: both torpedoes exploded uselessly in the vacuum between their ships. The missiles not expended in that effort kept going, attracted by the massive target just beyond.

Thirty-eight missiles made it through the cruiser's defensive screen, sailed through its nonexistent shields, and slammed into the hull. Her own shields were impacted in the exchange, though with minimal damage. Her rail guns were already on manual, and their operators wiped out three-fourths of the cruiser's broadside.

"Rotate!"

The heavy cruiser was spouting great plumes of hull plating, internal structures, and atmosphere as it slid off the starboard side of her display, flew beneath her feet, and rolled up the port side.

"Port weapons, fire! Ready helm."

Her final broadside included three Delfin torpedoes. They streaked through space with their smaller brethren and met no resistance from the wounded ship.

"Go!"

The *Phoenix* shot away, putting much-needed distance between it and the shockwave that would soon follow. Ekatya spun her chair aft and had a beautiful view. The destroyer was now an expanding cloud of debris, and the heavy cruiser was dying. Three massive explosions at the bow, midship, and stern marked the impact of the Delfins, dwarfing the smaller strikes of the missiles.

The two destroyers that had previously targeted them fled the destruction, heading back to the one remaining heavy cruiser and its attendant destroyers. Ekatya gave the order to follow and sent a warning to the *Victory* and *Thea.*

Those destroyer captains had missed their chance. Unnerved by the sudden loss of two ships, they did not realize what a target she now presented. A double Serrado Spin was physically tiring for the weapons teams. Manual operation of the rail guns added stress and mental effort to the burden. In addition, every person on her ship was currently feeling the effects of two back-to-back jumps. Her chest hurt from the dual impacts into her battle harness, and her spine was grateful for the cushioning of her chair. She hoped that none of her crew had lost their bracing holds, or Alejandra would have her hands full with fractures and blunt force traumas. They desperately needed a few minutes to recover, and the frightened Voloth captains had given them exactly that.

She rubbed her chest and watched the glorious light show put on by the heavy cruiser. Had the yield of the Delfins been kept outside the hull, lack of oxygen would have snuffed the fireballs. That they continued to billow, with secondary explosions distorting their shape, testified to the destruction of the ship's integrity.

At last the flames faded, the oxygen supplying them having dissipated into vacuum.

Six seconds later, the fusion core blew.

The display automatically darkened, saving their retinas as a small sun burst into life. It grew exponentially, spreading into a brilliant, perfect sphere, then winked out.

Cheers rang throughout the bridge.

"And *that's* how you use Delfin torpedoes," Ekatya declared, setting off another round of whoops. "Helm, navigation, well done. We couldn't have timed it better. Serrado to weapons teams, beautiful job! They'll be teaching this to cadets next year."

She pretended not to see Lieutenant Scarp wipe the sweat from his forehead. He was entitled to a little nervousness after the fact.

Her console lit up with an incoming private transmission from the *Thea.*

"Fuck me and take me for a ride," Captain Teriyong said with a grin. "That was one Hades of a tactic."

"Liked that, did you? Too bad we'll only be able to use it once. They'll never fall for it again."

"Once was enough. They're down four ships now. I don't think they counted on losing two of their heavy cruisers. If we're lucky, one of them was their flagship."

They weren't that lucky.

The remaining heavy cruiser pulled out before the *Phoenix* could get there, followed so quickly by the last four destroyers that Ekatya knew there had been no sudden change of command. Whoever was directing this battle was on that cruiser.

All five ships streaked away, heading for Alsea at top speed.

6

BLACKSUN BASE

As the publicly acknowledged lover of the Lancer's Lead Guard, Lanaril had become familiar with Blacksun Base. Fianna had secondary quarters there, taking up residence whenever Andira needed to spend time on base. Despite its foreign nature—a small community made up entirely of warriors—Lanaril grew to enjoy it and even feel comfortable in its environs.

The location was inspiring, high atop a mesa surrounded by ancient forest. In the distance, Blacksun's skyline sparkled and winked with reflected sunlight in the mornings, sliced silhouettes into the sky at sunset, and glowed with life at night. Closer in, the towering trees sheltered a winding maze of trails. Fianna knew them all, and though Lanaril was born and bred in the city, she was learning to appreciate the quiet beauty of these woods.

But never before had her transport been escorted in by fighters. Never had she been obliged to wait in her seat until she was visually cleared by armed warriors with orders to be certain she was who she claimed to be.

"Our apologies, Lead Templar." The painfully young Guard stood back, holding her door. "Thank you for your patience."

"I understand." She stepped out to join Lhyn on the bricks of the landing pad. "It's an unusual day."

"That it is. We're glad you're here. Today of all days, we need the bless-ings of Fahla."

"Today of all days, she is watching over us." Lanaril smiled with an assurance she did not feel. It was enough. The young Guard grinned back, relaxing as he closed her door and rejoined his three fellow warriors.

Not until they were out of earshot did Lhyn speak. "Do you believe that?"

"Yes, of course. Now, if you ask whether I believe her regard is a guar-antee that neither of us will lose someone we love . . ."

"I'm not asking," Lhyn said shortly. "I know better."

They exited the landing pad and walked south along Aerial Way, an ancient road constructed when Blacksun Base was little more than a collection of wooden barracks. Though the barracks had long since given way to gleaming domes of glass and stone, Aerial Way was unchanged, its surface still paved with the original flagstones. It circled the base, hugging the cliff edges and wide enough for six warriors to run abreast. Fianna used it as a running route when she was short on time or wanted to enjoy the open views.

A cool breeze brushed past, laden with the dry, aromatic scent of the surrounding trees. Wisps of clouds lingered at the horizons; in another hantick, even those would be gone. Soon the breeze would cease and the heat of the day would begin.

If Lanaril closed her eyes, she could almost convince herself that it was a normal summer day. She would meet Fianna in a few ticks, and they would continue south, taking one of the trails that switchbacked down the mesa to vanish in deep forest.

With her eyes open, such imaginings were impossible. Straight ahead, just before the mesa's edge curved west, a Voloth ground pounder loomed over the road in menacing stillness. Three more were positioned at the southwest, northwest, and northeast corners.

"They look better in Alsean colors," she said, breaking the silence. "But I cannot stop seeing them for what they were."

"I know. I hate them, too. And these aren't the only ones here. They're just the visible ones." Lhyn swept her hand outward, indicating the carpet of trees below. "Andira said there are twenty more hidden away in there. This base is the most well-protected location on Alsea right now."

For good reason, Lanaril knew. Not only was their head of government here, but their secret and strongest weapon as well.

Divine tyrees, a weapon. It was anathema to her. She and Andira had argued about it, first good-naturedly, then with increasing depth of feeling until they agreed to leave the topic off the table. They valued their friendship too much to continue down a path that could only lead to damage.

Of all people, Alejandra Wells had been the one to help her see it in a different light.

"When we make a vaccine," she had said in one of their sessions, "we take a virus, modify it, and use it to our advantage. We take the most frightening, dangerous parts of life and turn them into a blessing."

"Yet this is precisely the opposite," Lanaril had insisted. "Taking the most beautiful blessing of Fahla and turning it into a dangerous weapon."

"No, no. Salomen is the healer modifying the virus. The virus is the lie the Voloth Empire tells its military. If she can take the power of that lie away from them . . ."

"I would never have thought of it in those terms."

"That's because you see the world in terms of its creator. I see it in terms of universal building blocks."

Lanaril gazed up at the motionless ground pounder. The base of its blocky platform hung twenty paces above the ground, and the platform was at least two stories thick. It was an enormous, terrifying weapon, yet all she could think was, *This is a virus we modified.*

"Rax is in that one," Lhyn said.

"He's here? I thought he would be in New Haven, keeping his people calm." She had grown to respect Rax Sestak, a quiet, unassuming man despite his role as leader of the Voloth Empire settlers. His pursuit of templar studies had earned the regard of many, and his protection of Salomen had earned the timeless gratitude of many more.

"Andira wanted him here in case she needs him in negotiations. In the meantime, he's acting as a consultant and backup weapons specialist."

Lanaril turned to look at her.

"I know, it surprised me, too." Lhyn was still watching the immense machine. "I'd have thought that would be his worst nightmare, acting against his own people again. He said his people are here."

There was immense depth of meaning in that simple statement.

"How things have changed," Lanaril said.

Lhyn tilted her head back, looking up toward the battle they could not see. "Not enough."

At the next cross path, they turned inward, winding past the administrative building and between barracks until they ended at a grassy quadrangle. The quad was the heart of the base, used for exercises, trainings, and games in the mornings and evenings. In the afternoons, it became a park where base residents ate midmeal and sprawled in the sun for a well-earned rest.

There were no shouts or chanted cadences this morning. Hundreds of warriors ringed the grassy verge, watching the group at its center. As Lanaril and Lhyn approached, the nearest Guards shifted aside to let them through.

The divine tyrees were sitting, standing, and lying beneath a large awning stretched across a temporary frame. It was not solid fabric but a screen, allowing for a clear line of sight to the skies above while providing shelter from what would soon be intense summer sun. At one side of the shaded area, Corozen Micah presided over a table heaped with equipment, supplies, and refreshments. Head Guardian Gehrain was with him, responsible for ensuring the safety of the tyrees. Fianna had reported his extreme disappointment at being denied the chance for glory that she and Ronlin enjoyed, but his rank dictated his responsibility.

What she had not said, but Lanaril understood, was that she and Ronlin were more expendable.

Learning of Fianna's role in this battle had been one of the worst moments of her life. For all her concerns about being courted by a warrior, the thought that her best friend would send her lover to die had not crossed her mind.

She had avoided Andira for five days, furious, heartbroken, and afraid of what she might say. On the sixth day, she had entered her study for the first appointment of the morning and found Andira waiting inside. With her front down and her emotions bared, Andira made it clear that Fianna was anything but expendable.

"It doesn't help," Lanaril murmured as they trod the close-cropped grass.

"What did you say?"

"Nothing important." Seeking a diversion, she added, "I never imagined seeing Salomen in a combat vest."

"Me either. But she looks great in it, doesn't she?"

"And that's something else I never imagined. If you're hoping to keep that relationship a secret, I advise you to never talk about Salomen around high empaths. Or mid empaths."

Lhyn stopped short. "You know."

"How can that surprise you?"

"You never said anything!"

"I was being *polite*." Glad to have something else to focus on, Lanaril faced her. "I thought you would tell me eventually."

Guilt filled the air as Lhyn kicked at a small seedhead. It exploded, tiny seeds dancing on the morning breeze as they drifted south.

"I wanted to." She looked up, meeting Lanaril's eyes with less remorse and more determination. "But it's still new. It changes practically every day. We're still trying to understand what we can do with it."

"What you can do with it? It's a tyree bond, Lhyn. Not a tool you can take apart to understand how it fits together."

Lhyn pointed to the divine tyrees. "That's a tool. And a weapon."

"Unfortunately. I mourn that it should be so, and hope the need will never come again. Nor do I believe this is what Fahla had in mind when she bestowed her gift."

"Do you think it's always a gift? Even if ours isn't, um, traditional?"

"By traditional, I assume you mean limited to two?"

She nodded.

"No templar worth their training would draw such simple lines. We are complex beings who carry the spark of Fahla within us, and Fahla is more complex than we can fathom. If your bond connects all four of you, it is not for anyone else to dictate whether it's acceptable."

Silently, Lhyn touched her hand, allowing the full impact of her relief and gratitude. "It doesn't connect all four of us," she said. "Well, it does, but it doesn't."

"I feel quite illuminated."

Amusement sparkled around her. "That was pretty nebulous, wasn't it? I mean, I love all three of them, but in different ways. Ekatya is mine in a way Salomen will never be, just as I'm hers in a way Andira will never be. But Salomen and I share things that Ekatya and I don't."

"And Andira?"

"The kind of friend I never imagined having. My chosen family. Not my lover."

"Intriguing." It was even more complex than she had thought.

"Salomen and Ekatya have the same sort of connection. No physical attraction, but a friendship so deep you'd think they grew up together." Lhyn was warming to her topic. "For me, Ekatya is fire and heat and passion. A love that challenges and changes me. Salomen is comfort and peace. She's a friendship that ignited, but where Ekatya is flames, Salomen is coals. A different, calmer kind of heat."

"Salomen is not coals around Andira. They're flames together."

"Right! All of these bonds are distinct, with their own characteristics and strengths. We call it a six-pointed bond. When we all Share together, we call it the seventh star." She drew a circle in the air, then stabbed her finger at an imaginary point near its top. "From the Shield of Alsea. The divine spark."

"Great Mother. The spark that healed you."

"I think it changed our brains. It didn't just heal me, it made structural changes in all of us. When we—" She stopped, brightening as she looked past Lanaril's shoulder. "Salomen. How are you feeling?"

"Terrified." Salomen came to a stop beside them and lifted both hands, greeting Lhyn first and then Lanaril. "Well met, Lanaril. Andira is hip deep in war council talks, but she asked that I apologize for her. She would have arranged for you to be here had she realized you wished it."

"I didn't know I wished it. Not until Lhyn came to find me."

"She has a way of seeing things we don't." Though Salomen's front was up, a sonsales could read the look she bestowed on Lhyn.

"I cannot believe any of you thought you could keep this a secret. For the love of Fahla, you may as well print signs and wear them."

The smile dropped. "What have you two been talking about?"

"Lanaril's perspicacity. She says you're a flame with Andira. Which you are."

"Are you speaking of the group Sharing?"

"No," Lanaril said. "You keep much behind your front, but love sits upon your face for anyone with eyes to see. And Lhyn has no front at all."

Though startled, Salomen recovered with admirable speed. "No, she doesn't. Neither does Ekatya. We knew it would come out at some point, but there hasn't been time to worry about the political repercussions."

With a sigh, she added, "I haven't wanted to think about yet another relationship being opened for public consumption."

"Two relationships," Lhyn corrected.

Salomen waved a hand in agreement.

"As a Lead Templar being courted by Vellmar the Blade, I certainly understand that," Lanaril said wryly. "I wish I could say it's no one else's concern. Unfortunately for that hope, you're the Bondlancer."

"I'm all too aware. I don't give a flying fanten what anyone thinks of me, but I do care what they think of Andira."

As if called by her name, Andira separated herself from the group and jogged over. "Lanaril, well met," she said rapidly, offering a double palm touch. She was proud, worried, and intensely focused as she turned to Lhyn. "Micah will bring out your combat vest and one for Lanaril. He'll also reiterate what I'm telling you right now: at the first sign of danger, you'll both be taken down to the war room."

"Andira—"

"This is not a discussion." She seemed to hear the tone of her voice and spoke more gently. "Even if you were willing to risk your own life, you brought Lanaril here. You're responsible for her."

"Is that why you suggested—you sneaky little shit!"

"Lhyn." Salomen set a comforting hand on her shoulder. "If the worst happens, Ekatya cannot lose all three of us. You know that."

"And if I lose all three of you? How am I supposed to live with that?"

Only now did Lanaril realize that Lhyn's acceptance, seemingly the product of experience, was in fact a thin veneer—and one that was rapidly disintegrating.

"The same way I might have to," she said. "You told me that waiting was the hardest thing in the universe. I came here with you because you're right, it is. So we will wait together. We'll face what comes together."

Lhyn looked skyward and shook her head, then faced Andira with a sizzling glare. "You'd better come through this intact, because I've got a few things to say about that manipulative dokshin you just laid on me." The glare crumbled when she reached out. "Please be safe."

Andira caught her hands and held them. "We're not a likely target. You know me, planning for all contingencies."

"I know." Lhyn's reddened eyes were the only outward sign of her fear. As she let go and reached for Salomen, Andira touched a finger to her earcuff and turned, giving them privacy while listening to whoever was currently demanding her attention. Lanaril had no such distraction, nor any excuse to leave.

"The whole idea of falling in love with a producer was that I wouldn't have to do this," Lhyn said, clasping their hands together.

"The whole idea?" Salomen's smile was soft. "I must have been mistaken."

"There may have been a few other tiny inducements. Very minor. Almost undetectable."

"Then I'm fortunate you're so skilled at seeing patterns and assembling the full picture."

"Do you know what I see in that full picture? The bravest shekking woman I know. You're not a warrior, but you're fighting. You're afraid, but you're fighting."

"You already had your fight." Salomen slid one hand along Lhyn's jaw. "And proved your courage. Let me go into this knowing one of us is safe, yes?"

"This is so unfair," Lhyn grumbled. "You're as bad as Andira. You just make it sound nicer."

"That might be the first time I've been accused of sounding nice rather than the opposite. Andira is right, we're low risk here. If the Voloth do send fighters this way, they'll target Blacksun, not the base. Injury or death is not what I fear."

"You won't fail."

"From your lips to Fahla's ears."

"She won't fail." Andira had rejoined them. "The *Phoenix* reported in. Ekatya took out two more ships. A destroyer and a heavy cruiser."

"Yes!" Lhyn chopped her hand through the air. "That's my Ekatya!"

"That's the good news," Andira continued. "The bad news is she scared them enough to run. They're on their way here. Ekatya's ships are harassing them every step of the way, but she says it's unlikely they'll get any kills in a running battle."

"Three against five." Salomen's lips compressed into a thin line. "We were hoping for better odds by the time they reached Alsea."

"It doesn't change the plan, tyrina. In fact, we have an advantage now. We know which one is their flagship. We know exactly where you should go."

7

SWARM

"What the Hades are they doing? I can't figure this out. There's a big piece missing."

Candini and Rahel were keeping station at their assigned location next to the space elevator cable, the lead fighter in a flight of four. Theirs was the lowest orbital position, close to a point of strategic concern: the port platform that anchored the cable. Whitemoon was also at risk, as a major population center nearby, but it was being guarded by a separate squadron flying in the lower atmosphere. Additional squadrons were supporting the original fleets of transports around Blacksun, Whitesun, and Redmoon.

"What piece?" Rahel asked. "The *Phoenix* fighters are here, we have the entire cable guarded—"

Candini pointed at the battle grid. "Their fighters. The heavy cruisers carried forty-five each. Where are they? They should have launched them at the minefield as soon as they saw the *Phoenix* fighters sitting out there alone. Yeah, they lost one cruiser right away, but if they'd launched immediately after, it would have been ninety against sixty. It was the perfect time to hurt the Fleet fliers before they could retreat back here. Now there are over one hundred and sixty of us up here and only forty-five of them."

"Maybe they miscalculated," Rahel suggested. "They waited too long, and now it's too late."

On the battle grid, eight ships swooped and dove in a deadly ballet that moved ever closer.

Candini scowled at it. "They haven't miscalculated much yet. Wiped out our minefield in one easy shot, upended two moons of planning—the stupidest thing was that heavy cruiser not running away before Serrado blew it to atoms."

"And blowing up its fellow ship right before." Rahel had only seen a representation of it on the battle grid, but that was a *glorious* tactic. Captain Serrado had the biggest horns in the galaxy.

"Yeah, but what I'm saying is, that was a captain's dumb decision. Not the battle plan. Their plan has been sound."

Rahel looked up through their transparent cockpit cover. The space elevator stretched away farther than she could see, dotted at regular intervals with four-fighter flights. "And you think their plan involves not releasing their fighters?"

"I think they'll release them when they get here. What I can't figure out is the strategy for holding them back. There has to be one."

Candini was a veteran of several battles with the Voloth. Rahel trusted her instincts. "You're making me nervous."

"I'm making myself nervous. I hate not knowing what they're thinking." With a frustrated growl, she activated the quantum com on the fighter command frequency. "This is Nightwing. I've got a feeling the Voloth are about to unleash something we didn't plan for. Stay alert. Expect the unexpected. Be ready to move."

"Helpful," Rahel commented when she signed off.

"If they're expecting dokshin to fall out of the sky, they won't be as surprised when it happens."

For all the forewarning, Rahel was still surprised when it happened.

The ships arrived in a whirl of sparking shields and flying weaponry, with the four Voloth destroyers teaming up on their Fleet equivalents. The *Thea* and *Victory* were focused on defending themselves, while the *Phoenix* held off the heavy cruiser and took shots at the destroyers whenever it could. It looked like a battle of attrition at this point, one that could easily be tipped either way.

The heavy cruiser broke off and ran, straight for Rahel and Candini.

"Oh crap," Candini said. "This looks—huh?"

The ship dove toward Alsea with the *Phoenix* in hot pursuit, descending far enough into the thermosphere for their shields to be outlined by friction heat. The two glowing spots carved out the base of a parabola and rose again.

On the battle grid, Rahel could see where that curve would lead them: right to the elevator cable.

"Shipper shit, it's a strafing run!" Candini activated the com. "They're going to strafe the elevator. Evade, evade! Get behind the cable!"

She slammed the control stick forward and shot away, leading their flight around the cable. Its shields would withstand the first strikes. Those of the fighters might not.

Candini swiftly positioned their fighter in a vertical stance, lined up with the cable and as close as she could get without touching its shields. The others found positions above them just in time.

The heavy cruiser sped out of the atmosphere, now flying parallel to the cable and spraying it with laser cannon fire in devastating bursts. The elevator's shielding lit up with blinding flares, but held—and protected the fighters sheltering behind it.

Watching the massive ship pass within a few kilometers, Rahel knew Candini's warning had saved lives. With their lack of space battle experience, she didn't think the Alsean pilots would have recognized that parabola for the start of a strafing run. Not until it became obvious, and by that time, it would have been too late.

"What in the ten purple fucks is that?" In her surprise, Candini spoke in Common. "It looks like they're ejecting a moon's worth of garbage."

A cloud of small objects were tumbling through space in the cruiser's wake. In the next moment, the *Phoenix* tore through them.

Brilliant bursts of light danced along its shields.

The great ship responded instantly, rolling away from the elevator and out of the main part of the cloud. Its missile launchers fell silent while the rail guns and laser cannons came alive, targeting the objects as it continued its chase.

"They're *mines*," Candini swore. "I've never seen anything like that!"

Their com lit up with a confirmation from the *Phoenix*'s weapons officer: the heavy cruiser was dropping thousands of tiny mines along the length of the elevator. They were of unknown configuration and appeared to be attracted not to pikamet radiation, but to the energy signature of shields. The *Phoenix* was destroying what it could, but the cruiser had to be its priority.

"Shekking wonderful. They won't have to sit here and fire at the elevator's shields; the mines will do it for them." Candini watched the cruiser as it continued its flight up the length of the cable. "I'll bet my best boots it's going to top out, come around, and make a second run down this side. And every one of those mines is a risk to us." She opened the com and barked out instructions. For each flight of four fighters, two would focus on neutralizing mines while the other two would run defense, keeping mines off the shooters' shields—and their own.

"This won't be anything like shooting drones," she warned. "They won't fire back at you, but they'll be trying to latch on to your shielding. And there are thousands of them. Don't get complacent and don't get caught. Now move before that shekking ship runs down our backsides. For Fahla and Alsea!"

She had their fighter in motion before she finished speaking, flying around the cable and straight for the swarm of miniature mines.

What followed was the most intense, adrenaline-filled, exhausting fight Rahel had ever been in. Their war games were nothing compared to this. Not even the Battle of Alsea matched it for sheer relentless pressure. The mines came at them from all sides, constantly chasing, and their numbers never seemed to diminish. She was using both fore and aft weapons, flipping back and forth more rapidly than she had ever been required to before. The mines didn't dodge fire like drones, but their smaller surface area made them difficult to hit.

Adding to the stress were the evasive maneuvers Candini was forced to fly. The fighters guarding them often veered away to save themselves, and they couldn't shoot mines that flew between them for fear of friendly fire damage. Candini was rolling, diving, and looping so much that Rahel couldn't remember what it felt like to fly a straight line.

Then it got worse.

As predicted, the heavy cruiser made a second strafing run. Rahel knew the *Phoenix* would try to stop it but couldn't spare a moment to glance at the battle grid. She only learned of its failure when the ship's weapons officer came on the com to warn them that another drop of mines was in progress—and that the cruiser had finally released its fighters.

"Shipper shit," Candini growled before calling out a new set of orders.

The *Phoenix* fighters continued to battle the mines, along with a third of the Alsean fighters. Candini took the remaining Alseans into combat with the Voloth.

It was quickly apparent that the mines recognized the Voloth fighters and left them alone, giving them an enormous advantage. They flew unimpeded while the Alseans battled both mines and fast, aggressive two-person fighters.

But Candini's forces held an advantage not even Fleet knew about: each of the flights she took into battle had one high empath gunner. While the other three fighters ran defense, the primary pilot worked to get within two or three kilometers of a Voloth fighter, depending on their gunner's personal ability. As soon as a fighter was in range, the gunner subjected its pilot to a paralyzing projection of terror.

The same weapon that had turned the Battle of Alsea was proven even more effective in space.

Neither the Protectorate nor the Voloth Empire knew the true range of high empaths. Lancer Tal had long ago planted erroneous data that projections couldn't reach beyond one to two hundred meters. The misinformation was particularly effective due to its method of dissemination: Lhyn's book, the galaxy's most widely read reference on Alseans.

Rahel had once asked Lhyn about her ethical comfort with that choice. After all, her devotion to academic integrity bordered on the religious. It had been strong enough to help her withstand torture.

"Before my torture, I don't know if I'd have done it," Lhyn said. "I might have asked Andira to find another way. But I spent two days having my bones broken because a Protectorate political party was afraid of Alseans. Not the Voloth, the Protectorate. After that, it was an easy decision. Am I comfortable with it? You bet."

What torture could not force from Lhyn, Lancer Tal received with a simple request. The results were playing out before Rahel's eyes.

Time after time, their flight chased down a Voloth fighter and watched it suddenly cease active movement, instead coasting on inertia in whichever direction it had been going when its pilot was mentally broken. One or two seconds after, the secondary gunner blew it to atoms.

It was unpleasantly easy. The mines were by far the most difficult part of the battle.

On three occasions, they ran down Voloth pilots flying in a too-close formation, enabling their high empath to break them all. Rahel destroyed four fighters and their eight occupants with less effort than was required for a level-three drone.

She had worried about this part of the battle, fearing in her darkest moments that it might trigger the trauma shock she had only recently put behind her. As she took two more lives with a press of her thumb, she felt nothing more than the grim satisfaction of completing a distasteful task.

Perhaps it was because this time, she didn't see the effects of the projection. Nor was she in charge of the high empaths. It was not her order that destroyed minds.

Distance, she concluded, helped a great deal.

In short order, they wiped out the entire wing of Voloth fighters. Not one escaped alive. Their own losses were limited to six fighters, all injured by mines before being hit by Voloth fire. An additional five lost their shields to mines but escaped further damage; these were sent to Alsea as backup for the squadrons protecting the cities.

Based on the reports she received, Candini was certain none of the Voloth were able to get off a distress call or any sort of warning. Their sensors had recorded no transmissions in the extremely short time between mental breaking and death.

The truth of Alsean empathic range was still a secret, and the Voloth had no more fighters.

"No rest for the weary," Candini called out. "Let's get these mines off our elevator!"

8

UNTHINKABLE

E katya chased the heavy cruiser all the way up the space elevator, helpless to stop its devastating attack. The laser cannon fire only softened up the elevator's shields; that didn't worry her. The mines were the true threat. Unfortunately, she had to leave this mess to the destroyers and fighters while she kept the cruiser away from them.

No one in Fleet had seen anything like these miniaturized mines. They were new Voloth technology. She could only imagine how much Sholokhov would want to get his hands on one. Hades, *she* wanted to get her hands on one. How did they pack such a powerful explosive plus shield sensors in that small package? How long had it taken to manufacture thousands of the things?

She had little time to wonder as the *Phoenix* hurtled after the cruiser, taking out as many mines as it could along the way. Before reaching the counterweight, she ordered Lieutenant Scarp to break off pursuit and cross to the other side of the elevator cable. There was no doubt in her mind that the cruiser would be making a second run. The ten fighters she had sent ahead waited near the counterweight, prepared to neutralize any missiles the Voloth threw at it.

To her dismay, this captain was smarter than the one she had killed back at the minefield. The cruiser did not pause, firing only a handful of missiles at the counterweight before coming around with Delfin torpedoes already blasting out of its launchers. Ekatya was forced into evasive maneuvers, while her own broadside was expected and almost entirely neutralized. A few shield breakers slipped through, but she was nowhere near getting this behemoth to the point where she could take it out.

She found some consolation in frustrating the captain's intentions toward the space elevator, inserting her ship in the firing line and preventing the second strafing run. She paced it all the way down, launching shield breakers and forcing it to defend itself rather than target the cable.

But she couldn't stop the dispersal of a second swarm of mines, or the fighters that suddenly appeared from the drop bays. They dashed behind the cruiser for protection and headed back up the elevator, swiftly vanishing from her range as she continued her headlong flight down the cable. The best she could do was warn Candini.

At the end of its strafing run, the heavy cruiser rolled away and shot off in a direction that made her heart leap into her throat.

Her navigation officer confirmed it: the cruiser was headed for a point directly over Blacksun. Her assurance to Andira that the Voloth had never committed an orbital bombardment looked very thin now.

"Get us there first," she ordered. "Weapons, be alert for a possible orbital bombardment. Prepare to divert all fire to neutralize planet-bound missiles. But first, let's give them a spin." If they went where she was expecting, she could get in front and have time for an offensive move.

She called the Alsean war council and shared her suspicions. Within seconds, she knew, the fighters and ground pounders surrounding both Blacksun and Blacksun Base would go on high alert. Even if her weapons couldn't stop all the missiles, the Alseans were not helpless. This battle was far less one-sided than the last one she had fought here.

The *Phoenix* had better engines and a much better pilot. They edged past the cruiser, which did not divert its course.

"Aft weapons, fire!" she called. "Helm to port. Starboard weapons, fire!"

The heavy cruiser captain had been expecting the attack and was ready with a defensive barrage. Shield breakers and rail gun projectiles filled the space as Ekatya ordered a rotation and another broadside. The expansive curve of Alsea flowed from one side of her display to the other, close enough at this low-orbit altitude that she could easily make out the distinctive ring of mountains around Blacksun Basin.

She never had the chance to order a second spin. Before her horrified eyes, the ship did exactly what she had feared.

"Orbital bombardment! Target those missiles!"

The automated defense system would not respond to missiles that were tracking away from them. Her weapons teams would have to fire manually, a difficult task when they were already handling shield breakers at a dizzying pace.

Still, they did her proud. She spun her chair to watch as the first rail gun projectiles tore away and closed the distance. The battle grid lit up, a succession of red circles indicating positive contact on every target.

But something was wrong. Where were the explosions?

"Did the sensors malfunction?" Commander Lokomorra asked.

"Tactical," Ekatya snapped. "Pull up the battle record and pick a target. Magnify and replay the moment of impact."

"Acknowledged."

A new square popped up over the battle grid, showing one of the missiles headed toward Alsea. A blur streaked in from the left on an intercept course. One second later, the missile blew apart like grass in the wind, nothing but shreds of material flying away from the impact site.

"Oh, fucking Hades," she whispered. "No, no, no! Weapons, recall all fighters! Those are bioforce missiles!"

This wasn't an attack on Blacksun.

It was genocide.

9

ANCHORED

Salomen had leaped twice already, both times failing to connect. In all their practice jumps, even during the war games, her target ship hadn't rocketed through space at quite these speeds, twisting and turning as it flew. She could sense the cluster of minds, knew where she wanted to go, but when she thought herself to the location, the ship was no longer there.

Andira kept encouraging her, telling her not to worry, this was merely battle jitters and she would soon find her feet.

She mostly believed it until Colonel Razine called from the war council. The news was terrifying: Ekatya was chasing the Voloth flagship toward Blacksun and suspected an orbital bombardment.

"Don't be afraid," Andira murmured. "No matter what you hear. Our mission is exactly the same."

Her lack of fear helped. If Andira wasn't frightened, then it hadn't happened yet.

She felt oddly detached, as if the horrific possibility existed in another time and place. Right here, right now, she was standing in the quad on Blacksun Base, feeling the diminishing breeze on her face and hearing the occasional buzzy call of a fairy fly. Radiating around her and Andira in geometric lines were thirty divine tyrees, all lending her their power. This was her reality.

"If one of those missiles gets through, will it hurt?" she asked. "Or will we wink out and never feel it?"

"Any missile that gets past Ekatya will be neutralized by our ground pounders or fighters. We prepared for this, tyrina. Let the warriors do their jobs. You do yours."

"They're coming." Salomen hovered in a nothingness of time and space, sensing the tangle of minds racing toward her. "I can feel them."

There were two glowing concentrations of emotions. One pulsed with fear, arrogance, and foreign hatred. The other also held fear, but largely of a protective flavor. The minds there were more determined than hateful.

One shone above them all.

Just as she leaped for the ship of foreign hatred, the other shot through space, curving directly in front of her. She fell into it, helplessly tumbling until she landed in a heap—on the bridge of the *Phoenix*.

Ekatya was there, staring at the upper display with horror coming off her in waves. She spoke in Common, her words rushed with urgency, then caught herself and added what sounded like instructions in a clear, deliberate manner. Despite the circumstances, Salomen was fascinated by the way her words affected the emotions of every officer on the bridge. They had been fearful, but now settled into a fierce resolve.

Ekatya spun her chair to face Salomen and stopped in shock. Her lips moved, forming a single word that she did not speak aloud.

Salomen?

Though stunned, Salomen managed to think herself across the bridge and up to the command chair. "You can see me?"

Andira's astonishment vibrated through their link. "Is that Ekatya?"

Salomen nodded her physical head in answer, just as Ekatya did the same in front of her.

"You have to do this quickly," Ekatya whispered. "Stop them, now. Whatever it takes, stop them."

Her emotional signature was warm and welcoming, despite the fear on its surface. Deep in its core was a spark Salomen recognized: a piece of Andira, embedded within. She had never seen it before, but now it glowed like a beacon, calling to her.

In her physical ear, Colonel Razine urgently reported something on their reserved channel. It wasn't important. What mattered was right in front of her.

"Salomen! They're firing bioforce missiles. Do you understand? They're planning to wipe out your civilization, down to the last child. We're doing what we can, but you have to go. Now!"

Reality rushed in, disintegrating the shock-induced bubble of calm. Salomen gathered herself, felt for the Voloth ship, made her leap—

And fell onto the bridge of the *Phoenix*.

Scrambling up, she tried again.

Finding herself once more at the side of Ekatya's chair, she lost hope. "I don't know what's wrong," she gasped. "I cannot make the jump. It's as if—" She reached out, drawn to that piece of Andira. "I'm being held here. I need more power."

Ekatya watched her hand, then looked up with an electric shock of realization. "From me?"

"It's Ekatya," Andira said at the same time. "You're anchored to her for a reason. Use her strength."

"From you," Salomen agreed.

Without hesitation, Ekatya snapped out a crisp sentence that had Commander Lokomorra turning to stare up at her in disbelief. She said something else, then made an impatient gesture. The commander swiveled back to his console and began calling out to the bridge.

"I've turned command over to Lokomorra. He's a little startled, but all we're doing now is defense. He'll be fine. Do you need me to open my shirt?"

"I don't think so." Her hand passed through clothing and connected with the life force beneath. It settled her, a burst of power that brought Ekatya's confidence into her blood. She envisioned it flowing through her, carrying away her toxic panic and replacing it with the strength of a trained warrior.

She focused, jumped—

And wept when she landed in the same place.

"It's not working!"

Ekatya closed her eyes, forcing down the frustration and fear. Her emotional control was riveting, a skill Salomen wished she could absorb as easily as the power.

In the space of one breath, her eyes opened and her signature flared with revelation.

"We need the seventh star."

10

SHELTER

Lhyn paled when Micah told her and Lanaril why they had to move. "Orbital bombardment?" she said as they hurried away from the quad. "It's a war crime!"

Her disbelief struck Micah as darkly amusing. It was interesting how the Protectorate didn't consider unprovoked invasion, slaughter, and enslavement a war crime. But shooting missiles from orbit? That crossed some sort of line.

"Does Ekatya know, or is she assuming the worst?"

"If she waited until she knew for sure, we'd have no time to get you to shelter," Micah said shortly. He possessed neither the time nor the patience for questions, even from Lhyn. Thank Fahla he only had two civilians on his hands.

The warriors streaming down the paths moved with purpose but no panic. They would shelter in the bunkers beneath the barracks, chipped out of the mesa in the earliest days of the base. The rocks from those excavations now paved Aerial Way.

He led Lhyn and Lanaril down a different, smaller path.

"We're going to the war room," he said, cutting off the question Lhyn was drawing breath to ask. It was deeper and far more hardened than the bunkers. That room and others on its level were currently housing some of the most important people on Alsea.

"I've been to the war room. It's over there." She pointed toward the towering administration building.

"That's not the only entrance."

"Escape tunnel. It wouldn't have just one entrance." Lanaril dredged up a smile. "Don't look so surprised, Colonel. Blacksun Temple has secret underground entrances, too. You could have included us in your shelter plans."

"The temple is a primary target," he reminded her.

Her smile fell, revealing the fear it had masked. Kicking himself as a dokker's ass, he tried to make amends.

"Fahla has a special love for her temples. I believe she'll protect them today, as she did in the Battle of Alsea. But we couldn't base our plans on faith."

"We just left our Lancer, Bondlancer, and the entire population of divine tyrees to face orbital bombardment with nothing more than combat vests. Faith is all we have."

That shut him down. His guilt at leaving Tal and Salomen behind could not be assuaged by any rational argument. Yes, Tal had made it an order. Yes, he was a coordinator of the shelter plan, and yes, he had been designated—over his objections—as a senior leader of what they euphemistically called Alsea Ascendant. It was absurd, the idea that he could be a founder of the second civilization after abandoning the leader of the first.

Faith was indeed all they had.

He wondered if Alejandra knew. How quickly did battle data get to the chief surgeon? There were so many things he hadn't asked her, so many conversations yet to be shared. And one in particular she was adamantly unwilling to have.

She had returned to her suite a hantick after walking out and said she couldn't speak of it then. She understood why he brought it up, appreciated his motives, but asked him to respect her need for time.

Time. He could almost laugh. Time was the one thing they did not possess. If Alsea Ascendant was put into motion, his desire to have a child would no longer be a choice. It would become an imperative, with or without Alejandra's participation.

His earcuff activated with the voice of Colonel Razine.

"Orbital bombardment has commenced. The Phoenix *is defending and*

has recalled all fighters. We're sending most of our fighters as well, including those guarding Blacksun."

Before he could recover from the surprise of leaving Blacksun undefended, she added, *"The missiles are not nuclear. They are genetic disruptors, designed to exterminate Gaians on a planetary scale. Prime Scholar Yaserka confirms Captain Serrado's assessment: given our genetic similarities, they will exterminate Alsean life as well. This is an extinction-level threat. No missile can be allowed to explode in our lower atmosphere."*

Micah stopped in the middle of the path.

"What is it?" Lhyn asked.

He seized her arm and dragged her with him. The hidden entrance was at the end of this wall. "No time. Move! Ekatya was right, but they're firing a different kind of missile."

"A different—what other—oh, no." Lhyn's horror roared through their skin contact, weakening his knees. "Not bioforce."

Reaching the boulder that served as an anchor for the wall, he tapped a four-point pattern into a patch of what appeared to be lichen. The patch rotated in place, exposing the smooth scanner hidden on its back side. He pressed his palm to it and spoke rapidly. "Corozen Lintale Micah, Colonel, Alsean Defense Force."

A tiny light blinked blue before the boulder slid back, silent as a ghost despite its size. Beneath it, stone steps descended into a lit passageway.

"I don't know the name," he said, nudging her forward. "Some kind of genetic disruptor—"

"And you're leaving them out there?" she shouted, spinning on her heel.

He caught her as she tried to run past. "Lhyn!"

"Let me go, you shekking—you're leaving them to die!"

The fury blasting off her skin loosened his grip. She was enraged enough to strike, raising her fist in an untrained attempt that he easily caught.

"Lhyn, stop! I don't want to hurt you." Pulling her back to the stairs was like trying to carry a frantic winden. She fought him every step of the way.

"You're killing them!" Rage shattered into icy shards of terror and grief, breaking her voice. "Micah, please!"

Lanaril's eyes were red as she watched. He could only imagine the beating her senses were taking, but she would not raise her blocks. Sensing Lhyn's pain was the only way they could honor it.

"Go," he grunted, wrapping an arm around Lhyn's twisting body. "I'll bring her. I have to close the door."

She hurried down the steps, leaving him to wrestle Lhyn through the doorway. The boulder slid into place above him, cutting off the sunlight, breeze, and every scent and sound of a living Alsea.

They were safe. He had done the worst of his duty.

Lhyn went limp, her fight vanishing the instant the door sealed. The sudden dead weight nearly overbalanced him, but he managed to get one arm under her knees and lift her while taking a step down, saving them both from a headlong tumble.

At the bottom of the steps, he crouched and set her on the flagstone floor. She slumped in place, her face turned away.

"How could you?" she croaked.

"It's my duty. Do you think I wanted to?"

He had meant to speak gently, but the accusation bit deep. She looked up, calm despite the streaming tears, and shook her head.

She needed to live. Not just for Ekatya's sake, but also to keep alive the memories of Tal and Salomen should their plan fail. Lhyn was the storyteller, the scholar of traditions and histories that shaped their culture. She would be the repository of stories that were not yet written.

If his burden was to lead, hers was to remember.

He was gathering the words to tell her when she stirred to life, scooting back to rest against the rough wall.

"Bioforce." Her voice echoed hollowly in the narrow space. "They're called bioforce missiles. They're supposed to be a deterrent between the Protectorate and the Voloth Empire. Neither side has ever used them against a population. I don't—why would they do it?"

Lanaril knelt in front of her, resting a hand on her leg. "Why were you tortured? Because they fear us."

"This can't happen. It can't!"

"Trust in Fahla. Trust in Ekatya. You know she will do her best, and her best is very, very good."

She let her head thud back against the wall hard enough to make Micah wince. "Ekatya will do whatever it takes. She'll ram that shekking ship if she has to. If my choice is to lose her or watch Alsea die . . ."

Micah's blood froze. If Ekatya rammed the flagship, Alejandra would die with her. There would be no time to eject escape pods. Even if there were time, the pods would be defenseless against four still-active Voloth destroyers with angry captains looking for revenge.

Would Fahla be so cruel as to give him a second chance and then take it away?

"Micah."

He twitched at the voice he hadn't expected to hear again.

"Bring Lhyn back. We need her in the link. Hurry."

Tal was still giving instructions as he seized a startled Lhyn, pulled her upright, and pushed her toward the stairs. Despite his rough handling and the lack of information, she ran up ahead of him.

"We're coming," he told Tal, and slapped his hand against the biolock. Light and fresh air poured in as the boulder slid aside.

Lhyn bounded out and faced him. "What's happening?"

"Salomen is with Ekatya. But she cannot reach the Voloth ship. Ekatya said to tell you they need the seventh star."

Her eyes widened before she turned and took off at a dead run.

Micah followed as quickly as he could, but her legs were longer and younger. She vanished around a corner in the path.

"Beauty precedes age," Lanaril said.

He nearly fell over his feet, shocked by her presence beside him. "What are you doing out here? You're supposed to be safe!"

"Safe is relative. I agreed to be on the shelter list because you were right, the survivors would need their Lead Templar. But the seventh star? This is Fahla, acting before our very eyes. I won't miss the chance to bear witness." She increased her pace, leading him by half a step. "Keep up, Colonel."

He cursed all stubborn scholars and called Gehrain. Lhyn would need to be equipped with an earcuff, enabling her to join the quantum com call that Ekatya had established with Tal and Salomen. "Since she's going to beat me there by half a length," he finished.

"I'll take care of it, Colonel."

By the time he and Lanaril came within sight of the quad, Lhyn was already sprinting between the lines of divine tyrees toward the brilliant glow enveloping Tal and Salomen.

"Great Mother," Lanaril panted. "It's brighter than a molwyn tree."

"It's thirty-two divine tyrees." Micah took some comfort in the fact that he might be slower, but she was breathing harder.

"Thirty-three," she corrected. "Soon to be thirty-four."

Gehrain met Lhyn halfway. Even at this distance, Micah could see her fidgeting while being fitted with the earcuff and wristcom. As soon as it was done, she shot away like a rail gun projectile.

Only in the last strides did she slow down. It was difficult to distinguish anything when she stepped into the shifting light, but he thought he saw her lift her hands.

Then he was falling, pushed backward by the energy pulse that blew across the quad. A flare of white light left him blinking away spots as he stared into the faultless blue sky.

"Fahla, my Goddess," came a murmur from beside him. "I kept your faith." Lanaril picked herself up and let out an incredulous laugh. "Did you see it? Like a bolt to the stars!"

He rolled to his knees. "I saw a flash," he began, and stopped.

In the center of the quad, Lhyn stood motionless with Tal and Salomen.

But there was no light at all.

11

FLAGSHIP

No sooner did Lhyn's hand touch the back of her neck than Salomen's shackles fell away. Power sparked at her fingertips, a surfeit of unquenchable strength.

She did not hesitate nor pause for a word of greeting before making her leap. Empty space flashed by at the speed of thought, and she splashed into a new river of emotions.

Look for the highest concentration of arrogance, Alejandra had said. *The minds that don't care how much harm they do.*

There was a great deal of arrogance on this ship, but relatively little was accompanied by entitlement. In fact, considering the high levels of hatred, she sensed a surprising amount of unease. It seemed that not every member of this crew agreed with genocide, even of a species they had been taught to abhor.

She opened her senses, letting the currents drift past while she sifted through emotions. The misery and fear were heartbreaking, but she had to set them aside. Those were surely the slaves. She couldn't help them, and they were not where she needed to go.

There. A pocket of . . . not hatred, but dislike, distaste, and callous indifference. Here were the minds that didn't care. They brimmed with the arrogance and entitlement she expected while adding a heaping dose of ambition.

She leaped, landed—

And stared openmouthed at the three figures who had landed with her.

"Well, this is a surprise," Lhyn said.

Andira blinked rapidly, then shook off her shock and began looking around their new environment.

Ekatya was already moving to the back of the busy room. Unlike her bridge, with its expansive space and central dais of three concentric rings, this bridge was smaller, more crowded, and divided into five levels that ran the width of the room. Each level held several workstations staffed by Voloth officers, all facing the display on the front wall. Though large, it offered little of the immersive sense conveyed by the hemispheric displays of the *Phoenix*.

Still, the split view of Alsea and the *Phoenix* was compelling enough. It was clear that both were viewed as enemies. While Salomen could understand that for an opposing ship, she had no comprehension of minds that saw a living planet and its entire population as hostile adversaries deserving death.

She watched Ekatya glide up the levels and noted that the higher the officers sat, the more ornate their uniforms became. The fifth and highest level was also the most spacious, housing two chairs side by side. Both resembled thrones more than command chairs, with intricately cast metal legs, backs that towered over the heads of their occupants, and cushions of deep blue. Behind them, matching blue banners draped across the wall.

Ekatya stopped beside the chair on the left, occupied by a stout man with soft jowls and hard eyes. He wore the fanciest uniform in the room and barked orders with towering arrogance.

The man in the second chair was thinner and outwardly relaxed, watching the bridge with silent disdain. His uniform was different, less ornate but topped with a flexible metal collar that draped onto his chest.

"This is the captain who's been giving me such trouble," Ekatya said, pointing at the stout man. "Stop him and you stop the ship. For the moment, anyway."

Though on the other side of the room, she kept her voice low, trying not to be overheard by her own officers. Salomen was surprised by her quick adaptation to occupying two spaces at once, but then remembered: she and Lhyn had both done this many times before.

"Can you make him remorseful?" Andira asked doubtfully. "He feels as if he may be beyond that."

"Everyone has something to regret," Lhyn said. "Even psychopaths, though they may only regret not doing more to benefit themselves."

"Try alarm," Andira suggested. "Fear that he's harming himself with this."

Salomen thought herself to the Voloth captain's side, wanting no interference between them.

It took little effort to slip into his mind and great effort to stay there. Her skin crawled, every instinct screaming at her to back out. No amount of training could prepare her for immersion in a man who wanted her entire species dead.

Stopping Alejandra Wells had been a matter of compelling obedience and overriding her instinct to help. She had succeeded completely with the first but only partially with the second. In the end, Alejandra had found a way to help despite the restrictions.

Obedience wasn't an option with this man, not when he was the one giving orders rather than taking them. For now, she needed to override his compulsion to destroy and take pleasure in the deaths of others.

She would have to go much deeper than she had with Alejandra.

Steeling herself, she reached in, gripped his will in a firm hold, and projected the alarm Andira had proposed.

Stop. It's the wrong choice. It will ruin you. Stop!

He stiffened. With wide, fearful eyes, he called out a staccato series of words.

"Good. He's stopped the bioforce missiles." In a louder voice, Ekatya said, "Commander Lokomorra, don't trust it. Be prepared to neutralize another barrage if necessary. In the meantime, put me through to that ship. I want to talk to the captain."

Salomen blew out a relieved breath. How had they ever thought she could do this alone? The plan had always been for Ekatya to issue the commands while she compelled obedience, but having Ekatya here made it so much simpler. Having Andira and Lhyn here as well gave her confidence. They would end this nightmare.

Her inexplicable anchoring to Ekatya suddenly made sense. She was never meant to be here by herself. All along, this had been a task for the four of them.

The thinner man snapped an irate question, sparking an argument. Salomen had assumed he was the executive officer, but he neither acted nor felt like a subordinate.

An officer in the middle of the room spoke up, only to be summarily silenced by the thin man. The captain reacted with icy anger, and the argument escalated.

Ekatya scowled. "Whoever that man is, he had the authority to reject my call. The captain is not happy about it."

"I'm not sure the captain is the one we need to control," Lhyn said from the front of the room. "I think that's the political liaison."

Next to her, Andira narrowed her eyes. "Explain."

"Rax Sestak said the hangers feared the officers, but the officers feared the political liaison. He's a spy for the Empire, reporting back on who is loyal and who isn't. If he thinks you're disloyal, or even insufficiently loyal, look out. But Rax didn't know the liaison had a place on the bridge. He didn't know anything about the setup here. I'm only guessing."

"That was the problem with our access," Andira said. "None of our settlers were officers. Their knowledge only went so far."

Watching the men closely, Ekatya gave a sharp nod. "It's a good guess, based on what they're saying."

"And what I'm feeling." Salomen tightened her grip. "The captain hates that man, but he's afraid of him, too."

"Enough to overcome your hold?" Andira asked.

"No. But only because I'm so deep that he'll probably never—" She swallowed, revulsion rising in her throat. "He may never stop being afraid after this."

Andira was suddenly beside her, the touch of her phantom fingers matching the physical reality of their bodies. "You're doing exactly what you need to, tyrina. I know it's hard."

"I don't want to feel sorry for him. He's trying to kill our world. But I'm holding his will in my hand."

"If it were me, I'd kill him. He's fortunate you're the one with the power. He may not be the same after this, but he'll still be alive."

"Though not with his rank intact," Ekatya said. "That political liaison is the equivalent of Admiral Greve. He's about to take command."

"I cannot hold them both!" Why didn't Andira have these powers, too? She would be so much better at handling a fluid situation. And two of them projecting would be more effective than one.

The will in her grip made a desperate attempt to escape. She squeezed, instinctively strengthening her projection.

The captain lost all control and screamed at the political liaison, his face mottled with anger that came naturally and terror that did not.

"Salomen, back off a notch," Ekatya said.

She tried, but the fear of losing her hold made finesse impossible. As soon as she lightened her touch, the captain's will resurged. This deep, in his very core, the battle for control felt like life and death to both of them.

She would not be the one to die. Determined, she clenched her fist and ended his resistance.

With a cry of rage, he flipped open a compartment in the ornate arm of his chair and pulled out what looked like a small disruptor.

"Salomen!"

"I'm trying!"

The political liaison produced a weapon from somewhere on his body. Before the captain could raise his arm, a bolt of energy sizzled across the space and impacted his chest.

Salomen cried out at the pain of it, echoing the captain's scream as a hole melted through his torso.

When his smoking body slid to the deck, she dropped with it, her fist clenched around a will that was no longer there.

"Salomen. Salomen!"

She tried to answer Andira's terrified call, but had no voice.

The deck gave way beneath her, and she fell into the emptiness of space.

12

DEEP DIVE

"Shipper shit." For the first time in the battle, Candini was rattled. "Oh, holy fucking fuck."

Rahel didn't understand. Even the news of a possible orbital bombardment hadn't affected Candini like this. But between that report and the one they had just received, she had veered from anger to outright fear.

"What are bio—"

A new call interrupted her, this one from the Alsean war council.

They were moving at top speed before it finished.

Rahel sat in stunned silence while Candini rolled and ducked their fighter out of the minefield, barking orders along the way. Half of the Alsean fighters would continue mine patrol. The rest would follow them back to a geosynchronous orbit between Blacksun and the *Phoenix*. Their new orders: to save the entire planet.

No great task, she thought. *Just don't miss. Ever. Or you'll watch Alsea die and know it was you who let it happen.*

"Don't let the stress get to you."

"Suddenly you're empathic?" she snapped.

"Hey. I'm not the enemy here."

She covered her eyes and tried to center herself.

Her imagination took advantage, serving up a buffet of horror. Her mother and Sharro, disintegrating in their Whitesun home while Little

Mouse wailed between them. Salomen and Lancer Tal, burning alive in each other's arms. Alsea, rotating beneath her while its beautiful hues of blue and green turned a sickly brown.

One of her hands was pulled away. Candini had cleared the minefield and locked in their course, giving her a free hand to hold Rahel's. As if she were a child in need of comfort instead of a battle-hardened warrior.

Against her will, in complete abandonment of her pride, Rahel squeezed her hand and took a shuddering breath. Hardened? She was cracking apart.

"Let it go," Candini advised. "Whatever it is you're thinking. Let it go. This is the same thing we've done all along. Find a target and eliminate it. Find another target and eliminate it. You can't think about the big picture. Think about your job and do it. That's all they need you to do."

"How am I supposed to not think about the big picture?"

"The same way you have been. Back there, shooting mines and neutralizing Voloth fighters—were you thinking about the space elevator crashing back to Alsea?"

She shook her head.

"Then that's what you keep doing. Let the higher ranks and fancier salaries worry about the big picture. Our job is to do what they tell us. Right now, that means eliminating targets. One at a time."

There was fear in Candini's touch, but it was controlled, kept at bay by a dense layer of determination.

Candini would not let this happen. She was the best pilot in the quadrant. Possibly in the whole Protectorate. Alsea had put her in charge of the fleet, even named their single-seat model after her. She would get them in position, and Rahel would take the shot. They would do it together, as they had from the start.

She licked her dry lips and nodded. "I'm all right. Thank you."

Instead of releasing her hand, Candini squeezed it harder. "It happens to everyone. Happened to me once, at the worst possible time. I'll tell you the story after the battle, when we're celebrating back on Blacksun Base. Deal?"

"That was manipulative. Worthy of a captain." Rahel had found a shred of humor.

"Captain Serrado did say I needed to earn my reputation."

"You already have." She let go. "Get your hand back on the control stick, you're making me nervous."

～

It was anticlimactic to arrive at the coordinates and have nothing to do. The Voloth flagship had ceased launching its bioforce missiles, though it was certainly launching everything else. It rolled and swooped, spraying firepower while the *Phoenix* danced around it, dodging some hits, taking others, and firing its own weaponry.

"Glad we're not in the middle of that," Candini said. "They could put our entire fighter fleet between those two ships and chop it to pieces."

"I hate sitting on my hands like a merchant with no wares. We could be back at the elevator, cleaning up mines."

At least one thing was going right: the Fleet destroyers were harassing their Voloth counterparts so relentlessly that the remaining fighters on mine patrol were able to work without fear of being targeted. Even though it was still two against four, the *Thea* and *Victory* were working smoothly as a team, making life difficult for the Voloth captains.

"Sure. And the moment we leave is the moment those dokkers start up again. Captain Serrado said not to trust it, and I wouldn't even if she hadn't warned us."

The heavy cruiser fired another set of Delfin torpedoes, sending the *Phoenix* rolling away.

Candini let out a string of curses. "How many shekking Delfins do they have? They must churn them out of a factory like sweets from a bakery."

"Too many. Did you notice anything odd about that last call?"

"From the *Phoenix*? No, why?"

Rahel shook her head. She couldn't put it into words, but the weapons officer had not sounded normal. "It felt as if something's not right on the bridge."

"Seemed fine to m—crap!"

A new set of missiles had launched from the Voloth flagship. Unlike all the others, these did not target the *Phoenix*. They were headed straight for Alsea.

"Bioforce missiles! Ready weapons!" Candini ordered the fighters.

"Remember, let the *Phoenix* get what it can. We're the second line of defense. And do *not* let any missile go below the red line!"

They were positioned at a lower altitude, out of the line of fire. It gave the *Phoenix* room to move and react, while also giving them time to coordinate and choose their targets.

Of the twenty missiles launched, the *Phoenix* destroyed seventeen. Studying the battle grid, Candini called out fighter assignments and took one missile for their own team. She and Rahel were the primary pilot and gunner; the secondary was off their starboard wing. They had no tertiary. If two of them missed, there would surely be no time for a third attempt.

Rahel wiped her sweaty hands on her flight suit before gripping the control stick. On her targeting screen, a green dot approached the central square. It didn't evade the way a drone would, nor fire back like a fighter. It simply traveled in a steady dive, a single-minded carrier of death.

At the bottom of her screen was a menacing red line, representing the altitude below which she could not fire. Destroying the missile above that line would harmlessly disperse its payload into space. Below it, the air currents in Alsea's atmosphere would carry the contents until they circumnavigated the planet, eventually filtering down to rain death on every city and town.

The war council's instructions were clear: if they could not destroy a missile in time, they had to let it go. It would instantly devastate Blacksun but delay the effects across the rest of the planet. Maybe, just maybe, their scholars could find a way to stop those effects in time. In the worst-case scenario, it would give them enough of a window to evacuate survivors off the planet—assuming they kept the space elevator intact, which was why half the fighters had been held back to clear mines.

But nothing would save Blacksun.

The red line began to climb upward. They were rapidly approaching minimum altitude.

Rahel blocked out everything but the geometric shapes on her screen. Nothing existed save this target. She and Candini had done this a thousand times and with much harder shots. She would not miss.

Candini dipped them into a steeper dive, magically sliding their target into the perfect location.

She squeezed off her shot and watched, dry-mouthed, as the dot exploded into red sparks indicating a clean kill.

"Got it! Told you!" Candini let out a whoop as she pulled up from their dive.

Rahel barely heard her words or their secondary's relieved congratulations. She was too busy fighting down the wave of fear that struck the moment her shot impacted. The red line hadn't even reached the bottom of her targeting square. They had saved Blacksun with room to spare, but her body didn't know that.

She held up her right hand and watched it shake. "My heart is pounding so hard I can feel it in my fingertips."

"It doesn't show," Candini assured her.

There were advantages to working with Gaians.

Though Candini had expected more missiles to be fired while they were in pursuit—and had her second-in-command ready to assign teams —they were able to return to their prior position before another volley came out.

This time, the *Phoenix* only missed two. Both were far enough away that Candini let other teams take them.

"Why so long between launches?" Rahel wondered. If she focused on details, she wouldn't think about what they were doing.

"I don't know, but given what's inside them? They probably can't be loaded with the automated systems. It has to be by hand. You don't want anything to go wrong while you're putting one of those in the launch tube."

It was an unlooked-for advantage. By the sixth launch, Rahel had overcome her fear. She could view them as just another target, and an easy one at that.

Hubris, Sharro would call it. Tempting fate and Fahla.

She and Candini had destroyed their fifth missile and were pulling out of their dive when the panicked cry came over the com.

"Negative contact! Target green!"

Three other teams had been in pursuit of missiles. One had not made the shot. The missile was active and below minimum altitude.

Blacksun was gone.

Rahel stared straight ahead, seeing nothing and feeling only a sense of blank disbelief.

"Not on my watch," Candini snapped. She threw them back into a

54

dive so abruptly that had Rahel not been strapped in, her head would have hit the cockpit cover.

"What are you doing?"

Candini didn't answer, instead sending their secondary to support another team and ordering her second-in-command to take over as defense coordinator.

Their fighter screamed through the air at speeds it was not built for. Rahel noted the readout in her peripheral vision and dismissed it. Whatever Candini had in mind would probably kill them anyway.

"We still have a chance," Candini said grimly. "A small one. But we're going to try."

"Try what? We can't shoot it."

"No, but we can take it back up and then shoot it."

"With what?"

"The grappler."

Rahel goggled at her. "That's meant for low and no gravity, not full gravity! And not ridiculous acceleration."

"Our fighter isn't meant for this airspeed, either, but we're doing it. Have you got a better idea?"

"Not a shekking one."

"Then flip your screen to the ventral view. And thank Fahla we've got one of the modified grapplers."

Shaking her head at the audacity, Rahel prepped her controls while Candini called in their intent.

"You're insane, Nightwing," she said. "But that's why I like you."

No other pilot on Alsea would even consider this. Likely no one in Fleet, either. But Candini was unafraid, and Rahel found new faith. Perhaps it was simply that even now, she could not accept the loss of Blacksun.

Above them, the Voloth flagship had not launched another set of bioforce missiles. They probably assumed the job was done. Even if millions of lives weren't at stake, she'd want to make this work just to prove them wrong.

"There it is," Candini said. "Ready grappler."

A slim, silver cylinder flew daintily ahead of them, looking far too innocuous to be a civilization killer.

It was odd, the things that crossed one's mind while staring disaster in the face. Rahel watched sunlight reflect off the metal casing and marveled at the fact that all of Alsea's defenses were working against these things, but only she and Candini were seeing one with their own eyes. Everyone else had worked from battle grids and targeting screens.

Candini crossed over the top of it, then steepened her dive to match its trajectory and speed. Gradually, she closed the gap.

"Almost there," Rahel said. The missile was growing larger and larger in her screen, close enough now that she could see alien lettering on its side. "Thank Fahla it's such a small diameter. We can get our grappler around it."

"Because there sure as shek aren't any convenient handles or magtran rails to grab." Candini was watching the same view on her screen, forgoing any other flight data in favor of getting this right.

"There. Hold steady." Rahel wiped her sweaty hand on her flight suit. It was going to need a wash, she thought absently as she grasped the control stick. Now repurposed for the task, it acted as an extended arm. The grappler was her own body, reaching out from the bottom of their fighter. She had practiced this so many times on the space elevator that it had become second nature.

A press of her thumb opened the jointed hooks.

"Turbulence!" Candini called.

Vibrations spread through the airframe, jostling the grappler and forcing Rahel to pull it back. One hard hit against the missile was all it would take to break a hook. If that happened, all was lost.

The vibrations grew worse.

"We're in a downdraft. Under a cloud mass. The air should get calmer when we clear it."

"How long?"

"Don't worry. We have time."

"I can see the shekking ground, Candini. I can see the Silverrun River."

"We have time."

"How long?"

The jostling lessened.

"Three pipticks. Two. One."

They were in smooth air again, and Rahel did not wait one piptick longer. Without letting herself think, she slipped the open hooks around the shining cylinder and pulled the trigger.

The grappler closed.

"It's in!"

"Good job, Red. Let's get the shek out of here."

Slowly, so gradually that Rahel wanted to scream, Candini leveled out their dive. They were almost brushing the tops of the Snowmounts before she began to climb again. After calling in their status, she said, "Keep an eye on that grappler."

"As if I could look at anything else?" If the power of her stare could keep the grappler intact against the acceleration forces it was now enduring, Rahel was guaranteed success.

"We're past the worst part. It survived the start of the climb. The stresses won't get worse than that. They'll get easier." Candini cleared her throat. "There's just one problem."

"One?"

"The missile's engine is still in operation."

"Isn't that a good thing? It's helping us take it above minimum altitude."

"That's a good thing for this part of the plan. It's not a good thing for the next step. The engine exhaust burned out our shield generator."

Rahel looked away from her screen for the first time. "We're going to shoot this thing with no shields."

A single nod was her answer.

"What are the chances that we'll get shredded?"

"Pretty high."

"Can we release it and run while someone else shoots it?"

"We're too far away."

"Can we release it and run while *we* shoot it?"

"We can try. The problem is, missiles like these use gravitational sensors. The moment we let it go, it's going to turn right around and head back to Alsea."

"So we take it higher up—"

"I think it's on a timer. As a backup for the impact detonator. The Voloth wouldn't build or buy something like this and take the chance that it might be a dud. We're carrying a live bomb."

"Shekking Mother on a burning boat." She laughed. "I must be insane. I've truly lost my mind, because this is actually funny. Of course it's on a timer. Why would it be anything else?"

"Rahel." Candini looked over with a solemn expression. "It's been an honor to fly with you. You're the best gunner I've ever had, and a good friend."

Rahel held out a hand, smiling as Candini took it in a firm grip. "The honor has been mine. You opened a whole new world for me. I've loved every tick we've flown together. And you're a wonderful friend, even if you won't leave me alone about my hair."

"All I ask is that you *try* the spikes—"

"It's not going to happen."

Candini's smile vanished. "No, I guess not. I won't be able to talk you into that tattoo, either."

"You already talked me into that."

She brightened. "I did?"

"I was going to tell you after the battle. I wanted to put a phoenix on my back. A two-dimensional version of my mother's sculpture."

"That would be stellar! I knew you'd see it my way."

"I usually did. Eventually."

With a final squeeze, Candini released her hand. "We're approaching minimum altitude. I want to give us some breathing room before we release it."

"Give us a lot of breathing room. If we're going to die anyway, take it as far as you can."

Rahel tried to absorb every detail of the view. They had left the last wisps of clouds far behind and were climbing into the welcoming darkness of space. Millions of stars blazed around them, comforting and familiar.

Once, these stars had been an impossible dream. Now they were home.

"Thank you, Fahla," she murmured. "You have blessed me beyond anything I deserved. And thank you for helping me die with honor."

"You've always been honorable," Candini said quietly.

"No. I tried, but I didn't always succeed. But this? It's been a good day. I saved Captain Serrado, and we saved Alsea. There's no better way to go."

"No, there isn't."

Candini called in the success of the missile's capture but did not speak of the likely results of its destruction. Rahel understood. She didn't want to spend her last moments listening to second guessing or final goodbyes, either.

They flew in silence, gaining precious altitude as an unknown timer ticked down. She remembered her earlier terror and marveled that it now seemed so far away. That had been a fear of failure, but she had not failed.

Her heart beat calmly, her breathing was slow, and she felt as peaceful as if she were back in the Whitesun warrior caste house, centering beneath one of the potted trees.

She wondered what it would be like to meet Fahla. Surely the goddess would be proud.

"Ready grappler," Candini said. "Then flip to the targeting screen. Use aft weapons; I'll jump the moment you fire."

"I'm ready."

One breath, then another.

"Release it."

Rahel depressed her thumb and watched the missile fall away. A tap to her board returned weapons to the control stick; a second tap brought up the targeting screen.

Candini had been right. The missile was already turning toward Alsea.

"Fire!"

The shining metal case filled her entire target square; this was a point-blank shot. She took it just as their fighter leaped, running from debris that exploded from the point of impact.

Another breath, and another . . .

She flinched as Candini let out a whoop of victory.

"Shek, yes! Who's the best? Who's the best pilot in the whole galaxy?" Candini pummeled her thighs and whooped again. "What a ride!" Swiveling, she pointed both forefingers at Rahel. "Now you *have* to get that tattoo."

Rahel stared, her mind scrambling to catch up. She wasn't going to die?

She wasn't going to die.

Laughter bubbled up. "I'll get it tomorrow."

"Too bad I can't take you back to the *Phoenix*. I've heard Dr. Wells is the best tattoo artist in the quadrant. She'd probably love—"

Rahel's heart jumped as the proximity alarm blared. Something tugged at her chest, hot and then cold. The cockpit was a blizzard of debris.

Candini scrambled for the controls, swearing as she fought to right the tumble they had been thrown into.

Too stunned to move, Rahel watched with distant interest as lights flashed on both consoles. More alarms sounded, then a voice warning about loss of atmosphere.

Her chest was freezing.

She tried to rub it, but her hand caught on something rough. Looking down, she found a large piece of metal protruding from her flight suit.

That would probably explain why it was so hard to breathe.

"Oh fuck. Rahel!" Candini threw off her harness and scrambled out of her seat, bent over beneath the cockpit cover. "Hold on. I'm going to get help. I just have to seal the hole first. Hold on, all right?"

She pulled a can of sealant from the emergency kit and stretched back, her hip brushing Rahel's shoulder as she sprayed the hole behind the seat.

Rahel looked down again, fascinated by the incongruity of the metal in her chest. This time, she studied it more closely.

Had she been able to get enough air, she would have laughed. It wasn't shrapnel from the missile. It was a piece of sabot from a rail gun projectile. In the end, she would die not from her heroic final act, but from the sheer bad luck of being in the wrong place without shields.

She coughed, and oh, shek, that was white agony.

Candini crouched beside her. "It's sealed. We don't have engines or even thrusters, but we're in range for a pickup. I'll get you—Rahel!"

When had her eyes closed?

She dragged them open again and tried to smile. "Tell them . . ."

Tears rolled down Candini's cheeks. "Tell them what?"

"Tell them . . . it didn't hurt."

13

DIVIDE AND CONQUER

Tal reeled from the conflict of two wildly different awarenesses. Her physical body stood on the grassy quad, Sharing with Salomen. Lhyn's hand still touched the back of her neck. The breeze wafted across her face and lifted a few wisps of hair, carrying with it the first scents released by the heat of the day.

But she had also just landed in a heap on a hard surface. There was no grass, no breeze, and Salomen was not in her arms.

She remembered empty space and a blurry, fleeting glimpse of stars. She remembered a ship glowing with the emotional output of more than a thousand minds.

With a sharp inhale, she remembered Salomen's cry of pain.

"Salomen!" She pushed herself to her hands and knees, saw the limp body lying within arm's reach, and scrambled over.

"I don't know." Lhyn was already kneeling on Salomen's other side. "But I can feel her standing here. I mean, physically."

Ekatya crouched at her head. "She's still conscious with you?"

"As far as I can tell. She's upright, at any rate. Salomen, I know you're in there. Say something!"

Tal tried to tell Lhyn not to bother, but the black hole in her chest sent desperate tendrils into every part of her body, trying to fill itself. Her words were sucked into the gaping chasm, along with her breath and most of her strength.

"That doesn't sound conscious to me," Ekatya said.

"She'd have to be, or none of us would be here. Somehow, she's still holding the Sharing together. The orbital jump, too."

"Then where is she? What the Hades happened?"

They looked to Tal for answers she could not give. If she moved so much as a muscle, she would surely collapse into the singularity.

Mindwalking required an enormous amount of power. Jumping to orbit multiplied that exponentially. Salomen took it all with her when she jumped, leaving only a shell behind.

That shell was now dark and empty. There was a heartbeat, breath, and balance, but the vibrant spark of life was nowhere to be found. Their bond was amputated, a devastating loss that left Tal hanging in a silent maelstrom.

She wanted to scream. They had poured so much time and effort into saving Salomen from the responsibilities of a warrior, and for what? So she could break under a burden that should never have been hers?

Why hadn't Fahla given those powers to the warrior instead of the producer who couldn't hurt a fairy fly? Had it been her, she would have killed that shekking captain without a second thought. Then the political liaison, then every breathing body on that bridge until she found one less evil and more malleable. She would have been death incarnate, wreaking Fahla's vengeance, and Salomen would never have been hurt.

The black hole sucked down her rage and eagerly looked for more. In the seething emotional storm, Lhyn's voice sounded distant.

"She was deep inside him when he died. You felt it, didn't you? I think part of her believes she died with him."

"Part of her?" Tal snarled, ignoring her flinch. "This is more than part! It's everything! Everything!"

"Andira." Ekatya spoke gently. "She's not gone."

"She is! I cannot sense her." Did they not understand what that meant?

"But we're still in the Sharing," Lhyn ventured, bravely trying again. "So she must be, too."

Ekatya looked around in dawning realization. "She brought us back."

Only now did Tal perceive the details of their location. Where before

62

there had been nothing but a deck, their bodies, and a featureless sea of gray, she now saw the expansive space of Ekatya's bridge. They were halfway between the central dais and the lift doors, sprawled on the hard surface of the lower display. Alsea shone beneath their feet, a glorious beauty sculpted in blues and greens and wrapped in ribbons of white.

A memory escaped the gravity of the black hole. They had fallen through space together, hadn't they? Salomen had cried out, and they had fallen.

"She was anchored to you," she said. "Before we brought Lhyn into the link. She must have held on to that anchor when we fell."

Lhyn brushed her fingers down Salomen's cheek. "You made sure we landed in a safe place. Typical, always taking care of us." She looked up, her features hardening with determination. "We need to take care of her."

"And how do you propose we do that? She's not here! Wherever she went, none of us can follow."

"Why not? We're all in the Sharing. She *is* still here. Somewhere."

"I don't sense her!" Tal rubbed her chest. "It's as if my heart has been torn out."

Lhyn's brows drew together. "Does it hurt?"

"Of course it shekking hurts, what do you think?"

"I think—"

Alsea slid away, flying across the deck and up the port side. Flashes of light streaked through the velvet blackness, but none blossomed into an explosion.

"Those were bioforce missiles," Ekatya said darkly. "The political liaison took command."

Tal twisted around to see better and froze at the eye-popping vision she had somehow missed before now.

"Ekatya," she croaked. "You're glowing."

Ekatya looked down at herself. "No, I'm not."

"Not here. There." She pointed.

In her command chair atop the central dais, Ekatya's physical body sat amid shifting, shimmering curtains of light, brighter than a burning molwyn tree.

"Stars and Shippers. How—?"

"You're not only Salomen's anchor. You're anchoring the combined power of all the divine tyrees."

One ring below, Commander Lokomorra called out an order as if nothing were amiss. An officer in the third ring responded crisply.

"Can't they see it?" Lhyn asked.

"They see it." The bridge officers were awed and wildly curious, but their training held firm. Tal was about to explain when the realization hit.

She could sense them.

Where Lhyn's logic could not penetrate, empathic knowledge slipped through. No one but Salomen was capable of this range. Tal would not be sensing the crew unless she and Salomen were still linked on some level.

"I know this is difficult," Ekatya said. "But we need—"

"She's here!"

Ekatya hesitated, thrown off by the sudden reversal. "Are you sensing her now?"

"No. I'm sensing them." She gestured at the officers.

"Because we're still in the Sharing," Lhyn said in a rush. "That's what I've been trying to tell you."

"Thank all the stars, then. Andira, listen. She stopped the flagship long enough for our fighters to get here. The *Phoenix* just neutralized seventeen of twenty bioforce missiles. The fighters caught the other three. We have two lines of defense now."

"Defense, but no offense." Tal picked up Salomen's limp hand and cradled it between her palms. "At least she bought us time."

"It's more than that." Lhyn was vibrating with suppressed energy. "Don't you see? Your chest hurts. Mine does, too. Ekatya?"

Ekatya rubbed her chest thoughtfully. "I didn't notice before. Too used to it, I guess. Why is it hurting when you're here?"

"Because Salomen isn't. Not on this plane." She turned to Tal. "You're seeing this, not just sensing it. You're showing the same symptoms, experiencing the same things Ekatya and I do in our bond. On our side, we're feeling what you and Salomen do. We're even feeling her absence. All the disparate abilities and consequences of our bonds have merged."

"How does that benefit us?" Ekatya asked. "There must be a way we can use it."

As if it had simply been waiting for the right question, Tal's mind snapped into focus. She saw their tactical situation unfold like a map, revealing a few poor options and one clear path.

"We already have," she said. "Thanks to Lhyn, we know who's in charge of that ship. We know how to get to him."

"Except we're here," Ekatya noted.

"Yes, and you're there." She indicated the command chair in its sphere of coruscating light. "We have a physical presence to work with. The political liaison wouldn't take your call before. He'll take it if you say you want to discuss terms of surrender."

"Um. Whose surrender?" Lhyn asked.

"Ours. For now. We only need to stall them long enough for you to find Salomen."

Lhyn's eyes rounded. "Me?"

"All of our disparate abilities, remember? Ekatya and I are the warriors. We'll deal with this side. Wherever Salomen is, it's not a warrior she needs now. She needs a tyree."

"You're her tyree."

"So are you."

"Not like you! You're her divine tyree. What can I do that you can't?"

"Make her your sole responsibility!" Tal exploded. "Do you think I want to send you in my place?" She held up a hand in silent apology and forced a calmer tone. "You were right. Part of her thinks she died with that captain. Even fully trained healers won't let themselves be caught in a dying mind, and Salomen was deeper than any healer has ever gone. Her instincts took her somewhere safe. Somewhere she could recover from the shock. I don't know where that is any more than you do. We have the same chance of finding her, but you have the *time*."

Lhyn stared at her, frightened and doubtful, but Ekatya understood.

"Andira would give her left arm to be the one to bring her back, but she's responsible for everyone on that planet." She pointed to Alsea, which had flipped over their heads and was now on the starboard side. "I'm responsible for everyone up here. You're the only one free to be what Salomen needs."

"You know her heart," Tal added. "Let that lead you to her."

"You have got to be joking. I don't even know—"

"Share with her."

"I *am* Sharing with her!"

"On the physical plane, yes. Now do it on this one."

"I—oh, fucking stars. Really? But we're not—"

65

"It's time," Ekatya said. "I'm sorry I made everyone wait. But if Fahla exists, she's beating me over the head right now with all of these clues. Go get Salomen."

Tal nodded. "Go get her."

Lhyn looked between them and swallowed hard. "Okay. I'll do my best." With tentative movements, she slipped one hand beneath Salomen's neck and stroked the other down her jaw. "Is this—?"

"You're in the right position," Tal assured her.

"Good." Still she hesitated, anxiety filling the air before a surge of determination forced it aside. "Here goes nothing," she mumbled, and leaned down to touch their foreheads together.

Tal watched and waited, still clinging to Salomen's hand. There was no time; she had to trust Lhyn and let go. Yet even on this spiritual plane, her fingers would not obey.

Lhyn gasped, the inhale as large as if she had been holding her breath. In the same moment, her emotional signature winked out.

"Great Mother!"

"What?" Ekatya demanded.

"I know where they are." Had she realized Salomen was *there*, she wouldn't have sent Lhyn. A sonsales Gaian should not have been able to find that path.

But Lhyn had followed a tyree bond.

"They? Lhyn found her?"

"Yes." Awash in sudden gratitude, she kissed the back of Salomen's hand and laid it on the deck. Her bondmate was not alone.

"Can she bring her back?"

"If Salomen is willing."

"Then it's done," Ekatya said decisively. "She won't say no to Lhyn."

Alsea whirled around the bridge displays again. Flares of light streaked beneath them, a terrifying reminder of the stakes.

"They need to hurry," Ekatya added as they climbed to their feet. "I don't know how long I can string out a surrender."

"I have an idea for that." Tal inspected the glowing body in the command chair. "How do you feel about impersonating a goddess?"

It was almost comical, the way Ekatya looked exactly as shocked as Lhyn had a moment ago. She stared at her body, then shook her head in resignation. "I don't suppose we can bring Lanaril up here?"

"Certainly, if you can convince the Voloth to take a short break from trying to destroy Alsea."

"Shek! Of all the people—" Ekatya lowered her head and pinched the bridge of her nose. "You'd better give me a light-speed training in how to be Fahla."

14

SURFACING

When Lhyn found herself in a heavy, liquid darkness, her first instinct was to fight. She thrashed uselessly, terrified by her blindness and disorientation.

Then she remembered Salomen and Andira telling the story of how they had held Micah in mental stasis after he was shot. The Path of the Return, Andira had called it.

This fluid darkness was exactly what they had described.

She forced herself to relax. Sure enough, her body floated upward. Black turned to gray, gray turned to soft green, and she broke the surface with a relieved gasp. Treading water and breathing hard, she searched for a familiar dark head.

The ocean stretched to the horizon in all directions, and Salomen was nowhere to be seen. But straight ahead was a rocky island that seemed to exist for one purpose: to provide a habitat for the great tree whose branches reached higher than any mountain she could think of.

It was physically impossible. A tree this tall would crack and shatter under its own weight.

"It's not real," she said aloud. Craning her head back, she tried and failed to find the topmost branches. "But my stars and asteroids, what a magnificent sight."

The tree's massive roots had broken the cliffs into large boulders. One root, thicker than she was tall, grew right into the water just ahead of her. She swam for it and climbed onto the rough wood.

No water dripped from her clothing. She held up her hands and turned them over.

Dry as a bone.

"Metaphorical," she reminded herself.

The width of the root made walking easy. She followed it up, down, and up again until it rounded a boulder and joined the great trunk.

There, at the juncture of root and trunk, was Salomen.

She had looked like a queen on the flagship bridge, standing straight-backed beside the captain with a fierce expression as she bent his will to hers. Now she sat against the trunk with her back bowed, legs drawn up, and forehead resting on her crossed arms. Though she must have heard Lhyn's footsteps on the bark, she gave no sign. Nor did she stir when Lhyn settled beside her.

"I'm sorry you're here," she said in a muffled voice. "So sorry."

"I'm not. This is hands down the biggest intellectual ride I'll ever take."

Salomen rolled her head to look at her sideways. "Lhyn, you're dead."

"No, I'm not. Neither are you."

"Then why do I not sense you?"

"Because we're in some sort of pocket reality? I mean, this is a Sharing within a Sharing. There has to be a point where the biological connections don't apply."

Abruptly straightening, Salomen flung out an arm to point at the water. "I've been here before. With Corozen. But there was nothing above the surface then, because he hadn't fully Returned. The moment I saw my Sharing tree, I knew it was over."

"This is the tree you see when we're Sharing?" Lhyn rubbed the bark beneath her hand. "Wow. I'm envious. You're so much more literal than I am." Her hand stilled. "Wait, this is your Sharing tree. I'm seeing through your eyes. The link is working even in here, but without the empathic aspect."

"There is no link!" Salomen cried. "I couldn't manage it. I couldn't hold him without forcing him too far. I'm dead and now you're dead and oh, Fahla . . ." Her head fell back against the trunk as she closed her eyes. "Please tell me it's just you and me. Tell me I didn't fail my whole world."

69

"It's just you and me because I'm the one who came after you. Ekatya and Andira are still out there fighting because they're the tactical brains. But they need you. You have to come back. You're not dead, Salomen! You only think you are."

She might have been speaking in Terrahan for all the indication Salomen gave of hearing. This was not her brave tyree, standing tall against a threat. This was a broken woman convinced of her failure.

Her stomach twisted with recognition. She had felt this way once, alone in a windowless room, in pain and utterly bereft of hope. Ekatya's appearance had saved her sanity. At the time, what she had needed most was assurance that she would not die alone.

But this was almost the reverse, wasn't it? In a way, Salomen *was* dead. This wasn't a windowless room she could be rescued from. It was the Path of the Return. She had been flung here by a terrible blow, too deeply linked with a soul when it died, and Lhyn's appearance had made it worse, not better.

With a stifled groan, Lhyn recognized the logic trap. The choice to go back could not be made unless Salomen believed that choice existed. Yet she had taken Lhyn's presence as proof that it did not.

Sometimes, irony was truly unpleasant.

"This is the afterlife, isn't it?" she asked.

"Yes," Salomen responded dully. "Or at least, the doorway to it. I thought I'd meet Fahla here, but—" She fell silent.

"But what?"

The answer came in a whisper. "If I failed Alsea, then she's—" She swallowed. "Busy. And I'm probably the last person she'll come for."

Lhyn thought her heart might crack right down the middle. But sympathy was not what Salomen needed now.

"If I'm dead, why would I be here? I'm not Alsean."

Salomen's eyes opened, her expression thoughtful as she stared at the water. "I don't know. Perhaps our tyree bond makes you Alsean enough?"

Lhyn shook her head. "I might accept that if we'd sealed our bond, but we haven't."

The sound that came from Salomen was an awful semblance of a laugh. "Because Ekatya wasn't ready. Now she never will be."

"Now she is," Lhyn corrected. "That was the last thing she said before sending me in here after you. She said Fahla was beating her over the head with clues. You need to come back with me so we can finish this battle and seal our bonds."

"I wish I could. You have no idea how much I wish that."

"Salomen, listen to me. Maybe sealing our bond will get me here eventually, but what we have right now is an enhanced communication between specialized parts of our brains. But if I'm dead, so is my brain. I'm not of your species, so I should be in a Gaian afterlife. Right?"

Salomen didn't answer, but her brows drew together.

"Therefore, if I'm here, I can't be dead." Lhyn waited for the clear logic of that to sink in.

"Nobody comes here if they're not dead."

"You did. So did Andira. So did your father and Nikin, all to help Micah."

"We came to the water surface, not to this." Salomen slapped her hand against the root. "And we're all Alsean."

"That was my point!"

"You're a sonsales Gaian. You cannot do what we did for Corozen."

"I'm a sonsales Gaian in a tyree bond with an Alsean. Andira said I should follow my knowledge of your heart. I did, and it led me here. Our bond led me here. You're trying to say that our bond makes me Alsean enough to come here if I'm dead, but not Alsean enough to come here while I'm alive and still linked to my living tyree. You can't have it both ways."

Salomen looked away in stubborn refusal.

This time, Lhyn didn't stifle her groan. She let her head fall back, thunking it against the trunk and hoping it might knock loose a brilliant idea.

Her breath caught. The tree.

This tree was a manifestation of Salomen's literal mind. She didn't need a better argument. She needed *evidence*. Literal, physical evidence.

She put a hand to her neck, terrified that it might not work in here. For one heart-stopping moment, she felt nothing. Then she shifted her fingers and exhaled in relief. The tree might be metaphorical, but her pulse was not.

Bark flew out from under her shoes as she scrambled to her knees. "Give me your hand."

"What?"

"Give me your hand. I want to show you something."

Frowning, Salomen held out her hand.

Lhyn folded down the fingers, leaving two extended, and pressed them against her carotid artery. "Feel that? My heart is still beating. I'm no spirit. I'm on the Path of the Return with you because I'm Sharing with you in your mindwalk. Our bond brought me here, Salomen. Not our deaths. Our *bond*."

Salomen stared at her with wide eyes, then felt for her own pulse. "Oh," she whispered. "I have a heartbeat."

A tiny smile tilted her lips. It was barely enough to bring out the beautiful lines at the sides of her mouth, but Lhyn recognized it. Salomen could not deny the evidence of her own senses.

"Thank the stars for that," she declared. "Andira is already so panicked she can hardly think straight. I don't want to imagine the condition she'd be in if you didn't have a pulse. Or the condition I'd be in." She rose and extended a hand, then held it up and stared in startled realization. "I touched you! And you touched me!"

"So?"

"So Ekatya and I couldn't do that before. It's new to this link."

Salomen gestured around them. "We're on the Path of the Return. Andira physically held Corozen here, and I held her. That's not new."

"I'm Sharing with you on the *Phoenix*. Touching your neck and jaw. Andira was holding your hand. It *is* new."

She looked up through the branches, allowing herself a moment to absorb the incredible truth: this was the afterlife. She would have given anything to stay ten ticks longer, but Alsea was depending on them.

Fahla had a twisted sense of humor, as Salomen was fond of saying.

"Come on, heart of mine," she said, offering her hand once more. "As much as I'd love to explore this place and write the greatest paper *ever*, we have to go."

Salomen let herself be pulled upright. "But it won't help. I don't have any more control now than I did before. Our plan won't work."

"It already did. They lost their flagship captain. You stopped the bioforce missiles long enough for our fighters to arrive. Right before I came in here, they caught three missiles the *Phoenix* missed. You didn't fail your whole world, Salomen. You saved it and gave us a second chance. Our stubborn warriors are figuring out what to do next."

She saw the moment when reality hit.

"Oh, Fahla. They're still fighting!"

"Yes. So how do we get back?"

Salomen raced down the root. "Come on!"

Lhyn gave chase, rounding the boulder in time to see her dive from a frightening height and slice into the water with barely a splash.

"She needs to teach me how to do that," she grumbled, and leaped off with considerably less flair.

Beneath the surface, Salomen caught her hand. They descended from green to gray to black, and though Lhyn could no longer see, she did not fear.

Like her pulse, Salomen's grip was no metaphor. It was proof.

15

UNTHINKABLE TRUTH

The Voloth flagship fought on, though not nearly as fluidly as before. It had lost its captain, and while that man had been reprehensible, he was also an excellent tactician. Ekatya considered his death a serious wound to the ship.

Unfortunately, no tactical ability was required to fire wave after wave of bioforce missiles.

Though concise, Andira's instructions still took too much time. They lost more time preparing Commander Lokomorra, but could shave no corners there. Once Ekatya went live on the com, she would not be able to speak without her words being shared across the Alsean system, the Voloth Empire, and the Protectorate. She was depending on Lokomorra to take care of everything without further guidance.

When he was ready, she adjusted her open call to Andira's divine tyree unit to include all bridge communications, translated to High Alsean. She also asked her ship's computer to mute incoming voice signals from Andira, Lhyn, and Salomen. Her brain had done a remarkable job of filtering the double communication, but she would need unbroken concentration for her upcoming performance.

In the meantime, Andira had updated Lanaril and brought her into the call. Ekatya thanked all the stars that she had come with Lhyn to Blacksun Base.

"It's enough to make you believe, isn't it?" Andira asked.

"Shut it," she grumbled.

"You need not believe in Fahla to be convincing." Lanaril spoke as calmly as if she were in her temple and not standing with Alsea's last line of defense. *"I'll do everything I can to help."*

With their preparations complete, they were forced to watch another launch while the political liaison ignored her offer of surrender.

She supposed it shouldn't be a surprise. He was already breaking every rule of civilized warfare. Refusing surrender was minor compared to murdering a planet.

If Salomen returned from wherever she was, she could jump to the flagship and compel him to accept the call. Once they had him on the com, they could end this. But Salomen remained motionless, and Lhyn hadn't moved either.

"We can't keep this up," she said. "We need to go on the offensive and hurt them enough for a call to get priority."

"If we go on the offensive, we'll be leaving planetary defense to the fighters," Andira said. "This is difficult enough. Making them the sole line of defense is an invitation for disaster. I hate to say it, but we're better off fighting defensively and giving Lhyn time."

The flagship fired yet another wave of bioforce missiles. This time, the *Phoenix* managed only sixteen interceptions, its worst effort yet.

The battle was taking a toll on Ekatya's weapons teams. Diminishing accuracy was a sign of both physical and mental fatigue. Knowing that an entire planet depended on their every shot was too great a burden to bear for long.

"Fighter teams intercepting," the weapons officer reported. "Positive contact on one. Two. Three."

Ekatya waited, her stomach dropping at the too-long pause.

"Negative contact. The fourth missile is below minimum altitude."

Andira did not speak, but her horror was a black weight on Ekatya's soul.

It was impossible to accept, she thought numbly. Millions in the city would die. Blacksun Base would be affected by the fallout within minutes. Lhyn, Andira, Salomen, Lanaril—they were all there, standing outside.

Her grandfather had once told her that ghosts were simply people who didn't know they had died. By that definition, Lhyn and Salomen were already ghosts.

Andira and Lanaril were not. They knew they were dead. But the far worse fate would be watching their civilization die first.

"Nightwing is in pursuit."

Her head snapped up. What could Candini and Rahel possibly do?

"They are attempting to grapple the missile and return it to target altitude."

"They have a modified grappler." She hadn't even thought of it. "Bigger reach and reinforced. Stars and Shippers, it might be possible."

"Your warrior and mine." Andira's eyes were brimming with the desperate hope that brightened their link. "It has to be a sign. It has to."

"May Fahla guide and protect them," Lanaril murmured.

Ekatya recognized the first line of an ancient prayer. She was trying to remember the rest of it—something about walking in dark places—when her comm officer spoke.

"Commander Lokomorra, the flagship has accepted our call."

"Captain?" Lokomorra asked.

"I'm ready." She wasn't, but there was no other option.

"Put it through to Captain Serrado, voice only," he ordered.

A soft click sounded in her internal com, followed by a voice she recognized from the flagship's bridge.

"Captain Serrado. No video? Is something wrong with your systems?"

"It's been a busy day." She should not have been capable of this kind of calm, but was grateful that her emotions had shut down. "We've had minor damage. Is something wrong with yours?"

"Not at all. I didn't want to talk terms until you understood the true stakes. Now that we've broken your defense, we can proceed. I am Commodore Vataka, at your service."

"A commodore, I'm honored. The Voloth Empire didn't think a captain was good enough to face me?"

Vataka hesitated for a telltale second before replying. *"Our captain has fought well and bravely. His job is done. Authority to treat with the enemy falls to me. Captain, would it surprise you to know that the Empire has developed a counteragent for the payload we dropped in Alsea's atmosphere?"*

"No, that doesn't surprise me," she said in disgust. "But it does explain why you waited until now to accept my call. This isn't a battle, it's extortion."

"It is a strategic master stroke. If the Alsean government agrees to our terms, their planet will live. Minus the population of Blacksun, of course. But in the larger picture, that should be an acceptable loss. Better a city than a civilization."

She could easily predict the terms on offer: lifelong slavery in exchange for the right to keep breathing. And the Voloth would have access to Alsea's nanoscrubbers, evening the playing field between them and the Protectorate.

"I will never agree," Andira snarled. "Neither will the Council." She clutched her chest and spun around, her fury gone in an instant. "Tyrina!"

Lhyn and Salomen were climbing to their feet.

"Are we too late?" Salomen barely got the words out before being scooped into a fervent embrace.

"No." Andira's voice was little more than a gasp. "But Goddess above, we need you."

"I have the authority to discuss those terms with you and convey them to the Alsean Council." Ekatya pulled Lhyn into a quick side hug, the most she could allow herself in this fraught moment. "Do you agree to a cessation of hostilities in the meantime?"

"I will allow it. Our destroyers are standing down."

On the battle grid, the four Voloth destroyers broke off their attacks and flew toward the flagship.

"Commander, notify the *Thea* and *Victory* and tell them to stand down." Eliminating the remainder of those mines was now top priority; she trusted him to give the right orders. Silently, she gestured at Salomen and pointed to the flagship on the display.

"We need to jump back to their bridge," Andira said. "Can you get us there?"

"I think so. What aren't you telling me? What happened?"

"Commander." Mindful of the open call to the flagship, her weapons officer spoke quietly. "Nightwing has captured the missile and is regaining altitude."

Andira must have heard from the war council at the same time. "Yes!" she shouted, punching the air with both fists. "Thank you, Fahla!" Her relief nearly overwhelmed their link as she flung her arms around Salomen again. "You missed a lot, but it's all right now."

Ekatya would have danced a damn jig if she'd had time. Instead, she muted the call. "Salomen, get us over there *now*."

Shocked realization spread across Salomen's face, but she nodded.

This jump was easier than the first one. One moment Ekatya was looking at her bridge, the next she was staring at Commodore Vataka. The captain's corpse had been removed, but no one had yet cleaned the blood from the deck—or his chair.

"Yuck." Lhyn scrunched her nose.

"Force him," Andira said. "Obedience this time. We'll work with him, not against him."

Salomen asked no questions. Barely two seconds later, she said, "I have him."

"Commodore Vataka," Ekatya said immediately. "I have called a ceasefire. Tell your ships that this battle is over. Inform your crew that no more bioforce missiles are to be fired. Not today, not ever."

"You heard her," he barked to his startled bridge officers. "Stow all remaining bioforce missiles. Inform the captains that the ceasefire is permanent."

They hustled to obey. Ekatya allowed herself a deep breath, then another.

That, she thought, might have been the easy part.

"I've been informed that our communication system is repaired," she said. "I suggest we go to visual. In fact, given the historic nature of these talks, I believe we should open this communication for all interested parties to observe."

Dialogue between opposing military forces was never conducted on an open channel. The results, yes, but not the means of arriving at them. She had phrased her command carefully, using the pride of the Empire to give Vataka a justification that would allay the suspicions of his bridge officers.

"Pride," Andira told Salomen. "Gleeful agreement. This is exactly what he wants, to have his conquest broadcast in real time."

Ekatya spared a moment to admire the two Alseans, who were taking multitasking to new heights. They were standing on the planet, listening to translated communications on their earcuffs, and acting on them here in orbit. At least she had the advantage of needing no translation.

Vataka agreed with alacrity. Despite the confirmation from her comm officer, Ekatya took a chance and dragged open her physical eyes. The duality of vision was dizzying, but she saw enough before letting her heavy lids shut once more.

"Well, Captain? I'm waiting. Your reputation is legendary. I'm eager to see this legend for myself. Now that you've surrendered," he added smugly.

"Engage visual," she said.

The split view that appeared on the flagship's smaller display showed the result of Lokomorra's preparations. On one side was the standard visual communication, transmitted from her command console. On the other was a view typically reserved for official or celebratory transmissions, sent from a cam mounted above the lift doors and taking in the entire bridge.

Both showed the blinding glow that enveloped her body. What could easily have been dismissed as data manipulation in the closeup was made far more convincing by the wide view.

She heard several gasps on the flagship bridge. It did look rather impressive.

"What is the meaning of this?" Vataka demanded. "What trick are you attempting?"

"There is no trick." It was decidedly odd to see herself speaking on that display, with her eyes closed and head resting against the seat back. "I am not Captain Serrado."

Lhyn put both hands to her mouth, admiration chasing astonishment as she realized their plan.

"You certainly look like her," he snapped. "Minus the visual effects."

"Commodore Vataka, engage your full bridge view and add it to this communication."

"Do it," he ordered his comm officer. He was startled and angry, but still under Salomen's control.

"Dual transmission engaged."

"Excellent," Ekatya said. "Now we can begin. For those watching now and all who will watch this recording in future, allow me to summarize our situation. Commodore Vataka of the Voloth Empire has agreed to a ceasefire after firing bioforce missiles on Alsea. He tells me he has authority to treat with the Empire's enemies, but I am no enemy."

Fucking Hades, how was she supposed to pull this off?

"Captain." Lokomorra's voice was quiet in her physical ear. "Candini was successful."

Thank all the stars. With that last piece in place, she tuned out the commands he was issuing to operations and medical. A ceasefire meant time to deal with the aftermath, and she was glad to leave that in his hands.

"With Captain Serrado's permission, I have inhabited her body," she said. "To the Alseans, I am known as Fahla. You know me as a Seeder."

The Voloth bridge officers murmured amongst themselves. She was pleased to note that her own crew didn't turn a hair.

"Excited belief," Andira urged Salomen. "Whether or not he personally worships the Seeders, his empire acts in their name. This is a coup for him."

"He does worship them," Salomen said. "But he fears deception."

"Work with that. If you can, remove the doubt gradually. The belief will be all the stronger for being natural."

"We've heard of the Seeder known as Fahla," Vataka said. "I would like to make her acquaintance. But surely you understand the Empire will need evidence that you are who you say you are."

"Allow me," Lanaril said. *"Let's give Salomen time to remove that doubt."* She began speaking, her careful enunciation making it easier for Ekatya to hear and memorize.

"For an Empire that claims to act in my name and the names of my brethren," Ekatya repeated, "I should think faith would be enough. But no matter. You ask for evidence? You shall have it, in the form of a gift. Commodore Vataka, I give you the gift of truth. Mine . . . and yours."

The guidance continued in distinct phrases that burned themselves into her brain as she understood Lanaril's inspiration. Looking at Salomen, she echoed the first.

"I am the goddess of compassion and family, though I suspect that means little to you."

Her gaze settled on Lhyn. "I am the goddess of wisdom, learning, and inner strength. That, I'm afraid, is also of no interest to you."

Andira knew where this was leading, nodding as their eyes met.

"Today you woke the goddess of judgment, protector of her people. I am no goddess of war, though you may mistake me for one if you do not choose wisely. Tell me, Commodore. Do you truly believe you act with divine approval from the Seeders?" Going off script, she added, "Speak the truth with no prevarications."

A direct command. Under Salomen's compulsion, he had no choice but to obey.

"No," he said. "Some in the Quorum do. Most don't."

Two-thirds of the bridge officers turned to stare in open shock. Vataka had uttered an unthinkable truth.

Confident now that they had crossed that line, Ekatya spoke for herself. "Yet you claim that approval. Your government tells its people that by serving it, they are serving the wishes of the Seeders."

"Yes."

"Explain why you and your government claim an approval you know is a lie." An order, not a question.

"It's done," Salomen said. "He believes. He's eager to please her."

"It's a useful fallacy." Vataka spread his hands in an expansive gesture. "The Empire's reach depends on it. We're controlling too many worlds. Our citizens are outnumbered thirty to one by slaves and hangers. If they ever rose together, the Empire would fall in a day. Fear and military might keeps most of them down; fear of acting against the Seeders does the rest. And pride," he added with a touch of his own. "I've often said we should value the power of pride. Some think fear is more powerful, but I don't agree. People will do anything as long as they can convince themselves they're right and justified. If they think they have divine approval? So much the better."

By now, the few officers still working had given up. Vataka had the unwavering attention of every person on the bridge—and everyone else watching this broadcast, both in the Protectorate and the Voloth Empire.

"I see," she said. "When you told your crew to enact genocide against an entire planet, they thought they were doing what was right."

Most of the officers looked distinctly uncomfortable. Several were visibly frightened. A few were angry, but she didn't know if that anger was directed against Vataka's earlier lies or the truth he was now speaking.

Andira was on the same wavelength. "They're mostly horrified, but three of them want him to stop talking." She pointed to two officers on the fourth landing and one on the third. "Him, her, and her."

"Commodore, I appreciate your honesty so far. Some of your officers do not. They don't believe your people deserve the truth. The man just below you. The woman to his left. And the woman in the center of the third landing. Remove them from your bridge."

In retrospect, she should have phrased it more carefully.

Vataka whipped out his disruptor and squeezed off three shots in rapid succession. Screams rent the air, both from the dying officers and those terrified by the lethal violence. Next to the third victim, a man dazedly wiped viscera from his face.

Salomen let out a wordless cry, her distress flooding their link.

"You couldn't have stopped him," Andira said hurriedly. "You cannot risk losing your control. It's not your fault."

"I know." Salomen's voice shook, but she kept her hold.

"They are silenced." Vataka replaced his disruptor.

What was Ekatya supposed to say to that? *Good job, not quite what I meant?*

"I accept your proof," he continued. "Captain Serrado could not know the identity of the other three Political Bureau officers on this bridge. No one in this task force knew that. You are who you say you are, and I am proud to serve."

Make that *Good job, I always wanted a homicidal worshiper.*

"Then let us continue," she managed. "You have shown me your dedication to the truth. I am pleased. Tell us now, did the Alseans attack your people before you attempted to take this planet by force the first time?"

"No."

The bridge officers gaped at each other, confirming a Fleet Intelligence theory: not even citizens or lower-ranked officers knew the whole truth.

"Did you ever send a peaceful envoy to treat with the Alseans, as you told your people?"

"No. That was a lie."

"Did the Alseans even know of your existence before you attempted to invade their planet? To enslave and exterminate them?"

"No."

"Fuck me," whispered one man. The others were silent, but their expressions matched his words.

"Tell your people the truth now. Why did you invade Alsea the first two times?"

"It has strategic importance. It's close to the Protectorate border and rich in natural resources. But the critical reason was its people. Alsean empaths would have been invaluable slaves. Possibly even turned the tide in our war with the Protectorate."

An officer on the first level dropped her head into her hands.

"How many of the planets you have attacked were truly a threat to your Empire?"

"I don't know. Many of our records predate my work with the Bureau." Eager to provide some kind of answer, he hurriedly added, "But in the twenty years I've served? Three, maybe. That is, they could have been a threat if we hadn't put a stop to their technological development."

"Fuck *me*," said the officer who had sworn earlier. "It's all a lie? *All* of it?"

The others appeared just as stunned. Ekatya found herself reluctantly sympathetic.

"How many of your envoys have been attacked during your tenure?"

He laughed. "We don't send envoys. We send intelligence gathering teams to determine which worlds are worth our investment. Primitives rarely even know we're there."

"One last question, Commodore. We know why you attacked Alsea the first two times. This third time, you violated all norms of civilized warfare by using bioforce missiles. You attempted genocide against a peaceful people. Why?"

"Do you want the official answer from my government? Or do you want the answer I believe?"

"I'm interested in both."

He looked happy to hear that. "Officially, we were ensuring the enslavement of the Alseans, access to their nanoweaponry, and the stripping of their resources. I'm sure that's all true, but they're not the real motivating forces. They're what procured political support. The real motivation is that the current Quorum leaders are afraid to look weak. Being beaten by a tiny planet full of primitives, which then signed a treaty with you—that is, with the Protectorate—it doesn't get weaker or more humiliating than that. This was supposed to be a lesson to the Protectorate and to those in the Empire who might be inspired by

Alsean resistance. Resist our might and you'll be wiped out of existence."

"Now that, I believe," muttered the *fuck me* officer.

A shiver ran down Ekatya's spine, leaving her dazed with the realization. It was done. They had not merely stopped this attack; they had destabilized the Voloth Empire. This entire conversation was public. The Empire would never be able to contain the damage.

"He values pride," Lanaril said. *"And contributing to his Empire. Salomen's job will be easier if we tell him . . ."*

Ekatya listened carefully.

"When you base an empire on lies," she repeated, "you build it on sand. It cannot hold against the tides of time. You have brought the truth to your Empire, Commodore Vataka. History will record you as the man who helped to save it."

Lanaril had a rather loose definition of saving, she thought with an internal smile. But Vataka glowed, proud to be singled out for his belief.

"It's time to finish this. Lancer Tal," she said, cuing her comm officer to make the prearranged addition to the call. "My Chosen. I see that Blacksun remains untouched."

The Voloth bridge officers goggled at that. She wasn't sure if it was because their attempted genocide hadn't worked, or because Fahla had put the leader of Alsea on the line.

Andira shook her head, smiling at the impromptu political boost. "My Goddess. The sun still shines on Blacksun, thanks to two courageous warriors who captured the missile mid-flight. We thank you for watching over us."

Now that was a brain stunner Ekatya hadn't prepared for: having Andira speaking High Alsean right in front of her while simultaneously hearing her voice over the Voloth com, distorted by the translator.

"I will always watch over you. Alsea is under my protection," she said, cringing the moment the words were out of her mouth. She had probably just influenced the next two thousand cycles of Alsean culture.

Lanaril came to her rescue once again, feeding her the right lines.

"But you must never grow complacent. Your brave warriors committed that act on their own, with no aid from me. My influence lies on the spiritual plane, not the physical."

Those might be the most truthful words she had uttered in the last fifteen minutes, and they weren't even hers.

"Spiritual aid is still an aid, and one we value greatly." Andira had the audacity to wink at her. "Your wisdom has seen us through trying times. I pray it shall ever be so."

"Is your emissary ready?"

"Yes, Fahla. She and her team can be there in a tentick."

"Very good. Send her."

"This is our best chance," Lanaril said. *"It's time to teach the Voloth a few truths."*

Surely it was the height of irony that Ekatya was letting a religious leader speak for her in the middle of a battle. Her self-image might never recover.

"Commodore Vataka."

He snapped into a respectful posture. "Yes?"

Lanaril spoke fluidly, pausing at regular intervals to allow her to repeat the words.

"You recently referred to the Alseans as primitives. Among my brethren, we use that term differently. To us, primitives are those who act as you acted earlier today, before you understood the power of truth."

He had been stiffening, but at this he relaxed and smiled.

"Your Empire has been primitive throughout its engagements with Alsea. Its cruelty toward its own people has led them to become cruel in turn. But the most primitive thing about you is your belief regarding the Termegon Fields."

She could practically see the electricity running through the bridge crew at the mention of their afterlife paradise.

"You believe that only citizens may enter the Termegon Fields upon death. This may be the greatest lie you tell yourselves. It is certainly the greatest lie you tell your hangers and slaves. The Termegon Fields are not for sale. You do not buy your way in with citizenship in the Empire. You earn your passage. Each time you act with compassion or kindness toward those less fortunate, every day that you live in truth and seek a higher truth, you take a step closer to our home. Think about that. Who is likelier to enter the Termegon Fields? Your citizens? Or your hangers and slaves?"

Though not a warrior, Lanaril had delivered a hammer blow to the officers. More importantly, this was a message to the hangers and slaves making up the majority of the flagship's crew complement, as well as the crews of the four destroyers. For the next part of their plan to work, they needed those crews to stand aside.

"I have asked the Alseans to send an emissary to your ship to discuss terms of truce. I suggest you use this opportunity to repair some of the damage you have all done to your chances at a happy afterlife." Speaking on her own now, Ekatya let her anger show. "You have attempted genocide against a peaceful people under my protection. Not a single person in this task force will set foot in the Termegon Fields unless you make a change today. Greet this emissary with peace and honor."

"I will," Vataka said shakily.

"You will? Or your crew will?"

He drew himself up. "My crew await the arrival of your emissary. She will be received with honor."

"Good. You may yet salvage your fates."

16

BACK TO THE BEGINNING

A flash of green light.
Darkness.
A flash of green light.
Darkness.

A vibrating hum, steady and somehow reassuring. Voices, one closer and another farther away. She could not make out the words.

The familiar pressure of emotions. Fear and worry. Desperation.

The green light flashed one more time and ceased, replaced by an overall brightness. The hum intensified.

A slight bump set off a wave of agony. Had she any voice, she would have screamed.

The hum died away. Now there were scraping sounds and hurried, staccato words. More emotions crowded around, their worry controlled by intense focus.

" . . . lucky it didn't clear the hull. You'd never have sealed the hole."

"I don't fucking feel lucky. I'm alive because her body stopped it. Get her out of there!"

"First Pilot, you're not helping. Give us room."

She recognized some of the voices, but could put no faces to them.

One snapped out orders, her tone conveying perfect confidence in herself and the obedience of everyone around her.

Beneath that confidence was a black hole of terror, controlled and hidden but ready to swallow everything the moment it was freed.

A prick to one arm. Then to the other.

"Give me the laser cutter."

"Dr. Wells, are you sure—"

"It's going to take a small body and small hands, so unless you want me to shrink yours with this?"

"There's no need for threats. I understand your stress—"

"You understand nothing. Now follow Candini's example and *give me room.*"

Confidence-over-terror brushed against her legs.

"Stay with me, Rahel."

The quiet, caring tone unlocked a face in her mind. She opened her eyes to find that same face looking down at her in surprise.

"She's conscious!" Dr. Wells called. "My sainted Shippers, how are you conscious? Dammit, I wish you weren't."

She tried to ask why, but all that came out was a tiny sound in the back of her throat.

"There's a piece of sabot going through the hull and your chest. I have to cut you free. I'm sorry, but I can't give you anything to help with the pain. You've lost too much blood and your pressure is too low."

Sabot. Yes, she remembered that.

She was sure she had died. Instead, she was . . . on the *Phoenix?*

There was something about the *Phoenix*, some reason she had not expected to be here. She couldn't remember.

"It will take about thirty seconds. I'll try to stabilize as I cut, but there will be vibrations. I'm sorry, Rahel."

Dr. Wells vanished from her field of view. A high-pitched whine rose from behind her.

Her chest caught fire.

The voice she had been missing burst out of her in a hoarse scream. Then another. She had never experienced an agony like this.

A tempest of grief and fury swept over her and was immediately locked down by ferocious determination.

The whine stopped. The fire did not.

"Clear! Ready transport!" In a softer voice, Dr. Wells spoke into her ear. "One more jar. Then you can relax."

She appreciated the warning.

It didn't help. Her body was shifted forward and lifted, sending another wave of flames through her. She had no strength left to scream.

They laid her on something soft, positioned on her side, and the wave mercifully ebbed. After the flames, this pain was nothing more than standing barefoot on hot sand in the summer.

"The worst is over. Stay with me, all right? After this, I'll be furious if you give up now."

She tried very hard not to give up as they brought her down to the shuttle bay deck.

But the lights dimmed, and she couldn't turn them back on again.

17

EMISSARY

From her position in the copilot's seat, Vellmar had an excellent view of the Voloth flagship they were approaching.

"Fahla on a funstick, that thing is ugly," she muttered.

"True words." Her pilot, an older warrior from Whitemoon Base, shook his head. "I used to think the *Caphenon* and *Phoenix* were what all Gaian ships looked like. Beautiful. Curvaceous. Then our destroyers arrived, and I thought, eh, not every ship can be a work of art. They're nice enough, but I don't want to stroke them."

Vellmar chuckled. "You wanted to stroke the *Caphenon*?"

"I did stroke it. Took a tour back when it first opened for viewing. Someday I'll fly on that ship," he said with certainty. "But this? What a bucket of bolts. It looks like someone gave a group of children some building blocks and said 'Go now, make a ship from these.'"

"It did a lot of damage for a bucket of bolts."

"Eh. It needs to be blown back to its constituent molecules. Or better yet, towed into the sun."

"I think Lancer Tal has a better use for it."

"If she keeps it, I'm not flying on it. We're still four lengths away and already my skin wants to crawl off my body."

Vellmar watched a bristling row of rail gun barrels slide past her side window and wondered whether Lancer Tal had taken that into account. If they succeeded in seizing this ship, how many Alseans could bring themselves to serve on it? There was already a waiting list of applicants to crew the *Caphenon* once it was raised. This would be a much harder sell. It was more than the ugly appearance or its provenance; it was what the crew had tried to do. Genocidal intentions were surely embedded in its bulkheads.

Rubbing the back of her neck, she silently admitted that it gave her the shivers, too. She was not looking forward to boarding it.

The shuttle bay came into view, its vast doors open and waiting. She listened to her pilot converse with the Voloth bridge and tried to shake her sense of flying straight into the jaws of a predator.

A small fish, Rahel had said.

In their last conversation before battle prep closed the communication lines, they had wished each other luck and offered a few words of encouragement. Rahel's had been typical of her: pragmatic and somehow poetic at the same time, with a dash of dockside wisdom.

"You're a small fish," she said of Vellmar's strike team. "But a lethal one. One thing you learn growing up by the ocean: size isn't everything. Ever see a firefin?"

Having grown up by landlocked mountains, Vellmar had not. The image Rahel showed her was of a rotund little fish the size of her fist, its body covered in iridescent swirls of green and blue while its fins were flaming orange and red.

"There's enough neurotoxin in one of these to kill fifty Alseans," Rahel had announced. "Nothing eats a firefin. Even the biggest fish take one look and flee. The Voloth still don't know that size isn't everything, or they wouldn't come back. Be a firefin."

Perhaps she *was* flying into the jaws of a predator, Vellmar thought. But that predator would regret taking the bite.

She sent a silent wish of luck to her friend, somewhere out there among the fighters still guarding their world, and unfastened her harness. Standing up attracted the attention of the twelve Lancer's Guards seated in the main cabin. These were her finest, and she was proud to have them at her back.

"Listen up," she called. "Lancer Tal says the bridge crew is quiet and noncombative. We have control of their commanding officer. That doesn't mean we have control of the rest. Captain Serrado just destroyed their belief system. That will knock the fight out of most, but a few will fight even harder. Never underestimate the determination of those desperate to avoid admitting they were wrong."

"Is that really Captain Serrado?" Senshalon, her second-in-command, voiced the big question. "It didn't sound like her."

"She's acting." Dewar had one arm wrapped around the medic's pack on the seat beside her. "She wouldn't be chatting with that blindworm like one captain to another. She has to sound like a goddess."

"I've never heard a goddess speak," Vellmar said. "I couldn't say what one sounds like."

Senshalon snorted. "Lead Templar Satran is your lover. Don't tell us you don't know what a goddess sounds like."

The shuttle filled with laughter as Vellmar tried and failed to keep the blood from rushing to her face. "Someone needs to teach you the difference between literal and figurative."

Lanaril would be highly amused at Senshalon's comment. Vellmar wished she were in Blacksun Temple now, telling her. They had lost four precious days together, all for nothing. She had been based in Whitemoon on the assumption that their ship infiltration would occur near the space elevator, so of course the Fahla-damned blindworms had tried to bomb Blacksun instead. Her pilot had put their shuttle through an unplanned speed test getting them into position in time.

She held up a hand, quieting her warriors when Lancer Tal's voice sounded in her earcuff.

"Vellmar, a bridge officer named Onruang is coming to escort you. You can trust him as much as you can trust any of these officers. He's unhappy and hasn't been afraid to verbalize it."

"In front of that commodore?"

"He's only shot four people so far." Lancer Tal sounded darkly amused. *"And none of them for repeatedly saying 'shek me.' Onruang will bring you to a conference room off the bridge. I expect to see all eleven of you walking through here, understood?"*

"Do you expect our uniforms to be clean as well?"

"That would be ideal." Her voice grew serious. *"Onruang is obeying his orders to escort you, but he was lying when he agreed to ten warriors each. His loyalty is to the ship and the Empire. He'll take precautions."*

"I understand. We'll be ready."

The shuttle bay was nothing like that of the *Phoenix*. Vellmar had been to Captain Serrado's ship several times, first to visit Rahel and more recently to practice moving through it with her team. She liked the enclosed bay with its exit tunnel and green guidance lights.

This bay was pretentious, open to space as if advertising that the Voloth didn't need thoughtful, protective design. Inside, nine shuttles were lined up in rows of three, each as bristly and unattractive as the flagship. A large square outlined in blinking lights was clearly the landing area for incoming shuttles. Shelving lined the bulkheads, reaching from the deck to the distant ceiling and packed with crates held in place by crisscrossing metal bars.

Two force fields kept the bay pressurized. One dropped as they entered, then reactivated behind them. For a few stressful pipticks, they were trapped between fields. Then the inner field dropped, and they flew into the massive bay.

Vellmar let out a soft exhale. "That's the first wall to climb. Glad we didn't have to fight our way in."

"It wouldn't have been difficult. Just a matter of forcing the right one." Senshalon was behind her, peering over her shoulder. "Look at that. Ten soldiers for us to see and fifty more hiding in those shuttles."

Vellmar had just finished her own count, dismayed at the number of emotional signatures flaring all over the bay. A six-to-one disadvantage was more than she had prepared for. Worse, most of them were nervous, which made them unpredictable.

"How are we going to empathically force sixty soldiers?" Senshalon asked.

"I think we'll have to be ready for something a little quicker and more permanent."

He patted the knives at his hips. "That's why I brought these."

"Or, maybe they'll be remorseful and walk us to the bridge with no problems."

"Sure," he said skeptically. "And maybe dokkers will learn to sing."

When the shuttle landed, she touched palms with the two Guards who would remain with their pilot. "If I give the word, or fail to check in at the appointed times, don't wait. You know your duty."

"Yes, Lead Guard." Neither Varsi nor Corlander were happy with being left in the safest place. On the other hand, if they did have to carry out their alternative duty, it would make their names. In the event that Vellmar couldn't bring her team back, they would force the nearest capable Voloth to bring down both force fields, depressurize the bay, and drop a package on their way out. It was a rigged Delfin torpedo from the *Caphenon*, and Captain Serrado had assured them that exploding it in the bay would cripple the flagship. After that, the *Phoenix* would finish it off.

As much as Vellmar wished she could follow that plan from the outset, her orders were clear. She led her ten Guards down the ramp and stopped in front of a shorter man in a ridiculously fancy uniform that might as well have been a sign reading *I never get out of my chair.* The profusion of braids and buttons would surely catch on the first tight corner he tried to walk around.

"Lead Guard Vellmar," he said in perfect High Alsean. "I am Operations Master Onruang. Welcome to the *Vengeance.*"

She managed not to roll her eyes at the ship's name and chose instead to be grateful that they wouldn't have to use their translators. "You speak High Alsean. Good, that will save time."

"Every officer on this crew has an Alsean language chip."

"What about the hangers and slaves?"

Though he kept it off his face, his disdain at the idea was suffocating. "They don't need it."

"And the fifty crew members hidden in your shuttles? Do they also have Alsean language chips?"

This time, he couldn't hide his reaction. "I, ah. They're for your safety."

"Dokshin. They're here in case we do anything to threaten you or your ship. The agreement was for ten warriors each. Mine are behind me." She raised her voice. "I am the Alsean emissary, sent by Lancer Tal and Fahla herself. You shame yourself and your commodore by not receiving me with honor. Bring your people into the open or we'll go back the way we came and you can explain your failure to Commodore Vataka."

It was an exceedingly effective threat. Within a tick, fifty armed soldiers had emerged from hiding at the call of their commanding officer.

"Better," Vellmar said. "Tell me, Master Onruang. Are you ashamed of your part in the attempted genocide of a peaceful people?"

He looked her up and down, noting her combat uniform, the

disruptor at her hip, and the throwing blades sheathed along straps crossing over her chest and back.

She doubted that he recognized the sword grip hanging from her opposite hip.

"Your people may be peaceful, but I know a soldier when I see one. Yes, I'm ashamed. I never believed the Empire should lower itself that far, even for a race that deserved it. To hear you never knew we existed . . ." He shook his head. "I'm a proud officer of the Voloth Empire. But I'm not proud today."

Truth. Not that she expected any different; Lancer Tal would not have led her wrong.

"Your words are welcome. I would now like to hear from your soldiers. Each of my warriors will ask the question. Answer honestly."

Onruang nodded to his soldiers. "Do as she says."

Her Guards spread out, and a hum of voices rose as the question was asked and answered of the first ten.

"Lie."

"Lie."

Both Senshalon and Dewar crouched in ready stances by the soldiers they had questioned.

"These two are not ashamed of genocide," Vellmar said. "I will not have them at my back."

Onruang sighed. "They were good officers," he said reluctantly, before drawing his disruptor.

Two shots sizzled through the air. Two bodies thudded to the deck. Fifty-eight soldiers took a simultaneous step backward, fear rising off their bodies in a nauseating stink.

Vellmar held herself still. She had heard the stories from Rax Sestak and his fellow settlers. She had seen Rax's scars and watched Commodore Vataka kill three bridge officers on an open com call. Even so, it was difficult to swallow the casual, lethal violence that seemed a normal part of life in the Voloth military.

No wonder Rax and his settlers were so happy in their little village.

"You." She pointed to the eight who had passed the test. "Stand over there."

They trotted to the designated space, relief making the air sing around them.

"Warriors, proceed."

Three soldiers failed this time. Vellmar fully expected the rest to run when three more smoking bodies joined the first two, yet they stood in place, awaiting their fate in silent resignation.

Even fantens fought the slaughter, she thought.

Their fear made them dangerous. They now knew their lies would be detected, yet were too terrified of Onruang to run or fight back. The only option left was to attack the ones exposing them.

"Warriors," she barked. When she had their attention, she pointed at her own eyes, a signal that came closest to the warning she needed to give them.

Get a target lock.

"Proceed."

Her warriors moved forward. Before any of them could ask the question, two soldiers screamed their defiance and drew disruptors. One died with a blade in his heart and a hand clamped around his wrist. His weapon hadn't cleared the holster.

The other, a sturdy woman with tattoos around her eyes, cleared her weapon but lost it when Senshalon snapped her wrist, tore the disruptor from her grasp, and threw it across the bay. He then broke her other wrist, leaving her incapable of using any weapon.

Onruang shot her anyway, his emotional signature radiating disgust. Vellmar wasn't certain whether it was from her attempt at murder under the flag of parley, or because she had been bested by a primitive in hand-to-hand combat.

The remaining soldiers realized they were doomed no matter what. Five drew their weapons. Two were shot by their fellow officers; three more died from Alsean weapons.

The carnage was shocking and far more than she had expected before they even left the shuttle bay. Somehow, she kept her voice level as she said, "We still need to ask. Continue."

No more Voloth failed.

When there were twelve corpses on the deck and forty-eight trustworthy soldiers standing at attention, Vellmar turned to Onruang. "Now we can go."

He put them in the center, with twenty-four soldiers ahead and an equal number behind. They followed the first group out the double doors and into a broad corridor with a ceiling so low that it made her want to duck. It was another difference between this ship design and that of the Pulsar class. If she used her sword in these corridors, overhead strokes would be out of the question.

The air smelled different as well, old and dry with a metallic tang. She vastly preferred the clean, woodsy scent of the *Caphenon* and *Phoenix*.

But the low ceilings and stale air were minor discomforts compared to the sheer empathic weight of this place. In the shuttle bay, she had focused on the immediate danger of the soldiers and tuned out the rest. Now she cast her empathic net wider, looking for hidden dangers, and sensed heavy echoes of pain, fear, horror, and despair. She had worried about the genocidal intent, but the bigger issue was the cycles upon cycles of misery that had soaked into the physical structure.

They would have to crew this ship with low empaths and sonsales.

The lead soldier stopped in front of a lift, which chirped at him and slid open its doors.

"No," she said. "We won't use lifts."

Onruang raised his eyebrows. "It's a long walk."

"Lifts can be redirected. Or stopped. They're traps with only one exit. We will not use them."

"Lead Guard, I assure you it's perfectly safe. I'm the Operations Master. Nobody will be redirecting or attacking this lift without my authorization."

She crossed her arms and waited.

"Fine," he said impatiently, though it was only for show. In truth, he respected her suspicion.

They walked down the corridor for what felt like half a length before arriving at a door marked with reflective text Vellmar could not read and a glyph that she could. The symbol for a ladder was apparently the same on both Protectorate and Voloth ships.

As the door slid aside and the first soldiers entered, Vellmar activated her earcuff. "Stay alert," she said in a low voice. "This is only a slightly more open trap than a lift."

The metal steps rang loudly under the impact of twenty-four pairs of boots. She watched the first group of officers trot upward, then led her team after them, Onruang at her side. The rungs were just wide enough for two.

Unlike the spacious, circular brace shafts on the *Phoenix*, this shaft was square and cramped, designed to accommodate the ladders and nothing else. Where the *Phoenix*'s ladders were vertical, passing through holes in landings at each deck, these were closer to very steep stairs. Each ended at a small landing, where one could either step forward to the door or turn around to climb the next ladder.

It was crowded and noisy, and Vellmar hated it. Looking upward, all she could see were switchbacking ladders full of soldiers. Below was a similar view, alleviated by the comforting sight of her warriors.

She slowed her pace.

Onruang grew suspicious as the leading group pulled ahead. "Planning something?"

"I don't like being constricted," she said shortly.

"I'd prefer that you keep up."

"I'd prefer not to have your soldiers' backsides in my face."

Though his expression did not shift, he was faintly amused. Nothing more was said as the open space grew to two, three, then four empty steps. That was as far as she could push it, given his rising wariness, but she was satisfied. Now she had room to maneuver.

They had climbed six decks when she sensed the danger. Somewhere above them, perhaps three decks away, an individual was approaching the shaft entrance with a disturbing mix of lethal intent and confident anticipation. One against sixty could only mean—

"Incoming!" she shouted, racing up two steps to the next landing. Onruang kept pace, distrust and an absence of fear showing that his motivation was solely to stay with her. He did not believe her warning.

The landing was clear, the soldiers ahead already on the next ladder but turning at her call. Senshalon and Dewar gave them no chance to move, having run up directly behind her and Onruang to take up the remaining space on the landing.

Vellmar slapped a hand against the control pad and thanked Fahla when the door slid open, revealing a wide passageway. She flung herself through, followed instantly by Onruang, and her warriors poured out in a steady stream. Determined to keep up with their superior officer, three Voloth crowded behind, too close for her to stop them.

The fourth was a hair too slow.

She stepped in front of him and turned at the same time, smashing her elbow into his jaw. It would have been a disorienting blow for any Alsean, but Gaians had lighter skeletons. He staggered back, falling half-conscious into the soldiers behind. That gave her enough room to kick him in the chest, sending the tightly packed mass clear of the door. Before any of them could recover their balance, she closed the door and shot the control pad for good measure.

"What the—" Onruang began hotly.

"Take cover!" Vellmar paid him no attention as she and her team crouched against the bulkhead, putting their backs to the door and arms over their heads.

For a frozen piptick, the four Voloth officers stood baffled. Then distrust expanded into sudden understanding, and Onruang dove to the floor.

His officers had barely joined him when a tremendous explosion blew through the ladder shaft, shaking the deck beneath their feet and bending the door outward. Several passing crew members screamed as they stumbled, then collected themselves and fled.

The ensuing silence was deafening. Even if Vellmar hadn't registered the sudden disappearance of emotional signatures in that shaft, she would have known the death toll by the lack of any sounds of pain—and the scent of burnt flesh and hot metal now clogging her nostrils.

Above her, the malign intent shifted to satisfaction and moved off. Whoever had ambushed them had no idea of their failure.

Well, that certainly took care of her numbers problem, though it introduced a new one. There was a variable on the loose with access to explosives and no concern for collateral casualties.

Onruang was so shocked that he sputtered. "I didn't authorize that!"

"I know."

"How dare they?! I issued orders for every member of this crew to respect your passage unless I said otherwise! They disobeyed!" It took him several pipticks to arrive at the next realization. "They must have killed every officer in the shaft!"

Vellmar stared at him in disbelief. He was more upset about the insult to his authority than about the tens of soldiers who had died under his command. And this was the one she was supposed to trust? What did that say about the other bridge officers?

"Vengeance," he snarled, and spoke a rapid stream of Common.

She thought he was making a vow before her wristcom kicked in and fed the translation to her earcuff. No, he was not swearing to avenge his fallen officers. He was issuing orders to the computer to put the ship under lockdown. When that was done, he ordered his security chief to find the bomber immediately, then called Commodore Vataka and assured him that everything was under control, a statement he believed.

A shrill alarm blared in the corridor, repeated itself twice, and was followed by an automated message. All personnel were to return to their quarters and remain until further notice.

"Does that include the weapons teams?" Vellmar asked.

"Getting ideas? Don't bother. Essential personnel are locked down at their duty stations."

"Great Mother," Dewar mumbled next to her. "They lock up their own crew."

"Only when necessary. Though I've never had to include officers in a lockdown before. It's usually slaves and sometimes the hangers."

Vellmar exchanged an incredulous glance with Dewar. These people were barbarians.

"Don't even think about trying mind control," he added. "We may be down to four, but I have trusted officers watching us through security cams. If you attack me, or if I act out of character, they have instructions to seal off the corridor and depressurize it. I'll die, but you'll die with me."

He was not bluffing. She nodded her understanding and gestured at the ruined door. "Who would have access to explosives like that?"

He scowled. "The chief of security and officers above three ribbons."

"How many officers are above three ribbons?"

"My orders are to get you safely to the bridge, Lead Guard. I don't have to answer your questions along the way."

"No, you don't. I was merely wondering who would have both the access and the willingness to kill you along with us."

Judging by his surprise, that had not even remotely occurred to him. He was accustomed to ironclad control over those beneath him—which, given his rank, accounted for nearly every person on the ship. She knew that much from Rax's lessons on the Voloth military power structure.

"And since you just ordered a lockdown, whoever it was knows you're still alive," she added. "The question is, will they be relieved or disappointed by that news?"

"Shek me," he muttered, looking up and down the quiet corridor before eying her with sudden interest. "I think you should meet my second while I ask her a question. Vataka was right about one thing. You would have made invaluable slaves."

The shame he felt at his Empire's actions did not extend to the system that had benefitted him. In any other situation, he would gladly enslave them and abuse their empathic powers.

"Alseans don't take well to slavery," she said icily.

"We noticed that. Vengeance, encrypt location data for me and the three officers in my immediate vicinity. Restrict access to myself and Commodore Vataka. What is the location of Submaster Bakshi?"

Shock rippled through the air, chased by rising anger.

"That's not possible. Recheck."

The anger crested with a vehement curse as he slammed his fist against the wall. "I don't need you to question my second," he spat. "She's in the Political Bureau. There's no other way she could encrypt her location data. Now listen here, I don't trust you any more than you trust me. But if you're smart, you'll stick with me. I can still get you to the bridge. Bakshi has no interest in obeying those orders."

"She's the one who just killed forty-five of her fellow officers?"

"With considerable help from you, yes."

She glanced pointedly at the bowed door, which had barely held back the force of the explosion. "Would you rather I had left that open?"

The answer was self-evident, to his obvious annoyance. "Don't tell me you didn't enjoy it."

"I didn't drop that bomb." She spoke quietly, imitating a tone she had often heard Lancer Tal use to great effect. "I will not apologize for saving my warriors from the actions of yours."

He glared, his jaw tight and anger radiating from every pore.

"That said," she continued in the same tone, "We will stay with you."

"Thought you might." Imperiously, he held up a hand for silence while listening to an internal communication. "Chief, I couldn't care less about incomplete compliance right now. It's the officers I'm worried about, not a few hangers and slaves."

Vellmar sincerely hoped those hangers and slaves were acting on the commodore's revelation. A rebellion on this ship could only benefit her goals.

"Round them up and bin them. I'll deal with them later. Send a squad to the captain's mess and make sure you pick the ones who hate Bakshi. She's trying for a takeover. Yes, that's what I said, now get going!" He ended the call and gestured irritably at the foremost security officer. "Change of plans. We'll go through the stables. Take point."

They moved down the eerily silent corridor, then cut through a cross passage to a hallway so narrow they could barely walk two abreast. Vellmar scanned it as far as she could sense, wincing at the empathic echoes that pressed sticky, bleeding fingers into her thoughts. They were stronger here and more difficult to filter out, especially given the bright red bursts of immediate fear and the dark misery all around them. There were slaves behind these bulkheads.

If the ship designers shared Onruang's disdain for the threat they posed, security coverage here was probably thinner than in the more open public areas.

She dropped a hand beside her leg and signaled the warriors behind her: *Project obedience.* Three fingers pointing forward meant they would focus on the security officers ahead. She would take care of Onruang.

His mind might have been made of paper for all the resistance it offered. Projecting both obedience and a desire to please, she spoke in a low tone and hoped it wouldn't be picked up by nearby cams. "Your security net has blind spots, yes?"

"Yes, of course. No net is perfect."

"And as the Operations Master, you know where the blind spots are."

He puffed up. "There's nothing on my ship I don't know about."

"Are there any nearby?"

"Right up there," he said, pointing ahead. "It's a dead end leading to slave quarters."

"Take us there and stop."

They gathered in the tiny stub of a corridor that ended at one door and had two more on each side. It was so small that not all of her warriors fit. Those who did not stood on guard, affecting nonchalance for the sake of the security officers watching the cams. This would have to be quick.

She didn't need to give the command to her warriors. They had rehearsed this many times and knew exactly what to do.

Before Onruang could utter a word, she seized his jaw, slid her hand behind his neck, and pressed their foreheads together. With no care for possible damage, she drove deep into his will and rewrote it from the bottom up. Not even during the Battle of Alsea had she been so ruthless. But she needed more than simple compliance. She needed intelligent, proactive support.

This close, she heard the faint voice in his internal com. The security chief was surely checking up on his disappearance.

"You're fine," she whispered. "You merely wanted a private moment with me."

"I'm fine, Chief," he said in Common. "Just wanted a bit of privacy to enjoy the scenery. Have you *seen* their emissary?"

A tinny laugh sounded, followed by a few short words that sounded like a sign-off.

She stayed a few pipticks longer, strengthening her control. When she withdrew, he blinked at her in lustful adoration.

"Did I tell you how good you look in that uniform? Like a big hunting cat with claws." He reached out, intending to touch one of the sheaths crossing her chest.

Disgusted, she stepped away. Though she had practically guaranteed this response with her words, that didn't make it more tolerable.

But it did give her an opportunity to put on a show for the officers watching through the cams.

He followed as she backed into the main corridor.

"You said we'd make invaluable slaves. What would you do if I were your slave?"

"If only you were," he purred, looking her up and down. "I'd worship you the way you should be worshiped."

"How?"

Had his will been intact, he probably would have reacted the same way. She allowed his grasping fingers to brush her breasts, let him bring his mouth close to hers—and then seized his right hand, thumb pushed into the pressure point between his third and fourth knuckles. She twisted his hand and yanked it across her body, turning at the same time and shoving her other thumb into his elbow. A quick thrust pushed his elbow above his shoulder and forced him up on his toes.

Still turning, she pulled down as she went, ending by standing behind him with his arm extended and every joint locked. He was now bent at the waist, off balance and no threat at all.

She could have stopped there and proven her point, but the misery pulsing through the bulkheads gave her too many mental images. Why had Onruang known there was a blind spot here? How many slaves had he abused in that corridor stub where no one could see?

Pushing his arm forced him to lower his head further and step forward in an attempt to relieve the painful pressure. She offered no respite, marching him across the corridor until his head banged into the bulkhead in full view of any security cams in the area.

"Don't *ever* touch me or anyone else without their consent," she snapped. "That includes slaves."

"I won't," he managed in a strained voice. "I thought you wanted it."

"You thought wrong. And you call that worship?"

She let go and stepped back, ostentatiously brushing off her sleeves. He straightened, grimacing as he gingerly rotated his elbow and wrist.

"At least he had the right animal," Senshalon said. "Vallcat Vellmar."

She smiled at the old nickname, a tiny bit of normality in this extraordinarily dangerous place. "Call me that again and I'll push you into the wall, too."

"I'd be a little harder to manage."

The other three security officers were watching their Alsean counterparts with a telltale eagerness. They now had four turned officers and a much better tactical position.

She extended her hand down the corridor. "Take us to the bridge."

18

INVISIBLE THREAT

The *Vengeance* was two ships in one, Vellmar thought as she followed their guides down yet another short corridor. There was the wide open, pretentious part, exemplified by the shuttle bay. Then there was this maze of cramped spaces containing machinery, storage, processing areas, and slaves. An unmistakable stench attested to the presence of sewage.

Just past the sewage treatment, they entered a ladder shaft even narrower than the first one. "Officers don't use this," Onruang said. "It runs through the slave quarters. Bakshi won't expect to find us here."

"I thought you said we were going through the stables?"

Ahead, the officer on point chuckled.

"It's slang for slave quarters," Onruang explained.

"Too bad forced obedience doesn't include basic decency," Dewar muttered behind her.

The four officers clanged up the metal steps, making no effort to be quiet. Vellmar held out her hand and gestured palm downward, silently ordering her warriors to tread lightly. It helped that their boots were soft-soled. Voloth military boots seemed designed to make as much noise as possible.

They did not sound like a group of fifteen. They sounded like four arrogant officers who had never considered stealth.

The leading officer stopped at a landing and reached for the door panel. On the other side of the door were nine emotional signatures bearing none of the arrogance of officers and much of the feel of slaves, with a strong layer of desperate determination.

"Stop," Vellmar said. "Step back."

He obeyed instantly.

She squeezed past the two officers still on the ladder, positioned herself to the side of the door, and tapped the control pad.

As the door slid open, a metal bar sliced through the air where the soldier's head would have been. Vellmar caught it and twisted, bringing a skinny body stumbling forward. It was a young man, so thin that he could muster no resistance as she spun him around, pulled him against her, and put the bar beneath his chin. Then she marched him out into the corridor.

Eight sets of fearful eyes stared up at her.

"Shekking Mother! They're *children*."

Her warriors crowded out to see.

The eldest was the one in her arms; she didn't think he was more than sixteen. The youngest gripped a hammer in her fist and looked to be Jaros's age. All were armed with various builder's tools.

She released the boy and held out the metal bar. He looked up, cautious but hopeful, and she nodded.

He accepted the bar.

Holding up her hand, she pointed at her wrist and activated the speaker. "It's all right. We won't harm you."

The voice of Lhyn Rivers spoke from her wristcom, a calm stream of Common that alleviated their fear.

"I'd like to ask you some questions, if you'll stay with us. If you want to run, that's all right, too. But I hope you won't."

"What about the beaters?" the oldest boy asked.

"The beaters?"

He pointed to the stairwell behind her. "Security officers. They're the ones who hand out most of the punishments."

She thought of Rax's scars, imagined them on these tiny bodies, and clenched her fists. "We have four officers with us, but they won't harm you either."

The little girl snorted with all the cynicism of a weary adult. "You can't promise that."

"Yes, I can."

"You have Operations Master Onruang with you," she said. "Nobody gives him orders except the captain and the commodore."

"Master Onruang," Vellmar called.

The clang of boots on metal heralded his appearance in the doorway. Sturdy and well-fed, clad in his fancy uniform festooned with ornaments, he looked like a different species than the skinny children in their plain brown trousers and shirts.

"No further, please," she said. "For the sake of the children."

He folded his arms over his chest and glared at them, but did not step past the threshold.

"It's true," the eldest gasped. "The stories, they're true! You can control their minds. That's why they want to wipe out your planet."

Vellmar took a chance and crouched down to their level. "Yes, it's true," she said softly. "But don't give that away. There are other officers watching us on security cams."

He looked from her to Onruang, then gave a delighted laugh. "Not here, they're not. This cam's been broken for days. They haven't fixed it because it wasn't a priority, what with the battle and all. That's why we set our ambush here." Turning to the little girl, he added, "It's all right, Enzi. They can't hurt us now."

She eyed Onruang. "Can we hurt him?"

"You can try," he snarled.

"Master Onruang! You will not hurt these children or any slave. Not ever again. Or I will be very displeased."

"I'm sorry." He dropped his head, radiating dismay.

While the children looked on slack-jawed, Vellmar said, "No, you may not hurt him. He's taking us to the bridge. We can't get through the locks and security measures without him."

"Too bad," Enzi said. "We wanted him to die."

Never would she have imagined such cold malice in a child. Then again, the girl was not as young as she had first thought. Her emotional signature bore the maturity of someone older and far too experienced.

"They're malnourished." Dewar was beside her, looking at the children in horror. "Mother of us all, do they not feed their slaves?"

"They feed us." Enzi's sneer twisted her face as soon as she understood the translation. "Enough to keep us alive so we can serve them. Not enough so that most of us can't be bribed with an extra portion."

Dewar unslung her pack and knelt, setting it on the deck. "I have food. It doesn't taste very good, but it will give you strength and energy."

That was all it took to win their trust. They crowded around, eagerly accepting the energy bars. Vellmar had thought they would cram the food in their mouths, and while two did, the others took small bites and blissfully savored them.

She wanted to kill every officer on this ship.

"Why were you here?" she asked. "I can only imagine the penalty for attacking officers."

The eldest boy spoke up. "To find you. Everyone's been watching the broadcast. Everyone knows you have a Seeder goddess on your side. You can take us back with you."

"We were being escorted by forty-eight security officers until a few ticks ago," she pointed out. "How did you plan to get through them?"

"They never look behind them. Not at us. We're invisible until they need us. We planned to hit them from behind, take one disruptor each, and fight. If you joined in, we could have taken them all."

Enzi twirled her hammer in one hand while taking a bite of her energy bar. "Good for kneecaps," she said through a mouthful of food.

"Then we heard about the bomb and that the masturbator was down to three beaters."

She tapped her wristcom, wondering if the translator had gone awry. "The masturbator?"

One of the younger boys laughed, spraying crumbs. He instantly clapped a hand over his mouth, then examined his palm and licked it.

"Master Beater," the eldest explained.

Her smile set off a round of chortles, though it wasn't the joke that amused her. Onruang had never realized that his disdain for the slaves was returned in full. Abuse of power and bodies had earned their fear but not their respect.

"Some of us stayed behind to watch where you went. Once we knew where you were going, we came here." He pointed down the corridor. "Onruang was taking you to the bridge by way of the master chef's kitchen and the captain's mess."

"Did you consider the consequences of failure?" she asked.

Several of the children looked blank.

"She means did we worry about what would happen after," Enzi told them. "If we couldn't get the Alseans to help."

Nine heads shook back and forth.

These children had embarked on a suicide mission. They would be free or die in the attempt, and it was clear from their emotional signatures that they were prepared for either outcome.

"Tell me something," Vellmar said. "If we released all the slaves but kept the hangers and officers in lockdown, what would the slaves do?"

"Go to the officers' mess," said one.

Several giggled.

"Some would tell on you," the eldest said. "The ones in favor with the officers. They get bigger quarters and extra privileges for, um, doing things. Some of them are more powerful than the hangers. They'd sell you in a heartbeat."

There went that idea.

"Do you know any way to shut down the weapons rooms?" It was unlikely, but—

"Yeah," he said. "Cut the power. Rail guns and automatic loaders don't work without it. They could still load the launch tubes by hand, but the loaders won't feed any new missiles to the rooms. Wouldn't affect the laser cannon, 'cause that's run from the bridge, but the weapons rooms are on a different circuit."

"You know a lot about it."

"We're in operations. We're the ones who fit best in the maintenance spaces. I don't know how to cut power to the whole circuit, but I know someone who does. Cutting power to the officers' quarters would keep them in lockdown, too."

He spoke the truth, or at least believed it. She had found a useful ally.

Better yet, she had found an invisible threat.

"If you could cut power to the weapons rooms, how many missiles would they be able to shoot before running out?"

"Only what's already in the launch tubes. Missiles stay in the armory. The loaders run behind the bulkheads and deliver one at a time."

"Couldn't they pull apart the bulkhead and get the missiles out of the loaders?"

This was apparently quite funny.

"It's hangers and officers in those rooms," Enzi said when she stopped laughing. "You think they get themselves dirty clearing jams? Or take the risk? That's a slave job. They don't know how to do it. Most wouldn't even fit."

Vellmar was beginning to understand that Rax and his settlers were more privileged than she had thought.

"If I can get the right slaves released, the ones who can help you, can you cut the power? Shut down the weapons rooms and lock down the officers?"

"Yeah." The eldest boy stepped closer, his breath fragrant from the winterbloom flavor of his energy bar. "But you have to promise to take us back with you."

She held a fist to her heart. "On my honor as a warrior, I promise that if you help me take this ship, I will bring you back to Alsea when this is over."

It would be a bureaucratic nightmare. Lancer Tal might strangle her.

He copied her, holding a fist to his underdeveloped chest. "It's a deal."

"How are you going to release them?" Enzi demanded.

"Master Onruang, can you open the doors to specific slave quarters from here?"

Onruang nodded, eager to please after his earlier chastisement. "I'll call them in. They can be remotely released."

She addressed the children in a lower voice. "Can you get where you need to go on your own?"

Their faces fell. Obviously, they had not considered this. "We're on lockdown," one of the middle children said. "They'll catch us as soon as we go into a monitored area."

"Then you'll need escorts." She had hoped to take the officers on the bridge with her, but this was more important.

The children were agog when the three security officers greeted them courteously—as instructed by their Alsean handlers—and swore to help in any way they could.

"Bend down," Enzi ordered one, testing her control.

When he bent over, she lifted a tiny fist and swung for his face.

Vellmar caught her arm. "No. You have power over them, just like they used to have power over you. If you abuse it, you're no better than them. Do you want to be like them?"

Agonized indecision flared through her emotional signature. She badly wanted to hurt them, yet could hardly bear the disgust at thinking of herself that way.

Scowling, she stepped back. "I'm nothing like you."

The eldest boy addressed his little company. "Remember the cams and the other beaters. We can't be seen ordering these three around. If anyone sees them obeying us, we're done for."

Enzi's eyes widened. "That's true. We have to be careful."

That, Vellmar thought, might be a more powerful incentive than moral superiority. "And you need to be fast. We don't have much time. Give Master Onruang the names you need."

The children conferred and came up with four names, then watched in gratified amazement as Onruang ordered the releases in his normal arrogant tone. He even provided the plausible explanation that they were required for repairs and would be escorted by security officers.

"Mind control," Enzi said happily, chewing the last bite of her energy bar. "Neat trick."

19

COMMAND DECK

Tal listened to Vellmar's report with burgeoning hope. Her Lead Guard's task had been the most dangerous of them all, rife with potential for catastrophic failure. Not only had she brought her team through with no losses so far, she had also turned Operations Master Onruang and eight security officers, including the chief and four others who had met them at the captain's private dining room.

And she had made allies who were even now conducting their invisible sabotage.

"Submaster Bakshi is a concern," Vellmar added. *"She wiped her tracking data, which is only possible at her rank if she's a Political Bureau officer. Onruang doesn't know where she is. But she has her own agenda, which might include taking over the ship. He's sent backup to guard the bridge access but isn't certain they're trustworthy. He also thinks she's the one responsible for killing those forty-five officers."*

"He doesn't know? What about the security footage?"

"It's conveniently missing."

Tal relayed this to the three women standing beside her on the flagship bridge. With her physical body still on the broadcast, Ekatya could not respond verbally, and Salomen was too busy controlling Commodore Vataka to engage in conversation. Her strength was flagging with this prolonged projection.

Lhyn was the only one able to answer.

"We're outside our realm of knowledge," she said. "The Bureau looks like another layer of control, this one over the officers and so secret that even Protectorate Security isn't aware of it. Or if it is, Sholokhov never mentioned it to Ekatya."

Ekatya nodded.

"On the *Phoenix*, the only people who can erase tracking data are Commander Cox, Commander Lokomorra, Ekatya, and Admiral Greve."

Ekatya pointed to Vataka and drew a line across her throat.

"Bakshi is coming after Vataka," Lhyn translated.

"Who is not only her superior officer on the ship," Tal mused, "but also her superior in the Bureau. She's making a big play. If she can neutralize him, get this ship back under control, and finish the bombing of Alsea, she can expect a great reward back home."

"And she's willing to take a great risk to get it," Vellmar said. *"Starting with wiping out her own officers and attacking the third-in-command. If she brings Alsea down, the Empire won't give a fanten's fart about her crimes. But if she fails, she's a dead woman. This is a do-or-die strategy."*

"Which makes her extremely dangerous." Tal did not like this at all. "How far out are you?"

"Ten to fifteen. We're climbing through a brace shaft now."

"All due haste, Vellmar. Salomen is tiring. We need to finish this."

She ended the call and watched Ekatya's glowing body on the display. Having made the excuse that she was called to another world but would return to this one when her emissary arrived, Ekatya had gratefully fallen silent. But the divine light still shifted around her, making even her skin glow, and Tal watched it for any sign of fading. She was extremely concerned about Salomen's endurance. Her tyree had already been halfway to death and back; how much farther could they push her strength?

"There's another option," Salomen said in a strained voice. "I could force him to set the ship to self-destruct."

"Salomen, no!" Lhyn gasped. "You'd never recover."

"I thought I failed." She took a harsh breath. "When you came to get me. I cannot face that in reality. I won't. It was torment."

"You'd rather be responsible for the deaths of everyone on this ship than for the death of Alsea," Tal said.

She gave a single nod.

"That is not your burden to carry, tyrina. It's why we have our backup plan with the Delfin torpedo. As a failsafe in case things go wrong here."

"You cannot tell me . . . that you wouldn't do it if you were me."

"In truth, I can. Because I did consider that as an absolute last resort. Then I spoke with Ekatya about it. She said that unless Voloth protocol was radically different from that of the Protectorate, it takes two ranking officers to initiate the self-destruct. Given what we've seen of Voloth paranoia, I'm starting to think it may take three."

Ekatya held up three fingers and nodded emphatically.

"There's only one of us with these powers, so yes, I can tell you that if I were you, I wouldn't force that. It's a mathematical impossibility."

Raw, jagged dread drained from their link, pushed out by golden relief. There was so little she could do to help her tyree fight this battle, but at least she could set her mind at rest. That Salomen would even consider such an option was a testament to her failing reserves.

Silently, she willed Vellmar to hurry.

"While we're waiting, I need you to prepare to pull out," she said. "If Bakshi does what I think she will, Vataka may die. You cannot be inside him when that happens."

"No." Despite her fatigue, Salomen managed to smile. "I don't want a second trip."

"Not that I ever want to chase Salomen down the Path of the Return again," Lhyn said, "but I wouldn't mind a second trip of my own. Do you know what it cost me to leave without having a good look around? I'll spend the rest of my life wondering what I missed!"

Salomen let out a wheezing laugh. "I knew it."

"Can you blame me?"

"No, but you couldn't publish . . . that paper. Some things are not . . . meant for study."

"Salomen, please hold on." Tal reached for her nonphysical hand, found it clenched, and wrapped her own hand around it. "Just a little longer."

Silently, Lhyn picked up her other fist.

"I feel . . . as if I'm breaking apart. Don't let me go."

"We won't." In their physical world, she concentrated on moving her thumb to brush it across Salomen's lips. "Do you feel that?"

"Yes."

"You're still here. Still in my arms. You're solid. As soon as you let go, you'll be all right."

"Fahla, I'm dreaming about it. Letting go."

Tal muted her earcuff, assuring their privacy. "Did I ever tell you about the time Micah used an immobilizer on me?"

"What? No!"

Delighted with this resurgence of energy, she continued her blatant distraction. "It was before I met you, when I was feeling the effects of a broken tyree bond."

Now she had Ekatya and Lhyn's attention as well.

"After we left?" Lhyn asked.

She nodded. "I was in terrible condition. I should have been seeing a healer, but I wouldn't tell anyone what was wrong. I wanted to escape everything—the weight of my position, the decisions, the expectations. My life. I repeatedly slipped my Guards and ran away. I used to jump in my personal transport and fly to the Snowmounts for a solo trail run."

Salomen's breathing was still labored, but she was focused. "How does this . . . lead to using—?"

"Micah decided to teach me a lesson about what could happen if the wrong person found me alone. He set up an ambush. I was too cocky to realize that the ambush I sensed wasn't the real one."

Ekatya's smile held a melancholy edge. She was enjoying the tale, but hated being the reason behind it.

"You mean you were too arrogant to believe a low empath could get the better of a high empath," Lhyn said.

"I prefer my words, thank you."

Salomen let out a tiny chuckle.

"I began to stalk him, thinking I would teach him a lesson about trying to catch me unawares. That's when I walked into the trip wire."

Ekatya tried to stop her grin, but her amusement sparked across their link.

"I dropped like a rock. Couldn't even blink. I didn't know what to think, because if I couldn't trust Micah of all people . . ."

"You would have been alone," Salomen whispered. "Truly alone."

"Yes." The tale had suddenly gained significance. "Then he freed me, and we had a shouting match. I threatened him with prosecution. He told me to go right ahead, but at least I'd know that one person tried to tell me the truth. That was when I finally realized I wasn't alone after all. There was still one person I could talk to."

In her physical body, she felt the touch on her lips. "You will never be alone again," Salomen said firmly.

"Don't hurt him when this is over."

"I'd never hurt him. But I will have . . . a talk with him."

"Poor Micah. How long will it take him to recover from that?"

Salomen's smile slipped at the sounds of muffled shouts and weapons fire. "Is that—?"

"Get ready to let him go." Tal unmuted her earcuff as Vataka bolted from his chair.

"Onruang," he barked. "What is happening?" He scowled at the bridge doors while listening to what was clearly an unsatisfactory answer.

"Lancer Tal, Bakshi is there. She's disabled the security cams, but one of Onruang's people got out the call before going silent. If she's openly killing officers now—"

"She's closed the exit behind her," Tal finished. Bakshi had set herself on a course with only two possible endings.

"Move faster," Vataka snapped. Outside, the weapons fire had ceased, leaving an ominous silence.

The bridge doors opened and a short-haired woman marched in, leading a stream of security officers. With her average height and plain appearance, she was the sort who would be overlooked, a zalren blending with her surroundings until she chose to strike.

"Bakshi is on the bridge with twelve armed officers," Tal said. "I don't know how many she left outside."

Ekatya winked out and reappeared in the open bridge doors. She looked around, then turned and held up four fingers.

"Strike that, she left four guarding the doors," Tal corrected. Fahla, she envied Ekatya's ease of movement with this incorporeal form.

Vellmar acknowledged the message at the same time that Commodore Vataka spoke.

"Submaster Bakshi," he said in an unimpressed tone. "You do not have authorization to be on the bridge. Leave at once."

"What happened to you?" Bakshi asked. "You were the rising star of the Bureau. Now you've bared your throat for the Protectorate and some twinkly lights on a faked video link."

"You've seen the same evidence I have. Captain Serrado could not have known those names."

"She didn't know any names, she just pointed out bodies!"

"The correct ones! Do you think a Seeder would trouble herself with all of our names?"

"She certainly seems to know yours. You betrayed the Empire and nearly lost us this battle."

"I am *saving* the Empire!" he cried. "Open your eyes and look past your ambition. We came here once and lost an entire invasion group down to the last bolt, bar, and slave. We came again and lost every mobile asset from the Third Fleet. What else could have defeated us but the strength of the Seeders? Now we've come for the third time, and so far we've lost two heavy cruisers, two destroyers, and every one of our fighters. The mines didn't get through to the elevator, and we can't get a missile through to Alsea. There's our explanation." He pointed at the display. "It's insanity to continue down this path! Do you want to curse the Empire and ruin your own afterlife?"

"I don't know about my afterlife, but I know about yours."

"Salomen, get out," Tal said.

Ekatya appeared in front of Lhyn and turned her away, silently shaking her head.

"Commodore Vataka, with the power vested in me by the Political Bureau, and in keeping with my duty to serve the Empire—"

"What the fuck do you think you're doing?" Vataka snarled.

Salomen bent over, hands on her thighs as she wheezed. Without her influence, Vataka was no longer trying to convince his underling of the truth as he had seen it. His fury at her effrontery filled the room.

"I'm removing you from command and putting an end to this charade," she said, signaling her officers. "Take him to the brig."

"Belay that order!" Vataka roared.

"They don't answer to you," she said smugly. "They answer to the Empire."

"I didn't do any of this! It wasn't me!"

She let out a contemptuous snort. "I suppose Fahla made you do it?"

The officers came up both sides of the room, converging on the fifth level. Before they cleared the second step, Vataka whipped out his disruptor.

His bolt missed Bakshi, who dove to the side and came up shooting. The bridge officers hurled themselves to the deck as disruptor bolts sizzled over their stations from two directions.

It ended quickly, with a close-range shot from a security officer who took advantage of Vataka's single-mindedness.

Tal was forever grateful for Salomen's exhaustion. Vataka's head blew apart in a pink spray that flew right through her insubstantial body, but with her head down and eyes closed, she was blissfully unaware.

In their physical realm, she was a dead weight slumped against Tal. Her pained, rasping breaths sounded as if they were drawn from the very bottom of her lungs.

"You're all right." Tal needed all her strength to brace her larger bond-mate and keep their connection intact. "You let go in time. Just relax and breathe. Don't look at him."

The disparity between their physical and spirit selves had never been more stark. Though Salomen's body was taxed to its limit, her spirit self was already recovering its balance. Despite Tal's advice, she glanced at the corpse before turning away with a grimace. "I cannot go back in," she croaked. "I don't have the strength."

They all felt the truth of that, as well as her misery in admitting it.

"You had more strength than anyone could ask. Rest now. You've done your task. We still have options." Tal looked at Ekatya, who gave an affirming nod.

"Submaster Bakshi." Her voice rang out from the display.

"Ah, *now* you find your words." Bakshi holstered her disruptor and walked toward the top level. "Interesting timing you have, Captain Serrado."

"I will not waste my time on an unbeliever. Your murder of one who was trying to do right has sealed your fate."

"I'm in charge of the ship holding the missiles that will turn Alseans to ash. I'd say I've sealed your fate. You'll go down in history as the captain who let this planet die. It's fair, isn't it? You only ever beat us by treachery. Now that the odds are even—"

"The odds are not even. You're not in charge of that ship."

Now on the fifth level and unwittingly right next to Ekatya, Bakshi gave a derisive laugh. "Maybe you should open your eyes, Captain. There's been a change in command."

Ekatya's spirit self looked daggers through her. "I've seen no handover of command, only murder many times over."

"The cost has been higher than I hoped." Her emotions belied the outward display of regret. "But we are all children of the Empire. We owe our lives to her. If necessary, we owe our deaths as well."

"But not your own, I notice."

"I risked my life getting here. That I stand here while he lies there"— she pointed at the headless corpse—"doesn't mean I wasn't willing to die. It means that you're no Seeder. *Our* Seeders are helping me. And your so-called Emissary, wherever she is, will soon be as dead as everyone else who tried to stop me." Regally sitting in Vataka's chair, she added, "Weapons, Operation Ash is still in force. Fire missiles."

On the fourth level, an older officer rose shakily from the floor. "Which missiles?" she asked in a trembling voice.

"I said Operation Ash. The bioforce missiles, you useless drip of snot! What kind of bridge did those two run?"

"Uh . . . Commodore Vataka ordered those to be stowed. They're back in the armory."

"Seeders save me from crawling idiots." Bakshi looked toward the ceiling, her mouth twisted in a scowl. "Get them back *out* again. And fire what we have until then!"

"I wouldn't do that if I were you," Ekatya said.

"Comms, end this transmission and open a properly secure one to our ships."

"Your weapons rooms won't fire more than once."

That stopped her. "Belay that order. What do you mean?"

"You have one shot left. Choose it carefully."

In the physical world, Salomen had recovered enough strength to lift her weight off Tal. "What is she doing?" she whispered.

Tal caught Ekatya's eye, silently asking the same question. They needed her to stall for time, but this was a tremendous gamble. If the slaves hadn't succeeded, she would lose the credibility her goddess persona had earned thus far.

Ekatya lifted her hands in a *Do you have a better idea?* gesture.

No, she didn't.

Bakshi was studying the display with narrowed eyes. "You can't possibly have managed that level of sabotage. Even if you are a goddess, you said you can't affect things on the physical plane."

"No, but I can help your people see the truth."

"Like Vataka?" she sneered. "Comms, end it. Fire missiles!"

The display reverted to a battle grid.

Freed from her constraints, Ekatya swore. "That didn't gain us much."

"Uh . . ." the weapons officer ventured.

Bakshi snapped something short, inspiring a hurried and apologetic explanation from the weapons officer. But with the transmission down, the translation was no longer in effect.

"What is she saying?" Tal demanded.

"That the *Phoenix* still has mostly hard shielding, so firing missiles would be a waste of resources," Ekatya answered. "She's recommending shield breakers."

Bakshi growled out an order.

"She says 'do your damned job.' I don't think Bakshi has much bridge experience. Definitely none in battle."

"I think I could do better," Lhyn remarked.

"The comm officer hasn't opened a channel to the destroyers. Bakshi belayed the first order but didn't repeat it. He's taking her literally instead of showing any initiative. It's passive resistance. And the destroyers aren't making any moves. They're waiting to see how this plays out."

The display showed a broadside of weaponry slicing toward the *Phoenix*, which responded with a barrage from its rail guns.

"That's only half a broadside. What is this weapons officer playing at? Either the sabotage worked and she's trying to draw it out, or she's passively resisting, too."

The *Phoenix* had no trouble neutralizing the attack.

"Bakshi hasn't given her pilot a command, either," Ekatya reported. "He's sitting on his thumbs. They haven't even turned to present their starboard side. I think this crew is quietly mutinying."

"Can you blame them?" Salomen asked. "They've watched five officers die on this bridge."

Bakshi snapped out an order.

A second set of shield breakers launched toward the *Phoenix*. Tal swore, desperately racking her brain for a way to buy more time.

"No, look!" Ekatya's elation sparkled through their link. "That's not a full broadside either. It's less than half."

Only now did Tal see that these weapons were sparser than the previous barrage.

"What—?"

"They did it. They shekking did it! This ship has two standard launch tubes per room, just like mine. Those are the shield breakers that were already reloaded in the second launcher. Remember, they were firing both bioforce missiles and shield breakers. They took out the bioforce missiles, but not all of them reloaded their tubes." She stopped to listen as her ship's defenses responded.

"It wasn't that they only had one shot left, it was that they had one shot per tube," Tal said slowly, realization setting in.

"If that's the end of it, we're in excellent shape to take on those destroyers," Ekatya announced.

The weapons officer made a trembling report, setting off an incandescent level of anger in Bakshi. Tal needed no translation.

Lancer Tal, the slaves said their weapons sabotage was successful. I don't have any way to confirm it—"

"I do." Tal was happy to set Vellmar at ease. "Bakshi tried to fire them without much luck."

Thank Fahla. They said they burned out the whole area, so it won't be an easy repair. They're working on the lockdown now. My teams are in position. Can you tell me Bakshi's exact location? And her officers?"

"She's in the commodore's chair. Her officers are lined up along the levels, five on each side of the bridge and two standing by the bulkhead behind her chair."

Five, five, and two, I have it. We're moving now. Tell Salomen and Dr. Rivers to close their eyes."

Tal was leading Salomen and Lhyn to the back corner when an explosion rocked the bridge. Smoke poured through the half-open doors, and the bridge officers were on the floor once more.

Bakshi's rage shifted to vicious glee as she spoke in triumphant tones.

Lhyn was more subdued. "She said she looks forward to telling Captain Serrado that her emissary didn't see the detonator on the doors."

20

ENDGAME

"It's there." The Voloth chief of security grinned, his teeth the most visible part of his face in the dim exit shaft. "Just as he said."

Vellmar had to give Onruang his due. The man was a psychopath, but he knew his ship and his second. He had predicted that she would repeat a successful strategy and rig the bridge doors. The four officers she left behind were only the first line of defense.

"Can he trigger it from there? Take out the doors and guards at the same time?"

"Yes. He says it will only eliminate two, but the others should be surprised enough to be easily neutralized. He awaits your permission."

"Senshalon," she said softly.

A quiet scuff behind her meant he had drawn a blade. "Ready."

She crossed her arms over her chest and pulled two blades from the topmost sheaths. With the tip of her right knife, she indicated his projection target: one of two emotional signatures bracketing the door ahead.

"Target acquired," he murmured.

She focused on the left-hand signature. "Freeze."

After the Battle of Alsea, training in both types of terror projection—freeze and flee—had become mandatory for high empaths in the protective services. She detested it, but this was easier than any of her practices. The soldier's unshielded mind crumpled like a dried leaf.

"Frozen." Senshalon confirmed his own success.

She tapped her guide's arm with a knife hilt and nodded.

"Master Onruang," he said. "Proceed."

An explosion roared dully on the other side of the thick door separating them from the bridge, bringing with it a barrage of fear and the muting effect of shock. The bridge officers had been frightened so many times in a short period that some were losing their ability to cope. It made sense, she thought. Her tours of the *Phoenix* had shown that a bridge crew was mostly scholars and builders, with a scattering of warriors. They might be trained for combat, but for most, it was a kind of combat fought from within a massive, impervious ship. Not the kind that took place right over their heads.

Nearby, she sensed a savage triumph that had to be Bakshi.

"They're down," her guide reported.

"All teams, go."

He repeated her order into his com, then slid open the door and pulled aside the banner that hung in front of it. As light and noise poured into their narrow passage, Vellmar caught a glimpse of the bridge over his shoulder. Straight ahead were the backs of the two throne-chairs she had seen on the broadcast. Slender hands dangled over the armrests of the one on the left; beside it sprawled the headless body of Vataka.

The lower stations were empty, their operators crouching on the deck. It gave Onruang's team a clear sightline from the main doorway to their targets on the right side of the bridge. Vellmar and her team would take the left side.

Ahead of her, the security chief did a credible dive-and-roll out of the emergency exit hatch. He came up on one knee and shot the nearest officer on the fourth landing.

Vellmar was close on his heels, turning the moment she emerged to sink a knife into the frozen guard's heart. On her right, Senshalon did the same to his.

She yanked out the bloody blade and refocused on Bakshi, projecting simple confusion to delay the woman's response. One step and a quarter turn put her in the proper orientation, and she sent both knives across the bridge in quick succession. The first lodged in the throat of the woman closest to the main doors. The second, glistening from its previous use, took down the man next to her.

Trusting her warriors to neutralize their own targets, she kept moving, reaching the commodore's chair just as Bakshi leaped out of it and turned. Projected confusion shifted to instinctive horror when she caught sight of the warriors pouring out of the emergency exit—a bridge access Onruang had accurately guessed she would not consider a high risk. It was meant solely for the four-ribbon officers, who could run down the exit shaft to a luxurious, high-powered escape shuttle. That shuttle required cleaning and maintenance, and lowly hangers or slaves doing the work could not be allowed to dirty the bridge with their presence. Thus, the exit shaft had a second entry from a brace shaft.

Bakshi had not rigged this door, clearly believing that two guards close by and ten more lining the walls would be enough for the unlikely threat. In addition, Onruang had pointed out, she wouldn't want a bomb so close to the command chair she had stolen.

By the time the frightened woman drew her disruptor, Vellmar had already extended her sword.

The first stroke severed Bakshi's wrist, her fingers still clutching the weapon. The second sliced across her throat, leaving her a dead woman standing. She stared, all fear erased by stunned acceptance as a curtain of red streamed down her throat and into her collar.

Even as her body crumpled to the deck, Vellmar threw a third blade at an officer who had taken cover on the right side of the bridge, shielding himself from Onruang's team. He was not shielded from a well-placed knife, however, which struck in the one place exposed to her: his shoulder. He jerked back with a cry, a natural response but a fatal mistake. Her fourth blade sent him to the deck with a severed trachea.

She drew a fifth and cocked her arm, scanning the bridge for hostiles. The air stank of burned flesh, with a tang of hot metal indicating missed disruptor shots that had struck bulkheads instead. Fear bombarded her senses, as well as a few flashes of weary satisfaction from bridge officers.

Interesting.

There were no more threats. Her warriors had done their jobs with speed and precision, aided by the surprisingly effective security officers. Ten bodies lined the walls, two lay at her feet, two more slumped behind her, and all of her warriors were still standing, though Senshalon grimaced as he held a hand clamped against his shoulder. Dewar was already unslinging her medic's pack, preparing to treat him.

She fervently hoped Lancer Tal had heeded her advice. If Salomen had seen this, her friend might never look at her the same way again.

"Master Onruang!" she called, sheathing her blade.

He stepped through the damaged doors. "Yes, Lead Guard?"

"Please see that these bodies are removed from the bridge. Then make sure no one enters or leaves. And get my knives back."

He snapped his fingers at two nearby officers and pointed. They jogged over to pick up Bakshi, but not before Vellmar had cleaned her sword on the woman's fancy uniform jacket.

It was a Yulsintoh blade. She would no more retract it while bloodied than she would jump from a moving transport.

"Well done, Vellmar. Very, very well done!" Lancer Tal sounded delighted. *"You even kept your uniforms clean."*

She hooked the retracted sword back on her hip, trying not to smile too broadly at such effusive praise from her oath holder. "Thank you. Please tell me Salomen didn't see it."

"She did not. And she's extremely relieved to know her task is truly done. Goddess above, I'm glad to see you here. I don't—" She stopped. *"We've had some unpleasant surprises along the way. Having this work so perfectly . . ."* Once again, words failed her.

"I understand." Had she been forced to bring Lanaril into a battle, she'd be lucky to string two words together.

"Thank you." Lancer Tal's voice was crisp once more. *"Be aware that the pilot, weapons officer, and comm officer have engaged in a quiet sort of mutiny against Bakshi. You may find them supportive."*

"We still have to embed the directive."

"Yes, but it should be relatively easy. They're waiting for you. Go be our emissary. I'll tell Lanaril you're all right."

Too many words crowded her throat. This was not the time, nor was Lancer Tal the person for a message of love. But she had seen and sensed so much pain on this ship that the thought of Lanaril's serene smile made her physically ache.

She pushed down the image and surveyed the sea of wary faces looking between her and the bodies being carted from the room.

"I am Fahla's Emissary. Your ship is locked down, including all officers. Your weapons rooms will not fire. I'm taking control of this ship and taking it out of the fight. I'd like your assistance in that, but I won't threaten you to get it. My hope is that this is the last violence we will see today."

Quickly, she outlined her terms: they could remain on the bridge and work with her, or they could be removed and put under lockdown until a prisoner transfer could occur. This lockdown would not take place in their own quarters but in the slave quarters.

That had been Dewar's idea, and it was diabolically effective. At her first mention of the lockdown option, half the crew rose from their chairs. Upon hearing the phrase "slave quarters," all but two sat back down.

She sent those two away in the company of a security officer with a quiet order to put them in the brig. Onruang had warned her that any officer who accepted her offer had either an abusive relationship with slaves or a profitable one. Either way, he advised her not to allow it.

She did not understand this culture and hoped she never did.

"Given that all of you have been complicit in the attempted genocide of my people," she said, "I'm sure you'll understand that I can't trust you not to betray us. Each of my warriors will implant an empathic directive in you. The instruction is simple: you will not be able to harm Alsea or any Alsean. That's it. It's painless, as our Voloth Empire settlers can attest."

Every remaining member of the bridge crew stared at her in shock. So did her turned security officers.

"Excuse me." A woman on the fourth level lifted a hand.

"That's the weapons officer," Lancer Tal said.

"Yes?"

"Could you explain what you mean by Voloth settlers?"

That was not the question she had expected. "The prisoners from the Battle of Alsea. Your government abandoned them after the battle. The ones who survived with their minds intact were given permission to make their homes on Alsea. They've built a nice little village and created their own municipal government."

Far from clearing up the shock, her explanation seemed to do the opposite.

"Good Fahla, they didn't know."

"We were told there were no survivors," the weapons officer said, confirming Lancer Tal's realization. "They said you killed them all, down to the last one."

"Your government lied to you. Again. One of the survivors taught me everything I know about Voloth ships and military structure. He's the elected spokesperson of the village."

An older man spoke up. "We were firing bioforce missiles on our own people?"

"Does that change the immorality of it for you?"

He at least had the grace to not only feel shame, but allow it to show. "I never thought it was moral. But questioning orders isn't good for one's career."

"Or life, today," someone muttered.

"I'm going to arrange for Rax to address the Voloth fleet through the Phoenix. *It will take a few ticks. Get busy with those directives."*

"Enough. We need to move on. Either accept a painless empathic directive to leave us alone, or spend time in the slave quarters."

It was amazing what that threat could accomplish. The officers meekly lined up at the front of the bridge and awaited their fate.

Vellmar walked down and pointed at the weapons officer. "You seem more courageous than the others. Step over here, please. I'll embed your directive and you can tell them they have nothing to fear."

With trepidation she almost managed to hide, the woman stepped out of line. She appeared to be middle-aged, inasmuch as Vellmar could judge age in Gaians, and about Lanaril's height.

"I have two sons," she said quietly. "They're back home, waiting for me. If that makes any difference in the mercy you show."

"I have two mothers. They're on that planet." Vellmar pointed at the display. "Waiting for me to come home. That made no difference in the mercy you showed today."

It hit hard. Clearly this woman had never once considered that Alseans might have families they cared about. She dropped her gaze, unable to look Vellmar in the eye. "What they told us about you—they made you sound like a threat to the galaxy. Monsters who couldn't be allowed out of your system."

"Do you know the irony of that? We don't *want* to leave our system. Perhaps someday, but we're not the ones who invade peaceful worlds and murder entire civilizations."

The officer nodded, sniffed, and held up her head. "I'm ready."

"I promise you, it won't hurt." Vellmar slid her hands into position and rested their foreheads together.

She was gentler than she had been with Onruang. This wasn't a rewrite of a resistant will, but the simple addition of a new layer.

Less than one tick later, she withdrew. Every bridge officer was watching intently.

"Well?" a younger man demanded. "Are you still you?"

"Shades of our Seeders. Yes, I'm fine. The only thing that hurts is my heart."

"She damaged your heart?"

"No. I did. We all did." She faced them. "You can't tell me you were comfortable with this mission. Bioforce missiles? Even the Protectorate agreed not to use them. Since when are we worse than them?"

Many of them averted their eyes.

"I passed on those orders knowing they were wrong, but I didn't think I had a choice. Now the idea makes me sick. I'd rather die than give another order like that. But that's all she did." Looking back at Vellmar, she added, "Thank you for your mercy."

"You're welcome." Though she didn't know how merciful it truly was. When this officer returned home, would her government accept her? Would it allow her to rejoin her children, or would it conduct medical experiments to determine the physiological effects of an empathic directive, as Rax and his settlers suspected?

It was not an issue she could afford to worry about. These officers had made their choices, coerced or not. Now they had to face the consequences.

She kept watch, along with her turned security officers, while nine of her ten warriors completed the directive implantations in shifts. With his arm in a sling, Senshalon could not manage the necessary contact.

When it was done, she had a nearly complete bridge crew and full control at last.

"Call the *Phoenix*," she said. "Use an open channel and the translator for High Alsean to Common. It's time to speak to Fahla."

21

PATH OF THE RETURN

F ahla probably wouldn't grin like an idiot.

But it was difficult to hold back when Vellmar capped off the most precise military assault Ekatya had ever witnessed by pressing both fists to her sternum and bowing her head in the salute given only to the Lancer—and now, apparently, a goddess.

"Fahla, my Goddess," she said with a perfectly straight face. "I am Lead Guard Vellmar, your emissary to the Voloth flagship *Vengeance*. This ship is now under Alsean control."

With that opening statement, sure to reverberate through Alsea's history books, she sat in the commodore's chair as if born to it.

"She just made her reputation." Andira's pride could have been seen a light year away. "Give me a tencycle to teach her, and she'll be an unbeatable candidate for Lancer."

Salomen shushed her. "Don't distract Ekatya."

She was leaning against Andira, one arm wrapped around her shoulders as if she needed the support even on this plane. Despite her obvious exhaustion, she was transformed with relief and a muted joy.

Ekatya certainly understood that. It took all of her command experience to keep the euphoria out of her voice.

"Well met, Emissary," she said in High Alsean. "I had hoped your path to the bridge would be easier. Yet you stand before me having caused fewer deaths than the last person in that chair."

"From what I've seen here, my warriors and I have more respect for these people than their own superior officers. Or their government." Vellmar waved a hand, indicating the bridge officers. "These officers are not my enemies. While it's true that they obeyed reprehensible orders, it's also true that the Voloth military structure punishes questions and resistance. I don't blame them for choices made under duress. They are free to return home as soon as we can arrange transportation."

"Does that offer apply to the hangers and slaves as well?"

"They had even less choice than the officers. Alsea has no interest in taking prisoners or punishing anyone. We merely wish to end this and prevent it from ever happening again." Vellmar lifted her chin, the picture of a victorious commander. "To that end, the Alsean government offers the following terms of surrender to the remaining destroyers: lay down your arms, give control of your ships to us, and we will give you safe passage home."

She paused to let that sink in.

"We understand you may not trust this promise. Your government told you that we're monsters who killed every one of the soldiers in the last invasion. That was another lie. The survivors asked us for asylum, and we granted it. I now invite Rax Sestak, former Weapons Specialist First Class, Third Pacification Fleet, to speak for those survivors."

Ekatya's comm officer patched in the quantum com call from Blacksun Base. Rax wore the uniform he had used in Salomen's march and looked agitated.

"There was a time when I believed what the Voloth Empire told me," he said in Common. "It's how I was able to fire mortars and missiles at Alseans who never knew we existed. But when they won the battle, they treated us better than the Empire ever did. We're all hangers. The Alseans gave us land to build our own village. They gave us the means to grow our own food. They gave us freedom and rights. When I was attacked by four Alseans who believed lies about us, the government put them in prison. It protected me, a Voloth Empire hanger, because my assailants broke the law. I love Alsea, and I will never go back to the Empire. None of us will."

His face was replaced with footage of villagers. "You've been lied to repeatedly. I know you probably think I'm being forced to say this, so let me show you who we are. This is New Haven, our village. We built every brick and board of it ourselves. I made this video two moons ago, when Lancer Tal told me I might be talking to you."

Images shifted across the display as he took his viewers on a virtual tour of the village, showing the settlers in their homes, eating in the dining hall, laughing and relaxing on its back deck, working in their kitchen garden.

"They're stunned." Andira tilted her head toward the bridge officers. "They didn't believe it at first, but this is making a difference. Visual proof of one more lie."

"Two," Lhyn corrected. "Rax and his people are alive, and Alseans aren't vicious primitives."

"Three," Salomen said as they watched the settlers raise their hands in a village vote. "Hangers are capable of self-government. They don't need the Empire."

Ekatya's head went back in surprise. She had thought this was an excellent strategy two moons ago, but now—had Andira really planned it out to that level? If the hangers on the four destroyers were drawing the same conclusion, this might tip the balance.

"I won't say it's been easy." With the video finished, Rax was back on the display. "But it's much easier now that we know they aren't monsters, and they know we aren't. I'll tell you one thing about the Alseans: they keep their promises. If they say you'll go home safely, then you will."

Time to step back in. "I also keep my promises," Ekatya said. "Here is mine. If you surrender your remaining ships, you will return to your homes unharmed. But if you do not, Captain Serrado will send every one of you back to the atoms from which you were created." She injected a bit of snarl to her voice. "The moment the Voloth Empire sent its ships into this system, it lost them. Your only choice now is how your ships will be lost. Decide."

After a fraught silence, the display shifted to show an additional broadcast. Glaring out at them in standard quantum com format was a female captain who spoke in clipped tones.

"The Voloth Empire ship *Fury* will never be taken by a primitive species. We do not accept your alternative and will not give you the satisfaction of destroying us. We choose a third option. *Fury*, set self-destruct."

The broadcast blinked out.

On the battle grid, the two destroyers closest to the *Fury* veered away in either a wise act of self-preservation or a desperate run for the base space exit point.

Ekatya tensed, waiting to see which it would be. If they fled, she needed to be free to fight. Salomen would have to break the Sharing.

A quiet inner voice observed that she had just crossed the line. For a Fleet captain, the only defensible choice was to let those ships go. She had already fulfilled her mission objective. Further aggression could not be justified and would end her career.

But she had made a promise as Fahla. For the sake of Alsea's future, she needed to keep it. This attack had to be a total loss for the Voloth Empire.

The third ship altered course, chasing after its fellows, and Ekatya mentally cast away her uniform.

"Vessel of Fahla," she murmured in High Alsean. Salomen would understand the reference. "Prepare to end—"

All three ships slowed to station keeping.

" . . . this battle," she finished in a shocked mid-sentence reverse.

Andira, Salomen, and Lhyn looked at her with equally questioning faces. She could do nothing but smile at them.

A new captain appeared on the display. "This is the Voloth Empire ship *Questor*. We will not fight a Seeder and those under her protection. We surrender."

In quick succession, the other two captains followed suit.

To Ekatya's surprise, the display lit up a fourth time, showing a man with a beard that rivaled Lokomorra's.

"This is the *Fury*." He cleared his throat nervously. "We have removed our captain and canceled the self-destruct for our ship. We swore an oath to die for the Empire, but we won't die for lies and pride. We won't spend eternity outside the Termegon Fields. We surrender."

"Dear goddess," Salomen whispered. "It's over."

"Fucking stars, I can't believe it." Lhyn was equally stunned.

Andira leaned her head against Salomen's shoulder and let her eyes close.

"In the name of Alsea and its people, I accept your surrender and reiterate our promise," Vellmar said. "You will be returned to the Voloth Empire as soon as we can arrange transportation. In the meantime, Alsean delegations will be sent to each of your ships. I expect them to be met with honor and courtesy. My government's leaders will discuss details with you soon. For now, let us rest and care for our wounded."

"Ronlin is already on his way to the *Fury*." Andira straightened, taking charge once more. "That looks like the most important one to get under control first. Ekatya, is it safe to end the Sharing?"

She nodded and spoke for the broadcast. "You have chosen wisely. I now return control of this body to Captain Serrado."

Too short, probably. Too curt for a goddess who was leaving her people after a miraculous appearance to protect them. She should have signed off with grand words of wisdom or some kind of reassurance, but Salomen had been holding this link to the point of exhaustion and beyond.

Concentrating, she lifted her heavy physical hand and made the signal.

"End broadcast," Lokomorra said.

"Broadcast terminated," came the confirmation.

Freed at last, she took in a relieved lungful of air. "Thank all the stars, I'm glad that's—"

"Wait! Don't go!"

That voice did not belong on her bridge. "Candini?" she blurted, drawing a sharp look from Andira.

Running footsteps pounded across the deck. "If you really are Fahla, you can't let her die!"

"Who are you talking—"

"Rahel! She saved that whole fucking planet and she's dying in surgery. She took a sabot to the chest and Dr. Wells won't stop trying, but she's losing the fight. Please, tell me this isn't a trick. Tell me you can save her!"

"She took a sabot to the chest?" Ekatya repeated stupidly. She didn't understand. The last she knew, Rahel and Candini had destroyed the bioforce missile and—

"We lost our shields." Candini's voice was hoarse with emotion. "The missile burned out the generator. I didn't drop altitude in time. I was too busy celebrating and it's my fault. Help her, please! She shouldn't have to die because I was *stupid*."

The memory hit then, of Lokomorra calling out orders to operations and medical . . . for a fighter retrieval. Oh, Hades. It had been Rahel all along.

Hurriedly, she explained to the others. Even expecting the blow, she was physically stunned by Salomen's response. Her horror roared through their link, turning Ekatya's bones to ice.

"No. No, not her. Andira!" she pleaded, grief shifting to desperate trust. "Don't let me lose her. Not another one. Not her!"

It was a terrible burden, one Andira could not possibly carry. She would be forced to shatter Salomen's heart and her own at the same time. Ekatya braced herself; this would hurt all of them.

Andira faced her bondmate with calm determination. "Can you hold this link much longer?"

"To save Rahel? As long as it takes!"

"I have an idea. I don't know if it will work," she cautioned. "But it's worth a try. Micah, get Healer Wellernal. Tell him we need his empathic healing skills. He'll have to join our Sharing and direct it through this link." She paused, listening to the response.

"Captain Serrado? Fahla?"

"We're working on it, Candini." Ekatya had underestimated Andira's tactical mind, but it was still a long shot. "I can't guarantee anything, but we'll do what we can."

"We brought Wellernal here for the divine tyrees and as part of Alsea Ascendant," Andira told her. "He's one of our strongest empathic healers." She turned back to Salomen. "Channel his knowledge the same way you've channeled the divine tyrees. Push it into Ekatya and help her project it."

"Into me? I can't project!"

They ignored her, too focused on each other.

"He has the skill," Andira said quietly. "We have the power. You just need to direct it into the only physical body we can push it through."

"Push it—yes!" Salomen lit up with hope. "Yes, I can do that! If he can tell me what he's looking for and where I should focus."

"Could someone explain to me—"

"You'll be our outlet," Andira said. "A vessel through which Salomen can direct Wellernal's healing skills. Get to the medbay and be ready to apprise him of the medical situation."

"Oh, is that all."

Her sarcasm was lost on the two Alseans, but Lhyn caught it and gave her a wobbly smile. "It's the day for miracles, isn't it? What's one more?"

"Ready yourselves." Having been given a path to follow, Salomen was wasting no time. "I'm taking us back to the *Phoenix*."

Ekatya had barely processed her words before she fell through the deck and into the vastness of space.

She tried to take in all the details of this extraordinary journey, but it passed too quickly, leaving her with fleeting impressions.

The galactic arm flashing past, a brilliant ribbon of stars she could reach out and touch.

The gleaming hull of her ship rushing toward her.

The glimpse of over one thousand minds, a heaving mass of living, *feeling* individuals, their emotions creating a beacon in the darkness. Was this what Rahel sensed? No wonder it overloaded her.

A river of emotions rushing over her as she dove through her ship—

"Fucking Hades," she gasped. "That was intense."

She was crouched on the deck, head hanging down as she tried to settle her stomach. Her subconscious recognized the smooth surface beneath her boots before her conscious mind caught up. This was the lower display of her bridge, now showing Alsea's untouched perfection as they kept pace above it.

"I'm sorry." Salomen was breathless. "I couldn't protect you the way I did before. Too tired."

Kneeling beside her, Andira shook her head. "Don't worry about us. Save your strength for Rahel."

Ekatya climbed to her feet and examined her body in the command chair. It felt as if she had left days ago, yet nothing had changed.

Standing at the base of the dais was Candini, hands pressed together and held against her lips as she watched Ekatya's glowing body. She was still in her flight suit, her face cut and bruised and her spiky hair matted with blood. The medbay staff must be overwhelmed to have allowed her to leave in that condition.

Then again, Ekatya thought, she probably hadn't waited for permission.

"Commander Lokomorra," she said. "I need to get to Rahel's surgery bay, but I can't walk. Have a mobile chair brought and get me there as soon as possible."

"I'll get it!" Candini spun around.

"Hold on, First Pilot," Lokomorra said. "You have no authority here. The medbay staff won't respond to you."

"I need to do something!"

"You already have. Now shut up and let me do my job."

While he called for the chair, Ekatya realized that she'd never had the chance to tell the others why she was in charge of the battle group.

"Andira," she said urgently. "You need to know. Rahel saved Alsea in more ways than one. Admiral Greve was two pipticks away from removing me from command. Rahel took him out of the equation. She shouldn't be on this ship."

Surprise electrified their link as Andira scanned the bridge. "I didn't notice he was gone. Why didn't you say anything?"

"I was a little busy!"

"What does 'took him out of the equation' mean?" Salomen demanded. "Did she—"

"She sedated him."

"Thank Fahla." Her head dropped back. "Rahel, you grainbird. Couldn't you keep out of trouble for five ticks?"

Andira watched Ekatya with a knowing look. "That's still assault. Against the battle group commander. And she danced off your ship to join Candini?"

"I deported her," Ekatya said with a shrug.

The tension and exhaustion was affecting both of them. When Andira gave a great snort of laughter, Ekatya had to clench her jaw shut to keep from doing the same.

"You deported her," Andira gasped. "Goddess above, what a shekking mess. She'll survive, you know she will, if only to cause me the biggest headache of this entire battle. Vellmar invited slaves home for evenmeal, we'll have hangers and officers asking for asylum, I'll be working day and night for the next moon dealing with captured ships and prisoner transfers, but getting Rahel off this ship will be the worst of all." She sobered. "Greve will press every button he has to punish her and you."

"He won't have the chance." Lhyn drew Ekatya into her arms and rested her chin atop her head. "You're done, aren't you?"

Ekatya nodded, her jaw clenched for an entirely different reason.

These were likely the last minutes she would spend on her bridge, and she hadn't even been in her body for most of them.

The lift doors opened, disgorging two nurses. One guided the mobile chair across the bridge at a jog while the other ran ahead to the dais. To their credit, they only hesitated for a moment upon seeing her glowing body.

"Has anyone touched her?" asked the lead nurse.

Lokomorra rose from his station. "No. Captain—"

"It should be fine. There's light but no heat. Commander, would you —" She lowered her voice. "I'd rather it be you putting me in that chair."

"Of course." He stepped up to her level and carefully touched her hand, testing the contact. "No heat or shocks," he announced. With gentle movements, he detached her battle harness, slid his arms beneath her, and lifted her out.

The nurse had pushed the chair up the dais and parked it behind him. Lokomorra had only to turn and deposit her, but Ekatya could hardly see through the haze in her vision. She was torn between the physical sensations of her body being handled by two people in two different locations. One surrounded her with comfort and understanding, the other with respect and care—but for all his care, Lokomorra was taking her from the place she loved.

"It'll be all right," Lhyn said. "I'm so sorry it's ending like this, but you have a whole new life waiting. With no Greves or Sholokhovs."

She nodded and sternly told herself to focus. Rahel's life was in the balance and she was mourning her damned command chair? Time for that later.

"Let's go," she said, extracting herself from Lhyn's embrace.

The nurses took that as a command, pushing her body down the dais and across the bridge. Candini trotted beside it, while Ekatya led Lhyn, Andira, and Salomen close behind.

The four of them barely managed to crowd into the lift before the doors shut. Ekatya wondered idly what would have happened if Andira, the last one in, hadn't quite made it. Would she be carried along, half in and half out? Or would the lift have left her behind?

She was getting punchy, she realized. If she was losing the ability to think clearly, how much worse must it be for Salomen?

The doors opened again, revealing the surgery bay level of medbay. It was controlled chaos, with staff hurrying this way and that, but most seemed to be coming or going from one bay in particular.

"Ah," Andira murmured. "Healer Wellernal just joined us."

"Well met," said a male voice. *"Colonel Micah has apprised me of the situation. I'll do my best, but I need more specifics."*

"Healer Wellernal, this is Captain Serrado. I'll get you those specifics in one tick."

She followed her body into the surgery bay and stopped short at the scene.

"Oh, no." Lhyn clutched her hand.

Salomen was silent, but the icy blast of her fear made Ekatya shiver.

Rahel was surrounded by a thicket of equipment, lights, and medbay staff, two of whom were working furiously over her supine body. Bright surgery lights spotlit her abdomen, open from top to bottom and showing white bone and glistening tissue in places Ekatya was fairly certain they did not belong.

The floor of the bay was littered with so many blood-soaked items that the staff had simply kicked them to the sides rather than take the time to pick them up. She didn't know a body could contain that much blood. Was there any left in Rahel's veins?

"Dammit!" Alejandra threw another bloody item to the floor. "Sponge! And who the *fuck* let this crowd in here? Get out!"

A nurse placed a fresh sponge in her palm. Without looking up, Alejandra stuffed it into Rahel's abdominal cavity.

"Get Candini into a treatment room and everyone else out," she growled, both hands moving with a swift steadiness Ekatya marveled at.

"Dr. Wells," she said. "I may be able to help."

"Unless you've got a spare Alsean liver in your pocket, you can't help. Leave my surgery bay, Captain."

"Um. Dr. Wells?" an attending doctor ventured. "I think you should look at her."

"For the love of—" Alejandra glanced up, then did a double-take.

"Phoenix, add Dr. Wells to this call. Dr. Wells, I have Healer Wellernal standing by. We're going to try empathic healing, but he needs specific details of the issue."

"Dr. Wells?"

"Healer Wellernal." Alejandra was still staring at Ekatya, eyes wide

138

above her mask. She gave a quick shake of her head and returned to work, now speaking in High Alsean. "I've got a foreign object penetration through the right chest and into the abdominal cavity, resulting in comminuted fractures to the seventh through tenth ribs and punctures to the liver and lower lobe of the right lung. Bone reconstruction is under-way. The lung is sealed and stable for now; it's not the priority. The liver is irreparable. We've been stopping bleeders left and right, but the force of impact sent a shockwave through the entire organ. It's practically lique-fied. Every repair causes another tear, and I've run through most of my blood supply." Though her hands never stopped, her breath hitched. "I don't see a solution."

"*I understand,*" he said gravely. "*Lancer Tal, if you could arrange blood donations from our fighters, that would buy us time. Dr. Wells, the type?*"

"Type two light."

"I'll take care of it." Andira stepped aside and began speaking to the war council.

"*Captain Serrado, you must sterilize your hands.*"

"Scrub and gown the captain," Alejandra snapped in Common. "Move it!"

One nurse rushed her body through the door and down the hall while the other tugged Candini in the opposite direction. Ekatya stayed in the surgery bay, afraid to get too far from Salomen and risk their link.

"Phoenix, mute." Her internal com went silent, cutting off Wellernal's instructions on increasing Rahel's energy stores for the healing. "Record message for Commander Lokomorra. Commander, keep our fighters out for now. We need the bays for Alsean fighters. We're asking the pilots and gunners for blood donations for Rahel Sayana. Have guides ready to bring them to the medbay as soon as they arrive. Send message. Unmute."

A soft chime confirmed that the message had been sent.

Alejandra called out orders for injectors to be loaded with what sounded like twelve different compounds. Staff scurried in all directions, two of them running out of the room.

"Captain," a nurse said in her physical ear. "I need to cap and mask you first. May I?"

"Go ahead. Thank you for asking."

The nurse's touch was brisk, twisting up her loose hair and tucking it beneath a cap. Ekatya gritted her teeth, hating the duality of sensation.

She hated it even more when the mask went over her nose and mouth.

"I know," the nurse said kindly. "It's not the most comfortable thing, letting someone do this for you."

"You sound as if you speak from experience."

"I do." Her chair was turned in place. "May I touch your wrists? Thank you. You're under the decon projector. Now spread your fingers— good. Three, two, one . . . done. Leave your arms out; I'm gowning you next." The nurse turned her chair again and began pulling the gown over her uniform sleeves. "Dr. Wells put us through an exercise to remind us how patients feel. We undress them, flip them to change sheets, manipulate their bodies for treatment. It's easy to forget what it's like on that side."

Efficient fingers secured the gown behind her neck and tucked the loose sides between her body and the chair.

"Gloves next. Lift your hands, ninety degrees at the elbows. Good." Tugging the gloves over her fingers, he continued, "So she made half of us wear blindfolds while the other half prepped us for surgery, just like this. Then we switched. I can tell you that nobody liked being on this end of it. Doctors and nurses prefer to be in control."

"Captains are worse," Ekatya admitted.

"I've heard that." A final tug set the second glove in place. "One more trip under the decon."

While her hands were being positioned, a message chime sounded in her ear.

"Phoenix, play message."

"Captain, consider it done. I only wish I could donate, too."

Belatedly, she remembered that Lokomorra was one of Rahel's closest friends. When this was over, she would need to check in with him.

"All set," said the nurse. "Hands up. Don't touch anything."

Ekatya watched her body come back through the door, capped, masked, gowned, and with gloved hands held up in front. It hardly looked like her, a disparity that was surprisingly helpful. That body was no more than a physical container.

"Bring her over here." Alejandra indicated a place to her right and switched to High Alsean. "Healer Wellernal, we've pumped Rahel's system with as much as her blood volume can carry. The captain is in position."

"*Captain Serrado, let Dr. Wells guide your hands. Bondlancer?*"

"I'm ready." Salomen stood on the other side of the table, next to the orthopedic surgeon.

Ekatya sidled up to Salomen. From her position by Rahel's legs, she could look up and across to her body, sitting in its now-elevated chair beside Alejandra.

"*Dr. Wells, begin.*"

It was the oddest thing in a very odd day, watching Alejandra guide her physical hands over Rahel's exposed organs. They made a shocking contrast: her hands the light green of clean gloves, Alejandra's so coated in blood that the green only showed at her wrists.

"Here. This is the one that won't stay closed."

She wrinkled her nose as her hand touched something smooth and warm. There was a reason she wasn't in medicine.

"*Yes, I feel it.*"

"So do I. I've felt this before." Salomen glanced at Lhyn, standing by Andira near the doorway. "But this is a hundred times worse."

"*It's a grave wound. A terrible disruption to the balance her body seeks. Our job is to restore that balance. It will take time, Bondlancer. Don't try to rush it. Focus and let it happen.*"

"I am." Salomen held her spiritual hand over Ekatya's physical one, then lowered it until they occupied the same space.

Time seemed to slow. Except for the orthopedic surgeon still piecing together ribs, the staff came to a standstill. The room was quiet but for the click of tools and soft whirs of equipment Ekatya couldn't name.

"Sucking Seeders." A nurse's exclamation was jarring in the silence. "Do you see that?"

"Quiet," Alejandra snapped.

She did see. The light that had been shimmering around her body— so shocking at first, now almost normal—had sunk back into her skin. It vanished for a second, then reemerged from her hands, all the previous brilliance focused in a narrow beam that made the surgery lights seem dim. Rahel's liver glowed, lit so brightly that Ekatya had to swallow her nausea and look away. Bodies should not be open like this.

"My stars," whispered a doctor. "She *is* Fahla."

Ekatya waited for Alejandra's inevitable growl at the disobedience. When it failed to manifest, she looked up curiously.

Alejandra was staring in wide-eyed shock at their hands.

No, she was staring at that awful, dark red gash in glistening tissue—the gash that was slowly sealing itself.

"Salomen," she murmured. "Is that really you?"

"Me, thirty-three divine tyrees, Healer Wellernal . . . and possibly Fahla, I don't know." Salomen's voice was equally hushed. "I never knew empathic healing could work like this."

"Had I said it wasn't possible, would you have tried?" Healer Wellernal sounded euphoric. *"It has never worked on this scale before now. Can you feel it? The rebalancing?"*

"Yes. It's—I can hear it. The symphony. As if there were instruments missing, but now they're starting to play in the background."

"Good, good, that's how many interpret it. Well done, Bondlancer. Focus on the music. Listen to it swell. It grows louder, more assured."

Salomen winced. "Louder, but that note—"

"Another bleeder. Sponge!" Alejandra blocked the new flow and held out a bloody hand. "Biosealant."

"Dr. Wells, wait. Don't seal it yet."

"I don't have any blood to spare," she warned.

"You will in a few ticks," Andira said. "The first fighters are already in your bay."

"I apologize. I should have listened more closely when you spoke of lique-faction. Spread Captain Serrado's hands; make sure they cover as much surface area as possible. Gently!"

"Acknowledged. Captain, like this. Yes, barely touching."

Ekatya wrinkled her nose again. For the love of flight, she was practically cradling Rahel's liver.

"Bondlancer, we must focus more broadly. Instead of bringing in the missing instruments, we will increase the volume of the symphony. The liver tissue is too fragile for repairs. Focus on solidifying the whole."

Salomen nodded, forgetting that he couldn't see.

"Dr. Wells, we have three donors in the medbay now," reported a nurse. "More are on their way. They're lined up out there, waiting for clearance. Type two light is one of the most common blood types among Alseans."

"It's the only common thing about her," Alejandra said.

For an uncomfortably long time, Ekatya watched nothing happen.

Salomen was so intensely focused that she appeared frozen, eyes closed and hands spread. But her fear and grief had disappeared, submerged beneath determination and a kind of deep, spiritual joy that Ekatya associated with flying.

Or listening to the symphony of a Sharing, she thought.

"Now," Healer Wellernal said. *"Seal the bleeder."*

Alejandra wasted no time. "Done," she said not half a minute later.

"Is it holding?"

"So far."

"Good. You're doing wonderfully, Bondlancer. On the biological level, we're repairing microtears and even individual cells in the capillary walls, strengthening this organ from the inside out. How are you feeling?"

"I'm all right."

"You'd say that if you were on the verge of unconsciousness," Andira said.

"Don't ask me to stop. If I pass out, so be it. At least I won't wake up knowing Rahel died because I didn't try hard enough."

Andira and Lhyn looked at each other, then moved in unison to stand behind her.

"Give her everything you have," Andira said softly. "I'll be here if you fall. I'm right here, right now."

"And I'm right behind you." Lhyn touched the back of her neck, an echo of their true position on Alsea. "We'll both catch you."

"I know." Salomen made a gulping sound that was somewhere between a laugh and a sob. "I know you will. Ekatya, I'm sorry."

"Why?"

"Because when I cannot hold on any longer, we'll be here. And you'll be there."

"I'm fine. Besides, if I weren't here, who would be Fahla's Vessel by proxy?"

"Isn't that the truth and a half," Lhyn said. "Thank all the stars you're there. But we need to work on your title. Vessel by Proxy doesn't chime my bells."

As if activated by her words, alarms sounded on two machines, their different tones blending in an urgent call.

"Salomen, stop! Healer Wellernal, we've lost too much blood. She's below minimum levels."

"Don't panic, Bondlancer." In their Sharing, Wellernal felt Salomen's instant terror as easily as the rest of them. *"That simply means we've used all of Rahel's energy stores in the healing so far. Her body cannot fuel further progress until we replenish her blood volume and add more nutrients."*

"What does that mean? We stand here and wait? How long can she survive this way?"

"A surprisingly long time," Alejandra said. "There are machines in this room running her bodily functions for her. We've taken the load off her systems and outsourced it until she can handle it again. My worry was the blood loss that I couldn't stem, but she's stabilized. It's still not good, but it's not getting worse." She flexed her fingers and released a breath, tilting her head as a nurse moved in to blot her brow. "All right, let's prep for the incoming blood. We need to preload it. And turn off those alarms."

After confirming Rahel's weight, she called out a series of incomprehensible names and numbers. Four staff hurried to the counter at the side of the room, pulled vials from various cabinets, and began loading slender injectors.

Ekatya blamed her exhaustion for the fact that it took a full minute to understand what was happening. She looked up at Alejandra with new awareness. "You did that in your head."

"Did what, calculate dosages? Of course."

"Calculate weight-based dosages. Of drugs you don't normally use during surgery, judging by the fact that you had to send runners for some of these." And in the middle of a very difficult surgery that was surely taking an emotional toll.

"Are you just now realizing I'm good at my job? I thought that was why you recruited me."

The nurse who had helped Ekatya dashed through the door, one blood bag in each hand. His arrival set off a new flurry of activity as the bags were quickly hung and injected with whatever complicated mix of compounds Alejandra had ordered prepped. Within seconds, the blood was flowing into Rahel's body.

"Look at those numbers." Alejandra had never sounded so relieved. "Healer Wellernal, we've had a blood delivery and we're already back in what you'd call the blue zone."

"Excellent. Bondlancer, do you hear the difference?"

"I do. The symphony is much clearer."

"I believe we're ready to heal that big tear."

Alejandra didn't wait for instructions before moving Ekatya's hands to the area in question.

Once again, it slowly sealed itself, millimeter by agonizing millimeter. Ekatya held her breath, waiting for the tissues to split open elsewhere.

"My sainted—" Alejandra gave an incredulous laugh as the tear closed and faded with no repercussions. "Goddess above, Mother of us all, Great Mother, and anything else that applies. This is working!"

"It feels as if that was the worst of it. Are there more tears you couldn't seal?"

"No, we sealed the rest, but I don't trust them. Salomen, do you have enough power left to check my work?"

"As much as you need."

Ekatya squinted at her doubtfully. There had been a slight tremor in her voice, and she could see it in her hands as well. If even her spirit self was showing the strain, it must be debilitating indeed.

Andira caught the look and shook her head.

Over the next twenty minutes, more bags of blood arrived, and Salomen strengthened the seals of at least ten sizable tears in Rahel's liver. Then they turned to the lung. When that was repaired to Alejandra's satisfaction, she tried to get Salomen to stop.

"She's out of danger. We have the blood, her liver is in better shape than mine, we avoided resection of that lobe of her lung—it's just closing now. You should rest."

"No," Salomen said stubbornly. "I'm seeing this through to the end."

"I can hear how tired you are."

"If you were the one doing this, would you stop now?"

Alejandra hesitated. "No. All right, how about this? Let me do the closing, and you can seal each layer as I go. You'll still accelerate her healing, but it won't cost you as much."

Having agreed on a compromise, they set about their work. Ekatya sat obediently, letting her hands be moved this way and that and trying not to look too closely at the gleaming layers—red, grayish-white, and pink—that she hoped never to see again.

"Look at that. Her skin tone is perfect," Alejandra marveled as she moved Ekatya's hands over the final seal.

"Alejandra?" Salomen's voice was a low rasp.

"Yes?"

"I'm done."

Ekatya had no warning before the bright lights of the surgery bay blinked out.

She fell into darkness and never knew when she hit bottom.

22

ILL-TEMPERED

Before she opened her eyes, Tal knew two things. One, she was in a bed. Two, she smelled hyacot twigs. Which added to three: she was in a healing center. The only question remaining was whether she was still on Blacksun Base or back in the city.

She opened her eyes, took one look at the high ceiling, and knew she was in the city.

Thank Fahla. That meant things were under control. Micah would have kept her secured on base otherwise.

Turning her head, she found Salomen next to her, so deeply asleep that not even a residual buzz of emotions tickled their link. Her color was normal and her expression untroubled, making her look cycles younger.

"Good," Tal whispered. "You needed it."

As she rose up on one elbow, a startling sight came into view: Lhyn lay on Salomen's other side. She was in an adjacent bed, but had moved so far to the left that her body was now in the crease formed by the two mattresses. One hand was wrapped around Salomen's arm, and her forehead was furrowed, as if she were uncomfortable even in sleep.

Tal slid backward, not wanting to disturb either of them, then slipped out of bed and padded into the bathroom.

Three neatly folded piles of clothing waited on a bench, the shoes beneath them a clear sign of which belonged to whom. Salomen's favorite sandals were there, as well as the comfortable shoes Lhyn usually wore in her suite.

She smiled at the polished boots beneath the third pile. Micah knew her well.

A hot shower left her tingling and awake. She dressed quickly, ran a dehumidifying comb through her hair, and tiptoed out of the room.

Micah was leaning against the opposite wall of the corridor, arms crossed over his chest. "It's about time," he said.

"For the love of Fahla, I just finished the mindwalk to end all mindwalks, on top of a battle. You'd begrudge me a hantick of sleep?"

"A hantick?"

She gestured at the nearest window. "The sun is still high."

"Tal, you fell unconscious *yesterday*. It's been twenty-two hanticks." He nodded at her silent shock. "You four are the last ones. All the other divine tyrees were up and about by the ten-hantick mark. Wellernal said you were fine, but . . ." He scratched his jaw, discomfort shivering the air around him. "Not even after you abused stims did you sleep this long. I didn't like it."

"Am I the first one up? Of the four of us?"

He nodded. "Ekatya and Lhyn aren't resting as well as you and Salomen. Though Lhyn is doing better since we moved her. The healers didn't know about your connection and put her in a separate room. She was thrashing in her sheets before Wellernal came in and realized what was wrong."

Tal leaned against the wall beside him, unable to look him in the eye. "I didn't think about it. The moment Lhyn joined our group Sharing . . ."

"Everyone knows now."

"Are you angry that I didn't tell you?"

In her peripheral vision, she saw him turn to look at her.

"I've known about you and Ekatya since three moons after she left the first time. Am I angry that you found a way to resolve it without hurting anyone? No, Tal. I'm not." He sighed. "It's been too long since we shared our lives over a bottle of spirits. I know I'm partly to blame for that. Are you angry that I didn't . . . see you?"

She held back her first response. He had asked honestly and deserved an honest answer.

"I was. And ashamed to be so. Ekatya helped me understand why I was reacting that way. But I'm happy for you, Micah. She's a remarkable person. Worthy of you," she added, remembering Alejandra's work in the medbay. "She barely blinked at the idea of ground-to-orbit empathic healing."

"Oh, she blinked." His tone prompted her to face him. Smiling broadly, he continued, "She said that as soon as she can come down, she'll be lighting every rack in Blacksun Temple."

"Those racks are going to be busy. How is Rahel? Ekatya?"

"Rahel hasn't woken yet, but she'll make a full recovery. Ekatya is in the worst shape of all of you. She has no tyree with her. Alejandra is doing everything she can to make her comfortable, but—" He stopped, suspicion coloring his emotional signature as she glanced at the closed door of her room. "No, you don't. I will not allow you to go up there. Ekatya's not awake, but Admiral Greve is. He thinks Rahel acted on your order."

"If I'd known to give that order, I would have." She let her head fall back against the wall. "Shek. I cannot leave Salomen, but I cannot bear the thought—Micah, she's carried a heavier burden than any of us. When does it end?"

"When you and she make it end. And you will. For now, focus on your own recovery."

"What is the status of the—"

He held up a hand. "No. I'm not giving you status updates, security reports, or anything else. The war council is handling it. You put good people in place; let them do their jobs. Your job now is to take care of yourself, Salomen, and Lhyn."

"They're sleeping! What am I supposed to do, sit there and watch them?"

"That's exactly what you're supposed to do," he said with irritating calm. "Perhaps with a good book in your hands. Salomen needs you for her recovery. Lhyn needs Salomen since she cannot reach Ekatya. Now, I've ordered a meal appropriate for someone who drained herself of every iota of energy and then didn't eat for more than a day. Shall we dine in your room? It'll be like old times. Don't worry about them," he added, pointing his chin toward the door. "Wellernal says his bondmate could play her long bells in there without waking them."

She scowled, remembering the "old times" with far less nostalgia. It was just before the Battle of Alsea, when he was furious with her for abusing stims and had punished her in his own quiet, effective way.

"You're enjoying this," she accused.

"I'm enjoying the fact that you're awake and grumpy. You worried me, Tal. All thirty-three of you dropped like you'd been shot. Wellernal was the only one left standing. It looked like a Fahla-damned massacre. I thought—"

She recoiled at the distinct flavor in the air, metallic and stale like old blood. Though his words had failed him, Micah's emotions spoke of remembered terror.

"Micah," she murmured.

He shook his head.

"I'm all right. We're all right."

"You are now. So give me some time in your ill-tempered company."

When he put it like that, how could she stay grumpy? He was right; there was little she could do at the moment.

"At least tell me those ships are under control," she insisted.

He pursed his lips, then gave up with a sigh. "Fine. Not only are they under control, the Council is already wrestling with the issue of asylum. It seems there are quite a few Voloth who would rather throw themselves on the mercy of Fahla than go back to a collapsing, vengeful government."

"Collapsing?"

A healer's assistant came around the curve of the corridor, pushing a laden table toward them.

"I suppose it would be simpler to tell you a few things than keep deflecting," Micah said with a martyred air. "Since you're making it so difficult."

She didn't bother hiding her triumph. It really did feel like old times.

23

PHOENIX

Rahel woke with a contented hum, her subconscious recognizing the familiar touch before her conscious mind identified the emotional signature.

She opened her eyes to a comforting sight: Dr. Wells sitting on the stool beside her, smiling as she trailed her hand down Rahel's cheek before pulling back.

"I hoped that might help you wake in a good space," she said. "Looks like it worked."

"It did," Rahel rasped. Her throat felt like a desert.

"Don't talk until you've had this." Dr. Wells raised the head of her bed and held out a water packet.

With a grateful nod, Rahel sucked up the too-small amount of water. She wanted more, but knew from experience that the packets limited their output. Handing it back, she cleared her throat and tried her voice.

"How did I get here?"

"You don't remember?"

"I remember the impact. Debris everywhere. Candini getting it under control. That's all." She tilted her head at the cloud of relief. "Is that what I'm supposed to remember?"

"You woke twice. Once right after we retrieved your fighter, the second time about four hours ago. It's normal to be missing some short-term memory after a significant physical trauma."

"That doesn't explain why you're happy about it."

Dr. Wells hesitated. "I had to cut you free. I'm glad only one of us remembers."

Cut her free?

She inhaled with the flash of memory and looked down at her chest. "The sabot. There was—did you get it out?" What a ridiculous question. The medshirt lay smoothly on her skin; of course it was out. But how was she alive?

"We got it out and pieced you back together, with a little extra help. Your mother says Fahla always watched over you. I believe her."

There was a wealth of meaning beneath those words, but Rahel could not parse it. Too tired to ask, she lifted her collar instead and checked the damage. Where metal had once protruded, she saw only healthy skin and a red line running from the base of her sternum to her pelvic ridges. A second scar started at the top of the first and arced down to the right, following the curve of her ribs.

"I've been working on minimizing the scars," Dr. Wells said apologetically. "If I'd done a normal closing, they wouldn't be so prominent. The accelerated nature of your healing meant we bypassed that part of the treatment. I'm afraid you'll always have them, but give me another week and they'll hardly show. Please don't mention them to Salomen. Not for a while, at least."

"Salomen? Why would she care if I have scars?"

She listened in stunned silence to a story straight out of a templar's fever dream. Had a high empath been telling it, she might not have believed them, but Dr. Wells spoke nothing but the truth. Her next truth was equally improbable: five Voloth ships currently at stationkeeping, with bridge officers newly loyal to Alsea and a significant number of crew now devout believers in Fahla.

"I always said she was Fahla's vessel." Rahel brimmed with pride. "She can't tell me not to call her that now! To think she claimed she wasn't a fighter."

"She certainly fought for you. Right up to the very last moment."

Her smile dropped at the reminder. Salomen had burned herself out and still wasn't awake more than a day later.

"Oh. That's why you don't want me to mention the scars."

Dr. Wells nodded. "It would hurt her to think she harmed you in any way."

"Harmed me? I don't care about scars. I never expected to live." She lifted her collar again. "Huh. Maybe I should put the phoenix here instead."

"The phoenix?"

"I promised Candini I'd get a tattoo. I wanted a phoenix on my back, like Mother's sculpture. But now . . . Salomen would never see the scars if they're hidden by flames and feathers."

With an odd pulse of yearning, Dr. Wells indicated her medshirt. "May I?"

"It's your work. Go ahead."

Dr. Wells opened the shirt and traced an invisible pattern on her abdomen. "How big?"

"Um. I don't know, I hadn't given it serious thought. Big enough to cover those scars?"

The pattern shifted, moving to her right side. "You have two wounds. Entry and exit. If you wanted to make a powerful statement, you could put the body here. Mostly on your back, for the flat canvas, with the head resting on your scapula." She slipped her hand under Rahel's shoulder. "But its wings would reach around. One across your back, the other curving to this side." Her warm hand wrapped around Rahel's ribs, barely skimming the surface on its way to her chest. Then she drew a finger down to her stomach. "It could drop a flaming feather here, and you'd have enough to cover all three scars. A phoenix, embracing you."

Rahel caught her hand. "Right before the sabot hit, Candini said you're the best tattoo artist in space. Would you do it?"

The yearning blossomed into cautious delight. "You don't want to hire an Alsean artist?"

"I want it to be someone I love."

"Rahel . . ."

"I woke up knowing I was safe and loved. My subconscious knew who you were before the rest of me caught up. I was thinking how unfair it is that you don't know that. You can intuit exactly how I want my phoenix to look, but you don't know how I feel unless I tell you." She pressed their hands against her heart. "I don't have a name for what you are to me, just like I could never put a name to what I have with Sharro. What do I call someone who fills so many roles?"

"Your friend," Dr. Wells whispered.

"My friend, my mentor, another adopted mother, a healer who put me before her own comfort. Fahla, I'm glad I didn't die in that surgery bay. Not for myself. I was ready to Return, even before we destroyed that missile. But for what it would have done to y—"

"Don't." Her voice was harsh, yet she made no attempt to pull away. "The only way I managed that surgery was by refusing to think of the likely outcome. I still can't think of it. Don't say it."

"I'm sorry."

She closed her eyes and gave a tiny shake of her head, regret and exasperation pouring through their skin contact. "No, I am. You're telling me something beautiful and I'm—dammit." Gently, she freed her hand and began pulling the medshirt back together. "I prayed to the Seeders once, like the naive fool I was, never imagining they wouldn't answer. Never imagining that their response would be to take my son." With the sides lined up, she sealed the shirt. "When I got the call about you, I took my team to the shuttle bay and stood there, watching the tractor beams bring in a mangled mass of metal, and I didn't pray. Not one word to Fahla, not one bit of hope that she might help. The only things between you and death were these hands"—she sat back, staring at them—"and a lifetime of expertise."

Rahel held out her own hand.

Dr. Wells clasped it and met her eyes. "Isn't it ironic? She answered a prayer I was afraid to voice. She was there, Rahel. I know exactly who was involved and what happened, but the science I'm aware of can't explain what I saw. There are a hundred reasons why you shouldn't be here and one reason why you are. I am so—"

Her breath hitched, and Rahel didn't know what to do. Dr. Wells hated feeling exposed. Even knowing that Rahel could sense her, she never acknowledged certain emotions aloud.

"I'm so grateful," she finished, wiping her eyes with her free hand. "I love you too, you brave idiot. Don't *ever* hurt yourself like that again."

"I'll try not to."

"Do more than try. Your poor mother, stars above, I feel for her. What you've put her through! I had to tell her. She's your emergency contact.

Now I know where your strength comes from." She shook her head again, this time in admiration. "I aspire to be like her someday. You'd better call her as soon as you're ready. She needs to see you. Sharro, too."

"I will." Rahel squeezed her hand once more and let go before she grew too uncomfortable. "But first, how are you doing?"

"Me? Fine, why?"

Rahel looked at her askance. "Who heals the healer?"

"Who has time?" she quipped. "Captain Serrado is still unconscious, I have half a million reports to write—"

"Have you spoken to Colonel Micah?"

She deflated. "Yes."

"Is he all right?" That slumped posture was alarming.

"Hm? Yes, yes, he's fine." She hesitated, then straightened with a pulse of determination. "I did the same thing to him that I just did to you. He told me something beautiful, and I turned it into something else. There hasn't been time to address it since then. It's weighing on me, but I don't know when I'll be able to see him. I won't do it over the quantum com."

"Would it help to talk about it?"

"Not subtle," she said with a scowl.

"No one ever accused me of that."

"And I won't be the first."

Rahel was a veteran of many evening discussions with Dr. Wells. She knew when to be quiet and wait.

Sure enough, after another minute of silence, it came spilling out.

"I researched it after I got over being angry," Dr. Wells finished. "Do you know what it takes? The surrogacy?"

Rahel shook her head.

"Five injections." She let out a scornful huff. "Five damned injections. I was envisioning days of three-way sex and forced interaction with some Alsean woman who can do what I can't, and all it takes is a daily injection to help bring the hormones up to the required levels. And five days of pleasure the surrogate can get at a pleasure house. It's so *simple*. He was giving me a gift, a way to have something he knew I'd want, and I walked out on him."

"But you went back. You apologized. I don't know Colonel Micah that well, but one thing I know for sure. He doesn't hold a grudge."

"Ha. If he did, we wouldn't have lasted three days." With a groan, she planted her elbows on her knees and dropped her face into her hands. "I don't know, Rahel. I want it, and I don't."

"I understand why you want it. Why don't you?"

Her head tilted up, chin resting in her palms. "My age. Wondering if I've forgotten how to be a mother."

"Truly? Scratch that one off your list. I can attest from personal experience that you'd be a fantastic mother. Loving and ferociously protective. And that child would always know where the boundaries were."

That earned a rueful chuckle. "Points taken. Here's another. Do I have the right to bring a child into my life when that life is starting over? I won't have much stability."

"That's relevant," Rahel agreed. "But Colonel Micah's life is very stable."

Dr. Wells stared at her, realization billowing off her skin. "Oh."

"What?"

"I didn't think of that. I'm not used to the Alsean—oh, shek. I won't be the mother, he will. I'll be the *father*." She laughed unsteadily. "I need to rewrite my brain."

"No, you'll be the mother. He'll be the father. The only things you need to rewrite are your definitions. You still think a father can't give birth or nurse his child." She grinned at the vision of Colonel Micah holding a tiny baby against his broad chest. "Any child would be lucky to have him for a father. And you'd both have a lot of help. Imagine him trying to keep his new baby out of Salomen's hands."

The humor fell flat.

"His baby," Dr. Wells repeated. "That's the biggest one. Where would I fit in? I don't know how to be a mother who isn't a mother. He'd have the physical, biological, and chemical connections with that baby, and I wouldn't even be a sperm donor. Some other woman would. Or some other man. For the love of flight, even that's not a given. Maybe I'm not as open-minded as I like to tell myself, because I cringe every time I think of a stranger having a connection to my child that I never will."

Though Rahel thought that was patently ridiculous, she knew better than to say so.

"Don't choose a stranger," she suggested. "Choose someone you know. Someone you have a connection to."

"Oh, of course," Dr. Wells said with cutting sarcasm. "Among the many Alseans I know so well. Who would—" She stopped, her eyes going wide.

Rahel waited for a count of ten before deciding that Dr. Wells was not going to speak it aloud.

"Yes, I'm offering."

"Rahel." Her feet slid off the stool's footrest. "Are you serious? You don't even know what's involved!"

"Five injections, I hear."

Her shock would have been amusing in any other situation. "You're on heavy medication. Probably euphoric from surviving. You can't be held—"

"Oh, stop. I'll say the same thing when you let me out of here. You've saved me twice now, and you think I'd hesitate to give you a gift that would mean so much to you? Something that's in my power to give? It would be an honor."

"But you'd be a *parent*. You've never given any indication that you want a family of your own."

"Being sansara doesn't mean I don't want a family. Maybe someday I'll meet the person I want to raise a child with, who knows? But in the meantime . . ." She shrugged, the movement setting off a wave of acute discomfort. "Ouch. Remind me not to do that."

"Don't do that."

"Helpful, thanks."

"I'll remind you if you need it. You may seem healed, but your body has been through a severe trauma. As we start dialing down the medication, you'll feel as though you've been hit by a shuttle. Which is a fairly close approximation of what happened."

"Thanks for the warning." She lifted a hand to rub her chest, remembered in time, and rested it on the covers. "I doubt I'd think of myself as a parent. An aunt, perhaps. Someone who visits and brings gifts."

Dr. Wells made no answer. Her emotional signature churned with a kaleidoscope of tumbling emotions, none staying ascendant for long— until a smile curved her lips. Leaning forward, she dropped a gentle kiss on Rahel's forehead.

"Thank you," she murmured, gratitude and love warming the air between them. "I don't know if I'll accept. But you've changed the equation. I need to think about it from this new angle."

"Take your time. I'll be here."

"Not for long, I hope." She quirked an eyebrow at Rahel's confusion. "You really do have short-term memory loss, don't you? There's a reason you weren't supposed to come back."

"Shek," Rahel groaned. "Greve."

"Yes. Greve."

24

NEGOTIATION II

M icah stayed for two hanticks, sharing first a meal and then several cups of shannel. Though Tal delighted in his company, she nevertheless spent the first tentick feeling awkward about speaking with him when Salomen and Lhyn slept a few paces away. He was family, but this was an entry into the innermost part of her life—and theirs.

Then she realized that he had chosen the seat facing away from the beds, giving the sleeping pair privacy while simultaneously allowing her to keep an eye on them. It was a typical Micah gesture, one that filled her to overflowing with affection. She teased him about it, he hit back in kind, and before she knew it, they had fallen back into their old roles.

She couldn't remember the last time they had sat and conversed like this, as if nothing were more important than sharing their stories and talking over the implications. It felt easy and right, healing in its own way, though she would never admit it. That would mean admitting he was right to enforce her unwilling day off. She still could not believe they were talking about their lives rather than the critically important situation in orbit. He had even confiscated her earcuff, wristcom, and reader card.

"Do I get them back now?" she asked when he rose to leave.

"Get what back? Ah, you mean these?" He pulled the earcuff and wristcom from a jacket pocket and examined them as if seeing them for the first time. "I think not. I've left orders that you're not to be disturbed, but I don't trust certain members of this administration to keep your best interests in mind." The hardware vanished back into his pocket.

"At least give me my reader card."

"There are five books sitting on that table," he observed.

"Micah!"

"Salomen said the book on top is riveting. She wanted you to read it so she could discuss it with you."

"That is hitting low," she grumbled. "I thought you were above emotional manipulation."

"When it comes to your health, I'm not above anything."

While she fumbled for an adequate answer to such unexpected honesty, he smiled and walked out the door.

"Asshead," she said in Common, then laughed at herself. For all her annoyance with his high-handedness, she had to admit it felt good. Micah may have been preoccupied and distant for a few moons, but his care for her was unchanged. This was proof.

She picked up the top book, sat on the bed next to Salomen, and began to read.

One hantick later, she was deep into the story and enjoying both the tale and the light buzz of emotions that tickled her senses. Salomen was either in a dreaming phase of sleep, or she was rising to the surface.

A tap on the door startled her. Frowning, she set the book aside and crossed the room.

Healer Wellernal waited in the corridor. "Well met, Lancer Tal. I'm glad to see you up and about. May I check on Bondlancer Opah and Dr. Rivers?"

"Yes, of course." She followed him to Lhyn's bed. "Do you have news of Captain Serrado?"

"I spoke with Dr. Wells half a hantick ago. Unfortunately, there has been no change."

"Meaning she still isn't resting properly?"

"Not as well as we could wish." He turned Lhyn's arm to expose the underside of her wrist and held a scanner against it. "We've considered chemical intervention, but this is such an unknown situation that we felt it best to let her body recover without interference."

The scanner's four readouts came alive, scrolling through numbers before settling on final results. With a satisfied nod, he clicked it off, rested his other hand on Lhyn's forehead, and closed his eyes.

"Good," he murmured.

Tal stepped back, giving him room to move to the head of the two adjoined beds. When he leaned over to pick up Salomen's wrist, she understood why the beds were pushed away from the wall. Given her position in the center, he had no other way to reach her short of clambering onto the mattress.

Apparently pleased with this scan as well, he pocketed the small device and touched his palm to her forehead. "Ah! She feels much better. This is a normal resting sleep, rather than recovery."

"And Lhyn?"

"Should be waking in the next hantick or so. Bondlancer Opah might sleep the rest of the day." He rejoined her on the other side of the bed. "May I speak with you? It has nothing to do with their health. It's a question of future applications."

Wary, she sat in one chair and waved him to the other. "Future applications of what?"

"Bondlancer Opah's extraordinary powers."

"I already know I won't like what you're about to say."

"What she did yesterday was unprecedented. The potential—"

"Stop there. Have you spoken to anyone else about this?"

He looked as if he had bitten into an unripe panfruit. "Colonel Razine required me to sign an Honor and Discretion form before she allowed me to leave Blacksun Base yesterday."

Thank you, Razine, she thought. That might have saved them all a great deal of trouble.

"She was right to do so. We cannot have the truth making its way to the Protectorate or worse, the Voloth Empire. If they knew our planetary defense hinged on a handful of individuals and one in particular—"

"Of course I understand that! I don't question the strategic necessities, not at all. But surely we could reveal Bondlancer Opah's healing capabilities without touching on the rest? Only to the healer community, obviously, and only for the worst of cases."

"No."

His mouth dropped open. "But—"

"You cannot possibly think she should be asked to give so much of herself again." Tal pointed toward the beds. "She still hasn't recovered from this effort."

"With respect, her exhaustion is from a combination of factors." He ticked them off on his fingers. "An orbital jump, extended use of empathic force, holding that link longer than any other before now—all of those must be considered as well as the healing."

"She was exhausted before the healing began, yes, but not to the point of losing consciousness. That was what put her over the edge."

"I'm quite certain the physical effort could be managed—"

"No!" She glanced at Salomen and lowered her voice. "Twenty-five hanticks and she's still not awake. And you say she might sleep the rest of the day. I don't *care* how much of that is from all the rest. That healing taxed her to the limit, and you would put her on a call list for your worst cases? Would you make her a virtual slave, existing only to help others?"

His head went back, betraying the anger his perfect front concealed. "I know you're recovering from a traumatic event, so I won't take offense at that. But I must tell you it's difficult when you cast such an aspersion. I am a *healer*."

"And one of our very best, which is why I asked for your assistance yesterday."

That smoothed his feathers. "Thank you. I was honored with your trust."

"Then let me trust you with a small insight into Salomen. She is no warrior, yet she fought like one yesterday. She is no healer either, yet she did the impossible with you. We ask and she gives, which makes it too easy to forget what she is."

"A producer? I know you don't believe her caste should limit her potential."

"Quite the opposite. Her caste defines her. There was a time when I thought she should have been a scholar, but I couldn't have been more wrong. Salomen is happiest when her hands are in the soil. She gave up too much of that when she accepted the title that came with our bonding. I will not ask her to give up more."

"I understand—"

"No, I don't believe you do. You look at your healing center and see

162

terrible cases that you cannot save, and now you look at Salomen and see a resource straight from the hand of Fahla, and you think it cannot go to waste."

By his expression, she had voiced his exact line of thinking.

"You tell yourself that you'll only ask for her assistance once every other moon, or once per moon at the absolute limit. She would never refuse. Never. Tell her it's a child, or a parent with young children, or an elder who still has much wisdom to share, and she would not be able to live with herself if she said no. Word would travel, because even with Honor and Discretion agreements, knowledge of multiple miracles could not be contained. Now once per moon is once or twice per nineday. Every healer who hears of it will think the same thing you do—they would never ask such a favor except in the most deserving and difficult of cases. They will all have the best of intentions, and they will kill her with them. Slowly, without meaning to, but the result will be the same. Her life will consist of giving everything she has to help others, and sleeping like the dead to recover her strength before she's asked to give again. She will never say no, and they will never stop asking."

Wellernal looked horror-struck at the picture she painted. "Lancer Tal—"

"I know you speak from a place of caring," she said, gentling her tone. "But you are also imagining an ideal situation in which we retain perfect control of the information. Unfortunately, we don't live in that world."

He slumped back in the chair. "Then it's all or nothing, and so it's nothing."

"I'm afraid so. If Salomen chooses to aid someone she loves, that would be different. But I will not allow anyone else to ask."

A sigh escaped as he glanced at Salomen, motionless in the bed. "You defend your bondmate well."

"Because I've already asked too much of her." At least she could assuage her guilt by making sure no one else committed the same fault.

"Did you ask her to save Rahel Sayana?"

"No, but I asked her to fight a battle."

"Would Alsea still be intact if you hadn't?"

"I don't know. It's possible that Captain Serrado would have stopped the flagship by ramming it."

He nodded gravely. "Killing herself and her crew, and severing two tyree bonds, one of them divine. Dr. Rivers would never have been the same. Neither would you. And because of that, neither would Bondlancer Opah."

Neither would Micah, she thought.

"Thus the picture changes. You didn't ask too much of her. You gave her a way to save everything she holds dear." He smiled, correctly reading her surprise. "You're not the only one who can think through a hypothetical situation."

"Apparently not. Thank you," she said sincerely. "I appreciate your care and insight."

"Thank you for listening." Though disappointed with the outcome of his proposal, pride in her regard seemed to bring some consolation.

She showed him out and stopped in the doorway, startled by the familiar figure striding down the corridor. "Aldirk! How did you get past the wall of security? I assumed Micah would put your name at the top of the blacklist."

Chief Counselor Aldirk gave a disdainful sniff. "He knows better. You've had a call from Director Sholokhov. He wishes to reopen negotiations given the changed situation."

"Oh, he does, does he? This might be the best part of my day." She held out a hand.

Aldirk pulled a Gaian pad from his inside jacket pocket and laid it in her palm. "I'm afraid this is only a loan. I'll be here while you make the call."

"You, too?"

"It's not a betrayal, Lancer Tal. We are all concerned for your health."

"Yes, I've noticed." She closed the door.

Resuming her seat, she set up the pad's virtual screen and put the call through. Bless Aldirk's efficiency; he had already activated the translator program.

Her call was answered quickly.

"Lancer Tal, a pleasure." Sholokhov adjusted the knot of his purple scarf of office and rested his hands on his desk. "We both have crowded agendas at the moment, so I won't take much of your time. Our funding situation has changed, thanks to a late vote in the Assembly. I'm pleased to say I am now able to offer you a Pulsar-class ship in exchange for ten years of service from ten high empaths."

"We appreciate the offer," she said. "But I'm afraid that window of opportunity has closed. We no longer have need of a Pulsar-class warship, given our recent acquisition of a Voloth heavy cruiser and four destroyers."

The lack of reaction meant he had expected her response. "Yes, I've heard all about your victory. Forgive me, I should have opened with my congratulations. You've struck quite a blow against the Voloth."

"Thank you."

"Of course, that blow was struck with the considerable assistance of the Protectorate."

"In accordance with our treaty, yes. We are grateful that the Protectorate kept its promises."

Thinned lips telegraphed his annoyance. "I begin to have a better idea of why that treaty is so advantageous to Alsea. Yet here you are, turning down another, equally advantageous agreement."

"I wouldn't have turned it down two days ago," she said, twisting the knife. "But one must adapt to changing circumstances."

"Yes, one must. It seems both of us have experienced a change in circumstances. I have something to offer besides a ship."

She waited.

"I've been reading some fascinating reports. First Guard Sayana made quite a name for herself, starting by assaulting a Fleet admiral." His bushy gray eyebrows rose theatrically. "She followed that performance by saving Alsea from a bioforce missile and nearly dying in the process. Now she's recovering on the *Phoenix* thanks to the skills of a Fleet healer and blood donations from half the Alsean fighter fleet."

Shek, she *knew* this was going to be the biggest headache of the battle.

"You surprised me with your lack of concern for Captain Serrado's career," he continued. "But I don't imagine Alseans would favor a Lancer who turned her back on their greatest hero of the battle. The warrior caste in particular would not be impressed, and I understand their support is critical to your position."

"Make your point, Director."

"My point is that you can't toss her aside the way you did Captain Serrado. Not without significant political repercussions. On my end, I have a very angry Fleet admiral pressing charges and demanding prosecution to the fullest extent of the law. The only reason Sayana isn't in the brig is that we'd have to push her bed in there." He steepled his fingers and gave her a small, triumphant smile. "So it seems you and I have something to negotiate after all."

25

AFTEREFFECTS

Ekatya opened her eyes to a light so blinding that it set off explosions in her skull.

She curled into a tighter ball, hands pressed to her head in an effort to mitigate the pain, and hissed out a ragged breath.

Pressure did not help. Letting go did not help. Controlling her breathing did not help, but counting breaths focused a small part of her mind away from the white-hot agony.

She had counted eighteen when a door opened.

Any distraction was good. She concentrated on the sound of the door closing and soft footsteps coming toward her.

"Dammit," someone whispered. "I was afraid of this. Ekatya, it's Alejandra. Can you hear me?"

Nodding was out of the question. She lifted a single finger and hoped it would be enough.

"I need to put you in the scanner. We couldn't do it until you were awake. Just hold on, all right?"

As if she had any choice.

She didn't remember the door opening again, but it must have, because multiple voices surrounded her. They spoke in low tones as her bed moved and the light changed and her bed moved again.

That her brain was not operating at its normal capacity became obvious when she found herself lying in the scanner without any memory of being lifted into it. Machinery hummed, Alejandra quietly gave orders, and this time she was aware of being transferred back into sheets that still held her body heat.

Too warm, she wanted to tell them. She craved something cold on her skin.

Her bed moved, the lights brightening and fading, and a door closed.

When cool metal touched her throat, she welcomed it as a relief from the heat. Only when she heard the hiss did she realize it was an injector.

"You should start to feel better soon," Alejandra said. "In the meantime, I'm going to try a different treatment."

Gentle fingers slid into her hair.

Her rigid muscles began to unlock one by one, pushing a groan of relief from her throat.

An exhale sounded above her. "Good. Relax, Ekatya. You're safe and you're not alone." Alejandra continued the scalp massage, using the lightest of touches, and Ekatya's body sank into the sheets.

The touch trailed over her forehead, along one side of her face, and down the length of her throat. It stopped briefly, then reappeared on her forehead and moved down the opposite side.

Ekatya lost all track of time, her world consisting solely of these touches and the pain they were steadily pushing away. Unfortunately, the gradual relief in her head allowed a new pain to surface: the ache in her chest, which felt as if a dokker had kicked her. Twice.

She pressed the heel of her hand against her sternum.

"She's stiffening up again," Alejandra said. "I've gotten her as far as I can. Try it now."

Try what? she wondered.

"Hello, tyrina."

Her eyes snapped open. "Lhyn," she croaked.

Lhyn crouched beside the bed, putting their heads on the same level. "Welcome back. I missed you."

Her heavy-lidded eyes and the telltale lines around her mouth spoke of insufficient rest, but her smile was beautiful.

"Are you here?"

"Not physically. Alejandra is acting as my proxy for the moment. I've got her on the com and you in front of me. And about time, too. This was my third attempt."

Unthinkingly, Ekatya caught the fingers trailing down the side of her face and held them against her cheek. "My body knows. That you're not here. Feels like we've been apart for months."

"As if Micah took a running start and landed on your chest with both feet?"

She nodded, opening her hand. The comforting caresses resumed.

"Healer Wellernal says it's because we exhausted all of our reserves and had nothing left to combat the separation pain. Plus, the physical repercussions are bigger because the link was so intense. Andira and Salomen are perfectly fine. I'm a lot better now that I'm seeing you."

"You're gorgeous."

Lhyn's eyes crinkled. "You're a little high on drugs."

"Doesn't change the facts." Her voice, raspy to begin with, was failing.

A water flask appeared in front of her, and she gratefully sucked up as much as it allowed. "How long?" she asked.

"Forty-six hours." Alejandra took back the flask and checked the diagnostic band on her wrist. "I had to run an IV line for hydration. You had all of us concerned."

"Especially Salomen," Lhyn said. "She feels terrible that it's been so much harder on you."

"She knew. She said it before we lost the link. That you three would be there and I'd be here."

Lhyn held out her hand.

As Ekatya reached for it, another, smaller hand moved into the same space as Lhyn's. She grasped it tightly, part of her knowing it wasn't the right one but the rest of her craving the contact. "I guess we need the foursome link to be able to touch each other."

"Salomen offered. We wouldn't let her. Neither would Healer Wellernal."

"I wouldn't either, if she were in my care," Alejandra interjected.

"When you get back here, I might not let you go for a day or two. Just giving you advance warning so you can prepare."

"Sounds like paradise." She squeezed the hand in hers. "Why did it hurt so much?"

"You were an outlet for a kind of power I can't even measure,"

Alejandra said. "It caused a massive disruption in both your brain chemistry and your neural activity. I did what I could while you slept, but we needed you to be awake to determine the exact treatment necessary."

"The injection?"

"Mm-hm. There's only so much I can do with chemistry, though. Natural healing is always best. You needed Lhyn. You'd have been much better off if we could have gotten you to Blacksun."

"Why didn't you?"

"Don't ask," Lhyn said. "You'll set off her temper."

Carefully, she rolled onto her back, still clutching Alejandra's hand. One look at the thundercloud on her face and she knew. "Greve. He relieved me of command, didn't he?"

The thundercloud darkened. "And confined you to the ship pending an investigation into whether you coordinated with Tal and Rahel to usurp his command. He also thinks you faked your performance as Fahla."

"Not that there are any regulations against that," Lhyn added. "I checked."

"How can he think that when our security cams recorded everything? I could understand if all we had was the broadcast, but . . ." She trailed off, frowning at their expressions. "What?"

"Funny thing about that." Alejandra gently pulled her hand free and resumed her treatment. "There's no security footage."

Perhaps something had rattled loose in her fevered brain.

"I'm not kidding. Greve told me, at high decibel levels and with unnecessary adjectives, that the bridge security record cut out right after you recalled our fighters to defend against the bioforce missiles. It didn't resume until you left the bridge."

"The lift? Here?"

She shook her head. "Everywhere you went, the cams stopped recording. There's no record of Rahel's healing. All my staff who saw it will swear to it, but Greve is paranoid enough to think there's a conspiracy and stupid enough to think I could or would fake her medical records."

"Not to mention faking yours," Lhyn said. "His current theory is that you sedated yourself."

"Right. That's my standard procedure immediately after a battle, when five captured ships are sitting off my bow."

Lhyn smiled. "Sarcasm means you're feeling better."

She was. Between Lhyn's presence and Alejandra's touch therapy, the pain had receded to the point where she could begin to think straight.

"If he thinks you faked medical records, why are you still on duty?"

"He has zero proof, for one thing. I suspect he only has enough pull with Fleet to remove you from command. Removing me as well would raise more eyebrows."

"Not to mention that he's terrified of her," Lhyn said.

"He should be," Alejandra growled. "Asshead."

"When did the surgery bay cams come back on?"

"The moment you passed out. The irregularities were enough for him to override my medical order sending you to the Blacksun healing center. I filed an objection, but it didn't have much weight when my order was based on a concept Fleet Medical doesn't recognize."

"Don't worry, Ekatya. We'll get you out of there. Rahel, too. Andira is negotiating with Sholokhov. She won't share the details, but it must be big. She's been talking to the High Council."

"And she's already gotten one concession," Alejandra said. "Greve can't haul you in for questioning or debriefing or whatever he'd try to call it. Rahel is exempted, too. He can investigate to his black heart's content, but only around the edges."

Ekatya sighed as the gentle massage moved to her scalp. "No wonder this works so well on Rahel. And here I thought she was the one I had to worry about."

Alejandra's furious expression eased. "She's already complaining about being kept in bed. I think she'd be practicing with her stave if I let her."

"Her stave!" She tried to sit up and was instantly pushed back down.

"Do *not* get ideas about moving until I say otherwise. I swear, you're as bad as Rahel."

"I told you not to set off her temper," Lhyn said knowingly. "What about her stave?"

"I had to confiscate it. I put it in my bridge console for safekeeping. If Greve—I can't let anything happen to it."

"I'll ask Commander Lokomorra to bring it to my office. That's probably safer than anywhere near you or Rahel right now."

"Thank you." She relaxed, the immediate emergency resolved. "I'm not worried about an investigation. Fleet only has to look at the first five minutes of battle footage to know Greve would have cost us two ships at the very least. Nothing I did as Fahla is actionable—"

"Oh, sister." Lhyn grinned, enjoying her use of Whitesun slang. "What you did as Fahla started a revolution. Fleet won't climb up your ass about that."

Alejandra nodded, confirming the outrageous statement. "The government went into freefall within hours of the surrender. Remember when Commodore Vataka said the Empire would fall in a day if the slaves and hangers revolted?"

"Yes?"

"He was right. They've been rising up on planets all over the Empire. The military hasn't responded because first, they're stretched too thin, and second, they're falling apart, too. Those ships don't run very well when the hangers and slaves stop taking orders. Neither do dirtside detachments of soldiers."

Ekatya stared at her, speechless. "I started a revolution?"

"On the scale of an empire."

"Fucking Hades."

"Yeah," Lhyn agreed cheerfully. "I think you might have some pull with Sholokhov now."

❧

She was sitting up, brushing her teeth after an Alejandra-approved meal, when Admiral Greve strode in.

Lovely. Just what she needed to elevate the throbbing in her head back to a full migraine.

He stood at the foot of her bed and scowled. "Spit that out."

She stopped brushing, raised her eyebrows, and resumed at a slower pace.

"Oh, for the love of all that's holy. Are you a child? I gave you an order."

He stewed for another twenty seconds while she finished and spit into the bowl on her tray. Then she held up a finger, rinsed and spit again, and finally wiped her mouth with the napkin. "I'm on medical leave," she said, pushing the tray back on its swinging arm. "You want to give orders, do it somewhere else."

"I want to give you orders for the last few days I can before Fleet kicks you down to a garbage hauler or out altogether. I don't care what magical shielding you've had up until now, it's over. You'll never set foot on a warship bridge again."

"I don't think that's your decision," she said silkily.

Having nothing left to lose was an incredible freedom.

"Maybe not, but my report will have weight with the people who do make that decision. You know what else will have weight? The footage of you on that broadcast, playacting at being a Seeder." He shook his head in mock sorrow. "Some captains have a god complex, but you're the first to take it literally. Half of Fleet won't serve with you because you profaned our gods by pretending to be one. The other half won't serve because they're afraid you weren't pretending. Me, I think you really are that deluded. It doesn't matter that you won that battle. What matters is that you're politically toxic."

She let her disdain show. "I've been that for the past four and a half years. Nothing new there. Maybe you're right; maybe it doesn't matter that I won the battle. But you know what does matter? That you would have *lost* it. Badly. Ah ah!" She lifted a hand, her glare stopping his retort mid-word. "You want to talk political toxicity? Let's talk about an irrelevant admiral playacting at being a battle commander. Let's talk about who in Fleet will want to serve with a man who tried to send two crews to their deaths for the sake of his pride. If I'm toxic, you're radioactive."

A wave of red rose from his collar. "You knew what Sayana planned. You had to. She was never loyal to Fleet, she was loyal to you and Lancer Tal."

"She's loyal to Alsea. But the real problem is that she shattered your fantasy, isn't it?" This anger had a flavor of betrayal to it, and his expression confirmed her guess. "You enjoyed thinking she respected you. She deserves an acting award for that. It must have taken a truly creative imagination."

His jaw was so tight that he could have chewed the heads off tension bolts. "She playacted almost as well as you, *Fahla*. You two deserve each other. I can't tell you how happy I am to see both of you in here. She's getting a practice run at her future prison cell, and you're getting a practice run at your enforced retirement. Are you bored yet?"

"No, I'm still counting up the pages I'll have in the history books when they talk about the fall of the Voloth Empire. Don't worry, I'm sure you'll get a footnote." She gave him a smug smile. "I may be going out, but I'll go out on top."

For an intriguing moment, she thought he might choke. If he did, she planned to wait a good five minutes before hitting the medical call button.

"You're not fit to serve," he managed. "Fleet will be well rid of you."

"The captain who won a battle at three-to-one odds and started a revolution? They'll use me in recruitment posters."

"I detest you," he snarled. His fists were clenched in helpless fury, reminding her of a school bully whose bluff had been called.

"Fair enough," she said mildly. "I detest you, too. It might be the one thing we have in common."

Having nothing left to say, he spun on his heel and stalked out.

26

BLACKOUT

Two hours later, Ekatya was finally released from the medbay with strict instructions to go home and relax.

On her way out, she dropped in on Rahel but found her asleep. It was odd to look at her through physical eyes rather than from the spiritual plane. Even odder was the thought that two days ago, she had held this woman's liver in her hands.

She watched Rahel breathing, easily and deeply, and decided to never again think of open abdominal cavities and glistening organs.

She left no note or sign of her presence. Greve was too paranoid and Rahel's position too tenuous to risk it.

Entering her quarters was like revisiting a home she no longer lived in. Everything was achingly familiar, yet she wandered through with a sense that she was merely a guest, soon to leave. The computer responded only to the most basic of requests, locking her out of even low-level situation reports and reiterating the difficult truth: her life here was over. Her command codes were suspended, and without them, she had no more power on this ship than a VIP passenger.

Make that less power, she thought when an attempted call to her grandparents failed. Her quantum com allowance had been suspended along with her codes. Greve had trapped her on her own ship. She might not be in the brig, but in every other way, she was imprisoned.

Eventually, she settled down with a book, a recording of the Enkara Preserve on her display, and smooth instrumental music to help calm her thoughts. It was a quiet, peaceful evening, the sort she would have killed for a week ago. She received no guests and expected none, knowing that Greve had ordered the section chiefs to refrain from contact until the investigation was complete. Alejandra had been the exception as long as she was still in the medbay.

Not that Alejandra cared much for the order. Ekatya was startled when her matter printer activated of its own accord and presented a meal, a teabag, and a message on the display.

Eat everything. Doctor's orders. The tea is herbal and will help with the headache and chest pain. It also has anti-asshead properties.

Laughing, she carried the tea to her kitchen and added it to a cup of hot water. Four minutes later, she lifted the mug in a salute to her friend and sipped it.

Not bad. If it really did keep Greve away, she'd drink five liters.

When it was late enough on ship time to qualify as a reasonable hour in Blacksun, she stretched out on the sofa and let herself fall back, drifting through the open door into Lhyn's mind.

"Have you moved in?" she asked, looking around at the sumptuous suite that was not theirs.

Lhyn beamed at her from her seat at the dining table, which bore signs of a recently finished breakfast for three. "My stars and asteroids, I'm glad you're here! Wow, you look a thousand times better."

"I feel a thousand times better. Even more now that I'm seeing you." She rubbed her chest, where the ache had instantly lessened.

Salomen turned from where she had been peeling some sort of fruit in the kitchen area. "Ekatya! It's so good to hear your voice. You've been sorely missed."

"You can't see me?" she asked, disappointed.

"I think we'd need to be Sharing with Lhyn for that. Or I'd need some divine tyree power behind me." She set down the knife and wiped her hands. "I'm willing, but certain people are adamant that I do nothing more strenuous than drink shannel for the rest of the nineday."

"You're lucky I'm letting you peel that starfruit." Andira came out of the archway that led to the bathroom and dressing room, already attired for a day in the State House. "Ekatya, welcome back. Salomen speaks truly; it's wonderful to hear you. None of us relaxed until Lhyn made contact with you."

"Especially me," Lhyn said. "I got more rest after seeing you last night than during my twenty-six-hantick knockout."

"I can see that." Ekatya had already noticed her bright eyes and the lack of lines around her mouth. "You look even more gorgeous. Any chest pain?"

She shrugged. "Residual. Nothing worth thinking about, especially when I know you're coming home soon."

"Am I?"

In the kitchen area, Andira accepted a cup of shannel from Salomen and gave her a grateful kiss. "You are. I'm working on it."

"Lhyn said you were in negotiations with Sholokhov. Please tell me you're not letting him use me to get concessions out of you."

"I cannot tell you that." She took a sip and hummed happily.

"Andira!"

"What else is she supposed to do?" Lhyn asked. "Leave you in Greve's clutches?"

"No, but he has no evidence and no case. It's only a matter of time before Fleet offers me a compassionate discharge so I'll go away quietly. I won't accept unless they drop all charges against Rahel. That will be my price for leaving without kicking up a public cloud of dirt."

Andira set down her cup. "Why would you assume this is your problem to deal with?"

"Because it is! You can't let Sholokhov soak you for something I can—"

"Stop right there. Are you under the mistaken assumption that because you're up there alone, and we're down here, you're on your own? Do you truly believe I would leave you to handle this mess?"

"Oh, Ekatya." Salomen shook her head. "Think carefully before you answer."

"I—no, but—"

"Good," Andira interrupted. "Because I will bring both you and Rahel home. I am sick to death of watching you bear the worst burdens and being helpless to do anything about it. I'm not helpless now. I have leverage and I am *delighted* to use it."

"I'm afraid to ask. What are you giving him?"

Andira picked up her cup and smiled.

"She won't tell us," Lhyn said. "It's very annoying."

"It's confidential," Andira corrected. "And delicate at this stage. Sholokhov is pulling levers at Gov Dome. Until he's done, I cannot speak of it. Not even to you."

"Since when do we keep secrets from each other?" It was a low blow, but she was frustrated by her virtual imprisonment and the lack of information.

"Since it became a negotiation point."

"One of your concessions is that you won't talk to me about your concessions?"

"Yes."

"That makes no sense."

"I can tell you this much. Sholokhov has a special regard for you."

"Sure he does," she said dismissively. "That's why he tried to sell me to you for a pack of high empaths."

"He feels justified in treating you as he wishes, but no one else is allowed. When I refused to accept your career as an inducement to negotiate, he viewed that as an insult to you. I didn't value you highly enough. It made him defensive of you."

"You can't be serious."

"Like siblings." Salomen stole Andira's cup, took a sip, and handed it back. "As children, Herot and I fought and insulted each other on a daily basis. But if anyone outside the family insulted him, I made them sorry for it."

"You think Sholokhov views Ekatya through a familial lens?" Lhyn asked.

"It's more a sense of ownership, but the psychology is similar. He wants to surprise you with the deal."

"Now that I believe. Information is power to him. He always needs to have more of it than me."

"Mm." Andira hummed into her cup. "I think that for once, you might enjoy the surprise. And that's all I will say." She set the cup on the counter and straightened her sleeves. "I wish I could stay, but I have a meeting."

"About your deal?"

"Relax, Ekatya. Enjoy not bearing any burdens for a while. Read a good book. It did wonders for me."

"How long is a while?"

"Another day at least. Probably two."

"I'll die of boredom. I don't even know what's happening with the Voloth ships! Greve has me in an information blackout."

"I can tell you," Lhyn said. "Sit down and have a virtual cup of shannel with Salomen and me while Andira goes out to save the world."

"We already saved the world," Andira said. "Now we're saving Ekatya and Rahel."

27

THE DEAL

I t took three days.

Despite knowing that even three days was the equivalent of light speed when it came to political decisions, Ekatya chafed at the delay. She had gone from nonstop action to a full stop, and the mental whiplash was killing her.

She considered packing up just to have something to do, but couldn't bring herself to order the crates. Greve would know and interpret it as a victory. She would rather drop her possessions in orbit and hope they eventually landed than give him the satisfaction.

Cleaning the quarters, going through her storage, and recycling every unnecessary item left the space sparkling but took less than four hours.

Reading another book occupied two more hours, until the lead character made a decision so stupid that she couldn't continue. She had enough of that in real life and refused to subject herself to it in fiction.

A visit to the Blue Rocket turned out to be a mistake. The bar was full of crew celebrating their victory, but her presence notably reduced the volume. They smiled at her and lifted their glasses in acknowledgment, but she didn't need to be an empath to feel their awkwardness. She had been removed from command; what were they supposed to say? Not to mention that the last time they had seen her, she had glowed and spoken as Fahla.

Loathe as she was to admit it, Greve might have a point about Fleet crew serving with her after that performance.

She finished her drink and went back to her quarters. Better to be alone there than alone in public.

Visits with Lhyn helped considerably. They took turns at first, but having Lhyn appear in her quarters was like having a visitor in prison. She much preferred taking herself on a virtual outing. On the second afternoon, she found Lhyn in Lanaril's garden and enjoyed an oddly easy three-way philosophical conversation. Lanaril had begun writing a book after Salomen's uprising and was newly inspired by recent events.

"How can you claim Fahla's involvement when you know the truth?" Ekatya asked at one point.

Lanaril smiled as she listened to Lhyn repeat the question. "I know *a* truth," she answered. "You know another. Are they incompatible? Or are they simply different views of the same thing?" She gestured at the wall of the temple complex rising above them. "We can sit here and claim we see the temple in all its glory. But if we walk around to the front and look up at the grand entrance, we'll see what appears to be a different building."

The choice of illustration gave Ekatya pause. While she had viewed events in orbit, Lanaril had viewed them from the quad on Blacksun Base, where thirty-three divine tyrees generated a visible power that reached orbit.

We need the seventh star, Ekatya had said when Salomen couldn't complete the jump. Lhyn had known exactly what she meant by it. But Lhyn had also defined that seventh star as a representation of the divine.

"There is a touch of the divine in all of us," Lanaril said at the end of their discussion. "It's up to us to decide how to use it. Or whether we use it at all."

Ekatya thought about security cams that stopped recording and wondered.

By the end of the third day, she had written a long letter to her grandparents and completed her filings for commendations, award recommendations, and several promotions. The list was nowhere near complete, but without access to battle reports, she could only make recommendations for performances of which she was personally aware.

With the filings in the ship's communications queue and the letter to her grandparents saved to her pad, she settled down with a new book and her last bottle of Valkinon. After all, she would have no need to take Alsean wine back to Alsea. Might as well drink it now.

The bottle was half empty and she was nodding at the lead character's ruthless but correct decision when the mountain scene vanished off her wall display, replaced by the priority blue emblem and a prompt for her com code.

"This should be interesting," she muttered, setting aside her book.

She transferred the call to the far smaller display at her desk and entered her suspended com code. The emblem shrank, replaced by Director Sholokhov's com ID. With a tap, she accepted the call.

"Captain Serrado, this is a true pleasure." Sholokhov was at his desk, the large window behind him showing nothing but darkness. It seemed the man never went home.

"Director Sholokhov. I understand you've been busy."

"Enjoyably so. It's rare that I'm able to get so many things I want at the same time." He leaned back in his chair and folded his hands across his stomach. "What has Lancer Tal told you of our negotiations?"

"Only that you're having them."

"She is a woman of her word. Yet she manages to keep that from becoming a liability by choosing her words with great care. It's fascinating to watch. Do you remember informing me with complete confidence that she would never give me what I asked for?"

He waited, making it clear that he would not continue until she answered.

"Yes," she said shortly.

He reached offscreen and held up a pad, then tapped a control on his desk. Her display now showed the signature lines of a formal treaty document.

She recognized Andira's signature on the first line. Beside it and on the same level was the signature of the President of the Protectorate.

"Allow me to highlight what Lancer Tal has agreed to."

The document scrolled past too quickly for her to read anything until it settled on a numbered list. Only the first two items were visible, but they were enough to elicit an involuntary gasp.

"She gave you the high empaths *and* the heavy cruiser?!"

The text vanished, revealing the most overtly pleased expression she had ever seen on Sholokhov's face. "Everyone has their price. It's merely a matter of finding it."

"What in all the purple planets was worth that?"

"What every politician cares about most. Her position. Her power." He loosened the knot in his scarf of office. "Ahh. The end of a very good day. You're witnessing the intelligence coup of a lifetime. I've found myself contemplating the ironies atop ironies that enabled it. First Guard Sayana was the key, and you're the one who brought her aboard. You put her in a fighter when she should have been in the brig. Had she returned to Alsea safely, I would have had no leverage. Had she died in that fighter or on the operating table, I would have had no leverage. But Dr. Wells saved her, and that made her a dangerous liability for Lancer Tal. She could not allow us to incarcerate one of the great heroes of that battle. Do you know what else became a liability?"

Still stunned, Ekatya shook her head.

"The revolution you started. By the way, I must congratulate you on both your performance and your skillful elimination of any evidence in the security record. Impersonating Fahla was a brilliant strategy, one I would never have thought of."

"Thank you," she said faintly.

"How did you identify the Political Bureau officers on the *Vengeance*?"

This, at least, she was prepared for. She and Andira had concocted their explanation via Lhyn.

"My bondmate is the best anthropologist in the Protectorate. She's been working with the Voloth settlers on Alsea and learned about the political officers. She also reads body language like you read a book. She knew those particular officers were unsurprised by Vataka's statements and angry that he was making them. It was blind good luck that they turned out to be Bureau officers." As with all good lies, this one was at least eighty percent true.

"And you had her watching the broadcast while speaking to you on your com. Well planned. Though I suspect you didn't plan to start a revolution."

"I hoped that exposing the Empire's lies would destabilize its govern-ment. An actual revolution went well beyond my expectations." That was one hundred percent true.

"And mine, I admit. You're quite a wild card, Captain. Four and a half years ago, you disobeyed orders and saved the balance of power between the Protectorate and the Empire. This week, you eliminated Admiral Greve to avoid disobeying orders and completely upended the balance of power. The Empire is in shambles. Whatever rises from the ashes will be smaller and weaker than what we faced before. In the meantime, I have a top-of-the-line heavy cruiser in nearly perfect condition, since you never broke its shields. The databanks are full, the technology, weaponry, and engineering are untouched—I even have the personal logs of both the captain and commodore. If the revolution stumbles at any point, I have no doubt the information in those logs will enable me to push it along."

He reached up with one hand and drew the scarf from around his neck.

"Immediately after the surrender, more than half the crews of those ships requested asylum," he continued, carefully folding the scarf. "The Alsean war council was congratulating itself on procuring not only the ships but also the bodies and skill sets needed to operate them. Within forty-eight hours, the picture had changed." He set the perfect square on his desk and rested his hands atop it. "No surrendering officer wanted to go back home to be punished, but when the central government collapsed and individual planets began falling to angry mobs, those officers suddenly looked like they were on the right side of justice. The hangers are eager to return as well, either to take part in the revolution or to protect their families and homes from the fallout. The only ones who want to stay are the hangers who don't have families, and the slaves who don't have homes."

The realization must have shown on her face, given the amused glint in his eyes.

"Your revolution cost Lancer Tal her crews," he said. "She has enough for the destroyers. Not for the heavy cruiser."

"So out of the goodness of your heart, you offered to take it off her hands."

"Of course. Don't worry, it was a profitable deal on both sides. In exchange, we're restocking the armories of the *Phoenix* and providing maintenance for the next three years, by which time the space elevator dock should be able to handle the work. We'll also restock the *Caphenon's* armories when the Alseans raise it."

It took her a moment to catch up. He had buried the salient point so smoothly that it slipped right past her.

"Maintenance," she repeated. "You traded the *Phoenix*."

"An agreement that makes both parties happy, wouldn't you say? I have the ship she can't use. She has the ship she can. Oh, I forgot one detail. During a transition period of one Alsean cycle, we will crew the *Phoenix* with staff who will train their Alsean replacements." He paused, clearly enjoying himself. "I stipulated one non-negotiable point. You will remain in command as the first admiral of the new Alsean fleet."

She had lost all ability to hide her shock. "Why? Why would you do that?"

"Because it's time for you to leave. Your battle strategy this week was nothing short of brilliant. It was also extremely divisive and makes you a liability to the organization. Then there is the issue of Admiral Greve's charges. They don't get more serious than usurping command. You and I know the man is a gasbag, but he's still an admiral. Rank carries weight."

"So this is my inducement to leave quietly."

He inclined his head. "It would be of great benefit should the separation occur with good feelings on all sides."

"I'm going to need more than that."

At last the shoe was on the other foot. His eyebrows rose in genuine surprise. "I've handed you the perfect solution on a platter, including a promotion to admiral, and you want more?"

She smiled.

28

BREAKOUT

It was nearing the end of the night shift when Rahel heard a commotion outside her treatment room.

"Captain, I can't—you're not authorized—"

Her door opened. Captain Serrado was in uniform and exuding confidence as she addressed the security guard outside. "Since when do I need authorization to visit one of my officers?"

There was a long pause. "You're not in command, Captain. She's being transferred to the brig tomorrow."

"So? She has a right to visitation regardless of location. My suspended command doesn't suspend my access to public areas of the ship, of which this is one. Do you have a legal reason to deny both of us our rights?"

"No, Captain," came the subdued answer.

"Then I'll be inside." She stepped in and closed the door. The authority crackling around her shifted to delight as she met Rahel's eyes. "You look much better than the last time I saw you."

Rahel put a fist over her heart and bowed her head. "Captain Serrado, well met. I heard you were recovered, but it's nice to see it for myself."

"I feel the same about you."

"When did you last see me?" she asked curiously.

"Two days after your surgery. You were asleep."

"I've been sleeping a lot. Dr. Wells says it's normal, but I'm sick of it."

She indicated the mobile chair beside her bed. "And ready to walk more than fifty paces."

"Typical warrior," Serrado said with a grin. "Lives through a miracle and complains about how long it took."

"I don't complain around her—"

"That's not what I heard."

"—much," she finished.

Serrado laughed. "The truth comes out," she quipped, looking Rahel up and down. "How badly do you want to get out of that medshirt?"

"Before today, I'd have paid for the opportunity. Now that I know I'll be wearing a brig shirt tomorrow, I'm not so eager."

"No, I wouldn't think so. Brown would look terrible on you. I've arranged to have your uniform brought instead."

"Um. I appreciate the thought, but I can't wear it. Commander Cox said he didn't like it any more than I do, but he doesn't have a choice."

She leaned over and spoke quietly. "You won't be here tomorrow to wear a brig shirt. I'm breaking you out."

"You're—Captain," Rahel said with a sinking heart. "Don't get into trouble for me. This is temporary. Lancer Tal won't let the Protectorate take me."

"No, she won't, because I'm taking you to Blacksun." Serrado held up a hand, stopping the next objection. "You've trusted me this far. I'm asking you to trust me now. It's going to be all right."

There was no dissonance of untruth. Whether justified or not, Captain Serrado believed her words.

"I trust you."

The satisfaction spreading across her emotional signature had an oddly sharp edge. "Good. You won't regret it, I promise."

Rahel looked toward the door as another familiar signature approached. "Dr. Wells is coming."

"Right on time."

Aghast, she blurted, "She's involved, too?"

"I remember when you first came on board," Serrado said conversationally. "The one area where Commander Cox consistently said you needed improvement was working as part of a team. You've made admirable progress in that."

"I—thank you, but—"

Serrado watched Dr. Wells come through the door, a large medkit in hand. "Your team is here," she said. "We look after our own. Good timing, Alejandra. Have any difficulties?"

"None." Dr. Wells set her medkit on the counter and opened it. "Let's get you into proper clothes." She produced a roll of cloth and held it out.

"My uniform." Rahel ran her palm over the soft Alsean material and blinked back the sudden moisture in her eyes. She looked up at the two officers with their matching smiles and no longer cared whether this was doomed to fail. If it did, she would go down in uniform, supported by her oath holder and her friend.

She still had to be careful sitting up and moving to the edge of the bed. Once there, she could dress herself with only a few twinges. Dr. Wells had even brought fresh undergarments from her quarters, which felt divine after days of baggy medbay clothing. She had just sealed her jacket when her boots were presented, clean and polished.

"What else do you have in there?" she joked, gingerly bending to pull on the first boot.

"Finish dressing and you'll see."

Such happy excitement was a marked contrast to her friend's moods since the battle. She secured the second boot and rose with an expectant grin. "I'm ready."

The grin dropped at the sight of her stave in its holster. "Oh," she whispered. No other words would come through the blockage in her throat.

"I would never have let it come to harm," Captain Serrado said. "I put it in my bridge console for safekeeping. When Greve locked me out of the bridge, I asked Dr. Wells to take care of it."

"Commander Lokomorra passed it to me," Dr. Wells said. "It's been in my quarters for the past three days. I have your uniform from the fighter, too. Candini remembered that you'd brought it with you and went looking for it."

"Is this—?" She swept a hand down her body.

"The same one? No. I wasn't sure you'd want to wear it, given what happened. But I had it cleaned just in case. Your seat was torn to shreds, but the storage compartment was unscathed."

"My good luck charm. That's what Candini thought it was when she saw it." Rahel clipped the holster onto her belt and felt whole for the first time since waking after surgery. "If I'm going to Blacksun, then I can see her and tell her to stop feeling guilty. She keeps sending apologetic messages, but I can't get her on the com."

"Candini is the reason you're alive," Serrado said. "We were seconds away from ending the link when she alerted me to your situation. If Salomen had broken that link, she couldn't have made the jump again."

"Fahla was watching over you." Dr. Wells brought the mobile chair around. "Hop in."

"Are we going to the shuttle bay? I can walk to the lift."

Dr. Wells merely waited.

Sighing, she sat in the hated chair. "You're only drawing this out because it's your last chance."

"Is that what you think? I'm coming with you. Someone has to get you settled in the healing center."

"Let's go." Serrado opened the door and walked through.

"Captain—oh, no, you can't do that."

Rahel recognized the officer stepping forward, distress rising off his skin. She had worked well with DeValle during her cycle in security.

"Don't make me call Commander Cox," he pleaded. "I hate this, too, but I have my orders."

"I know you do," Captain Serrado said calmly. "Go ahead and call him."

Rahel tried not to show her surprise. Cox was involved as well?

DeValle stepped away to make the call, never taking his gaze off the captain. He returned with a looser posture and a much lighter emotional signature. "I don't know what's going on, but Cox said you're cleared to proceed to the shuttle bay and my duty shift here is ended."

"Thank you. My apologies for the difficult position Greve put you in. You handled it with competence and respect. Have a good night." Captain Serrado nodded at him and walked past.

"Are you going home?" DeValle whispered.

"Looks like it. Wish me luck."

"Good luck, Red. Don't catch any more sabots."

Rahel shook his hand and settled back in the chair, feeling far more optimistic about this adventure.

They crossed the lobby to the lift with no further challenges, only cheery farewell waves from the nurses at the main desk.

"Shuttle bay," Captain Serrado said.

With her command suspended, she should not have been able to order the lift to a restricted area. Which meant Commander Zeppy must have overridden the restrictions. Were there any section chiefs not taking part in this?

The lift doors reopened onto a nearly silent shuttle bay. No shuttles were in operation, and normal maintenance was a day shift job. The night shift staff were all in the office, two levels up.

"Captain," Rahel said as they passed behind the nearest shuttle. "Do you think it will be possible to get a few more things from my quarters at some point? I can't bear the thought of leaving Mother's sculpture behind, or my wooden daggers."

"I promise that you won't lose anything," Serrado said. "Your quarters are locked down. Not even Greve can get in."

That was baffling. "I thought he was conducting an investigation?"

"He was. That's been suspended."

"Just like your command," Dr. Wells observed, to the vast amusement of both officers.

"No, much better than that. I don't do things half-assed." Serrado pulled a pad from her sleeve pocket, gave it a few taps, and handed it to Rahel. "Hold this, please."

She rested the pad in her lap and decided she was better off not asking.

The shuttle bay had never seemed so large as they made their way across. Of course Serrado's preferred Alsea-capable shuttle was as far as possible from the lift. Worse, no one seemed to share Rahel's sense of urgency. Dr. Wells strolled along as if they were out for a walk on Deck Zero, and Captain Serrado was looking at every part of the bay as if committing it to memory.

Because that was exactly what she was doing, Rahel realized with a jolt. There was no coming back from this. Dr. Wells had already made her decision to leave Fleet, but had Captain Serrado decided to run rather than fight?

She faced forward, thinking furiously. Maybe this was Lancer Tal's plan. Rather than embroil the Alsean government in a political show-down, she was quietly slipping Rahel off the *Phoenix* and taking Captain Serrado with her. After all, they had five Voloth ships now.

Captain Serrado could take over the heavy cruiser and lead the new fleet.

The more she thought about it, the more sensible it seemed.

They reached the shuttle with no cries of "Stop!" coming over the bay com, no sound of running footsteps, no alarms of any kind. Rahel began to believe they might depart without fanfare.

"I can go from here," she said as Captain Serrado lowered the shuttle ramp. "Besides, it'll be easier for you to push the chair up without me in it."

"How considerate." Dr. Wells walked around to stand in front of her. "For such a terrible patient. Tell me, is it true that one of my nurses found you hanging from the overhead bar in your treatment room?"

"Um. You said it was for physical therapy. To increase my upper body strength."

"To shift your weight and position in bed, not to swing from!"

"I wasn't swinging! There wasn't any room to swing." Why were they talking about this instead of getting the shek out of here?

"And that's the real reason I want to get her to Blacksun," Dr. Wells confided to the captain. "Surgery I can handle. Physical therapy with an Alsean warrior? Not even Fahla has that much patience."

Rahel didn't hear the lift doors open over the sound of their chuckles. But she certainly heard the shout.

"Serrado! You're not going anywhere!"

Multiple emotional signatures registered on her senses. She counted six before they came into view, including two she wished she didn't recognize.

Admiral Greve strode in front of Commander Cox and four security officers, his face reflecting the triumph that oozed from his skin. "Thank you for being so predictable," he said. "I knew you'd try something like this. You've put yourself in the shit this time."

Serrado's emotions were not at all what Rahel expected. She wasn't afraid, worried, or even regretful. She was blazing with ferocious joy, a warrior finally facing the battle she had itched to fight.

"What is it you think I'm trying?" she asked, her calm voice belying the hurricane roiling the air.

"Seeders preserve us, you really are that arrogant. You're caught, Serrado. The ship's computer was programmed to notify me if you took

Sayana out of her treatment room or ordered the lift to the shuttle bay. Imagine my lack of surprise to learn you'd just done both." His smile was vicious. "You know what the best part is? I didn't have much evidence of your scheme with her before. Now I do. You're finished." He turned to the officers. "Take Captain Serrado back to her quarters and post a twenty-four-hour guard. And take Sayana straight to the brig. She doesn't need another night in the medbay."

"Belay that order," Serrado snapped.

The guards stopped mid-step, looking warily between the two ranking officers.

"You do not take your orders from her!" Greve shouted.

"Actually, they do." Cox was enjoying this almost as much as Serrado, though his face was impassive.

Greve rounded on him. "Don't link your shuttle to the wrong ship, Commander."

"Phoenix," Serrado said. "Respond on the shuttle bay com. Who holds command of this ship?"

The computer's voice resounded through the empty bay. *"The* Phoenix *is commanded by Captain Ekatya Serrado."*

Greve froze in disbelief, then broke loose with a jolt of rage. "Since when?" he snarled. "I don't believe this. You've manipulated the ship's records."

"Oh, no," Serrado said in a dangerously soft voice. "I haven't done anything with the ship's records. That's your game, not mine."

"What are you talking about?"

"I believe that's my cue." Commander Cox held up a pad, open to a document with the words *Department of Justice* emblazoned across the top. "This is a report detailing your violations of the rights and protections guaranteed to all members of Fleet. I compiled it after accessing your file space on the ship's computers."

Greve's face drained of color, a counterpoint to the shock vibrating through his emotions.

"It's my experience that someone who abuses power doesn't stop with legally sanctioned abuse," Captain Serrado said. "You had access to all security records with me in them. Those records included private and confidential conversations with members of this crew. You were obligated to delete them once you determined they had no bearing on my tyree bond or my relationship with Lancer Tal." She stepped forward, closing the space between them. "I suspected you couldn't resist keeping anything you thought might be useful. Or titillating."

The four watching security officers moved toward Greve, cutting off any avenue of escape.

Not that he was capable of running, Rahel thought scornfully. She was recovering from impalement and could probably still outrun him.

Greve's eyes shifted rapidly as he assessed his options. Unsurprisingly, he went for bluster. "Whatever you think you found in a search of my *private* files, you'll get nowhere with it. You didn't have probable cause. That search was illegal."

"You should be more aware of the laws you're breaking," Cox remarked. "Members of Fleet have no constitutional protections against warrantless searches of their workplace. They do have protection against searches of their private files, *if* those files are kept off the military installation. You're on a ship, Admiral. Using ship's resources to store your illegal records. Even if you tried to argue that they're still somehow protected, I have a warrant. What I found in your office was more than enough probable cause."

"Who did you get to push that warrant through, some ensign at Fleet Justice? I am an *admiral.* You've overreached."

"It wasn't an ensign." Captain Serrado held out her hand. "Rahel, the pad?"

She had forgotten all about it. Now wildly curious, she placed it in the captain's palm.

Serrado activated the virtual screen, showing a call in progress. "Director Sholokhov, have you heard enough?"

"Heard enough and read enough. This is quite a list, Commander Cox. And some very interesting footage." Sholokhov set a pad on his desk with a decisive click. "Admiral Greve, I've been many things in my life. An ensign was never one of them."

Rahel had never seen anyone turn quite that shade of green.

"Director Sholokhov." Greve's voice was weak. "I didn't mean—"

"Don't bother. I deal in information, and you have nothing to offer me. False protestations of innocence and piles of frantic lies don't qualify. As you so eloquently said to Captain Serrado, you put yourself in this shit."

"But I—"

"Commander Cox, take Greve into custody. I'll send a shuttle to collect him. He can wait in the brig."

"Yes, Director."

"Now wait a damned minute!" Greve stabbed a finger toward Rahel. "That woman attacked me on the bridge and she's been treated like royalty. Serrado ordered it, you know she did, and she wasn't even confined to quarters. You have no right to put me in the brig!"

"I have no right?" Sholokhov repeated. "Are you suddenly concerned about rights now? You're late to the party." A smile thinned his lips. "Rahel Sayana did not attack you on the bridge. I saw that footage. She laid you down as gently as a lover."

"Gah," Rahel said involuntarily.

Beside her, Dr. Wells muffled a laugh.

"I've also seen footage of her in an actual attack. I assure you, what she did to you wasn't even close." Effortlessly dismissing him, he turned to Serrado. "Thank you for bringing this to my attention, Captain. While I have you on the com, there's one more thing I couldn't tell you before. The authorization came in after our call. You're being awarded the Presidential Medal of Galactic Service."

That had not been in the plan, Rahel knew. The captain was dumb-founded.

Greve made a strangled sound, his shock shading to loathing.

"The Protectorate is sorry to lose you to the Alseans, but I'm certain you'll serve them with as much distinction as you did us. As a parting gesture, the President is pleased to bestow the highest award in his power. Are you familiar with the requirements?"

She nodded, apparently incapable of speech.

"I'm not," Rahel said.

His intense stare swung to her. "No, you wouldn't be, would you? It's the greatest honor a Protectorate citizen can receive. The requirements are such that only a handful have ever been given out. The Medal of Galactic Service is given for acts of such valor, distinction, or importance that they impact the course of history. It's difficult to imagine an act more impactful than instigating a revolution across the entire breadth of the Voloth Empire. Captain Serrado has made quite a mark on history. I hope she'll continue to do the same for your government." He turned back to

Serrado. "Am I correct in assuming you won't want to return to Gov Dome for the ceremony?"

"No, I can't," she managed. "There's too much to do here, setting up the new fleet. But I thank you for the offer."

"Of course," he said briskly. "I anticipated that and sent the authorization to Ambassador Solvassen's office. We'll hold the ceremony by quantum com. Expect correspondence from the Office of the President establishing a date and time."

"Yes, Director."

He gave her a nod in lieu of a goodbye, and the virtual screen went transparent.

"My sainted Shippers," Dr. Wells said. "The Medal of Galactic Service?"

"I'm as surprised as you are." A slow smile lit Serrado's face as she looked at the seething admiral. "Though I did tell you I'd be going out on top."

"Don't do what you're thinking." Commander Cox caught Greve by the arm. "I've heard what happens when Captain Serrado defends herself. Much as I'd enjoy seeing it firsthand, our chief surgeon is leaving the ship. You'd be getting patched up by her assistants."

"My staff are extremely capable, thank you," Dr. Wells said. "They're up to the task."

"I'd rather not get my hands dirty. Get him out of here. Commander, stay a moment." Captain Serrado watched with fierce triumph as the security officers marched Greve away. Not until the lift doors closed did she turn back. "I've been waiting four days to ask you this question. The cams that stopped recording—"

"It wasn't me." Cox hesitated. "Well, a tiny part of it was."

"I'm all ears. Dr. Wells and First Guard Sayana know the full circumstances and are cleared for this conversation."

"I'm all ears, too," Dr. Wells put in.

He glanced at them with a calculating shift in his emotional signature. "That explains where the sedative came from. And the training in how to use a Gaian injector."

"I have no idea what you're talking about," Dr. Wells said. "We were discussing security cams?"

Rahel put on her best innocent look.

"Work on that," he advised her before meeting Serrado's expectant gaze. "What I told Admiral Greve was ninety percent true."

"An excellent lie, then. What was the ten percent?"

"The bridge cams didn't cut out when I said they did. You spoke with someone named Salomen, who I assume is Bondlancer Opah, and said you needed the seventh star. There was a bit of conversation about logistical details, and then a light flare overloaded the sensors."

She stared at him in wonderment. "You altered the records to protect me."

"Greve was on the rampage. I didn't see the need to give him ammunition. Nothing you said to Bondlancer Opah endangered this ship, its crew, or the interests of the Protectorate. In fact, I suspect it was just the opposite, though I have no proof."

"I'm afraid you won't get any." She held out a hand. "Thank you, Commander. I'm deeply grateful for your support. More than I have words to express."

He shook her hand firmly. "Serving with you has been a pleasure, Captain. I hope you'll keep me on for the next Alsean cycle."

"Count on it."

"The next cycle?" Rahel looked up at Dr. Wells, who shrugged. They were equally in the dark.

Captain Serrado gestured toward the lowered shuttle ramp. "I'll tell you on the way. It's a Hades of a story."

29

COMING HOME

"I cannot believe they're finally coming home." Salomen shaded her eyes, looking into the sky for the first sign of the shuttle.

"It's been a long fight." Tal was focused not on the sky but on her bondmate, who wore a summer dress that bared her arms and shoulders. It offered plenty of tanned skin for the touch and a tantalizing glimpse of chest ridges and cleavage that taxed her self-control. Given the number of journalists waiting with them on the bricks of the landing pad, she could not afford to be caught with her eyes in the wrong location.

In another time and place, the Lancer ogling her Bondlancer would enhance both their reputations, but this was a serious event. Other than Vellmar, there was no Alsean more famously associated with their dazzling victory than Rahel Sayana. That she had been injured so grievously while saving the planet from a bioforce missile endeared her further. Her return was global news.

Her confinement, on the other hand, was a state secret. Tal would have shouted it from the front steps of the State House, but the Protectorate was embarrassed by Admiral Greve's battle-losing opening gambit and the fact that Rahel had removed him so easily. Alsean silence on the matter had been a useful tile to play during negotiations.

Salomen wrapped an arm around her shoulders and squeezed. "I'm proud of you."

"I'm a little proud of myself."

Laughter rumbled through her chest. "You deserve to be. You performed a miracle."

"The miracle was yours. I merely hammered out a new interplanetary agreement."

"Tyrina." Salomen turned, taking her by the shoulders to rest their foreheads together. "These journalists may not know what you did, but I do. So do Ekatya and Lhyn. Miracles are not only the province of the divine."

In her peripheral vision, Tal saw several vidcams hovering nearby to record the moment. At least she wasn't looking down Salomen's neckline.

"I love you," she whispered. "You inspire me to do the miraculous."

In answer, Salomen kissed her forehead, a gentle confirmation of their bond.

Since the battle, they had barely been able to be in the same room without touching. Something about that intense, high-powered Sharing had heightened their need for each other, an effect reported by the other divine tyrees as well. Healer Wellernal speculated that it would lessen with time, but so far it showed no signs of abating.

Lhyn had suffered quietly, having the same need with no means of relieving it. Tal and Salomen did what they could to help, but there was only one solution.

"There it is!" someone cried.

And that solution was here, Tal thought.

Anticipation increased her heart rate as the shuttle soared over the dome of the healing center. Even her breathing was affected while she watched it settle onto the landing pad and spin down its engines. The ramp lowered, and she joined the journalists and Guards in their exuberant applause when Alejandra Wells pushed Rahel out in the mobile chair.

Ekatya appeared in the doorway, tracking their progress, then looked over the heads of the journalists and straight into Tal's eyes. Her smile was radiant.

"She looks ten cycles younger," Salomen said quietly.

"She'll look fifteen cycles younger by tomorrow morning."

They held hands and watched Rahel answer questions, a cycle's worth of experience showing in the confident way she handled them. Ekatya was soon pulled in, as was Alejandra, and the planned five-tick event became ten. Then Rahel stood up from her chair, drawing a new round of applause.

"I'd like to say one thing," she announced in a clear voice. "I caught that missile, yes, but I only worked the grappler. First Pilot Candini is the one who made it possible. I don't think any other pilot, Alsean or Fleet, could have done what she did. And then she saved my life. If she's watching this, I have a message for her." She paused, allowing an expectant silence to fall. "Nightwing, you're still a wonderful friend and I'm still not putting spikes in my hair. But I *am* getting that tattoo."

"Oh, well done," Tal murmured as the journalists laughed. She felt an inordinate pride in this warrior, who had come so far and accomplished so much.

Still holding Salomen's hand, she stepped forward to offer formal greetings and a few words meant for public consumption. Salomen welcomed her sworn warrior home with a double palm touch—an act that floored Rahel and sent the vidcams into a momentary whirl—and Tal ended the event with a declaration that Rahel had family waiting inside.

While the Guards formed a protective rank around them, Alejandra ordered Rahel back into the chair and began pushing her toward the healing center doors.

"You have family waiting, too," Tal told Ekatya as they followed.

"My heart's about to leap out of my chest." She rubbed the body part in question. "But the ache is gone. I knew she was here before I landed the shuttle."

"She's missed you desperately," Salomen said. "She puts a brave face on it, though I don't understand why. She knows it hides nothing."

"It will take more than a cycle and a half of living here to overcome a lifetime of cultural training. Our instinct is always to hide our vulnerabilities."

"It's clear you're bondmates," Tal teased. "That sounded just like her."

The comment bounced off. "Hopefully, it's only the best bits that are contagious."

"Are you implying she has any bits that aren't the best?" Salomen asked.

That tease also failed when Ekatya caught sight of the crowd through the healing center doors. Alejandra pushed Rahel over the threshold to a new round of applause, complete with whistles and foot stomps from Vellmar and Candini. The waiting people surged forward, leaving one individual behind.

Lhyn stood still, her eyes locked to Ekatya's.

For her part, Ekatya didn't seem to notice anyone else in the spacious lobby. She walked as if in a daze, skirting around the edge of the crowd and dodging bodies without ever breaking her focus.

"Mother! Sharro!" Rahel cried, standing up from her chair in time to be enveloped in a taboo-breaking warmron with both women. They laughed and cried, profound relief and love broadcast for all to sense. Salomen brushed a knuckle beneath one eye, and Tal wanted to absorb the beauty of a reunion she had enabled through endless hanticks of high-risk politics.

But she could spare them only a glance, her attention drawn by Lhyn's sudden movement. Ekatya sped up at the same time, and they met behind the crowd in a silent explosion of joy that had every Alsean in the room turning to look.

Lhyn lifted Ekatya right off her feet, then set her down and wrapped her in a warmron so tight that the wing of a fairy fly would not have fit between them. Her eyes were closed and her face wreathed in a beatific smile, while Ekatya had her nose tucked into Lhyn's throat and looked as if she would never move again.

A squeal shattered the quiet.

Lanaril shifted the bundle in her arms with a delighted grin. "You felt that, didn't you, Periso? Your senses might not be developed, but you know love. Yes, you do!"

Rahel held out her hands and twitched her fingers. "Give him to me. I haven't seen my little brother in too long."

"Rahel Sayana, I did not raise you in a mud puddle. Show some manners," Ravenel scolded.

"Especially to the Lead Templar," Sharro added. "Who graciously agreed to hold our wiggly child so we could give you a proper greeting."

"Give him to me, *please*. O great and wondrous Lead Templar."

Laughing, Lanaril handed over her charge.

Rahel settled him in one arm and offered a finger for his tiny hand to wrap around. "Hoi, Little Mouse, well met! I missed you and your sweet baby scent."

"You're fortunate he's smelling sweet for you," Sharro said. "He wasn't five ticks ago."

"Did you drop weight for the big event?" She pulled him closer, rubbing her nose on his still-smooth forehead and making him burble with glee. "You might be a warrior after all."

Vellmar groaned. "Now you're giving warriors a bad name."

"You don't all evacuate your bowels before important moments?" Salomen asked innocently.

Lhyn's voice rose above the laughter. "See what I mean? You never think things like that are going to come out of her mouth."

"I don't know why; you've known me long enough."

"No, we really haven't." Ekatya was still wrapped in Lhyn's arms, her eyes sparkling as she smiled at them. "But we plan to."

30

A TOAST

"**B**attles end; bureaucracy is forever" was an old Fleet saying that Ekatya had never understood quite like she did now.

The preparations for a battle were nothing compared to those for decommissioning a ship. A printed list of the logs, reports, images, and other files being sent to Command Dome for historical conservation would surely reach from the *Phoenix*'s nose to its tail.

Every piece of artwork had to be taken down and packaged for shipment, meaning she could not walk down a corridor without tripping over another crew member carefully prying tile art from the bulkhead. She had personally boxed up the ship's bell from her office and the builder and commissioning plaques from the bridge.

Commander Zeppy had a team packing up the official plaques and insignia throughout the ship. More teams swarmed the corridors removing every Fleet identifier from bulkheads, doors, offices, and public spaces. Officers and crew in every section were looking for any other object that could be considered an integral part of the *Phoenix*'s short history and tradition, each of which required an explanation of its significance in writing. Her section chiefs vetted the selected objects and sent their reports to her for approval.

She had been reading many, many reports about many, many objects.

Because this was a handover as well as a decommissioning, all ship's systems had to be in top working order and signed off by the appropriate section chief. Every file not necessary to the running of the ship had to be pulled from the ship's computer. All ship's stores not included in the handover were being packed up. Every time she turned around, something else needed to be done.

On top of everything else, she was writing her final Command Operations Report covering the year to date. Given that this time period included the biggest battle of her career, her report contained a staggering amount of detail.

Having never yet met a pile of work she couldn't add to, she was also dealing with her relinquishment of command, retirement, award acceptance speech, and induction into the warrior caste. She was hopping from the moment she woke each morning until her eyes slammed shut at night, secure in the comfort of Lhyn's arms.

She had never been so happy.

The isolation that had haunted her since Admiral Greve's arrival was gone, replaced by Lhyn's company and the camaraderie of a crew working toward a common goal. There were still those who didn't know how to act around her, but she had been accustomed to that since making captain. Awe of rank and awe of possible divinity didn't differ all that much, she found. What made the difference were the walls that had fallen around her. Each time she spoke openly to an officer, crew member, or friend, she rejoiced anew in her freedom. Only now did she fully understand how caged she had been.

And yet, her cage had been virtual. Lhyn spent every day aboard one or another of the Voloth ships, working with slaves and some hangers, and returned to the *Phoenix* each evening with tales of cages that were all too real. The Alsean Council had asked for her expertise to help sort out the hundreds of requests for asylum, work, or repatriation. It was difficult but rewarding labor, and Lhyn buried herself in it.

All of that dropped away when they came together at night. Though Andira and Salomen had told them what to expect, they were still startled by the ongoing level of need.

"I don't think Alsean dartflies have this much sex," Lhyn mumbled into her neck one night, still breathing hard from her exertions.

"I don't think I like your comparison." Ekatya lifted a weak arm to rest it on Lhyn's bare back. "Doesn't the female dartfly eat her mate before laying eggs?"

"Well, yes. But only after she's joined with him for twenty hanticks straight."

Ekatya chuckled, remembering their explosive reunion in the State House. "We did beat that time, didn't we? If you don't count the sleep and food breaks."

"Food breaks we only had because Salomen made sure we were fed." Lhyn kissed her throat, then slid off to collapse in a heap beside her. "At least we're down to an hour now. This was practically a quickie."

"If only my crew knew your definition of a quickie. They'd be convinced of my divinity then."

"That's what it takes to convince them? I should have known. And here I thought it would be the way you took down Greve."

With some effort, Ekatya rolled over and snuggled in. "Not if they knew the truth."

What the crew did know was that Greve had been whisked off the ship in disgrace. Shocking disgrace, in fact, for no one could recall another instance in Fleet history when an admiral had spent time in a ship's brig.

"How *did* you manage that?" Andira asked during one of their too-rare quantum com chats. They had both been running ragged since the battle, though Ekatya thought she might have it easier. She only had to deal with one ship; Andira was handling five.

"I didn't," she said. "It never occurred to me to ask for brig time. All I wanted was to get him out of Fleet. But I think you're right about Sholokhov having a special regard for me. Those files Greve was keeping? One of them was a recording from before Commander Cox bought me that black market scanner. Before I found and destroyed the illegal cams in my quarters." The cams they now knew were installed by Greve's adjutant, thereby earning his own court-martial.

"No! Tell me he didn't. In your bedroom?"

"Thank all the stars, no. In the main room. But I had gotten ready for a shower and decided I wanted a cup of that spiced tea Salomen gave me, the one that takes a tentick to steep. I figured I'd start it steeping before my shower. I didn't bother putting on a robe to go out to the kitchen. Cox said the access log for that file was in the triple digits."

"He's fortunate to be out of Alsean space," Andira snarled. "If I'd known—"

"You couldn't have done anything. Not without endangering everything else you were working on. But Sholokhov did."

She had since given it a great deal of thought, trying to puzzle out why Sholokhov would come down so hard on an unimportant player. A gasbag, he had called him. Admiral Greve had meant nothing—until he saw those files.

The invasion of her privacy had offended Sholokhov's personal code, she concluded. Blackmail and murder were all in a day's work for him, but the file of her making tea in the nude had no purpose other than to titillate. It had no political or military value. It existed solely for Greve's masturbatory fantasies, which made it not merely an abuse of power but a waste of it.

Sholokhov had spent years playing terrifyingly dangerous games with her, one of which took the life of a promising young officer. He was frustrated by her lack of fear and compelled to prove his power over her again and again, yet she knew instinctively that deep down, he didn't want to win. He respected her for the fight. Had she ever surrendered, he would have despised her.

To his view, then, Admiral Greve had been put into a position of power over her but hadn't proven himself worthy of it. He had wasted her potential and topped it off by disrespecting her in the most puerile of ways. In doing so, he had earned the enmity Ekatya was so careful to avoid.

He was now paying for it in spades.

Public mortification was only the beginning of Greve's woes. Court-martial proceedings had already begun, with conviction guaranteed given the amount of evidence. Still, he could have walked away with a lenient sentence. Left to its own devices, Fleet would likely have retired him with full rank and benefits just to get him out and shut him up.

On the day of his first court appearance, Ekatya received a one-line message from Sholokhov.

At which rank do you suppose he last served satisfactorily?

With that, she knew what Greve's punishment would be. Other than prison time, the worst sentence for a convicted officer was dismissal—a dishonorable separation resulting in loss of pension, benefits, and voting rights. It also included a reduction to the last rank at which the officer was deemed as having served satisfactorily.

In the shuttle bay, Admiral Greve had pulled rank, huffing that their warrant was probably pushed through by "some ensign at Fleet Justice."

Ekatya deleted Sholokhov's message with a laugh, poured herself a shot of iceflame, and lifted it in salute to the future Ensign Greve, Retired, Protectorate Fleet.

31

CEREMONIES

The last time Salomen had been aboard this ship was in the chaos of battle.

It felt decidedly odd to sit here now and watch such calm proceedings. Lowering her blocks brought a river of excitement, anticipation, pride, happiness, melancholy, quiet regret—emotions that were in every way the antithesis of what she had felt before. She let them roll over her, enjoying the mostly pleasant flavors until their weight grew too pressing. With her blocks back in place, the gentle music of the ship's band seemed markedly louder.

On a screen above the temporary stage, the lyrics to this ballad were displayed in both Common and High Alsean. It was a love song, speaking to the seductive call of life in space, and many of the attendees were singing along.

She had thought the ceremony would take place on Deck Zero, given its incomparable aesthetics. What could be better than sitting in a land-scaped park where they could look up through the transparent hull to Alsea?

"Too impractical," Lhyn had said during their last quantum com call. "Deck Zero doesn't have any really big, open spaces. It's designed for privacy. Besides, they'll have to build temporary stands, and those are a lot easier to construct in the shuttle bay where they don't have to worry about crushing plants."

Salomen looked around the gray walls of the cavernous bay and concluded that practicality had its limits. The most aesthetically pleasing views in this windowless space were the two women flanking her in the front row. Then again, she admitted, she would think the same regardless of location.

The *Phoenix*'s shuttles and others that had brought so many guests were stationkeeping with the ship, leaving the deck open for the stage and seating. Occupying the floor-level chairs around her were the ship's senior officers, dignitaries from both Alsea and the Protectorate, her tyrees, and two people she had liked the moment she met them: Ekatya's grandparents. They sat beside Lhyn, wreathed in smiles and pride a sonsales could see. Her grandfather, wearing a Fleet uniform with a commander's rank insignia, sang with gusto.

Around three of the walls, tiered seats were full of *Phoenix* crew and those Alsean pilots whose special courage had earned them tickets to the event. The divine tyrees were there as well, their attendance one of the few public acknowledgments the war council could give them. Their private acknowledgment had taken place in the State House two ninedays ago, when Andira, Salomen, and the caste Primes awarded each of them the Sonalia Prize. It was the highest honor the government could bestow and came with a cash prize large enough to make a difference in their lives.

During a lull in the music, Lhyn leaned past Salomen to speak with Andira, sitting on her other side. "I haven't seen this many medals and ribbons since launch day," she said in a low tone.

Andira leaned over as well. "I haven't seen this many *ever*. Does Fleet award medals for successfully using the toilet?"

Salomen pressed her lips together, barely managing not to laugh.

"That's an Ekatya question. I dare you to ask her."

"Oh, I will."

"I suggest you wait until after she collects her latest medal." Salomen smiled at her bondmate, resplendent in her own dress uniform. The high-collared crimson jacket set off her bright hair and light eyes beautifully, and the Seal of the Lancer was all the more arresting for being the only decoration on her breast. Andira Tal did not need a chest full of medals to prove her worth or power.

"Though I'll admit I greatly prefer our tradition," she added. "Some of these people look as though they'll topple forward any moment under the weight. You look sleek and . . . edible."

A familiar thrill zinged through their link. "So do you, tyrina. You have a talent for choosing clothes that challenge my strength of will."

Lhyn's hand slipped onto her leg, palm up. "Seconded."

That was a different thrill, less familiar but no less potent. Salomen had not been in Lhyn's physical presence for a moon, making her hyper-aware now. She let their hands touch briefly, soaking up the emotional connection while cognizant of the many vidcams recording this event for Alsea and the Protectorate.

They had not gone public with their unusual bond, and now was not the time to do so. But it needed to happen soon, she thought. She hated secrets, Lhyn was a terrible liar, Andira deserved to love without reservation, and Ekatya had spent too much of the past cycle alone, concealing the most vibrant parts of herself. Even now, on this joyous occasion, it was the three of them together and Ekatya sitting apart.

But today was the last of it. After this, Ekatya would be free.

The ship's band ended on a quiet sigh of stringed instruments, and Ambassador Solvassen spoke from the podium. Salomen tuned out his voice, listening to the translation on her earcuff.

"Now that we've gotten through all the preliminary bits and too much talking on my part," he said to a swell of light laughter, "I'm very pleased to introduce Admiral Tsao, Fleet Commander, Sector One." He stepped back and applauded as the woman who had been sitting next to Ekatya moved to take his place.

She had a slim build, unlike most of the admirals in attendance, and gray hair pulled back in a no-nonsense style. This close, Salomen could see the scar that ran through her left eyebrow.

"Good afternoon," she said in a clear voice. "It took me sixteen days to get here for this ceremony. I'd like to state for the record that I'd have come if it took two or even three times as long. I've waited a long time for this opportunity to recognize Captain Serrado's courage, tactical brilliance, and selfless contributions to Fleet and the Protectorate."

Ekatya sat straight-backed in her chair on stage, her own dress uniform perfectly pressed and bearing a bewildering array of medals. She had listened to the first part of the ceremony with little outward expression, but now seemed startled and oddly shy.

Salomen leaned forward, fascinated by the change.

"Ekatya Serrado first came to my attention as a newly promoted full lieutenant. I was a captain at the time, and on the lookout for skilled officers that I could poach—I mean, encourage to serve with me."

This seemed to be of particular humor to the admirals and section chiefs in attendance, though Andira laughed as well.

"A service record surfaced in my pile with an unusual entry. Lieutenant Serrado had taken leave to visit her grandparents on Gaia, a trip that passes through some lonely stretches of space."

Ekatya's grandparents nodded in agreement.

"The public shuttle she was on had the misfortune of being stopped and boarded by pirates who ordered every passenger to hand over their bags for a search. Lieutenant Serrado refused. I should add here that there were four of them and one of her. I should also add that two of them were half again as tall as she is, and the other two were twice her weight."

Now the crew of the *Phoenix* chuckled, knowing the reputation of their captain and expecting the outcome of the story.

"They decided to teach her a lesson and make an example of her to the rest of the passengers. This is all on video, by the way, so I can tell you with certainty that it took exactly seven moves for her to lay all four of them out on the deck. Two were unconscious; the other two had multiple bone fractures. She sustained a bruised cheekbone and a sprained finger."

"Yeah!" someone shouted from high up in the crew section. Applause rang through the shuttle bay.

Onstage, Ekatya smiled.

"When it was over and the passengers had helped her restrain the pirates, someone asked what she had in her bag that was so valuable she would risk life and limb to protect it. She said, and I quote: 'Dirty laundry and some of the best chocolate I've ever tasted. It's for my grandmother. Nobody is taking chocolate from Grams.'"

Ekatya's grandmother rose from her chair. "It was *very* good chocolate," she said tartly.

This time, Salomen didn't suppress her laugh. Neither did the rest of the audience, especially when Ekatya blew a kiss to her grandmother. Tsao acknowledged the interruption with a genial nod and waited for the laughter to die down.

"I knew then that this young officer was only beginning to make a name for herself. Anyone who would take on four-to-one odds for dirty laundry and chocolate was not, in fact, fighting for dirty laundry and chocolate. She was fighting for her principles."

The mood in the shuttle bay was suddenly serious. Admiral Tsao leaned forward and spoke deliberately. "She risked her life for her principles. That kind of courage, that unwavering devotion to *right* versus *easy*, was what I wanted on my crew. So I recruited that young lieutenant. I have been privileged to watch her progress since then, and it doesn't surprise me that I'm standing here now to award her the Presidential Medal of Galactic Service. Because Ekatya Serrado never stopped fighting, no matter the odds or how unpopular or inconvenient her principles might have been. It has rarely been easy for her. But it has always been right."

Having gathered the attendees in the palm of her hand, Admiral Tsao took them through an overview of Ekatya's career. She skated through the early parts, going into more detail once Ekatya made commander and still more when she reached the rank of captain. Salomen listened closely, recognizing bits and pieces but hearing far more that Ekatya had never mentioned.

The stories gained depth, covering Ekatya's loss of the *Caphenon* in defense of Alsea and her subsequent command of the *Phoenix*. Finally, Tsao gave an extensive description of last moon's battle and the specific actions that had earned this medal. She ended by calling Ekatya to the podium and taking a slim case from her pocket.

"Unlike Fleet medals, I can't pin this to your uniform," she said, lifting out a large, gleaming disc hanging from a golden chain. "This isn't a medal to go beside others. It's one that stands alone, as you have." She hung the medal around Ekatya's neck and shook her hand. "Congratulations, Captain Serrado."

The shuttle bay exploded in applause and whistles as every person in attendance jumped to their feet. Ekatya's grandmother wiped her eyes with a lacy kerchief while her grandfather applauded wildly, ignoring his own tears.

Lhyn leaned against Salomen. "I'm so shekking proud of her. It's about time Fleet got its ass in motion."

"About time?" Andira asked. "Right at the end of time, I'd say."

"Thank you, Admiral Tsao." Ekatya's voice rang out over the shuttle bay com. "Of all the people who could have bestowed this on me today, I'm glad it was you. But I have to correct one detail. I didn't stand alone in that battle. I had the backing of the best crew in Fleet, two extremely skilled captains and their crews, Alsea's most formidable pilots—" She paused for the happy shouts from the pilots in question. "And most of all, I had Lancer Andira Tal, Bondlancer Salomen Opah, and my bondmate, Dr. Lhyn Rivers. Without them, none of this would have been possible." She raised her hands to them with a brilliant smile, inspiring another round of applause.

"Artful," Andira murmured. "She told the truth, but no one will understand it."

"That's our Ekatya." Lhyn blew a kiss and rested her hands over her heart. On stage, Ekatya mirrored the gesture.

In fact, Ekatya managed to tell quite a bit of truth in her acceptance speech. Her facility for choosing words that others would hear incorrectly —and in the way she meant them to be heard—was a talent she shared with Andira. The two of them were eggs from the same bird, as Lhyn said. There was a time when Salomen had found that intimidating and even threatening, but that was before she understood how a heart could love in different and complementary ways. She could no longer imagine Andira without Ekatya, just as she couldn't imagine her own life without Lhyn. They were far better together than apart, a lesson Fahla had apparently been determined to teach them.

She sometimes wished she could speak with Andira's mother, who had spent her life loving two men but only one openly. Of the three involved, only Corozen Micah had lived to see Andira take the same path.

"I feared for her," he had said when she asked him about it. "I couldn't bear the thought of watching her suffer the way I did. Then she met you, and I feared for you both if Ekatya ever came back. You would all try to do the right thing, and it would hurt each of you in different ways. Then she *did* come back, and I stopped being afraid."

"Why?"

"Because I could see the signs. You had never met Lhyn before, but by the third day of your bonding break, you made her your family."

"That's what a bonding break is for."

"Yes, and how many other people have you taken into your heart that quickly?"

None.

Perhaps a part of her had known back then, she mused, standing with the others to applaud the end of Ekatya's speech. Perhaps she had instinctively recognized the balance they would eventually find.

But she could never have guessed where it would lead.

In a well-timed move, the President of the Protectorate called in via quantum com, his image displayed on the massive screen as he congratulated Ekatya and lamented his inability to be there in person.

"Better not to speak at all than to tell such a transparent lie," Andira grumbled. "But she's making him look good." She watched avidly, her emotional signature alight with pride and a desire that no longer came burdened with guilt.

Salomen found this view far more compelling than the Gaian politician spreading his tail feathers onscreen. Leaning in, she kissed Andira beneath her ear and whispered, "I cannot imagine anyone else worthy of you."

The desire expanded and grew warmer, wrapping around the base of her spine. "Nor can I of you. Lhyn is a treasure."

"The Protectorate's most decorated starship captain and its most famous anthropologist. We have high standards for each other."

"Why wouldn't we?" Andira turned her head, their eyes meeting with an electric jolt that reverberated through their bond.

Even after a moon, the effects of their battle link had not fully dissipated and were unlikely to do so, according to Healer Wellernal. Salomen did not mind. The initial compulsion had settled into a background hum they could choose to ignore if they wished. Or they could let it grow, as they were in this moment, and enjoy the pleasure it brought them.

She pulled Andira's hand into her lap and leaned back, watching Ekatya with proprietary appreciation. Yes, Fleet and the Protectorate were belatedly giving her the recognition she deserved, but Andira had known her worth from the beginning. Now she was the Savior, beloved of all

Alseans—and the one person in the galaxy to whom Salomen would entrust her bondmate.

That trust would find a new level tonight, she knew. All four of them were poised on the edge before the jump, vibrating with anticipation and a delicious sense of the unknown.

She glanced at Lhyn, so close and still so untouchable, and smiled to herself. She could wait a few more hanticks. The expectation was part of the thrill, after all. Sealing their new bonds was an event that would occur but once in their lifetimes.

"We're doing things a little differently than usual today." Ambassador Solvassen was back at the podium. "Normally, the band would now play a rousing rendition of the Protectorate anthem and we'd end the ceremony with a final salute to Captain Serrado. But this is not a normal ceremony. I now invite Dr. Lhyn Rivers to the stage."

"Break an arm," Salomen said.

Lhyn's breath caught. "A leg," she managed, choking back laughter.

Salomen watched with a grin as she crossed the short distance to the stage and took the four steps in two strides.

"You knew that," Andira said.

"Of course I did."

At the podium, Lhyn shook Ambassador Solvassen's hand and turned to the crowd. "Many Fleet traditions date back to the days when ships sailed in water, not space," she said. "We still use them despite their having no practical application, because traditions matter. They make up the rich tapestry of our culture. At a time when Alsea is building new traditions, I'm privileged to narrate some of ours. Admiral Tsao, Captain Serrado, please come to the front of the stage."

The two women rose from their chairs and stood facing each other.

"Chief Warrant Officer Roris," Ekatya said, never taking her eyes off the admiral. "Report to the stage with the sword of command."

Applause swept through the tiered seats as Roris's friends celebrated the first official use of her new rank and her position of honor in the ceremony.

Roris marched down the center aisle of the floor seating, her white-gloved hands gripping a short sword in vertical orientation.

"Look at that," Andira marveled as they watched her pass. "A pre-collapsible sword!"

She executed a sharp right turn at the front, then a sharp left at the stairs before smartly stepping up and moving to a point at midstage. Once behind Ekatya and the admiral, she stopped and turned with precise footwork.

"Swords are not a part of modern Fleet weaponry," Lhyn said. "But they were indispensable during the early days of sailing on seas. A working sword was typically short and narrow, making it easy to carry and less likely to catch on rigging or other obstacles in the close quarters of a sailing ship. It had a plain, unadorned grip for the same reason, bearing only a simple guard for protection. It was lightweight and practical. Ceremonial swords were longer, fancier, and impractical, but it is not the ceremonial sword that survives today."

"Chief Warrant Officer Roris, present the sword of command," Ekatya said.

Roris stepped forward and held out the sword. Ekatya turned to her and nodded in acknowledgment as she accepted it with both hands.

"This sword belongs not to Captain Serrado but to the Ship of the Protectorate Fleet *Phoenix*," Lhyn said. "It represents the commanding officer's responsibility to her ship and crew, to protect them, guide them, and lead with integrity. Captain Serrado will now inspect the sword."

Turning toward the audience, Ekatya bent slightly and tilted the sword, its grip pointing downward. With a swift motion, she pulled the blade, leaving only its tip in the scabbard.

"A command sword must be returned in perfect condition," Lhyn said as Ekatya faced Admiral Tsao, rotated the sword, and bent a second time to inspect the opposite face of the blade.

"This symbolizes her care of both crew and ship, and the fulfilment of her duty."

Ekatya straightened with the sword held vertically once more.

"Captain Serrado will now close the sword as her last official act as captain and commanding officer of the SPF *Phoenix*."

Salomen heard the *snap* as the sword slid back into its scabbard. She did not expect the sound to have such an emotional impact, but found herself blinking back tears.

"The passing of the sword from Captain Serrado to Admiral Tsao represents her relinquishment of the duties and responsibilities of her command of the SPF *Phoenix*."

Ekatya took a single step forward, offering but not releasing the sword.

Admiral Tsao gripped it with both hands. "Captain Serrado, do you stand ready to be relieved of command?"

"Admiral Tsao, I stand ready to be relieved."

"Captain Serrado, I relieve you."

Ekatya let go and stepped back, her hands empty.

In her peripheral vision, Salomen saw Andira surreptitiously swipe a finger beneath one eye. She understood the emotion in their link. Even knowing that Ekatya was moving to a better place, the finality of this was difficult to watch.

"Admiral Tsao will now return the sword of command to Chief Warrant Officer Roris, maintaining the continuity of the sword's presence with its ship and crew. Normally, it would be taken to the captain's office to await its next holder. Since there will be no other Fleet commander of this ship, the sword of command will return to Tashar as a historical artifact."

Tsao offered the sword to Roris, who took it carefully in her gloved hands. "Chief Warrant Officer Roris, I entrust this sword to you for safe-keeping. Return it to my quarters, where I will see it safely to its next destination."

"Aye aye, Admiral." Roris bowed her head, turned smartly to the left, and marched off the stage. As she moved through the crowd, Ekatya retook her seat and Admiral Tsao stepped to the podium.

"With command of the SPF *Phoenix* now resting in Admiral Tsao's capable hands, we turn to the third part of today's ceremony," Lhyn said. "Admiral?"

"Thank you, Dr. Rivers." Tsao shook Lhyn's hand and watched her depart from the stage before announcing, "Captain Serrado will not be accepting new orders from Fleet. She is retiring today, but before I allow that, there is a small matter of record keeping."

Lhyn reached her seat and raised her eyebrows in a silent query for Andira, who shrugged.

"I don't know either," Salomen said as Lhyn sat down.

"Captain, evidence received by Command Dome has proven that the suspension of your command after last month's battle was an egregious abuse of power in the service of a personal agenda. That suspension has been struck from your record. In its place is a formal letter of apology from the Admiralty. As its chief representative here today, I would like to reiterate our regret for the injustice perpetrated in our name and in the name of Fleet."

"Oh my fucking stars," Lhyn whispered.

Clearly shocked, Ekatya could only manage a nod.

Admiral Tsao turned to the audience. "Fleet is a very large entity, encompassing individuals from planets all over the Protectorate. We have a saying, which I'm not sure will translate into High Alsean: a chain is only as strong as its weakest link."

"It translates," Lhyn called, setting off a wave of nods among the Alsean attendees.

"Good. We strive to elevate only our best, but as with any large organization, the ideal and the reality don't always match. Injustices do occur. They do not represent our ideals or our hopes. Captain Serrado, you *do* represent our ideals. Your retirement is a great loss to Fleet and a great gain for Alsea. I wish you the brightest of futures." She smiled at Ekatya before turning back to Ambassador Solvassen. "Ambassador, shall we begin the fun part?"

The fun part, it turned out, was a parade of speakers telling short stories about their experience working with Ekatya. Each of the eleven section chiefs spoke, as well as Commander Lokomorra and First Pilot Candini. Chief Warrant Officer Roris was also featured, along with a commodore and two admirals Salomen didn't know.

She noted an interesting trend: those who had not known Ekatya outside of her command persona told straightforward stories full of respect and admiration. Those who knew her better went for humor. She didn't think it was a coincidence that the stories grew funnier as time went on.

Ekatya returned to the podium for a few humorous stories of her own, exacting revenge in two cases for the tales that had been told on her. Then she delivered a speech aimed at younger members of Fleet, offering advice gleaned from a lifetime of service.

"In physical training, they tell you that if it's easy, you're not doing it right," she said at the end. "I've found that applies to most of life. Challenge yourself. Hold yourself to the highest standards, even if others around you don't. You can make it easy on yourself, or you can make a difference."

She paused, her gaze going to Lhyn.

"I chose to make a difference. And now, with the greatest respect for Fleet and the opportunities it gave me, I'm leaving. I've been asked to make a difference on Alsea, and I think . . ." A bright smile lit her face. "It's time for a new adventure. Farewell and good hunting."

The shuttle bay rang with shouts, whistles, and applause as every attendee rose to their feet.

Clapping madly, Andira leaned over and spoke in Salomen's ear. "I think she just received some much-needed closure."

Salomen nodded. "I think she feels better about Fleet now than she has in the past cycle."

"Admiral Tsao was astute. She turned a black mark against Fleet into a recruitment opportunity, all with a simple apology."

"Do you think that's why she did it?"

"Does it matter?"

The standing ovation lasted nearly five ticks, during which Ekatya descended from the stage to shake hands with and sometimes give warmrons to each of her former section chiefs. She ended in what appeared to be a heartfelt warmron with Commander Lokomorra, saying something to him that could not be heard over the continuing noise.

Salomen nudged Lhyn. "I know Gaians are free with warmrons, but it surprises me to see them at a military function."

Lhyn beamed at her. "She's not military. She just retired."

"What about them?"

"I think this falls in the cracks between ceremonies. It's not an official function right now. Besides, are they going to say no to her?"

Commander Lokomorra was laughing when he finally let go of Ekatya. She laughed with him, the past cycle's cares and burdens having vanished without a trace, and patted his shoulder affectionately before turning for the stage.

No, Salomen thought, there wasn't a person in this shuttle bay who would say no to her right now.

Ambassador Solvassen returned to the podium as the applause finally slowed and the attendees retook their seats.

"We now begin the fourth part of our program," he said. "The decommissioning ceremony."

The last shreds of applause died, leaving a heavy sense of solemnity.

"Such ceremonies normally involve speeches and long stories of the ship's history. But the SPF *Phoenix* is a young ship, entering service just two cycles ago."

Beneath the translation coming through her earcuff, Salomen heard two Common words she understood. In Protectorate timekeeping, it had been three years.

"The history of this ship is inextricably tied with the history of Captain Serrado's command. When Admiral Tsao recounted Captain Serrado's career during the award ceremony, she fulfilled that function of the decommissioning ceremony. There's little left to do now but the final acts. Distinguished guests, members of Fleet, I now present Vice Admiral Torokuok, Chief of Fleet Operations."

A white-haired man dripping with medals walked to the podium. "Thank you, Ambassador Solvassen. I'm grateful to be here on this momentous occasion. As the Protectorate Fleet transfers ownership of the SPF *Phoenix* to the Alsean Defense Force, we bid farewell to a ship that has served faithfully. It is both a pleasure and a comfort to know that this fine ship will continue to serve the same cause for her new owners: that of freedom and defense against those who would threaten it. This transfer cements the ties of friendship between Alsea and the Protectorate, and strengthens our shared determination to stand together in protection of those who need us."

He turned to face the cluster of Alsean dignitaries. "Prime Warrior Ehron, as you represent the Alsean Defense Force and the future crew of this ship, I wish you much success and offer our traditional good luck wish for any departing ship: Farewell, and good hunting." He paused for polite applause before adding, "This tradition dates back three generations, to the beginning of our war with the Voloth Empire. I sincerely hope that war has ended."

This time, the applause was longer.

Looking up to the raised seating along the walls, he said, "To you, the current members of this crew, I'm grateful for the smooth transfer of the SPF *Phoenix* and wish each of you continued success in your new assignments."

"We're staying!" someone shouted. In the same area, another crew member whooped.

"That was Roris's team," Lhyn said with a chuckle. "They were the first to request to stay on."

A few other voices popped up, some declaring "Me too!" while others cried "Wish I could!"

Torokuok waited for them to settle. "And now it is time. I hereby place the SPF *Phoenix* out of commission."

In the dead silence that followed, he stepped away and took his seat at the left side of the stage.

Ambassador Solvassen stood up. "Will Admiral Tsao and Dr. Rivers please return to the podium?"

"Part two," Lhyn murmured. She bounced back up the stairs, this time to stand side by side with Fleet's highest-ranking admiral. "In keeping with naval tradition," she said, "Fleet ships display the Protectorate flag and their commissioning pennant in the shuttle bay, the first place crew and visitors see when they board. These two items are the first to be raised when a ship is commissioned, and the last to be lowered at the end of its service."

Salomen turned toward the enormous flag hung above the shuttle bay office, directly across from the exit tunnel, and saw it with new understanding. Beside it, a colorful pennant spanned the same height but only a fraction of the width.

"Will the guests please rise?" Lhyn asked.

With a rumble, the audience stood.

"Officer of the deck," Admiral Tsao said. "Strike the commissioning pennant."

"Aye aye, Admiral," came a voice from the far side of the bay.

Accompanied by a soft drum beat, the slender pennant slipped down the wall. Before its tip could touch the deck, a crew member caught it in gloved hands and began walking backward. Three others stepped in as the pennant completed its journey, keeping its length elevated above the deck while the last man unclipped it from the line.

In sharp, practiced movements, the team folded it into a tidy triangle and presented it to a fifth crew member, who spun in place and marched to the stage.

"Admiral, the commissioning pennant has been struck."

"Very well. Prepare to haul down the colors."

"When a ship's colors are hauled down," Lhyn said, "it's viewed as a kind of death. The ship will never again sail through space under the auspices of the Protectorate. It will not be served by the same crew. It is a loss to Fleet, and as such is mourned with the traditional lament played at Fleet memorials. The melody you are about to hear is called 'Another Star Falling.'"

"Officer of the deck," Admiral Tsao commanded. "Haul down the colors."

"Aye aye, Admiral."

The band eased into a haunting melody as the flag began to sink. Salomen watched with a tight throat, startled by her reaction to an event she had expected to view as joyful.

Andira's hand rested on her shoulder. "It's a surprise to me, too," she whispered. "Fleet has some beautiful traditions."

Salomen reached across to cover her hand, needing the contact as they watched the flag descend. Two more crew members joined the original team of four to catch and fold it. They finished in perfect time with the song, their motions stilling when the last note faded into silence.

"Admiral, the colors have been hauled down."

"Very well. Close the log and secure the watch."

A whistle sounded over the bay com, followed by a different voice. "Watch is secured."

"Will the guests please be seated?" Lhyn said.

As the attendees took their seats, the two crew members holding the folded pennant and flag mounted the steps to the stage.

"Since it is now decommissioned, this ship can no longer be referred to as the SPF *Phoenix*. It is simply the *Phoenix* until commissioned and renamed by its new owners. In accepting the commissioning pennant and colors, Admiral Tsao is performing the last act of the ship's commanding officer."

"Poor Ekatya," Salomen murmured. "This should have been her."

"It might have worked out better this way." Andira watched Tsao acknowledge the crew members, who placed the folded cloths in her arms. "She'll be on the other end of it next moon, on a much more joyous occasion."

"Admiral Tsao will now present custody of the ship to Vice Admiral Torokuok," Lhyn said.

The two admirals met in the center of the stage.

"Vice Admiral Torokuok, I hereby deliver custody of the *Phoenix* to you." Tsao offered the pennant and flag.

"Very well. I accept custody of the *Phoenix*." Torokuok took the cloths, spun in place, and handed them to another officer. "Retire the colors."

"This flag and this pennant will never be flown again. They will travel to Command Dome to be preserved as two of the most important artifacts in the historical record of this ship. With the retirement of the colors, the decommissioning ceremony is concluded." Lhyn nodded to Ambassador Solvassen, who replaced her at the podium.

"Distinguished guests, members of Fleet," he said, "Vice Admiral Torokuok will now deliver the *Phoenix* to the Alsean Defense Force, represented here by Prime Warrior Ehron."

Ehron rose from his seat and mounted the steps to the stage. In his Alsean uniform and full cape, he stood out like a moonbird on the stage full of Fleet officers.

"Prime Warrior Ehron," Torokuok said. "Pursuant to the agreement executed between our respective governments, and as the Chief of Fleet Operations, I hereby transfer the *Phoenix* to the custody of the government of Alsea."

"Thank you, Vice Admiral. I accept custody of this ship in the name of the Alsean Defense Force." Ehron's High Alsean needed no translation, but Salomen thought she had heard wrong when he turned and said, "First Guard Vellmar, please come to the stage."

She shook her head. "Did he——"

Andira beamed. "She was due a promotion, don't you think?"

"And you didn't tell me before now?" She watched her friend stride up the steps carrying a folded square of dark blue cloth. Her dress uniform now bore an additional red chevron on each sleeve, a small change that meant so much.

Lhyn leaned over. "That closes some of the gap between her and Lanaril, doesn't it?"

"Yes, it does," Andira said. "I'm curious to see if anything comes of that."

Fianna stopped in front of Ehron and held a fist to her chest. "Prime Warrior, I present to you the banner of the Voloth Empire ship *Vengeance*, taken from its bridge in honorable combat."

"Thank you, First Guard. Admiral Torokuok, in accordance with the agreement executed between Alsea and the Protectorate, I hereby transfer the *Vengeance* to the custody of the Protectorate Fleet." He took the banner from Fianna and handed it to Torokuok, who examined it with more interest than he had shown in the ceremony so far.

"Thank you, Prime Warrior Ehron. I accept custody of the *Vengeance* in the name of the Protectorate government."

And that was that, Salomen thought. Endless days of negotiations that had left Andira hollow-eyed and sleepless, all wrapped up in a few sentences. Ekatya's medal ceremony and retirement had taken far more time than the official trade of two massive and extremely valuable warships between governments.

She would never understand politics.

The ceremony concluded a few ticks later with an invitation from Prime Warrior Ehron to join the celebrations being conducted on the ship. Crew members were invited to the main services corridor, which had been turned into a temporary party venue, while the senior officers and dignitaries would retire to the treaty conference room for what Lhyn said would be an event with less noise but better spirits.

The band played a peppy song, and the sound level rose as conversations began all over the shuttle bay.

Ekatya was suddenly there, throwing herself into her grandfather's arms for a lengthy warmron.

"I'm so proud of you, Katya," he said in High Alsean.

"Thank you, Gramps. It's been a *really* good day."

He laughed. "Yes, it has. You deserve it."

She squeezed harder before letting go and facing her grandmother. "Have I mentioned how happy I am that you could make it out here?"

"Two or three times. Come here and give an old lady a warmron."

"Still so bossy," Ekatya teased, obeying her orders.

"You'd better believe it. Got to keep these retired Fleeters in shape."

"She won't be retired for long." Lhyn opened her arms. "Come here and give a younger lady a warmron."

With a joyous smile, Ekatya nestled in and closed her eyes. "I plan to enjoy my retirement for at least a couple of days."

"Try one moon," Andira said.

Her eyes popped open. "A moon?"

"We've all earned some time off. Salomen has arranged for a little getaway whenever you're ready."

Salomen offered her best enigmatic look. "We'll talk about it later. Didn't someone say something about a party?"

32

IT'S TIME

"Do you think they'll ever realize that we couldn't wait to get rid of that death ship?" Vellmar asked.

Tal swirled the purple liquid in her glass. "They don't understand us well enough. I could call their President right now, speak the unvarnished truth, and he wouldn't believe me. They don't have our empathic senses, so they give no weight to them."

She sipped the drink, enjoying the fizz on her tongue. A Synobian Sparkler, Rahel had called it. Delicious.

"I've overheard a few conversations. They seem to think speaking Common means we won't understand them." With a tap to her earcuff, Vellmar subtly pointed her chin toward a cluster of admirals. "They're congratulating themselves on getting the better end of the deal. Maybe you should have asked for two ships."

"We already have two." The words still didn't sound real. Even after the negotiations and an entire moon of wrapping up details, she couldn't quite believe the *Phoenix* was theirs. "Why ask for more than we could possibly crew? Besides, the best deals are the ones your opponents think they won."

"I'll drink to that." Grinning broadly, Vellmar raised her glass of Alsean grain spirits.

"Here's to knowing who won." Tal touched their glasses together.

"And to you, for showing me the way."

"I just told you what I felt."

"You knew it was important. Your instincts were exactly right." She swallowed a mouthful of fizzing flavor, remembering her brief trip to the *Vengeance*. After Vellmar's warning about the empathic echoes embedded in its bulkheads, she had overridden Micah's vociferous objections and gone to sense it for herself.

That day would haunt her nightmares. The echoes were stronger than she could have imagined, a sensory cacophony of horrors. She had toured the ship in the company of thirty Guards, and every one of them had the same reaction: their skin crawled.

It was exponentially worse in the slave quarters, tiny rooms she wouldn't give to a fanten. The suffering and misery soaked into their bulkheads made her want to send that ship straight into the sun. Then she had stepped into several weapons rooms, confirming another of Vellmar's observations. Though these echoes were fainter, having been embedded in a shorter span of time, the murderous intent of soldiers firing genocidal weapons had left their mark. Mid empaths might not fully sense it, but they would sense enough to be constantly ill at ease.

She didn't bother going to the bridge.

Vellmar had been correct in her assessment that they could not have crewed that ship with anything but low empaths and sonsales. Ronlin's report from the destroyers was more encouraging: with relatively few slaves in service and no bioforce missiles in their armories, the smaller ships felt lighter and would be easier to crew.

After that visit, the solution to her problem with Sholokhov had been blindingly clear—as had a means of coming out ahead. Instead of trading the services of high empaths for a ship, she had traded them for a ship, two complete armories, two cycles of maintenance and repair, and a full cycle of operational responsibility and crew training, all while getting rid of a horror ship she didn't want and couldn't use.

And Sholokhov thought he had won.

"Thank you," Vellmar said, ducking her head. "I appreciate the trust you put in me."

"Perhaps you shouldn't thank me yet," she joked. "The more trust you earn, the more responsibility I'm going to put on your shoulders."

Vellmar pointed at the new chevron on her sleeve. "Isn't that how these work? I always thought—" She stopped when a familiar voice rose above the rest.

"Yes? It's a yes?"

All around them, heads turned toward the refreshment table. Micah held a laden plate in one hand, tilting dangerously toward the floor as he looked from Alejandra to Rahel and back again.

Alejandra nodded.

He dropped the plate on the table, let out a delighted whoop that silenced the room, and lifted her up for a full spin. She was breathless and laughing when he set her down and kissed her for all the world to see.

"Did he just ask her—Fahla on a funstick." Vellmar gaped as he turned to Rahel and raised both hands.

Tal's glass nearly slipped through her fingers. "Who asked what?" she said blankly, watching Rahel meet the familial gesture and rest their foreheads together. "What the shek is going on?"

"I have no idea. Damn, that woman can keep a secret."

Micah grabbed Alejandra's hand and pulled her toward them, Rahel trailing behind. The happiness pouring off him reached Tal's senses long before he did.

"Tal! I'm going to be a father!"

"You're—a father?" Mystified, she set down her glass and waited for some part of this to make sense.

"When did this happen?" Vellmar rounded on Rahel. "And you never said a word to me?"

"It wasn't my secret to tell! Besides, she didn't decide until a few days ago."

"Didn't decide what?" Tal demanded.

"Oh good, we're in time for the explanations." Lhyn had arrived with Ekatya, Salomen, and Lanaril in tow.

Alejandra spoke up, amusement dancing on her skin. "Micah and I have agreed to have a child together, with Rahel acting as my surrogate."

"I'll bear the child. Tal, I cannot believe she said yes. That *they* said yes." He thrust both fists in the air. "They said yes!"

Alejandra and Rahel laughed at his transparent joy, and Tal was pierced by a sense of loss. She pushed it down, reminding herself of Ekatya's words in the crater of Pica Mahal.

"I'm so very happy for you." She held up both palms. "You've found a different love, and no one deserves it more. No one deserves a family more."

"Thank you." He interlaced their fingers, elation and love pouring through their skin contact. But a flicker of concern marred the warmth. Leaning forward, he whispered, "You'll always be my first child."

She blinked back traitorous tears. "I know. You'll be a wonderful father to this child, just as you were to me. Fahla, what a day." She kissed his cheek, her momentary pain gone as if it had never been. "Micah, you're going to have a baby!"

"I know!" He squeezed her hands, laughing, and she had never seen his eyes so bright.

Twenty ticks passed in excited conversation, with everyone wanting to know details and Alejandra happy to provide them in explicit medical format. Ekatya was effusive in her congratulations, glad for Micah but overjoyed for her friend. Lanaril took Alejandra aside for a few hushed sentences that had the healer wiping her cheeks.

Salomen never left Tal's side, their hands always coming back to each other as they watched their family grow.

Then Commander Lokomorra arrived to whisk Rahel off for a congratulatory drink, and the group split up into couples as they remembered that this was a diplomatic function, not a family party.

For the next hantick, Tal and Salomen circulated among Protectorate diplomats and Fleet officers, performing their roles as expected before separating into different conversational groups. Tal spoke briefly with each of the Primes, then found herself alone with Vellmar once more.

She glanced at the new chevrons on Vellmar's sleeves, thinking of the changes that were rippling through the lives of everyone she knew. With a tap to one chevron, she asked, "How does it feel?"

"Fabulous. Like a dream come true."

"More than being Fahla's Emissary?" she teased.

"Ha. I never dreamed about that. Lanaril has been having fun with it, though. 'Emissary, you left your house shoes in the middle of the floor again. Emissary, would you bring me a cup of shannel?'"

Tal hastily lowered her glass as she laughed. "I can hear it!"

Her gaze fell on a familiar figure across the room. Ekatya was watching her, a small smile curving her lips before she hid it behind a glass and turned away.

Tal had only seen that smile once before, on their date. Now it appeared each time their eyes met.

"Taking that public yet?" Vellmar had followed her line of sight.

"I haven't even had a chance to talk to her, much less about something that big. But it's nice to know we finally have the option."

"Now that she's free of Fleet," Vellmar said knowingly.

And of Sholokhov, Tal thought. His ignorance of the true nature of their relationship had been critical to the negotiations. As long as he felt insulted on Ekatya's behalf, he was determined to extract concessions for her. Had he known she was a point of vulnerability, he would have been ruthless.

"Yes, now that she's free," she agreed.

"You're a lucky dokker, you know that? Most of us dream of having one tyree. You have two." Vellmar looked past Tal's shoulder. "And here comes one of them."

Salomen slipped an arm around her waist. "Fianna, do you mind if I take her away for a moment?"

"Certainly not." Vellmar plucked the glass from her hand. "You won't need that where you're going."

"Where am I going?"

Without answering, Salomen propelled her through the crowd. Once clear of the press of bodies, she asked, "Have you seen the bathroom? It's only for people using the conference room. Luxurious beyond belief."

"Ah, no," Tal began, wondering if she should stop this. She recognized the lustful determination searing their link—Fahla knew they had pounced on each other often enough over the past moon—but didn't think Salomen would act on it here, of all places.

"Then let me show you." A door opened at their approach. Salomen pulled her through, tapped a lock pad, and pushed her against the wall.

"Salomen, we're not—"

Her words were cut off with an aggressive kiss. She spent two pipticks trying to remember that they were at a reception, then kicked herself for wasting time and happily responded in kind.

"Dear goddess." Salomen pulled away, already breathing hard. "You are shekking gorgeous today, in this uniform and that crowd." She ran her hands up Tal's sides, her dark gaze following the movement with focused intent.

"So are you. I couldn't keep my eyes out of your neckline for most of that ceremony."

Salomen leaned in, lightly bit her jaw, and began kissing a path downward.

Her rare use of profanity was already arousing. The teeth closing on Tal's throat ridge were even more so.

She let out a groan. "We cannot do this here."

The grip on her throat tightened. For several pipticks, lost in their mutual passion, Tal thought they would throw all propriety out the airlock.

Then she was released, a gentle kiss soothing skin she knew would be showing a mark.

"No," Salomen said, straightening with a smirk. "We cannot. I was merely warming you up." She brushed a thumb across the mark she had made.

"Does this mean you're ready to leave?"

"Yes. I'm taking Lhyn to our quarters, and you're going home with Ekatya."

The sudden change of direction left her stumbling. "I'm—hold on."

"It's time."

Tal stared at her, a hand drifting to the heated skin on her throat. "What just happened?"

"Have you not seen the looks Ekatya has been giving you all afternoon? She's free at last, and it has opened a door she didn't realize was being held closed."

"Have you talked to her?"

"I don't need to talk to her. I have eyes. I also have Lhyn, who I've missed very much this past moon. She and Ekatya have finally sated their need after the battle. So have you and I. We're all rebalanced, and Ekatya is no longer burdened by serving two oath holders. It's time, tyrina."

She rubbed her throat. "And this?"

The heated look Salomen gave her could have set the room on fire. "A reminder. I'm going with Lhyn, but that doesn't mean I want you any less."

"Well, in that case . . ." Tal reversed their positions. "I don't think one reminder is enough."

33

THE LAST RITUAL

I n accordance with the new orbital safety protocols, the Alsean dignitaries had flown up in three shuttles: half the Primes and war council in one, half in another, and Tal and Salomen in the third. With them came Micah, Vellmar, Ronlin, and Rahel as additional military dignitaries, while Lanaril came as Vellmar's date.

The flight back felt substantially different with the addition of Ekatya and her grandparents, Lhyn, and Alejandra. Despite knowing only two people in the shuttle, Ekatya's grandparents took an active part in the conversation. Tal enjoyed their contributions immensely, especially the ones that made Ekatya groan.

At the State House landing pad, Vellmar and Lanaril left on foot to cross the park to the temple. Rahel hadn't returned with them, instead catching a ride to Whitesun with Candini. For the sake of Ekatya's grandparents, Tal led the remaining group on a scenic route through the State House, feeling a bit like she was trying to impress a date's parents.

Micah and Alejandra peeled off on the fourteenth floor, headed to Alejandra's usual set of rooms. Farther down the corridor, Ekatya gave Lhyn her bag to hold and helped her grandparents into their suite. She emerged less than five ticks later, and the four of them silently walked a familiar path.

Outside their own door, Ekatya and Lhyn looked at each other and nodded. Ekatya drew Salomen a few paces away, while Lhyn dropped her bag and came to Tal.

"The coming home ritual starts with her rank bars," she said. "Work your way down from there. The medals are mounted on three display bars, so that makes it easier. Let her put those away. She has a system."

Tal stared at her. "You're not doing it? I thought we would do our usual. Share and then—" She feebly waved a hand, only now realizing that she hadn't thought about the logistics.

"Not this time. It's her last coming home ritual as a Fleet captain. It needs to be you."

"Why?"

Lhyn tucked her hands into her trouser pockets, her emotional signature far too calm for this conversation. "Ekatya is very good at telling herself no. She's been denying herself for so long that I think she's forgotten how to say yes. Salomen says you're two seeds in a pod when it comes to that. You both need this ritual to help you say yes."

Tal had faced down a Voloth invasion with less trepidation than this. "I won't know what I'm doing. What if I get it wrong?"

"She won't know what she's doing, either. That's why you have to do it together. This is your ritual, too." Her smile held all the knowledge Tal wished she had. "It's not a test. It's learning about someone you love. The only way to fail is not to learn, and I know you won't do that."

"Fainting from nervousness would probably count as failure," Tal muttered.

Lhyn pulled her into a reassuring warmron. "You'll be fine. You love her. She loves you every bit as much. That covers a multitude of mistakes."

"I love you, too."

Her grip tightened. "Just not in the same way. And that's a good thing, because I couldn't handle all three of you."

"Can you handle Salomen?"

She pulled back, looking over her shoulder at the quiet exchange taking place a few paces away. "We haven't been telling ourselves no for nearly as long as you two have. We'll be all right."

Tal caught her hand as she stepped away. "Make sure she knows she's safe in your arms. If I'm good at self-denial, Salomen is even better at keeping herself safe. She can hide behind walls and make them look natural. Even to a tyree."

"I know. We're seeds in a pod, too."

"Lhyn, you have no walls."

"Not with you."

"No, you never have. Not from the first day. Long before you truly knew me."

"Make them look natural, remember? There's an interesting consequence of always telling the truth. People don't look behind it. They assume there's nothing there."

Tal thought of foursome Sharings and how surprised she had been to feel Lhyn's self-directed anger. Or her sense of inadequacy, or her conviction that she wasn't lovable . . .

With a start, she understood that Lhyn was even better than Salomen at hiding. She hid in plain sight.

"I see you," she said quietly. "So does she."

Lhyn leaned in to kiss her cheek. "That's why I'm safe. Love her well, all right?"

"To the best of my ability." Which she fervently hoped would be enough. "There's one more thing. She has nightmares about the battle. She'll need—"

"We talked about it. She told me what to do."

Of course she had. Salomen had arranged this whole evening; why wouldn't she have prepared for that as well?

"Andira." Lhyn held her by the shoulders. "She *is* safe in my arms."

She swallowed down the words crowding her throat and said the ones that mattered. "Love her well."

"I will. I promise."

Salomen looked up from her own conversation, then gave Ekatya a final word and a quick warmron before walking back. "Ready?" she asked, holding out a hand.

"I'm ready." Lhyn shouldered her bag and clasped their hands, anticipatory joy sparking from her skin.

"Goodnight, tyrina." Salomen tapped the side of her own throat. "Remember."

Ekatya joined her as they watched their tyrees walk away, hand in hand. "Do you get the feeling this is easier for them than it is for us?"

"The feeling? No. The absolute conviction? Yes."

"We've been together every night for a moon. That's more consecutive time than I've had with her in ages. I want this with you. I've wanted it almost since I met you, and it's still hard to let her go."

"I think that's the consequence of giving your heart twice. No matter which one we're with, the other still holds us."

Salomen reached the stairwell door and turned, holding a hand aloft. Lhyn blew a kiss.

Then they were gone.

"Right," Ekatya said. "Shall we?"

Tal followed her through the door, newly awkward in this suite where she had spent so many hanticks. The discomfort increased when Ekatya entered the bedroom. This was the point at which that door had always closed, while she and Salomen waited in the living area. She couldn't count the number of times they had looked out over Blacksun, sensing Ekatya's metamorphosis from the stressed, frustrated, grieving captain to the relaxed woman at home.

But Ekatya was none of those things tonight. This metamorphosis would be different.

She dropped her bag on the floor and looked back to the doorway. "Are you coming in?"

Tal stepped inside.

"It's funny, the things that come to mind at a time like this." Ekatya gazed out at the pink and orange sky, the sunset late at this time of the cycle. "As of today, the *Phoenix* is on Blacksun time. I'm done with ship lag. No more orbiting above Blacksun in full daylight while getting ready for bed. No more conversions between hours and hanticks. I never got used to it." She closed the space between them. "I need to ask you a question."

"Anything."

"What does this mean?" She touched the mark on Tal's throat. "I know it can't be what I assume."

"What do you assume?" Tal asked curiously.

"Salomen snuck you out of a high-level reception to give you that in some dark corner. In my culture, this would be a message to me. It would say she's marked her territory, and she's telling me who you belong to."

Gaian culture was consistently odd when it came to sexuality. "Does that sound like Salomen?"

"Not at all. That's why I'm confused." Ekatya drew a light circle around the mark.

"It's a message to me, not you. A reminder that she may be with Lhyn right now, but she still loves and wants me."

"You share each other's emotions. Do you need a reminder?"

"Did you need that kiss Lhyn blew to you?"

The lines in her forehead smoothed out. "Point taken." Her hand drifted down Tal's throat, ending by pressing on the center of her chest.

Tal held it in place. "Salomen is carrying the same mark. Didn't you notice?"

"Er, no. I wasn't really looking at Salomen tonight."

"I gave her the same reminder she gave me. Lhyn is probably asking about it right now."

"No, she's not. She'll already know." Her emotional signature abruptly dimmed as she stared at their hands. "But I didn't. I never do. Lhyn won't be having this problem."

Tal's chuckle startled her.

"What's so funny?"

"Us. Lhyn told me this would happen. She said we'd both be learning together. That it's not a test, and the only way we can fail is to not learn. I don't know what I'm doing either, Ekatya. But I want to learn with you." She touched the captain's bars with her free hand. "This is the first part of the ritual, yes? How do I take it off?"

With a burst of confidence, Ekatya stepped back, her hands going to her collar. "Let me."

"No, I'm supposed to—"

The bars were already in her hand.

"—do that," Tal finished.

"There is no 'supposed to.' We're learning, right? Besides, I need to do this." Ekatya turned the bars over, examining them. "I gave these to you three cycles ago. Do you remember?"

"I could hardly forget."

"You had just taken off my head and handed it to me. Kicked the anger right out of me, because I left you no choice. I judged you, made terrible assumptions—Hades, I honestly wanted to kill you. Or at least hurt you as much as I could before I went down. It's hard for me to remember that now, knowing what you must have felt at the time."

Tal nodded.

"But do you know what's easy to remember? That Sharing. The gift you gave me—it wasn't just sensing Lhyn's emotions for myself. It was knowing that I could trust you after all. That you had told me the truth, and I could finally make a decision based on all the facts. So I decided to give my loyalty to you."

"It changed everything," Tal said softly.

"But you didn't hold me to it. Fleet called and I left, and you never said a word about the promise I broke by leaving."

"You didn't break it. You've kept it all this time, at a terrible cost. This has been harder on you than any of us. I've wished so often that I could save you."

"And then you did." Ekatya held out the bars. "Andira Shaldone Tal, for the second and last time, I offer you my loyalty. And my love to go with it."

Tal's eyes stung as she accepted the small bit of metal. It was heavy for its size, a fact she had forgotten, but her hand remembered. The weight felt as familiar as if she had last held it yesterday.

"Either would be a gift beyond measure. Both together . . ." She cleared her throat, then shook her head. She couldn't get the words out.

Ekatya smiled, her eyes reddening as well. "Are you wishing I could feel you?"

"No," Tal rasped. "I don't wish anything when it comes to you. Everything I ever wished for is standing right here." With great care, she tucked the bars into her jacket pocket and sealed it. Then she pulled Ekatya in and showed her exactly how she felt.

"That worked," Ekatya said breathlessly. "Whew. Did it ever."

Feeling more confident, Tal ran a fingertip over her top row of medals. "How do these come off?"

Ekatya released the tab of her throat guard, then swiftly undid the other five down the front of her jacket. Holding it open with one hand, she pointed to three strips of shining metal on the inside. "The ribbons hang over a magnetized bar. These hold the bars in place. If you press the ribbon bar at both ends, it interrupts the magnetic charge long enough for this one to drop free."

"Easy enough." Tal spanned the top bar with forefinger and thumb and pressed the ends. It came off in her hand, the medals swaying on their ribbons, and Ekatya caught the inner bar.

She held it out. "Snap it back together so the ribbons don't slide off and set it on the side table. I'll put them away later."

The two bars came together with a click. "I want their stories," Tal said as she laid them down.

When the remaining medals had been safely removed, she checked the sleeves of Ekatya's jacket, found the tabs that held them shut at the wrists, and opened those. Then she pushed the jacket off her shoulders and hung it in the closet.

Turning, she paused at the sight of Ekatya in dress boots and trousers with a finely tailored white shirt. "Beautiful," she said. "You look different out of the jacket. More . . . accessible."

"Less armored?" Ekatya stepped forward and brushed her fingers over the bluestones that lined Tal's collar. "Do I need to take these off first?"

"No, they stay on."

"What do they signify?"

"That blue is my favorite color?" She smiled at the exasperated look. "It's also the background color of my family crest. And bluestones are rare and valuable, so these show my status. I've seen how you Fleeters need to shout your status with symbols nobody can miss. We prefer to be quieter about ours."

"Says the woman who wears a full cape embroidered with an enormous Shield of Alsea. Which probably took an army of crafters a moon to produce."

Tal opened her mouth, reconsidered, and had to laugh. "All right, I concede that."

"Why didn't you wear it today? I'd have thought you'd want to make an impression."

"There was no need. I wasn't in the ceremony. And sitting on a full cape for hanticks? No, thank you. I enjoyed relaxing in the audience and letting someone else play the role."

Ekatya looked at her with that same smile she had seen several times at the reception. "You are something else."

"Why?"

"Because you're the shekking Lancer and you don't need everyone to know it. You don't even need diplomats and admirals from another government to know it. You were the most powerful person in that shuttle bay, but you were content to sit in the audience and watch. With nothing but bluestones and this to mark your status." She ran her palm across the Seal of the Lancer, then slid it over the collar and up the length of Tal's neck.

Tal instinctively lifted her chin and was stunned by the passionate line of kisses searing their way up her throat. By the time Ekatya's lips reached her ear, she was having difficulty standing upright.

"You wear your power like a second skin," Ekatya murmured. "It's beautiful to watch. And very, *very* sexy."

Dazzled into immobility, Tal stood still while Ekatya unsealed her jacket, gently pulled it down her arms, and stepped away to hang it up.

"There. Now we're both less armored."

Tal held a hand against her throat. "You didn't kiss me like that on our date."

"I had different objectives then."

"Great Mother. I might not survive your objectives tonight."

"You'd better. I don't want to face Salomen's wrath tomorrow." Ekatya tugged her to the nearby bench and sat, crossing an ankle over her knee to reach her boot tabs. "I always take these off myself. Easier that way."

As she followed suit, Tal said, "The first time Salomen and I joined, she pulled off my boots and nearly exploded my head. That was the act of a subordinate, or so I'd been taught from my early training. She took a ritualized humiliation and made it erotic."

Ekatya stood up, boots and socks in one one hand and the other outstretched. "We had those, too. Things like being obligated to fetch whatever senior cadets told you to, including the textbook they forgot in their quarters on the other side of the compound. And Fahla help you if you were late to class. Fetching a senior's book was no excuse. Give me your boots."

She set both pairs in the closet, dropped their socks in the hamper, and returned to hold out a hand once more. This time, she led Tal to the bed before sitting cross-legged and patting the mattress beside her. "You wanted the stories," she said, picking up the top bar of medals. "These two you know. I had to ask for duplicates after leaving the originals on the *Caphenon*."

Tal touched the silver medal. "Extraordinary service performed for the

Protectorate," she recited, then moved to the red star. "And courage under superior fire. Fleet should have given you another pair of these after the Battle for the Stars."

"I have enough." She touched a third medal. "This is for covering my team when we escaped from Lexihari. It's hard to wear it when I lost Ensign Bellows on that mission." Shifting to a medal shaped like a chevron, she said, "This is from quite a bit earlier. Remember the story Admiral Tsao told about my promotion to lieutenant?"

They went through the medals one by one, and Tal enjoyed every moment of it. She had heard most of these stories during the medal ceremony, but not all, and none from Ekatya's lips. Each filled in a little more color of a life lived before they met.

"This one is special," Ekatya said, touching the last medal on the third bar. "It's the first I ever earned. It's for successfully using the toilet."

Her emotional signature curled in tight, quivering with barely suppressed glee.

Slowly, Tal turned her head and raised an eyebrow.

That was all it took. Ekatya snorted, then broke open with laughter, joyous and free. Just as she began to get herself under control, she caught sight of Tal's unimpressed expression and bent over again with a louder guffaw.

It was impossible not to join in, not when sparkling delight filled the room and tingled on Tal's senses. "Aren't you a hilarious little dokker," she said, trying to look severe.

"Well, I try." Ekatya wiped her eyes, still chuckling. "Lhyn told me. I'm shocked that you would engage in such unseemly conversation during a serious Fleet event."

"Hm. A sonsales could see how shocked you are."

"I bet. I haven't laughed that hard since I asked the lift to take me to Admiral Asshead's office." She paused, letting the expectation build.

"And?"

"It took me to waste reclamation. Where we process our sewage."

That sent Tal over the edge, which obliterated Ekatya's tenuous control, and they collapsed against each other. Ekatya slid backward, her upper body thudding into the mattress.

With a grin she couldn't erase, Tal straddled her. "You're stunning like this. Relaxed, happy—your emotional signature is *glowing*."

Her smile glowed as well. "You find emotional signatures attractive?"

"When they're like this? Fahla, yes." She slid a hand along her jaw, reveling in the intimate contact. "It shows here as well."

Ekatya looked up at her, open and trusting. "How are they doing?"

"I cannot speak for Lhyn, but—"

"But you know she's feeling the same as Salomen."

"They're . . . euphoric. Entirely at ease, passionate, and deeply intimate."

"Intimate? Already? We're the ones who have been waiting for three cycles!"

"Perhaps they had less protective armor than we did."

Ekatya mirrored her hand position and let her thumb brush Tal's bottom lip. "Do you know what Salomen told me in the hallway? That we're like one of Jaros's puzzles, except ours only has four pieces. Each of us is a corner piece, and we each interlock with two others."

The vision came easily: Salomen at Hol-Opah's dining table, assembling a flat puzzle with Jaros and smiling as she assembled an analogy with it. "An analogy based on seeing patterns. That's Lhyn's influence."

"I know. Fahla help us all, they're thinking alike." Her eyes danced with humor before growing serious once more. "She said she watched me during those ceremonies and thought no one in the bay would say no to me. That you had been saying no for far too long, and tonight I needed to help you say yes."

Tal closed her teeth on the thumb that had been caressing her lip and watched Ekatya's sudden, intense focus. A swipe of her tongue caused an intake of breath, and she let it go. "Lhyn said much the same thing when she told me about this ritual. Though we seem to have strayed from it by a length or two."

"Good," Ekatya murmured. "I want it to be something we create together. Andira, will you join with me now? Will you show me what a Shared joining feels like?"

Tal did not say no.

34

MORNING AFTER

The first thing Ekatya thought, when she opened her eyes to a room filled with light, was that Lhyn rarely let her sleep this late. She preferred to maintain ship time on her leaves; it minimized the disruption when she went back to the *Phoenix*.

She yawned and stretched, a pleasant soreness making itself known, and stopped with a squeak as the rest of her brain came online.

Lhyn had not let her sleep in, she was not on leave, and last night was not a dream, as her sore muscles proved.

Familiar voices drifted in from the dining area, correcting one of her assumptions: Lhyn *had* let her sleep. She was out there right now, chatting with Salomen. But Andira . . .

She turned her head.

Andira was watching with a soft smile, her eyes glowing in the light. "Good morning," she said, reaching out to clasp their hands.

"Is it still morning?"

"Barely. I refuse to feel guilty about it."

"How long have Lhyn and Salomen been here?"

"I don't know. I woke up earlier and those were already there." She pointed to the bench by the closet, now housing a neat stack of clothing. "I'm glad one of us remembered that I didn't have any other clothes."

Ekatya regarded the innocuous stack with dismay. Salomen had brought it for her bondmate. She had been in this room and seen them together, sleeping like the dead.

"It's all right," Andira said.

"I know. I'm trying not to feel like we've been caught."

"There's no need. Salomen is a holcat in the curing shed windowsill."

That was a new one. "A holcat surrounded by more than she can eat?"

"A sated, satisfied creature basking in the sun and contemplating what pleasure she'll give herself next." Andira fixed her with a pointed look. "I have rarely felt Salomen this kind of happy. Uncomplicated. Unalloyed by background concerns. Simply, deeply, blissfully content. She's happy for herself and for all of us. Don't bring a shadow to it by thinking you or I deserve any degree of shame."

"I don't." Wincing, Ekatya corrected herself. "I know intellectually that I shouldn't. But I also come from a culture that would tell me we've both betrayed our bondmates."

"While they betrayed us?"

The simple question brought her up short. "No. I'd never think of it that way. I'd judge myself, not Lhyn."

"And she would rightly call you a hypocrite." Andira softened her words with a kiss. "Let's join our bondmates for mornmeal. Or midmeal, which we're closer to. Then we can Share and put your mind at ease."

They showered together, an act that should have been more erotic than it was. But Ekatya could not forget who was waiting for them, and Andira made no attempt to touch her. This felt more like shipmates washing off in the locker room than lovers after a glorious night of passion. She mourned it, but could not behave nor think any differently.

Dried and dressed, they walked into the dining room and were greeted by two knowing grins.

"And we thought we slept in," Salomen teased. "You set a record."

Andira shook her head. "How soon they forget. The second day of our bonding break?"

"Oh, yes, that's right. That *was* a long night." Salomen stood, a glass of juice in her hand. "Drink this and kiss me, in that order."

Lhyn had risen at the same time and was offering a glass to Ekatya, who accepted gratefully.

"Was she this bossy with you?" Andira asked Lhyn.

Ekatya choked on her drink. How could she be so casual about it?

"Only part of the time." Lhyn seemed equally at ease. "The rest of the time, she was sweet and giving. Very concerned about my comfort."

"I'm only bossy with stubborn warriors." Salomen swept Andira into an embrace. "Good morning, tyrina," she murmured.

Ekatya turned away from their intimacy and found herself enveloped in Lhyn's arms.

"Stop that," Lhyn whispered. "Or I'll be forced to write a paper on the cross-cultural ramifications of swapping spouses between species."

The laugh came out of nowhere, a bubbling release born of relief. Lhyn was still Lhyn, and why would she have expected anything different?

She held on, burying her nose in Lhyn's throat and inhaling the familiarity of her fragrance. "I love you."

"I love you, too. Did you think that would change overnight?"

"No, but in all my imaginings of last night, I never got around to imagining this morning."

"That might be a good thing. Knowing you, you'd have worried yourself sick over it."

They took their usual seats around the table and served themselves from the generous array of options. Lhyn and Salomen had not yet eaten, a consideration that left Ekatya in a confusing blend of gratitude and guilt. Fortunately, the conversation steered away from the reality-bending event horizon of last night, enabling her to enjoy the meal.

She should have known better. Salomen was merely waiting for her to finish.

"I see you've learned how to mark an Alsean," she said, nodding toward Andira. "Were you as fascinated by her throat ridges as Lhyn was by mine?"

"Fucking Hades." Ekatya dropped her face into her hands, burning with embarrassment.

Andira laughed, disloyal dokker that she was. "I'm guessing not quite as fascinated, but close."

Ekatya eyed her through her fingers.

"To be fair—and accurate—I've seen Salomen's throat ridges before," Lhyn said.

"You have?" Andira gaped at her bondmate. "She brought out your throat ridges and you didn't join until last night? And you talk about me denying myself!"

Salomen sipped her shannel with a contented smile. "It shouldn't surprise you that Lhyn is thorough in her data gathering. Or that we would wait until you two were ready. The benefit is that she already knew what to do with everything above the waist. So did I."

Lhyn was *preening*. Ekatya lifted her head, watching in amazement.

"But she didn't mark you," Andira observed.

"I can't," Lhyn said. "I've tried. It takes too much pressure, and I can't treat Salomen that way."

"Not even if she wants it?"

"I don't want anything that would cause her distress," Salomen said.

"She senses it," Lhyn added. "It never gets to the point of me being distressed. Merely sensing my reluctance kills her arousal. It's fascinating, really. We come from a culture where good joinings don't happen without open discussions, self-knowledge, and enough confidence to say no. Or a partner who's both experienced and exceptionally skilled at reading body cues. But you have a powerful additional source of knowledge and a feedback system we lack. It makes your physical and cultural experience of sexuality different from the foundation up. Our first times, we fumble around trying to figure out what we like and what our partners like. Assuming our partner even cares, that is."

"I still cannot imagine that," Salomen interjected. "Being able to take pleasure in a joining when your partner does not."

"Nor can I." Andira reached for the shannel pot and refilled her cup. "We do still fumble in our early experiences, though. Tyrina?"

"Thank you." Salomen held out her cup. "She knows. I told her that story."

"Yes, so I know your use of 'we' is only accurate on the societal level." Lhyn raised her eyebrows. "*Your* first time was perfect. Salomen says you don't represent the norm. But she also says it doesn't take long for the fumblings to resolve into mutually satisfying joinings. One or two experiences and you're set. It can take us cycles."

"Tencycles, in some cases." Ekatya felt safer with this generalized discussion.

"Horrifying thought." Salomen tapped the side of her throat. "You didn't answer my question. Trying to avoid it?"

"Yes." As the others laughed, she acknowledged that avoidance would not save her. "All right, fine, they're incredible. Exotic and hot as—"

"A black rock on a summer day," Lhyn finished. "I know. Whew!" She fanned her face, and Ekatya had to pull the shannel cup away from her mouth or risk blowing it all over the table. Lhyn grinned, delighted with the results of her performance.

When the shannel was gone, they loaded up the dish cart for later collection and retired to the living area. Lhyn set out the cushions, Ekatya unsealed her shirt, and soon they were deep in the Sharing she had wanted for the last moon.

It took mere pipticks to confirm Andira's words: Salomen was happy in a way Ekatya had rarely felt. Discharging the burden of her role in orbital defense was probably a significant part of that, but it was obvious that she found great joy in loving Lhyn and knowing that Andira and Ekatya were no longer holding back.

Lhyn was equally happy, vibrating with the thrill of new discoveries and basking in a kind of love she had barely believed could happen to her once, let alone twice. Her radiance burned off any residual doubts Ekatya might have harbored.

Andira's emotions were familiar after last night's multiple Sharings, but Ekatya would never tire of sensing such exhilarated freedom and open-hearted love. That she was a cause of one and a recipient of the other was still astounding.

"You deserve it," Salomen said. "So does she. So do we all."

"Words for Fahla," Andira agreed. "We've walked a difficult road to be here. What we have, we've earned."

In their Shared unity, they were of one accord. By the time they let go and returned to their individuality, Ekatya felt weightless. She hardly knew what to do with herself. When was the last time she'd had no deadlines, no conflicts of duty and loyalty, no overwhelming concerns about her future or that of her loved ones?

When had she last felt this free of guilt or doubt?

"Come for a run with me," Andira said. "You need it."

A tentick later, she was running beneath the great trees of the State House grounds, burning off the energy that fizzed beneath her skin. It was so much sweeter than running in a ship's exercise room, and the company was beyond compare.

She gasped for air, driven to her aerobic limits, and still felt like laughing.

"Your emotional signature is like a fusion reactor." Andira glanced over with a grin, her breathing deep and even. "It makes me want to run faster."

"Please don't. I'm already close to death."

Andira's laughter forced her to stop, giving Ekatya a welcome reprieve. Their pace upon resuming was far more reasonable.

"I keep thinking I could have had this all along," Ekatya said as they walked their cooldown circuit. "If I hadn't left. I wouldn't have had to get here the hard way. Lhyn wouldn't have been tortured, you wouldn't have gone through the trauma of a broken tyree bond, I wouldn't have spent one cycle under Sholokhov's thumb and another under Greve's . . . but then I think of all the things we gained."

"It had to happen this way," Andira agreed. "For all that I wish we could erase some of those events, they brought us here today. Would I have challenged Salomen if you were here? I might have been too caught in wanting you. Without her, I wouldn't have survived Shantu."

"Rahel would never have met her." Ekatya was morbidly fascinated by the alternative path. "Shantu would be Lancer, and Rahel would be his Chief Guardian instead of saving Alsea with Candini."

"Candini wouldn't be here, either. Shantu would never have put a Gaian in charge of our fighters. And without you up there in the *Phoenix*, we might have lost Alsea in the first wave of missiles."

"We could have lost it even with me up there. The divine tyree unit wouldn't have Salomen. She'd still be untrained and unaware of her true power."

"Even if I had met her and everything else was the same, it wouldn't have worked without you and Lhyn. You wouldn't know about your own powers had Lhyn not been tortured. You might have discovered them eventually, but I doubt you'd be this far along in their development."

"It's enough to make me think Lanaril has a point." Ekatya wiped the sweat from her face.

"She usually does. Here's another one. Had you not left, you wouldn't have recruited Alejandra. She wouldn't be on the fourteenth floor right now, making Micah happier than I've ever seen him."

Ekatya tilted her head back, admiring the towering domes of the State House as they approached. "And finally healing from a wound she's carried more than half her life. Stars and Shippers, I hate the idea of being a kasmet piece in someone's game. But I can't argue with where we are today."

"We're in a wonderful place today. This way." Andira led her down a side path to a small clearing she hadn't known existed. A fountain plashed and burbled in the center, its wide, flat edge an invitation to sit.

It felt like a metaphor for all she had missed before now.

"Will I cause offense by dunking my head?" she asked.

Andira's answer was to plunge her own head beneath the surface. When she pulled out, it was with a twist that sent cold water splattering across Ekatya's chest.

"Gah!" Ekatya leaped at her, catching her by surprise. The ensuing wrestling match nearly ended with both of them in the fountain, hindered by helpless laughter. At last they gave up, leaning on each other to catch their breath before collapsing onto the fountain's edge. Ekatya dunked her head and made sure she withdrew with a proper sweep of wet hair, but Andira had turned away. The water hit her shoulders and back, not even causing a flinch.

"Feel better?" she asked.

"Much." Ekatya wiped her face and squeezed the excess water from her hair, smiling at the way Andira watched her every move. "I feel like I'm on a bonding break."

"I think we're allowed to feel that way. Salomen certainly does."

"That makes this so much easier. You knowing what Salomen feels."

"You can know how Lhyn feels as soon as you ask her."

"True. And if I have any doubts, they're gone when we Share." She planted her hands on the warm stone and leaned back, eyeing the Guards who stood at a discreet distance. "Did I just compromise your reputation?"

Andira's hesitation set off all her alarms.

"What? What happened?"

"Calm down." Andira reached for her hand. "You're going to need more than one day of relaxation, that much is clear. You're still hyper-vigilant."

"You didn't answer the question."

"I was trying to decide how to approach it." She nodded toward the Guards. "They know. The moment Lhyn joined our link at Blacksun Base, every divine tyree knew about her and Salomen. So did all the Guards watching over us. By the time that battle ended, they knew about you and me as well. Healer Wellernal knew when he joined. Then he had to move Lhyn into the room with us at the healing center, and all the staff knew. You have no front, so every Guard who has seen us this morning knows. And everyone we passed in the corridors. It won't be possible to keep this a secret."

"Then I *am* compromising your reputation." Her fear was rising, shadows of Greve and his traps darkening her spiraling thoughts—

Which came to an abrupt halt when Andira kissed her, in full view of the Guards and anyone else who might be in visual range.

Ekatya stared at her in shock. "What are you *doing?*"

"Stopping you. And showing you." She had not let go, her hand still cradling the back of Ekatya's wet head. "It's all right, I promise. I've already discussed this with the High Council and my communications advisor."

"You what!"

"Did you hear the part where I said we cannot keep this a secret?"

"Yes, but the High Council?" She needed to dunk her head again. No, she needed to dunk her whole body.

"Ekatya, please. Calm yourself. I'm not in danger."

"It feels like you are!" She was breathing hard, unable to accept that they were out here in public, acting freely. As if they had nothing to hide. She had done nothing *but* hide, for so long, with the stakes so high . . .

"Ekatya! Will you let me help?"

Her nod was instinctive. She hadn't fully processed the question.

Then she closed her eyes as warm comfort spread through her body, weighting her limbs and liquifying her muscles. The razor-edged fear disintegrated, leaving fatigue in its wake.

"Shek," she mumbled. "I could sleep right here."

"I'll hold you if you do. I'm so sorry, bana."

"Bana?" Her language chip provided the translation, but she had never heard Andira use the endearment before. Not with Salomen and certainly not with her.

"I won't call you that if you don't like it. It just slipped out."

"No, I like it." Her eyelids weighed ten kilos each. "What happened?"

"You had a minor panic attack. Small enough that a projection stopped it."

She dropped her head to Andira's shoulder, indulging herself in the protective embrace. "I've never had one before."

"Goddess above. You withstood an entire cycle of Greve's water wheel torture and never broke. One thought that I might be compromised and you went over the edge." Andira pressed a kiss against her temple. "You have an Alsean heart in a Gaian body," she murmured. "You and Lhyn both. I'm sorry, Ekatya, truly. I didn't mean to frighten you."

"It's not your fault. You tried to tell me. Let me go."

Andira released her, immediately and without question, and she let herself fall backward into the water. Her legs were still on the edge, anchoring her while the rest plunged into a welcome shock of cold.

She floated in sudden isolation, hearing only the muted thunder of water falling into the pool and letting it wash away the lassitude of Andira's projection. It had certainly stopped her spiraling terror, but it was also an injection of foreign emotion. She wanted to be herself.

Her pulse beat in her ears, slowing with the cold and her returning control. She floated longer than necessary, trying to push away the embarrassment at having a panic attack in front of the single strongest woman she knew. It didn't help to know that Andira felt that, too.

When she was ready, she held out a hand. Her eyes were still closed, but she trusted.

Her hand was clasped instantly, and Andira hauled her up.

Squeezing water from her hair for the second time, she said, "I'm all right. Just mortified." Which was deeply hypocritical of her, after all the times she had told Lhyn not to feel ashamed of her attacks.

"There's no need—"

"I know. You're right, I need more than one day of relaxation. What did the High Council say?"

Andira examined her, then shook her head. "Just like that?"

"Just like that. Tell me."

"Stubborn warrior." She gave in. "I asked my communications advisor to give them his conclusions. He said, and they agreed, that your status as the Savior puts you in a unique category. You—"

"The Savior?"

"After the battle, the media stopped calling you the Savior of Blacksun. You're simply the Savior now, chosen and temporarily inhabited by Fahla."

"I guess that would be a unique category." Her sense of humor was beginning to reassert itself.

"If the Lancer shares a dual tyree bond, and the other tyree is the Savior, Miltorin thinks that's a story that tells itself. Everyone on Alsea watched you save us last moon. They won't disapprove of our relationship, especially given that their Bondlancer is also in a dual tyree bond with their other favorite Gaian. If anything, this will enhance my reputation. It's not every Alsean who can land the Savior."

"Oh, is that what you did? Landed me?"

"You're here, aren't you?"

Ekatya looked back at the Guards, who had not moved. Then she slid her arms around Andira's shoulders and pulled her in.

"Yes, I am," she whispered against her lips. That she had surprised Andira gave her confidence, and she made their kiss last until she had shortness of breath for a much better reason.

When they separated, Andira was smiling. "Unique is right."

"I do try." Ekatya's skin tingled. She was exhausted from their run and her attack, yet exhilarated by coming out of it with enough flair to recover her pride. "Then you're going public?"

"I'm not doing anything without permission from you and Lhyn."

"Do it. You'll have Lhyn's permission two pipticks after asking. She doesn't deserve to be kept in the shadows, and I—" She stopped, now understanding her earlier trigger. "I've spent a cycle protecting everyone I care about by isolating myself. This last moon has been so freeing, but I still had to be careful about you because of Sholokhov. I don't know what he could have done once that treaty was signed, but finding out we tricked him would not have been good."

Andira nodded in understanding.

"But that ended yesterday. It's like I'm finally remembering how to breathe. The mere idea of being pushed back there, of being used as a weapon against you—I can't live that way. Not one day more."

"That won't happen." Andira's confidence left no room for doubt. "We'll defuse that weapon before it can gain any power. Perhaps going public will help others, too. I've wondered whether my parents would have acted differently if they'd had the option. It's not unheard of, but at their level of society . . ."

"Ensigns can do things captains can't," Ekatya said with a nod. "But captains can set new precedents."

Andira looked at her silently, a small smile playing at the edges of her mouth.

"What?"

The smile grew. "I'm glad you're home." With brisk movements, she stood and offered a hand. "Let's get back and clean up. You smell like a wet holcat."

"Charming. As if you're any better?"

They made their way to the main path, its colonnade of ancient tree trunks framing the State House at its end. Lhyn and Salomen were in that colossal building right now, taking her grandparents on a full tour.

I'm glad you're home, Andira had said. Not *I'm glad you're back.*

Alsea had felt like home for some time, but only now was it truly sinking in.

She never had to leave again.

35

NOT THE USUAL WAY

F ahla had a twisted sense of humor, Salomen decided.

Between the preparations for the battle, the recovery afterward, the normal hard work of Hol-Opah in high summer growth season, the additional work of her planned surprise, and the waiting—great Mother, the *waiting*—for Lhyn and Ekatya to return from their moon aboard the *Phoenix*, she had been more than ready for an unofficial bonding break.

She had not been ready for Ekatya's grandparents.

Nikolay and Elanor were smart, loving, fascinated by everything they saw in Blacksun, and relentlessly in the way. They had come a very long distance to see Ekatya and Lhyn, and while Salomen certainly understood prioritizing family, she was chafing at the unexpected delay.

"They don't know who we are, tyrina," Andira said. "Until Ekatya and Lhyn tell them, we have no standing."

"How are you so reasonable about this? You've been waiting longer than I have."

"Because I've been waiting longer than you have."

That was exceedingly unhelpful, a fact she verbalized with every bit of her annoyance.

What *was* helpful, she reflected later, was Andira's innate understanding of her, even when she didn't understand herself. Their joining had been fast and hard, burning off her frustration, and the sweet caresses afterward settled her in ways she hadn't realized she needed.

"You could move up the media announcement by two ninedays," she suggested, her cheek resting on Andira's thigh. "Then Ekatya wouldn't have to tell them."

Chuckles bounced the stomach she was stroking. "You've been in the State House too long. You're learning manipulation."

"Ha. You think I didn't know before? I merely chose not to use it."

"Most of the time," Andira said unwisely.

Corozen and Alejandra joined them for evenmeal that night, a lively and distracting event. They had already scheduled their creation ceremony, which earned Corozen a good bit of teasing from Andira. He bore it with genial ease, immune to any embarrassment.

"I've been ready for half a lifetime," he said. "So has Alejandra."

"No, I haven't. I've been ready for about six days." Alejandra picked up a forkful of mallowfish. "This is delicious! One thing I'm looking forward to here is the food. Mmm."

"Half a lifetime, six days." Andira waggled her hand back and forth. "Your sense of time needs to be calibrated, Micah. You'd better fix that before having a baby."

"Either that, or stop speaking for your partner," Salomen added.

Still chewing, Alejandra pointed the fork at her with a smirk.

"Yes, it reduces the risk of catastrophic error." Andira poked his arm. "Take it from one who knows."

"Now you're giving me relationship advice?"

"Who better?"

Alejandra dabbed the corner of her mouth with her napkin. "In his defense, I do understand what he meant. I've *missed* having a child for half my life. It might not make sense, given that Josue would have been an adult long ago. But he's frozen in time for me."

"It makes perfect sense," Andira said. "My parents are frozen in time for me, too. They would be the same age as Micah, but I cannot envision it."

Salomen looked over in surprise, having never heard that before. "Will that happen to me with my mother?"

"I think it happens to everyone. We remember them as they were, not as they would be."

"I don't want to remember her as she was. Frail and dependent—she hated that part of being ill. It wasn't her."

"Don't remember her at the end," Alejandra said. "I did that for far too long, and it suspended my grieving process. Remember her as she was before. The illness was a tiny fraction of her life; it didn't define her. If you imagine her before then, what do you see? Don't let yourself think, just envision it." She snapped her fingers. "Right now."

"I see her walking across the fields," Salomen said without hesitation. "With a long stride that left all of us behind if we let ourselves be distracted for a moment." She smiled, the picture coming into better focus. "She's wearing a frayed sun hat that's cycles past the fashion, but she's the one who taught me to value comfort over appearance. Her work gloves are tucked into her belt, because it's summertime and none of us wear our gloves until we need them. But we always have them with us. That's something else she taught us, to keep our tools nearby."

The focus became a little too sharp, and she cleared her throat. "She's pointing something out to me, saying we need to take care of that next, because she was always planning ahead—and she always said 'we.' I think that's what hurts the most about losing her. I lost that partnership."

"That's beautiful," Alejandra said as the others nodded. "No mother could ask for more than to be remembered like that."

"How do you remember Josue?"

The table went silent with wary expectation. It was a presumptuous question, but Alejandra had begun it. Salomen felt no compunction about turning it back.

"If you had asked me a cycle ago, I would have said 'badly.' Then I'd have told you the topic was not up for discussion."

"And now?"

One hand idly spun her glass of spirits. "Now I see him sitting on our front steps. That was where he liked to play with his toys, running them up and down the steps and inventing stories. Complex stories, given his age. He's smiling up at me. Always smiling," she repeated, her gaze far away. "He was a happy child. Every time I showed him something new, he thought it was the most wondrous thing ever."

"It probably was," Salomen said quietly.

"He made me laugh more than I ever had. You lost your partnership, I lost my laughter." She refocused, her emotions unburdened despite the topic. "Lanaril says part of the grieving process is finding the things we lost. Even though we can't find them in the same place."

"Even when they're not what we expected," Salomen agreed. "I found a partnership that surpassed my wildest dreams. Then I found another."

"I'm still learning how to dream." Smiling at Corozen, she added, "But I think I've found a good teacher."

He reached for her hand, his emotional signature a brilliant spiral of happiness and pride.

"That's one of his best skills," Andira said. "A toast, then. To laughter and dreams." She waited until they had drunk before adding, "And a creation ceremony brimming with both. Where will you be holding it? Here, the temple, or a pleasure house?"

"A pleasure house," Alejandra answered. "In Whitesun."

Salomen understood immediately. "Rahel."

"Mm-hm. Micah and I can do it anywhere. She needs—" She paused when Corozen choked. "Not what I meant," she said, patting his back.

Andira was grinning widely. "He's a little sensitive about these things."

Corozen held up two fingers in a rude gesture, which only made her laugh.

"Save that for the right time," she quipped.

"We're surrounded by children," Alejandra informed Salomen before raising her voice. "As I was saying, Rahel needs a more specific environment. Since she won't be taking the usual route of sexual pleasure, her surroundings are critical to the process."

"I'm still amazed that will work," Salomen said. "Rahel said it would, but we didn't get a chance to discuss details."

"It's fascinating." She leaned forward, sparkling with an intellectual eagerness reminiscent of Lhyn. "Gaians don't have any control over gamete production. For females, one hormone starts the process, another kicks in as the egg matures, and a complex interplay of hormones drives sexual receptivity to encourage fertilization. Your biology is almost the reverse of ours. The hormones that drive your gamete production aren't produced until you stimulate receptors in your brain with sexual pleasure. Then you limit fertilization with the maturation process. If you don't keep the hormone levels high for five days, the gametes will reabsorb without ever reaching maturity." She waved a hand self-consciously. "I'm sorry, this is telling you what you already know, but I find the whole thing so damned brilliant."

"Something new and wondrous?" Andira suggested.

She straightened, startled by the repetition of her own words. "Yes. Wondrous. Now that you're making me think of it, I suppose Josue got that from me." A smile broke across her face. "Here's something else wondrous, and this part you won't know. Being sansara means sexual activity won't drive Rahel's hormone production. That's not what activates her receptors. She needs comfort giving."

"So you're holding your ceremony where she's most comfortable." Andira had caught on. "Her own pleasure house."

"With the help of the people best equipped to give her pleasure. The injections will push her levels near where they need to be, but there's a limit to what synthetic hormones can do. She still needs to produce some of her own."

"Great Mother," Salomen blurted. "You're making this a family event. Ravenel and Sharro will be there, won't they?"

She nodded. "I can't be her sole provider."

"She'll be busy helping me with my hormone levels." Corozen glowed with joyous expectation. "It's not the usual way of doing things, but neither of us has ever done things the usual way."

His words stayed with Salomen throughout the following day. She had never done things the usual way either, and for that she had paid a lonely price. Now she was surrounded by people who stood together in their willingness to stand alone.

She was still pondering it at the musical performance that evening, sitting in their reserved seats with Lhyn and Ekatya beside them and Nikolay and Elanor one row behind. With the Voices of the Deep providing glorious vocals, the Blacksun Symphony played compositions chosen to represent the Battle for the Stars. Salomen was transported by the music and chorus, her throat occasionally tightening at a particularly beautiful or haunting passage. So lost was she in the memories that intermission came as a surprise, pulling her back with a jarring mental thud.

As the lights came up and people began moving toward the lobby, Lhyn let out a long exhale. "Fucking stars. I'll need a glass of spirits to get through the next half. That was—"

"Well chosen," Andira said. "If the intent was to put us right back in the battle."

"I can get that for you." Nikolay stood up and patted his pockets, then pulled out a credit chip. "Ah! I knew I had it somewhere. Ekatya, would you like one as well?"

"Yes, please. Something from the Whitesun region if they have it."

"Andira? Salomen?"

When they declined, Nikolay left with Elanor right behind him, stating that she needed to stretch her legs.

"I'm sorry," Ekatya said.

Salomen looked over in surprise. "For what?"

"For making us wait. Again. I thought I was done with that, but—" She dropped her head back with a frustrated groan. "I don't know how to tell them. Gramps is so proud of me and Grams is having such a wonderful time, and I can't—Hades, I'm sorry. Some Savior I am, eh?"

"You're not obligated," Andira said. "Only you know what's best for you and your grandparents. If the time isn't right, then it's not right."

"We have a lifetime ahead of us." Salomen's impatience had vanished in the face of such distress. "We can wait until they return home."

"I don't *want* to wait. I want them to know you. But they won't if I don't tell them."

"Why not?"

"Because you're not you when you're hiding."

Salomen looked from her to Lhyn, who nodded.

"You've been very reserved," she said. "Andira is more skilled at presenting open body cues and conversing naturally, even when she's holding back."

"Gramps says you carry yourself like an officer keeping a professional distance. Grams says she can't see past your eyes. It's an idiom from her region; it means—"

"I understand what it means." Salomen saw the reaction even as she sensed it, an instinctive withdrawal at her sharp tone. She looked over the audience below them, taking a moment to regroup.

"They think highly of you." Ekatya scrambled to fix the perceived slight. "Grams admires your perfect manners—"

"She thinks we could learn a few things from you," Lhyn put in.

"—and Gramps is dazzled that we're friends with the equivalent of royalty. Sometimes I'm a little dazzled by that, too."

"Ekatya." Salomen was disarmed by the last comment. "I'm not royalty. I'm a producer who fell in love."

"Oh, I disagree. I saw the footage of your march through Blacksun. You were the leader of your people."

"She's right about that." Andira slipped an arm around her waist. "I'll never forget how you looked, standing at the bottom of the State House steps. Like a warrior queen, Micah said. And you know how much it takes to impress Micah."

"These days, a mention of hormone injections would do it." Their laughter eased the tension jangling her senses, and she spoke from her heart. "I want to know them, too. They're your family. You know what family means to me."

Ekatya nodded.

"But I'm not like Andira. I cannot be open without being fully open."

"I know. Believe me, I understand what it's like to hide a significant part of who you are. You shouldn't have to." She scrubbed her face with both hands, exasperation making the air heavy around her. "At my medal ceremony, Andira said you arranged a getaway for whenever we were ready. Is it like a bonding break?"

"It is, yes."

"Then I'm ready. Grams and Gramps have seen most of Blacksun, and I can't relax here. Everyone sees me as the Savior. Maybe if we go somewhere quiet, it'll be easier. And if we're somewhere where it's just family, that will definitely be easier."

Salomen could hardly believe the solution had dropped into her lap. "We can go tomorrow, if you like."

"Done. What do we need to bring?"

She smiled. "Pack as if you were spending the moon at Hol-Opah."

36

SALOMEN'S SURPRISE

Nikolay and Elanor were delighted to be taken on a new adventure the next morning. Salomen and Andira found them waiting at the transport with Ekatya and Lhyn, their bags already loaded.

It required only a little maneuvering to make certain that the four Gaians sat on the right side of the transport, while Salomen and Andira took seats on the left. Andira had already instructed the pilot, who flew east for twenty ticks and passed over Blacksun Base before beginning a long, curving sweep north.

Ekatya noticed immediately. "You're laying a false trail, aren't you?"

"We couldn't make it too easy." Andira crossed her hands behind her head and stretched out her legs, the picture of relaxation. "I'd advise you to emulate me. Sit back and enjoy the flight."

"You don't know Katya if you expect that," Nikolay said. "She's not capable of sitting back."

"If you wanted that, you should have blindfolded her," Elanor added.

Salomen pinched Andira's leg. "Stop," she whispered. "You can think about that later. Not now!"

Andira lifted her shoulders in an innocent gesture that did not fool her one bit.

"Wait a tick," Ekatya said. "Now we're flying parallel to the Snow-mounts. We doubled back! Come on, tell me where we're going."

"And ruin Salomen's surprise? I think not."

The next thirty ticks saw her grow ever more suspicious. "If I didn't know better, I'd say we're going to Hol-Opah."

"Or we could be crossing the mountains to go to the west coast," Salomen pointed out.

"Or we could turn north again and fly to Koneza," Andira added. "It's lovely this time of year. Toasty warm days and crisp nights."

"Now you're throwing out decoys. Obnoxious Alseans."

"You know, *some* of us are enjoying the surprise," Lhyn said. "We trust our hosts."

Ekatya scowled. "That was low. I trust them, I just want to know."

"Katya. Settle down and wait."

To Salomen's amusement, Ekatya responded to her grandfather's order as if he were the captain and she an ensign. She said nothing more until their transport crossed the Silverrun River and began to descend.

"Ha! We *are* going to Hol-Opah, I knew it!"

"Close, but not quite," Salomen said.

"We're descending too soon," Lhyn observed. "We're not going to the house. The waterfall?"

"Even closer."

"Not the waterfall?" Ekatya's nose was pressed against the glass. "There's nothing else here. Unless you're planning a touch-and-go and this is just another decoy."

"I should have thought of that," Andira joked.

"Stay with me and I shall teach you my devious ways." Ekatya grinned at her, bright with humor and open love, and Salomen wondered how her grandparents could fail to see it.

She stood up as soon as the transport landed. "Leave your bags. The Guards will bring them later."

"Ooo, mysterious," Lhyn said. "They'd only need to bring our bags if we were sleeping here. Did you set up a tent? I hope it's pavilion-sized."

"Do you really think she'll answer that?" Andira asked.

"No, but I can't not guess."

"It would be like the Silverrun not flowing. An aberration of nature." Salomen waited for Lead Guard Ronlin to precede her, then led the others down the ramp. "We have a short walk, but there's shannel at the end of it."

"Shannel! I'm sold," Ekatya announced. She stepped onto the bricks and looked around. "You built a landing pad. And a trail?"

"Among other things." Salomen traded a conspiratorial smile with Andira as they set off down the gravel path.

It was wide enough to accommodate a crateskate, a requirement given the many loads of building materials that had traveled along this path from the landing pad. Three could walk comfortably abreast, and additional space on either side had been prepared for ornamental plantings. There hadn't been time, but she was looking forward to getting her hands in the soil this moon.

The path was straight as a sword from the landing pad to the edge of the forest, then wound between thick trunks of ancient trees on its way toward the Silverrun. As they passed beneath the first arching branches, Salomen identified the species to her guests and explained the law requiring producers to leave a natural buffer between the river's edge and their field borders.

"We cannot remove endemic species from the buffer. Not that we would wish to; most producers take pride in the age and health of their buffer lands. Many of these trees are over a thousand cycles old."

"Magnificent," Elanor breathed, gazing upward. "If I were a few cycles younger, I'd want to climb one. Is that allowed?"

"If it weren't, I'd have been in a great deal of trouble as a child."

Chuckling, Nikolay brushed his hand against a sapling beside the path. "How did you put the trail through here if you can't take out trees?"

"Exceptions are allowed up to a specific trunk diameter for each species. And only with permits from the caste house, which won't be approved without a good reason."

"What was your reason?" Ekatya asked innocently.

Salomen glanced over her shoulder. "Did you think that would work?"

"It was worth a try."

"Nikolay, Elanor, how terrible was she about birth anniversary gifts?"

They groaned in unison.

"A demon child," Elanor said.

"Impossible," Nikolay agreed. "We ran out of hiding spots by the time she was ten. After that, we took her gifts to work and kept them in our offices."

"But we had to bring them home eventually." Elanor took up the tale. "I resorted to locks. She learned to pick them."

"You picked locks?" Andira turned around and walked backward, grinning at an embarrassed Ekatya. "I'm impressed."

"Yes, but then Gramps ruined it. He told me it made Grams sad when I found my gifts before she had the chance to give them to me. And if Grams was sad, he was sad. I would have taken corporal punishment over knowing I made them sad."

Salomen laughed. "He knew your heart."

"And manipulated it. I was twelve!"

"I did only what any good parent should. You can't tell me you didn't use the same technique with your officers."

"Twelve, Gramps."

"A good age to learn self-restraint," Elanor said. "We got to you in time. Imagine if you had hit puberty any earlier!" She shuddered. "A demon child was bad enough. A demon adolescent? I'd have died young from sheer exasperation."

Salomen lost track of the conversation when she glimpsed her surprise through the trees. She kept moving, waiting for the others to notice, and smiled when the first blast of shock hit her senses.

"My stars and asteroids!" Lhyn burst out. "Salomen! You built a *house?*"

The second blast came from Ekatya half a piptick later. "When in all the purple planets did you do that? How did you do it? You can't build here."

The forest thinned out, rich soil giving way to barren rock dotted by shrubs and smaller trees. Ahead, perched on the edge of the canyon wall and overlooking the Silverrun River, was a two-story round house built on the traditional rural plan.

Salomen stopped their little group and pointed toward the rock beneath her feet. "This makes it an exemption zone. There's almost no soil needing to be held in place by the buffer species. We're well above the high water line. And there aren't many trees over the maximum diameter. You can see the ones we had to avoid—there, there, and those three over there. Otherwise, we were free to take out what we needed. But I hate taking down trees, so we only did what we absolutely had to." She turned and shaded her eyes. "Beautiful, isn't it?"

"It's stunning," Lhyn enthused. "What a perfect location. I can hear the waterfall. Is it right over the fall?"

"That was my original plan, but Prime Builder Eroles advised me to reconsider. The mist would be an issue during high flows."

"Both for weathering and lowering the temperature," Andira said. "We'd freeze in the winter. And have no privacy during the summer swim season."

Salomen resumed walking. "We're upstream. Close enough to hear it and be within easy walking distance, far enough to avoid the downsides."

Ekatya jogged up next to Andira. "This must be paradise for your runs. Do you head toward the main house or follow the river up the eastern boundary?"

"I haven't stayed here yet."

"Why not?" Lhyn was right behind them. "I know you were running around like a yardbird with twenty chicks after the battle, but—wait. When was this finished?"

"Last nineday," Salomen said. "My goal was to get it done before you came back, so we could spend our first night here together. I'm happy to include you in that," she told Nikolay and Elanor. "It's traditional for a new house to be blessed with the love and laughter of family on its first night. My father and brothers will be here for evenmeal as well."

"I'd have invited Micah and Alejandra, but they're a bit busy," Andira added.

Ekatya's forehead was creased. "You haven't even spent a night here? And you're housing all of us for a moon?"

Andira exchanged a glance with Salomen. "It's not that we're housing you," she began.

"We're bringing you home," Salomen said.

Lhyn and Ekatya stopped walking in a cloud of surprise. One step back, Nikolay and Elanor looked on in confusion.

"Home?" Lhyn said in a small voice.

Salomen ached at the longing she was trying so hard to hide. "I did tell you we weren't going to Hol-Opah. This is Hol-Tyree."

Ekatya stared up at the house. "Lhyn," she said urgently. "There's a seventh star over the front door."

Salomen would have worked twice as hard and for twice as long to live this moment again. The comprehension sweeping over both women, the submersion of Lhyn's longing and doubt beneath a wave of joyous belief, Ekatya's sudden and almost painful sense of belonging—even her happiest imaginings hadn't matched the reality.

"It was a gift from Ravenel," she said. "I tried to hire her, but she said the day she charged me for a sculpture was the day Rahel decided to be a merchant."

Lhyn laughed, then covered her mouth as the emotional overload began to leak out of her eyes. "But this is your family's land. How did—?" She waved her hand ineffectually.

"We had a family meeting and redrew our boundaries." Salomen pointed west and began a slow pivot. "This parcel starts at the head of the canyon, follows the river to just east of the plunge pool, and goes straight back to the field boundary. The landing pad marks the northern border. None of it can be planted, so it doesn't affect the holding."

"Your family gave it to you?" Nikolay asked.

"No, but they gave us a fair price. Andira helped me buy out my brothers' interests. Although . . ." She paused, still affected by the unexpected gesture. "Herot refused payment. He said he owed it to us."

"We don't agree," Andira said. "But he closed the door on the worst of his shame by giving a gift that was in his power. It would not have been a kindness to refuse."

Ekatya was shaking her head. "How are we supposed to accept this?"

"You accept because you're family," Salomen said.

It hung there, a statement of fact that stopped Ekatya and left her grandparents baffled. As the silence grew, Lhyn looked back and forth between them and finally blew out a determined breath.

"Right. We are. And I can't wait to get a look inside. But first . . ." She caught Salomen's hand and lifted it to her lips. "Thank you, heart of mine."

Salomen didn't quite know how it happened, but somehow she was in Lhyn's arms, receiving a loving kiss that started on her mouth and moved to her ear.

"That should blow things up nicely," Lhyn whispered.

She could not hold back the laugh. "I was leaving it up to Ekatya, you little dokker."

"Sometimes she needs someone else to take the lead. It's exhausting always being the captain." Lhyn let her go and turned to Andira. "Thank you. I love our State House suite, but it's never been mine."

"I know." Andira pulled her into a warmron. "You stayed because I didn't want you to leave. Now you have another option."

"Katya." Nikolay's voice cracked with uncertainty. "Is this another cultural difference?"

Trapped, Ekatya opened her mouth, closed it again, and straightened her spine with visible resolve. "So different that you probably won't believe it. But it's time. Salomen, you mentioned shannel?"

37

CULTURE SHOCK

In retrospect, Salomen thought, she should have been forewarned by Ekatya's reluctance.

With the exception of Herot, her own family had received the news with little surprise. Herot hadn't known Lhyn long enough to have seen the progression of their relationship. "But if anyone is going to form a tyree bond with an alien, it's my sister," he said wryly, before touching their foreheads together in a wordless blessing. "I don't have to understand it to know it makes you happy."

"It does."

"Then that's what matters."

Jaros had been overjoyed; he loved Lhyn and thought Ekatya was his ticket into shining space adventures. Nikin said he was only sorry he couldn't give the protective elder sibling speech, because "Lhyn can't hurt a fairy fly and there's little point in giving that speech to the Savior."

Shikal had held her hands and looked into her eyes. "You've learned to accept love," he said. "I should have known you'd take it as a challenge."

It was unusual, they all agreed, but Fahla never gave the gift without reason. In this instance, the reason was abundantly clear to all.

She had long looked forward to her first meal in the new house with all of her family. But in her imaginings, she had never considered that Nikolay and Elanor would not believe them.

"Surely you understand our concern," Nikolay said. They were seated around the dining table, where Salomen had sadly watched her canyon view go unremarked while Ekatya told her tale.

"I was afraid of it," Ekatya said carefully.

It was neither an agreement nor a refutation, but Nikolay didn't seem to notice. "You want us to accept that a goddess neither you nor we believe in has given her blessing for you to take a second partner. Yet you can't give us details on why you're so convinced or why we should be glad that you're breaking your marriage oath."

"She's not breaking her oath." Of the four Gaians, Lhyn was the only one who had retained her calm. "We held an Alsean bonding ceremony. We didn't sign a Gaian or Allendohan marriage contract. The wording and the cultural expectations are different. Ekatya hasn't betrayed me."

"Did you betray her?" he demanded. "Are you the one who started this?"

Andira laid a hand over Salomen's and gave a slight shake of her head.

She swallowed the angry retort that had been on the tip of her tongue. No, it was not yet their fight, but if Nikolay accused Lhyn again—

"No one betrayed anyone," Ekatya said sharply. "I can't believe you'd think that of me. Do you know how hard Andira and I fought against this? And for how long? Lhyn and Salomen practically had to lock us in a room together."

"Lhyn and Salomen," he repeated. "So it *was*—"

"Gramps!"

"Katya, you're asking us to take this on faith! You have incontrovertible proof but you can't tell us because it's classified? What in the name of flight could be classified about this?" His emotional signature hardened with suspicion. "Unless there really is something dubious about that change in your brain."

Now it was Salomen stopping Andira, whose protective instinct came roaring to the surface at Ekatya's palpable hurt.

"I spent a year and a half being tried and punished for this change in my brain," Ekatya said, using the Common words for time. "I never thought you'd pile on."

Suspicion collapsed into dismay. "I'm not. Katya, no, this isn't about your duty or loyalty. It's about you. We're worried about you."

She crossed her arms and said nothing.

"Katya, dear heart, you have to admit this is startling news." Elanor was obviously the peacemaker in the family.

"I don't see why it should be so shocking," Lhyn said. "The Protectorate doesn't limit legal recognition to any one type of bond. That's why we have marriage contracts."

"Yes, but the norm for us is one partner," Elanor said.

"Not on Allendohan."

"You told us in no uncertain terms how you felt about polygamy on Allendohan."

"No, I told you how I felt about women being seen as little more than breeding stock to increase the population. Polygamy is not polyamory."

"Is this polyamory? Do you love Salomen as much as you do Ekatya?"

"I followed Salomen into death," Lhyn declared. "I'm sorry I can't tell you more about it, but can you imagine me doing that for someone I didn't love? Yes, I love them both, equally and in different ways, and in some of the same ways, too." She rested her fingertips on Elanor's arm, looking at her with the earnest gaze Salomen had never been able to resist. "I'd be the first person to try to break this down to its constituent parts and classify each one, but it can't be done. The whole is more than the sum of its parts. You can either accept it or not, but you won't change it."

"What will change is Ekatya's happiness if you choose not to accept it." Andira had run out of patience. "She has answered every question with honesty and respect. There is little left for her to say, and she cannot alter her heart. You must decide whether this alters yours."

Ekatya looked up in alarm. "Andira—"

"No, I refuse to stand by any longer. I understand the need for time, but they're hurting you. I stood by and watched you hurt for a *cycle*. I won't allow it now, not even from them."

"This is not what I want!" Ekatya stood abruptly, her chair juddering along the wooden floor. "You're my family, my only family. I want all of you to—gah!" She gestured around the room, from its floor-to-ceiling windows to the creamy yellow walls reflecting an abundance of light. "Look at this place! It's so beautiful and peaceful, and I *need* that, if you only knew—" She held up a hand, her head bent, then stalked to the back door. "I need a moment."

The door snapped shut behind her.

Silence blanketed the room as they watched her stop on the other side, shoulders rising with a deep breath. She crossed the wooden deck to stare over the railing, a spike of awe marking the moment she saw the real view. Looking back over her shoulder, she caught Salomen's eye and mouthed something.

"She said, 'Fucking Hades,'" Lhyn translated. "Is it my imagination, or is she actually standing over the river?"

"It's not your imagination. We cantilevered the deck." Salomen took considerable pride in the breathtaking vista it offered. "Prime Builder Eroles said it would be a waste not to."

"I'd have to agree. And I think we've found Ekatya's new favorite place."

"So far. You haven't seen the rest of the house. She might find something else to love."

"She has a lot to love already," Lhyn said with heavy meaning.

Nikolay and Elanor did not respond, their eyes on Ekatya's back.

"I'll refresh our shannel." Salomen wanted distance from the relentless broadcast of three highly emotional Gaians.

She was not to get it. Elanor followed her into the kitchen dome, examining the room with interest while Salomen set the pot beneath the shannel dispenser.

"Ekatya can't cook, you know."

The unexpected statement startled a smile from her. "Yes, I know. I'm the only cook in this family. This is my domain." She leaned back, hands braced against the counter, and looked around with satisfaction. "I designed this from the ground up. It keeps everything I love about the kitchen dome at Hol-Opah and fixes all the shortcomings." It still smelled new, freshly cut wood and tile sealant vying with shannel and the rich, organic scents drifting in through open windows.

"You did a beautiful job. I'd enjoy working in here. Learning some Alsean recipes, if you wouldn't mind teaching me?"

"I would be glad for the company."

Elanor ran her finger across the leaf pattern of the hanging utensil rack. "Beautiful," she murmured. Slowly, she walked along the curved counter, her fingertips tracing the stonework. "You see, you say that and I can only take it at face value. I can't see past your eyes. Yet Ekatya asks me to believe that she doesn't mind sharing Lhyn with you because you love her just as much." Her eyes held the clarity of age and experience. "I'm sure you can understand why that might be difficult for me."

"No, I cannot. Do you not know or trust her? She's telling you the truth."

"She's telling us what she believes. Is it the truth? Only you know that."

The accusation was so unexpected that she did not immediately recognize it. No properly raised Alsean would stand in a host's home and accuse her of lying.

"Then you haven't heard a word Ekatya or Lhyn have said," she said shortly. "I'm not the only one who knows. That is the point of Sharing."

"Tyrina? Is everything all right?" Andira stood in the doorway, drawn by her simmering anger.

"Fine. Elanor was taking this to the table." She pulled the now-full shannel pot from the dispenser and held it out.

With brisk movements, Elanor carried it across the kitchen and thrust it into Andira's hands. "Would you mind carrying it out? We have a few more things to discuss."

Andira looked past her to Salomen, who hesitated before tilting her head in reluctant assent.

"Very well. If you need me . . ."

"You'll know." Salomen watched her go, appreciating the unfinished promise. She might be alone with Elanor, but she was never alone.

Elanor returned with both hands raised in a conciliatory gesture. "I spoke out of turn. Forgive an old lady for allowing concern to override courtesy."

"What does your age have to do with it?"

Wry amusement sparked the air. "Well, that's the first time that hasn't worked. You're a straight speaker; I like that." The sparks melded into resolve. "Let's be straight with one another. Ekatya is telling an impossible story that gives her everything she wants. Lhyn, bless her, she's so starved for love that she might see more than is there. I came in here to ask you, away from the others, if you'd be willing to Share with me. Show me how you feel about this."

Aghast, Salomen could only stare.

In the continued silence, Elanor's confidence wavered. "Have I offended in some way?"

"Offended? You want me to engage in an intimate act to prove myself?" Never in her adult life had she been so insulted. "If you cannot see the offense in that, I don't have the words to express it. When Lhyn told you she loved Ekatya, did you ask her to join with you to prove it?"

Elanor stepped back in a cold flash of horror, mortification following close behind. "No! No, I didn't mean it that way. Lhyn said Sharing isn't unusual amongst family members, and I thought—I'm sorry, I haven't said this right."

"I can hardly imagine a right way of saying that," Salomen snapped.

"Hades on fire, Ekatya will be so upset with me." Elanor rubbed her cheeks, then folded her hands and bent her head over them, regret rising like steam from shannel. She looked smaller in this pose, uncertainty draining the crackling energy that made her so like her granddaughter.

With a surge of determination, she crossed her arms, one hand cupping an elbow. "I sincerely apologize. Lhyn did say that Sharing is even more intimate than joining. But she also said she's done it with Lanaril, and I saw all of you do it at the bonding ceremony. I didn't realize—it's not like anything we do. Will you let me explain?"

No anger could withstand the overpowering broadcast of remorse, or the flood of relief unleashed by Salomen's nod. Elanor managed a crooked smile before turning toward the eastern window.

Hol-Opah's kitchen windows were small and faced northeast, providing little natural light. Salomen had designed her new kitchen dome with one large window over the prep area, looking south into the canyon, and the tall east window looking down the length of the deck. Both offered the light she prized, while one allowed a precious additional benefit: a view of her family outside.

Two were there now. Ekatya remained at the railing, one foot propped on the bottom rail and her forearms resting on the top. Beside her, Andira matched her position, standing so near that their shoulders touched.

"Sometimes I forget she's not my child," Elanor said. "I've raised her since birth. First with the help of her parents, when they were home on leave. Then alone with Nikolay after they died. I lost my daughter, but she left part of her soul behind. A beautiful, sparkling part who grew up to surpass all of us."

She crossed to the window and rested a hand against the glass. "Ekatya does not love easily. She was a lieutenant the last time she brought someone home. Before Lhyn, we were convinced she was bonded to her career. For her to say she loves Andira—that's not in question."

Then what was? Salomen wondered.

"And for our sweet, hyper-rational Lhyn to say she can't break this down and catalogue it? That's love, short and simple. Then Andira lost her temper with us for hurting Ekatya. I didn't realize we had, but she was right." Satisfaction danced along her skin. "Ekatya has always been the defender. Never the one protected, except by us. I don't know Andira well, but that—" A blunt fingernail tapped the window. "I recognize that, even on an alien."

Retracing her steps, she looked up with her weighted stare. "I don't see it in you. All this talk of balance and equal bonds—how equal are you in this? Do you love Lhyn the way she loves you, or are you making the best of it? Your bondmate is in love with another woman."

With a start, Salomen understood the true impetus behind that offensive request. "I'm the one you're worried about?"

"You're the one I can't see. If you can't maintain this, then it all falls apart and everyone gets hurt."

"Great Mother," she said blankly. When had she last misinterpreted emotions to such a profound degree? "Thank you for your concern, but I'm not good at making the best of things that wound me. I tend to fight back."

"Did you fight against this?"

She nodded. "Once, when I thought Ekatya was a threat. That was probably heard all over the State House. I went home to Hol-Opah—"

"Andira swears that's why there was a summer windstorm that day," Lhyn said from the doorway. "The next time you were that angry, the autumn rains began a tick later. You have to admit, the coincidence is remarkable."

Her presence was like sunlight brightening a shadowy corner. Salomen smiled into the warmth. "You're the one who says a data set of two is useless."

"Under normal circumstances, sure. Since when are our circumstances normal?" She crossed the kitchen in five long strides and settled against the counter, hip to hip with Salomen. "She's not a victim, Elanor. Those two would never have gotten past their honor if she hadn't pushed them together."

"Hoi! I didn't act alone."

"I did give Ekatya a few nudges," she conceded.

"And Andira."

"True, but not until—um. That night." Her voice dropped. "That was a memorable conversation."

"That was a memorable night." Lost in green eyes and vivid memories, Salomen nearly forgot the third person in the room.

"On second thought, I don't think Sharing would be a good idea," Elanor announced.

Salomen had the courtesy to refrain from laughing at her, but the reminder of that night did give her a possible solution.

"Perhaps I can share something else that may help," she said. "I've been having nightmares since the battle."

Lhyn's surprise showed on her face. She knew Salomen had not told anyone else of this issue. There seemed little point when the classification of battle details meant she could never explain what was so unsettling about the dreams. But Elanor didn't need to know details.

"I dream that I'm on the Voloth flagship," she continued. "Alone. I can see them destroying Alsea, and I know that if Andira, Lhyn, and Ekatya were there with me, we could stop them. But Andira and Lhyn are here, dying. Ekatya is on her ship, dying. It's my fault because I didn't bring them with me. I stand there helpless, watching everything and everyone I love burn."

"That sounds horrific," Elanor said sympathetically. "But why would it be your responsibility to stop it all?"

"That isn't important. The point is, it's a dream about catastrophic failure and loss, and it wakes me sweating and terrified every time."

Andira had thought she would have nightmares about the captain who died while she was deep inside him, or the commodore's headless body, or the three other deaths she had witnessed. Disturbing as those memories were, they paled next to her experience on the Path of the Return. Alone in her despair, knowing that she had failed and all of Alsea would pay the price—that had settled into a part of her psyche that sent tendrils to the surface at least thrice per nineday, though it was gradually improving.

"But a tyree bond is a physiological connection to your partner," she continued. "Andira wakes at the same time I do, because she senses my distress. By the time I get my eyes open, she has me in a warmron. I wake terrified, but it only lasts for a piptick before I'm surrounded by her emotional presence. No nightmare can stand against that kind of bone-deep certainty." She saw Elanor's lack of comprehension and added, "When Lhyn and I sealed our bond, we also sealed that physiological connection."

"I woke when she did," Lhyn said. "For about two pipticks, I was afraid I wouldn't be able to do what Andira could." Pride and love shone in her eyes when she looked at Salomen. "But we'd talked about it before. I pulled her head to my chest and surrounded her physically. I can't project, but I have long arms and legs—"

"And your scent," Salomen put in. One thing she had learned from her separation training was how vitally important both scent and touch were to the instinctive part of her brain. "My body recognized your scent, your skin, before I was fully awake." She turned to Elanor. "I don't know what kind of proof you need. But there are only two people in this universe who could pull me from those nightmares so quickly."

"Ah," Elanor said after a moment of silence. "I think I understand."

38

SANCTUARY

Elanor's understanding did not translate into acceptance, but she was willing to reserve judgment. Lhyn had somehow brought Nikolay to a similar place. With the strain thus reduced, Salomen and Andira led their long-delayed house tour, unleashing what they had awaited since the first brick was laid: the transparent delight from Lhyn and Ekatya at seeing their new home. Lhyn fell instantly in love with the upstairs room reserved for her office, in particular its window seat and built-in bookshelves, while Ekatya was speechless to find their bedroom full of niches housing plants from the *Caphenon*—a blending of Fleet and Alsean tradition. Both rooms were otherwise left undecorated, as was the bathroom on their side of the upstairs.

"Prime Crafter Bylwytin said it's not your space unless you can make your own choices," Salomen said as they stood inside Lhyn's office.

"The Prime Builder *and* Crafter? How many Primes were involved in this?" Ekatya asked.

Salomen held up four fingers. "Prime Merchant Stasinal made sure we had the best materials and fast deliveries. Prime Producer Arabisar helped with the initial clearing and landscape design. I only asked for recommendations, but they jumped in themselves. They enjoyed working on something that didn't involve politics."

"And had swift, tangible results," Andira added. "You wouldn't believe how quickly this went from bare rock to a complete house."

Salomen glanced out the window, a familiar itching in her palms. "There hasn't been time to work on the landscaping, but I have plans for this moon."

They hadn't fully decorated the downstairs either, with the exceptions of the kitchen dome and guest room. When Ekatya protested that she was career Fleet and didn't know how to decorate, Andira pointed out that she did know how to make decisions. "Bylwytin will be here in six days," she added. "She's bringing a specialist. They're looking forward to working with all of us."

"Your heads of government know?" Nikolay asked incredulously. His sweeping gesture encompassed the four of them.

"We're sonsales, Gramps. We can't hide how we feel. I'm not Andira's little secret."

"I'm not a little anything," Lhyn said, instantly defusing the tension.

After the tour, Salomen found her alone in her new office. "For someone who claims to be a social misfit, you're certainly smoothing the path today," she observed.

Lhyn folded herself onto the window seat. "You mean after I blew it up? My stars, this is comfortable. I may never get out of it. And I'm only a social misfit in the Protectorate. Not here."

"No, not here." Salomen slipped in beside her. "How is it that you're the calmest one in the house?"

"I like Nikolay and Elanor, very much. But I don't need their approval." With a delighted grin, she swung her legs up and rested them across Salomen's lap. Even at full stretch, her toes did not touch the other side. "Oh, look at that. It's wide enough for me! You did that, didn't you?"

"Of course. I also made the kitchen counters the right height for me." Her hands fell naturally into place. "Fahla, I missed this. Being able to touch you."

"Me too. Did you know this house has five bedrooms upstairs? And one downstairs? That's four guest rooms."

"I did notice that, yes."

"Are we planning to have that many guests?"

"We're planning to have that many children."

"I don't think Ekatya or I can help you with that."

Salomen laughed; she had missed this easy connection more than the touching. "You can help more than you imagine. You may even want to add to it, in which case our children will have to share rooms. Rahel says Commander Lokomorra would be an excellent sperm donor for Gaians."

"Mm." Lhyn wiggled into a more reclined position. "That might take some convincing. For me, at least. Have you heard from her?"

"No, but I don't expect to. Not for the next few days. Which reminds me, did you hear that four of the divine tyree couples had accidental pregnancies last moon?"

"No! A twenty-six percent rate? That's staggering!"

"They're staggered, that's certain. None of them had an inkling. Though it shouldn't have surprised anyone, given the compulsion we were all under."

"Did you—?"

She shook her head. "We were careful. But even with all the joining, neither of us reached that point. Andira wore herself to a dull edge after the battle, and I've been either in the fields or overseeing this. Our hormones certainly hit the right levels, but they didn't have a chance to stay there. Thank Fahla; we're not ready yet. Next cycle, I hope."

They fell into a comfortable silence, enjoying the simple happiness of being together without hiding. Salomen was thinking they should probably rejoin the others when Lhyn's emotional signature shifted to a slightly darker hue.

"I know this is our home too," she began. "But I need to feel that I contributed. So will Ekatya. I've saved up some cinteks from my government work. Ekatya will be making a good salary—why are you smiling like that?"

"We knew you'd feel that way. And you have more than a few cinteks in your account." Salomen enjoyed her confusion; it wasn't often she saw that on her scholar tyree. "Remember that award you said you didn't need? The Sonalia Prize comes with a cash component. Whether or not you publicly accepted, you still earned that." She squeezed Lhyn's leg, interrupting the surge of denial. "You risked your life with the rest of us. So did Ekatya, and we all know she didn't do it for the Protectorate. You helped save Alsea. Yes, you earned it."

Lhyn subsided. "Does Ekatya know?"

"Based on what I'm sensing, she's learning about it now. Along with her grandparents. As soon as she inscribes in the warrior caste and opens an account, her award will be deposited."

"Ekatya in the warrior caste," Lhyn mused. "It was inevitable, wasn't it? I remember our first day here, when Andira came to see us in the healing center. She and Ekatya were speaking warrior code even then."

Salomen leaned back against the window. She had put Lhyn's office on the north side, knowing her priority would be protecting books and scrolls from sunlight, but the wide expanse of glass still admitted a great deal of indirect light. A mid-morning breeze had set the ancient trees rustling, conversing in a language even Lhyn could not hope to decipher. Beyond the buffer, the verdant fields of Hol-Opah stretched toward darker foothills, which in turn gave way to the great peaks of the Snow-mount Range.

All her life, she had looked onto these same fields and mountains. It seemed miraculous that Lhyn and Ekatya, who had traveled the galaxy, could be content in this ordinary place. Yet their emotions made it clear: this was a sanctuary for Ekatya and a true home for Lhyn.

"Inevitable," she repeated, watching the trees speak. "Yes, I think so."

39

CREATION

"This is not what I thought we'd be doing our first day." Dr. Wells bent over, the buzz of her instrument preparing Rahel for another round. "We don't usually spike reproductive hormones with discomfort."

Rahel closed her eyes as the needles bit into her skin. "It's only uncomfortable for a little while. I needed you to finish. Every time I looked in the mirror after bathing, all I could see was that unfinished quadrant."

"For the love of flight, it's on your *back*. You had to make a special effort to see it and be bothered by it."

"No, I didn't. I'd glance at the mirror as I walked out of the bathroom and there it was. Glaringly obvious." Her shoulder blade twitched.

Instantly, Dr. Wells lifted the instrument. "Do you need a moment?"

"No, I'm fine. It's only that spot. It tickles."

"Tickles," she snorted. "Mm-hm. Hold on, let me finish this flame and I'll be switching colors." The instrument buzzed again, multiple needles stitching color under her skin. "If all you could see was the unfinished parts, how have you survived until now?"

"It wasn't unfinished before. It was just starting. When you drew the outline on my front, I admired it every day. I thought, 'Hoi, look at that, there's half my phoenix.' Then you drew the other half and I had a full phoenix." The needles hit another sensitive area and she exhaled, forcing herself to lie still. "Then you started filling in the colors, and every part of it was another piece of the picture. It was all building."

"Until all that was left was this." Understanding filled the air around her. "Then it wasn't a matter of building any longer. It just wasn't done."

"You understand."

"I'm a painter. There, take a breath while I change ink."

Her body sank into the bed as she consciously relaxed her muscles. She didn't have words to explain how much pleasure this process brought her. Watching her phoenix come to life was one of the most intense joys she had ever experienced. The transformation of her skin into a story—a story of transformation itself—made her feel as if her outside was finally matching her inside. She had been reborn so many times now, saved by fate and Fahla and people who loved her even though she made mistakes.

Saved by the woman who was brushing a gentle hand across her skin before resuming her art.

She could not imagine getting this tattoo from anyone else. It was too personal. Dr. Wells was an integral part of the story taking wing on her body, and for all her grumbles and mutterings, she found joy in this, too. It soaked into Rahel's skin along with the ink, a deep happiness that was new to them both.

Wanting to commit every part of this to memory, she opened her eyes.

Dr. Wells sat on a stool that had been delivered from somewhere inside the pleasure house, stools not being standard furniture in the ceremony suites. She wore a robe loosely belted over a low-cut nightgown, both made of a fabric so finely woven as to seem liquid. The deep green color brought out her eyes and brightened her smile, which was already brilliant these days. Her hair was out of its usual twist, pulled back in a loose tail that softened the sharp planes of her face.

She was intently focused on her work, bending over to add color, straightening to view it from a better angle, bending again, then turning to fetch a new sterile cloth. Though the nightwear had been a shock—Rahel had never been certain Dr. Wells actually needed sleep—this was day one of their creation ceremony. They were not in this suite as professionals or even visiting friends. They were here to create life.

The instrument buzzed, stopped, and buzzed again, background music to the sensual banquet of Dr. Wells's movements, the bite of needles as they spread their colors, and the complex, radiant emotions that filled the room. Rahel tried to soak it in, all too aware that this was the last time.

And all too soon, it was over. It had lasted another hantick, but even a full day would not have been enough. Dr. Wells laid the instrument on the bedside table, blotted Rahel's skin, and rested a gloved hand on her back.

The sudden silence added a heavy echo to her stillness.

"It's done," she whispered. "Rahel, it's beautiful."

"May I see?"

"Give me a moment."

This close, it was impossible to ignore.

"I'm sad, too," Rahel said. "I was so anxious to get it done, and now . . ."

"Now it is. I feel like this every time I finish a painting. Eager to put on the final touches, then depressed that it's done. This is worse, though. You aren't a blank canvas." Her hand swept up to Rahel's neck and rubbed gently. "Thank you. For asking me. I can't tell you how much it's meant to me, being a part of this. But I don't have to tell you, and that means even more."

"Sometimes it's nice not to need the words, isn't it?"

A small laugh accompanied the lifting mood. "Yes, it is. Never thought I'd say that. Here." She retrieved the hand mirror from the table. "Have a look while I coat it."

The mirror showed an unexpected addition: brilliant sparks flitting above the flaming wing and head feathers of her phoenix. "Hoi! That's what you meant when you asked—oh, I love them. I need these on the front, too."

"I knew you would." Dr. Wells's head was down as she spread the aftercare ointment, but Rahel could hear the smug smile. "And now you see my cunning plan."

"We need another session." It wasn't over. Joy spread through her veins, unleavened by any sense of loss. Adding the sparks would take mere ticks, but that didn't matter. What mattered was having something to look forward to.

"One more, yes." Dr. Wells met her eyes in the mirror. "But not until you've helped me make a child."

Rahel grinned at her. "I'm working on it."

40

SEEING

"No wonder Ravenel was so happy. It's spectacular, Rahel."

"Isn't it? Mother almost cried. She says it looks exactly like her sculpture, except alive."

Rahel sat shirtless in the courtyard of the pleasure house, enjoying the rare warmth. Whitesun was unpredictable in its winter weather, offering howling storms interspersed with calm but cold days and, once in a great while, days like today. The air felt as soft as late spring, carrying scents of warm soil that would be gone tomorrow.

Here in the courtyard garden, surrounded by the building's stone walls, it was balmy enough to disrobe in comfort. She had chosen a bench beneath her mother's favorite cinnoralis tree and was now turned to the side, allowing Sharro a good view of the finished tattoo.

"It *is* alive," Sharro said. "Every breath you take is proof." She traced a gentle path up the length of the vertical scar, then down the arc of the second incision. "I would not see these if I didn't know they were here. Do you think of them?"

"I never really did, except to worry about Salomen seeing them. It's a relief to know she won't."

"Perfect truth isn't always kind," Sharro agreed. "Some truths don't need a voice."

An elderly couple exited a ground-floor massage room across the courtyard, the man supporting his older companion. As they left the protected inner walkway to step into the sunshine, he looked up and waved.

Rahel was unconcerned about her seminudity, which was common enough in this courtyard. But Sharro was not working today. She should not be subjected to the social necessity of speaking with a client.

"There's a client coming this way," she said. "Shall we move on?"

Sharro leaned out to look around her. "Ah! No, Timjan is special. She's been with me since the beginning. May I show her your tattoo?"

"Sure." Rahel had to laugh at herself. Of all people, she should have known better than to make assumptions about who was a client.

The man's expression brightened when Sharro beckoned them over. He spoke to Timjan, who lifted her head but did not immediately look at them. Instead, she turned her head from one side to the other.

Only then did Rahel become aware of the rapid clicks. They were emanating from the center ornament of a brightly colored band around Timjan's forehead.

"She's echolocating!"

"Yes. Timjan wants others to know what is possible, so I can tell you this: when she was seventy cycles, she lost her sight and her tyree in the same accident. She's one hundred and eight now."

Not only a survivor of a broken tyree bond, but one who had rewired her brain. Impressed and fascinated, Rahel watched her approach.

It was clear that Timjan was mapping her route with the reflected sound waves, and equally clear when her echolocation revealed the bench on which they sat. Her bearing and focus changed, and soon she stood in front of them, looking directly at Sharro through milky eyes that saw nothing.

"I'd recognize that emotional signature anywhere! Sharro, well met." She held up a hand for a palm touch. "And who is this beside you? She's tall. Legs out to the pathway."

"Well met, Timjan. I'm very pleased to introduce Rahel Sayana. Rahel, this is Timjan and her son, Cullodren."

"Well met," Rahel said politely, reaching for her hand.

"Aren't you a surprise! I've been hearing about you for many a cycle now. Thought I might meet Fahla before meeting you." Timjan's palm was warm and smelled strongly of massage oil.

"I haven't heard about you. Sharro never speaks of her clients. Cullo-dren, well met."

He murmured a greeting, his touch revealing shyness and awe.

"Bah. She could speak of me; I have no secrets. I've lived too long to worry about keeping any. I can tell you something she doesn't know, though."

"What is that?" Rahel liked her already.

"When they announced on the news that you would recover, I was selfishly glad. Selfish, I say. Had you Returned, it would have been a long time before Sharro could give comfort again. I don't have that kind of time."

"You have another tencycle at least," Sharro said. "And you forget, I get comfort here as well as giving it."

"Hmph. From some. May I?"

"Please do."

To Rahel's great surprise, Timjan reached for Sharro's face and began a gentle mapping with her hands.

"It's a good thing you like this oil," she said.

"It always reminds me of the day I first smelled it." Sharro smiled, her eyes closed in pleasure. "That was a good day."

"Indeed it was." Timjan slid her hands down the sides of Sharro's neck, then dropped a kiss on her forehead before straightening.

Rahel watched her with new respect. Sharro allowed few clients to touch her and none that she had met before now.

"Yes, I'm one of the fortunate ones," Timjan said, revealing her higher empathic rating. "I came to her after suffering a broken tyree bond. She was barely past her Rite of Ascension and just starting work here. Too young to help, I thought."

She couldn't imagine it. Sharro was ageless.

"She saved my life that first cycle. Saved my sanity the second. By then, she was as much a part of my life as the blood running through my veins."

"I know what you mean," Rahel said. "She saved my life, too. And my mother's."

Her face creased into a grin. "You and I should talk."

"Before you start collaborating," Sharro said, "I thought you might enjoy seeing Rahel's new tattoo."

"A tattoo! What is it?"

"Rahel, will you stand up?" Sharro rose with her and positioned her in front of Timjan. "Timjan, your hand."

Gently, she set Timjan's forefinger against the tattoo and began to trace the outline.

"This is the phoenix Ravenel sculpted for her. It's wrapped around her, front to back, starting at this wingtip." She moved the finger back and forth, tracing out the wing and its angle. "Here, on the edges of the feathers, it's half feather and half flame. Yellow as a honeywood campfire. But here, as you go down toward the wing bone, it cools to an orange-red. Like a binberry when it's ripe enough to eat."

"Ah." Timjan nodded. "Yes, I can see it."

Sharro described every part of the phoenix, asking Rahel to turn in place so they could trace the rest. When they reached the head, she said, "Be careful here. Her artist only finished coloring it yesterday." She let go and stepped away, but Timjan's hand remained.

"I can feel it. Slightly raised still. Does it hurt, child?"

Rahel had not been called that in twenty cycles. Stifling a laugh, she said, "Not at all. If I'm not careful with the ointment, it can itch, but my artist is with me here. She'll make sure it's treated properly."

"Good. She works here?"

"No, we're visiting for a few days."

"Hmph. There's more in that statement than your words say." She dropped her hand. "But it's not my place to ask. Thank you for showing me your tattoo. I have it all in my mind now. When Sharro mentions you again, that's what I'll see."

She was too polite to ask, but Rahel could sense the longing.

"Would you like to have my face in your mind as well?"

Her eyes nearly vanished in the wrinkles produced by her toothy grin. "Anyone can see Sharro's hand in your raising. Yes, I would like that very much."

She placed her hands unerringly atop Rahel's head and began running her fingers through the short strands. "Hair like the burning clouds just after sunset."

"You can tell that from feeling it?"

Her laugh echoed off the stone walls. "No, child. Sharro has told me all about you. She has a gift for painting verbal pictures. Golden eyes like the hide of a winden," she murmured, tracing Rahel's eyebrows. "Ringed in the dark brown of molwyn seeds. Small, delicate ears, yes, she said they were the only small thing about you. Ah, the strong jaw. Straight from your mother, I hear." She slid her hands along Rahel's neck and out to her shoulders. "Thank you again. You've added images to my sessions with Sharro. Those are priceless to me."

She and her son left soon after, walking slowly but steadily through the courtyard toward the administrative wing.

"Another of your rescues," Rahel said. "How many lives have you saved?"

"Not as many as you." Sharro watched them go with an affectionate smile.

"I was just in the right place at the right time."

"To believe so gives no weight to the choices that enabled you to be in that place and time." She looked over, her smile growing. "And now you choose to be here. Not to save a life, but to create one. Shall we go inside and get started on that?"

41

FULL CIRCLE

Rahel could not recall ever being so pampered. Her medical needs aboard the *Phoenix* guaranteed comfort-giving sessions at least twice per week, but that did not compare to this.

Each morning, she went to the warrior caste house for stave practice, followed by a shower and a blissful hantick in the centering room. There she would lie beneath the exotic potted trees, surrounded by fellow warriors and the scent of cinnoralis, and let her energies reset.

Upon returning to the pleasure house, she would find either her mother or Sharro waiting. Sometimes they gave comfort, other times simply their company, which was a comfort in itself. On the third day, they left Little Mouse with a minder and came together. That enabled a wonderful session in which she rested her head on Sharro's lap, her legs on her mother's, and sank into the bliss of dual caresses. They surrounded her with love, for each other as well as her, and she could not imagine a finer feeling.

Colonel Micah and Dr. Wells would emerge from their bedroom in time to share midmeal, after which Dr. Wells would inject Rahel and check her hormone levels. They remained high, a fact Rahel could attest to given the tender swelling just beneath the curve of her molwine and directly above her opening.

The losslyn, it was called. The hidden seed.

Dr. Wells would then take over for another comfort-giving session, boosting the effects of the hormone injection. When that ended, Rahel retired to her bedroom for the purely mechanical requirement: stimulation of her molwine, focusing on the correct side for losslyn growth. It was necessary five times per day and became more pleasurable each time.

As Dr. Wells explained, they had created a positive feedback loop. The injected hormones increased her receptivity, which led to greater pleasure during masturbation, which led to higher hormone levels and thus more pleasure, all in service of the losslyn. She examined it regularly, fascinated by the idea that this unused and normally unseen part of her body was busily producing a sperm packet.

She tried not to think about the moment when she would have to release it.

Late afternoons found the three of them taking advantage of the pleasure house's offerings. Massage, aromatherapy, a soak in the hot pool followed by a cold plunge, and some of the finest rajalta ever poured in Whitesun were all included in the rental price of the ceremony suite. So was the excellent evenmeal delivered to their rooms, which they ate together while chatting about anything and everything. This, too, was part of the ceremony: the intimacy of knowing one another through questions and honest answers. The tradition was designed to build trust, and Rahel found it quite effective with Colonel Micah.

By the evening of the third day, she even managed to stop calling him that.

"What about me?" Dr. Wells asked.

"With him, it's just dropping the rank. With you, it's a whole different name."

"Work on it."

Rahel didn't point out that commands like that were precisely the reason she was still Dr. Wells.

On the fourth day, Micah shocked her.

It was after her hormone injection, while she lay with her head in Dr. Wells's lap. Their sofa faced the enormous window looking onto the courtyard garden, which was bending under the fury of another winter storm. Dr. Wells massaged her scalp while they watched the wind racing through the trees, and Rahel never wanted this ceremony to end.

She sensed Micah's approach long before he reached them.

"May I join you?" he asked.

Silently, she bent her knees, making room for him at the other end of the sofa.

"No. I would like to take Alejandra's place."

She goggled at him, her mental cacophony so loud that the only word she could utter was, "Why?"

He crouched down, bringing their heads level. "We have history, you and I. We've forgiven each other, yes, but I've allowed that history to stop me from fully participating in the creation of our child. Alejandra opened my eyes this morning, and she's correct. It was never solely her job to be your comfort giver."

"She's been my comfort giver since I joined the *Phoenix*. You and I don't have that kind of relationship."

"Not before," he said gravely. "Now it's different. Were we any other couple with a surrogate—"

"I'd be joining with you," she interrupted. "Or with a provider over in the joining services wing. I'm not any other surrogate. You don't need to do this."

"I want to."

There was no dissonance of untruth. Whatever Dr. Wells had said that morning had altered his thinking.

"Only if you're comfortable with it," he added. "If you're not, I'll go and leave you two in peace."

She had almost killed him. Helping Dr. Wells have a child was not just an act of love for her friend and mentor. It was also restitution for her crime.

"Do you know how to be gentle with a warrior?" she asked, only half joking.

A few ticks later, her head rested on a pillow in his lap while he received lessons in touching her from Dr. Wells. Rahel stared up at him, not quite believing she was in this position.

"Like this?"

His touch was so tentative that she cringed, squeezing her eyes shut. "That feels like a hairy watcher crawling on my face."

Dr. Wells laughed. "Not *that* gentle. She's not me. You can be a little firmer."

On his next attempt, Rahel let out a relieved breath. "Much better.

Thank Fahla, I don't think I could have withstood that for longer than a tick."

"That's not what I usually hear—"

"Oh, don't," Dr. Wells said with a groan.

He grinned down at Rahel. "I'm holding back the jokes."

It was easier after that, and soon he was touching her as if he had never been nervous. Dr. Wells took up a new position at the other end of the sofa, pulling Rahel's feet into her lap and beginning a massage.

Of the many surreal moments in her life, Rahel thought this ranked among the top three.

She uncrossed her hands from her stomach and pressed one against Micah's hip, where synthetic bone replaced what she had destroyed with a disruptor. When he showed no discomfort, she slid her hand upward. The skin beneath his shirt was smooth and warm, fully healed after she had burned it away along with several spans of intestine.

She had already apologized. Would it ever be enough?

The skin contact revealed no residual resentment. He was curious, calm, and understanding.

With her eyes closed, she didn't see him move until a weight came down on her leg.

"Where?" he asked in his deep rumble.

She picked up his hand and replaced it midway down her thigh, sliding it to the inside in a gesture that would have been sexual in any other setting. "Here."

Half a tick passed in marveling silence. Through the hand still pressed against his side, she felt the full impact of his wonder as each of them covered the once-grievous wounds they had caused the other.

"Your record said the shrapnel severed your superficial femoral artery." His quiet voice broke the stillness. "The healers called it fortunate that it was fully embedded, because if any of it had still protruded, you might have tried to pull it out."

"And if I had, I would have bled out before I could get to the healing center. They told me when I woke up." She opened her eyes to find him watching her. "I would have tried. Walking down that tunnel with it in place—" She stopped. "I would have tried."

"I'm glad you didn't."

"So am I." Dr. Wells gripped her ankles, a firm touch that reinforced her emotion. "When we focus on the things we wish we could change, we forget about the things that happened for the best."

"You sound like Sharro."

"I like Sharro, but no. That's from Lanaril."

Rahel nodded; they did have a similar philosophy. Regardless of its source, she understood the message. Another apology would not be welcome. This ceremony was about their future, not their past.

Remembering Timjan, she lifted her hand to Micah's face and closed her eyes once more.

"A strong jaw." She smiled at the realization. "Like me. Your child will have a strong jaw."

"Our child," he corrected.

"Our child," Dr. Wells said at the same time. "Yours, his, and mine."

Rahel mapped his face with her fingertips, her thoughts whirling with the tactile sensations and the sudden understanding that this child would be a blend of them both. Until now, she had thought of herself as a donor giving a gift, an involvement that would end tomorrow.

But their invitation was clear: her involvement did not have to end. She could be family.

"Our child," she whispered.

42

LOSSLYN

The fifth day was simultaneously the best and the worst. What was once novel was now a sublime routine, one Rahel reveled in while mourning its inevitable demise. Early morning at the caste house, a cup of rajalta with Sharro and Ravenel, comfort giving and conversation until midmeal . . .

Normal life would be a letdown after this.

She received her final hormone injection with a sudden bout of nerves, rubbing the injection site in an automatic motion that Dr. Wells did not miss.

"Does it hurt? Sting?"

"No, sorry." Embarrassed, she crossed her arms. "I didn't mean to worry you."

"But something's wrong."

Long experience had taught her the futility of deflection when Dr. Wells had this determined edge to her emotions.

"What if I can't?" she blurted. "I've never done it before. You've both put so much time and effort into this. My mother and Sharro, too. What if—"

Dr. Wells was shaking her head, concern evaporating under the shining light of confidence. "This isn't a matter of skill or experience. It's biology. Your hormone levels are optimal, your losslyn growth is right on schedule, everything is working as it should. We'll have a lovely last day here, and after a good soak and a massage, you'll go in there and catch a sperm packet." She squeezed Rahel's upper arm. "Don't worry. Your body knows what to do."

Her conviction was contagious, propelling Rahel through the rest of what was indeed a lovely day. The massage left her muscles liquified, a condition exacerbated by a long soak in the hot pool. They stayed until none of them could stand it a piptick longer, climbing out with loud exhalations of relief. These were soon followed by shrieks as they jumped into the cold plunge pool, with Dr. Wells exiting immediately and rolling her eyes while Micah and Rahel competed to stay in the longest.

"Bigger body, better insulation," Micah gloated when Rahel was forced to give up.

"But she has better sense," Dr. Wells retorted, comfortably wrapped in her robe. "Are you trying to freeze off important body parts? I have plans for those."

Rahel grinned as she toweled herself dry. "I'm going to remember this. The day she said I have more sense than you."

"She said better," Micah pointed out. "That doesn't mean more."

"I can't believe you're arguing about it." Dr. Wells held out a towel. "Get out of there."

That night's evenmeal and comfort giving were the easiest yet. Rahel settled into position with her head on Micah's lap, yesterday's awkwardness banished by honesty and a priceless physical connection. Dr. Wells took up her position at the other end of the sofa, and Rahel did her best to absorb every touch, word, and emotion of this final session.

She might have felt more bereft at its end had her task not loomed so large.

They moved to her bedroom door, where Dr. Wells held out a cylindrical container. "Give me a ten-tick head start."

"Is that all it takes to get him ready?"

She arched a brow with a wicked smirk. "I know which buttons to push."

"She does," Micah confirmed. He was already halfway there, judging by his emotional signature and the fact that he could barely look away from Dr. Wells.

Rahel hid a smile; she would get no good-luck wish from him.

"Let's make a child," she said, and stepped through the door.

One unforeseen consequence of living with a low empath and a sonsales was that she received regular secondhand doses of their arousal. Before she could pull off her second shoe, their levels had spiked. Dr. Wells hadn't wasted any time.

She piled the pillows against the headboard and sat nestled among them, comfortably reclined but elevated enough to see. The passion filling the suite was affecting her in ways it hadn't before. She felt heavy and wanting, highly aware of their activity and easily imagining herself with a phantom lover, someone who would do something about the pressure in her losslyn. It had been itching all day. Here in the privacy of her room, she was finally free to reach down and rub out the itch.

"Shek!" she gasped, curling up as every nerve in her body screeched its overload. "Oh, ouch, fucking fuck, that hurt."

As soon as the pain faded, she laughed at both her idiocy and her instinctive use of the Common swear phrase. Candini would be gleeful when she heard about it.

The next attempt was far more gentle. She drew her fingers down both pelvic ridges to converge on the curve of her molwine, barely brushing the sensitive ridge between her legs. When her body responded with immediate delight, she let a fingertip drift down and across the losslyn. That, too, felt extremely good.

Bringing her finger lower still, she circled her opening while using her other hand to gently stroke her molwine. Her eyes slammed shut as sparks flew up her spine and all the way out to her fingertips. Ten ticks? The way this felt, she'd be lucky to last five.

She lost herself in the sensations, clenching her jaw as they spiraled up and up. The thought occurred that she should have set a timer; she had no idea how many ticks had passed. Should she be delaying or hurrying?

"Shek it," she grumbled, and rubbed faster. *Your body knows,* Dr. Wells had said. Well, it certainly knew that it wanted release.

The building tension had pressed her head back into the pillows when a tiny voice reminded her that she needed to be able to see. With great effort, she lifted her head and cupped one hand in place, ready to catch the packet. Were she joining with a partner, their molwines would be in contact and her sperm packet would be expelled directly into the entrance of its destination. For this, her hand would have to suffice.

Her entire body was coiled and trembling. She was overheating, breathless and sweaty, every nerve straining for the signal—and then it came, a violent release that first folded her body double, then laid it out flat. As the painful pleasure rushed through her pelvis, something hit her palm.

She closed her hand on air.

Her body was still tingling when she bolted upright, terrified that she had lost the sperm packet.

It was lying between her legs, surrounded by glittering lubrication powder that had burst out with it. She grabbed the container off the bedside table, popped the lid, and bent forward.

"Oh," she whispered, startled by its movement.

She had seen footage before, but nothing compared to watching her own sperm packet slowly elongating, contracting, and elongating again. An iridescent sheen rippled over its surface, splashes of blue, green, and red swirling together and apart as it strove toward its goal. It had been created for one purpose and was doing its best to fulfill it: to crawl between the warm, lubricated inner ridges and find the egg.

But there was no warmth and no egg, only a cold, barren bed.

Feeling sorry for it, Rahel picked it up and set it inside the clear container, where a heated bed of artificial lubrication powder waited. "That will keep you toasty," she said, latching the lid.

It did seem happier, moving more smoothly and perhaps a little faster. She was still watching when the passion in the other bedroom broke through her concentration, reminding her of their unfinished business.

"You have a mission," she told the little packet. "Come on, let's get you delivered."

Dr. Wells answered the door wearing a robe tied so loosely that Rahel wondered why she bothered. "Did you—?"

Her eyes lit up at the sight of the container. She grabbed it and spun around, then turned back and pulled Rahel into a one-armed warmron.

"Thank you," she said hastily. "Have to go now."

The door closed behind her.

Rahel stood for a moment, amused by the whirlwind that had just blown past. Shaking her head, she turned for her room and a hot shower.

She was halfway across the living area when the wave of joy hit.

43

HEAVY TRUTH

A descending shriek accompanied the small body of Jaros Opah as he plummeted toward the plunge pool. The shrill sound cut off when he hit the water, leaving Vellmar to wonder whether he had stopped screaming or whether he was now terrifying fish and aquatic invertebrates.

"If we could record and amplify his scream, we could weaponize it," she commented.

Beside her, Lancer Tal chuckled. "True words. The Voloth would never know what hit them. We could have incapacitated them from the outside before boarding."

"That would have made things easier for me."

Jaros had surfaced and was now paddling toward Salomen, who treaded water while holding the floater ring for him. "Cheater!" he cried, his voice echoing off the canyon walls. "You're farther away!"

"I don't believe so," Salomen said with exaggerated innocence. "Are you sure you didn't jump farther away?" With a quick kick, she moved out of reach of his questing fingers, leading to an outbreak of giggles and accusations.

"For the love of Fahla." On Vellmar's other side, Lanaril tilted up her sunhat. "You two are on holiday. Can you not think like warriors for a hantick?"

"Can you not think like a templar?" Lancer Tal countered.

"At least templars know how to enjoy a free day." Sliding the sunhat down, she leaned back in her chair and dug her toes into the warm sand. "Ahh. There's nothing like sun on skin."

"You're not baring enough skin to benefit," Vellmar noted. "I could assist with that."

"Nice try. We've embarrassed Elanor and Nikolay enough already. They don't know what to think of a Lead Templar sunbathing nude."

"Not to mention a Lancer." Wearing only what she was born in, Lancer Tal stretched her arms overhead with a satisfied hum. "Ekatya did say they come from a more conservative part of the Protectorate."

"How is she so different?" Vellmar watched Captain Serrado sneak up behind Lhyn, bare shoulders showing above the water.

"She's Fleet."

"So was her grandfather."

"He's retired. I don't know, Vellmar. They don't always make sense to me."

The captain set her hands on Lhyn's shoulders and surged up, pushing her bondmate beneath the surface. Jaros gleefully joined the ensuing water fight, splashing first Serrado and then Lhyn as he switched sides without shame.

"That puts a lid on it," Vellmar said. "He'll never be a warrior. Too little honor."

As if to prove her point, Jaros turned and began splashing his sister, who hadn't even entered the fight.

"Ah, but you're assuming his mission was to support one side." Lancer Tal shaded her eyes, watching the flying water. "Perhaps the true objective was more subtle. Perhaps he wants a broader war."

Salomen dove under and reappeared on Jaros's other side, drenching him with a sweep of her arm.

"Good point. I think he's achieved it," Vellmar said as Lhyn splashed all three combatants in a flurry of indiscriminate flailing.

Lanaril let out a throaty laugh. "You really cannot stop yourselves, can you?"

For another laugh like that, Vellmar would keep joking all day. "A good warrior never overlooks an opportunity to learn. Lancer Tal just taught me a valuable lesson. I underestimated Jaros."

"Never underestimate Jaros," Lancer Tal agreed. "He's as devious as his sister while looking twice as innocent. He won over Ekatya's grandparents within five ticks of meeting them."

Downstream, on the broadest section of the pool's south beach, the rest of their swim party was finishing a late midmeal. The Opah men were dressed once more, as was Marinda, the woman Nikin was courting. Nikolay and Elanor had never removed their swimwear.

"I think all the Opahs have won them over," Vellmar observed. "They seem much more accepting of your bonds since meeting them."

"They were more accepting as soon as I mentioned the media announcement. Knowing that we're making this public put half their fears to rest. But yes, Salomen's family helped a great deal." Lancer Tal pushed herself out of the low chair and donned her short trousers. A loose shirt followed, which she sealed only enough to cover her breasts. "May I ask you to accompany me to the house? I have something to discuss with both of you."

Lanaril pushed back her hat. "You cannot do it here?"

"It's a conversation best conducted with chilled spirits." She gestured upstream, where the Silverrun tumbled over the rocky wall. "Shall we?"

Salomen waved as they climbed to the top of the waterfall. Whatever Lancer Tal had planned, she obviously knew and approved. Her wave was cut short when Jaros wrapped his arms around her neck, and she fell back with a theatrical gurgle.

Vellmar laughed as she followed the others across the new footbridge. It had been constructed at the same time as the house, along with the steps that now offered easy access up the canyon wall. Both were built from local stone, blending into the landscape while standing firm against the spring and autumn floods.

They emerged at the top of the canyon and continued down the narrow path toward the house. Native plants bordered it on both sides, fitting the landscape as naturally as if Fahla herself had placed them. They hadn't been there two days ago.

"When did Salomen have time to do this?" she asked.

At the head of their little procession, Lancer Tal spoke over her shoulder. "She and Elanor finished it yesterday, just before sunset. They've been doing quite a lot of planting over the past nineday," she explained to Lanaril. "It turns out that Elanor is a devout gardener. You can imagine how that's helped things along."

"Oh, yes. What an unexpected benefit." Lanaril's thin wraparound skirt brushed the ground as she bent to touch a scented herb. She rubbed a leaf, then lifted her fingers to her nose and inhaled. "Divine."

They mounted the wooden steps to the deck, where Lancer Tal invited them to sit while she fetched the spirits. Lanaril chose a chair facing downstream and pointed at the jar of small, flame-red flowers on the table. "Their State House quarters are always graced with the best bouquets the staff can create. Somehow, I find Salomen's little bouquets far more charming."

"She makes them with love," Vellmar said. "Perhaps we sense it, still lingering on the stems."

The look Lanaril gave her made her toes curl. "When you speak that way, I want to—"

"Here we are." Lancer Tal reappeared with three glasses in one hand and a bottle in the other. "Did I interrupt something?"

"Yes," Vellmar grumbled.

"Well, there's an unused guest room upstairs if you're still in the mood after this. It hasn't yet been sanctified."

"Where are Nikolay and Elanor sleeping?" Lanaril asked.

"In the downstairs guest room. They're blissfully unaware of room choices upstairs and no wiser when we come down for mornmeal. Nor do they wish to be." A practiced twist of the wrist opened the bottle, blue vapor emerging only to be whisked away by the light breeze. She filled the glasses, handed two across the table, and held hers up as she took her seat. "To Fahla and Alsea."

"To Fahla and Alsea," Vellmar echoed. It sounded so different as a toast, rather than a battle cry.

"Thank you for coming today." Lancer Tal set her glass down and leaned back, looking as rested and comfortable as Vellmar had ever seen her. "It may not be an official bonding break, but it feels like one when our friends are with us."

"It's an honor to be considered so." Lanaril set a hand on Vellmar's thigh, a casual gesture that still made her heart beat faster. "What sort of discussion requires these very fine spirits? And must be opened with a declaration of friendship?"

A smile flitted across the Lancer's face as she looked downstream, where the swimmers could be heard above the sound of the waterfall. "I've had time to slow down and think here. Think and watch and, perhaps, understand things I didn't before." Her gaze shifted to the little jar on the table. "Salomen put these canyon starfires on the dining table yesterday morning. They were closed then, so all we saw was this."

Gently, she bent the petals of one flower upward, showing their silver undersides.

"She said that's the source of their name. When they're closed, they're the color of starlight. When they open, they're like the star itself. A heart of fire."

"Starfires." Vellmar tilted a flower back and forth, captivated by this different view of a plant she had seen hundreds of times. "I didn't know that. It's a perfect name."

"Isn't it? I've watched Salomen and Ekatya unfold this past nineday, like starfires. They're both stunning when they're open and free. Absolutely beyond compare. I realized that I'm enjoying their freedom while imposing constraints on others."

Lanaril's hand tightened on her thigh. "Andira. Are you sure?"

"I'm sure that Vellmar deserves to make the choice."

Their attention swung to Vellmar, who felt like a first-cycle trainee being inspected. "What choice?"

Lancer Tal drew the flower from the jar and spun it slowly between her fingers. "When you told Lanaril about your role in the battle plan, she didn't talk to me for five days. She ignored messages, wouldn't take my calls—I had to resort to trickery to get her to see me. She was furious with me for risking your life."

Lanaril looked shamefaced. "It was not my finest moment. I regret that now."

"You have nothing to regret." She lifted the starfire to her nose and inhaled, then held it out. "But I do."

Vellmar accepted the flower automatically. There were undercurrents here that she didn't understand.

"Lanaril is a dear friend," Lancer Tal told her. "Losing her regard hurt in ways I didn't expect. The kindest thing would have been to let her be angry and work through it in her own time. But I didn't know if you would survive your mission. If you were killed, I feared losing her friendship forever. So I did the selfish thing. I told her the truth."

"Why was that selfish?"

"Because it burdened her with a secret. One she had to keep from you."

For half a piptick, she wondered why this was an issue when Lanaril kept a thousand secrets a day due to her temple work. Then the understanding hit: this was a secret about *her*.

It was a blow straight to her weakest point. Having convinced Lanaril to give her a chance despite her youth and far lower rank, she was ever aware of their differences and always striving to bridge them. Lanaril holding a significant secret about her, in concert with Lancer Tal, made that gulf seem wider.

"I understand that she can't share everything with me," she said, trying for an even tone.

"She can share this, if you choose it." Lancer Tal leaned forward, her expression shifting. Despite her short sleeves and damp, swim-tangled hair, she suddenly looked every bit the Lancer. "Be aware, though, this is a heavy truth. There is a good reason why I haven't told you, and why she agreed to keep the secret. She did it for you. She wanted you to enjoy your life unburdened by it."

Vellmar tilted the flower, watching the brilliant red-orange petals shift to a silvery white. "It sounds as if you're saying only one of us can live freely. Either Lanaril keeps your secret so I can stay happily ignorant, or I take this burden, whatever it is, and free her."

"It's not that great a burden," Lanaril said. "Nor is it something you need to know today. It will come naturally, in its own time. Don't do it for me."

"Of course I'll do it for you."

"Fianna—"

"What did I promise, that night in your garden? To take what burdens I could from you. If this is so big that it will affect how I live my life, I don't see how it can also be so small that you don't mind the burden. Can you give me skin contact and tell me that again?"

Lanaril's hesitation was answer enough.

She set the starfire back in its jar. "Tell me."

With an approving nod, Lancer Tal relaxed into her chair. "Lanaril and I have dropped our fronts with each other for a long time. I would like to do that now, if you're willing."

Of all the things she had imagined, this was at the bottom of the list. It was equivalent to a promotion. No, it was better than that.

"I would be honored," she managed.

The Lancer's front fell a moment later. Lanaril added her familiar emotions to the mix, leaving Vellmar so overwhelmed by the combination that she only belatedly realized her own front was still up. It took conscious effort to let it go.

Lancer Tal was *proud* of her. Vellmar didn't give a fanten's fart what this mysterious truth might be; it was worth it for that alone.

"When Lanaril finally spoke to me, I realized that her anger wasn't only because I was risking your life. She thought I considered you expendable."

Well, that was a confusing opening. "I am. We all are, in service to Alsea."

"That wasn't the issue," Lanaril said reluctantly. "This is not an easy thing to admit. In my fear of losing you, I lost sight of the truth. I believed that Andira . . . didn't care about you." Relieved at getting the worst out, she spoke more quickly. "I thought she couldn't, not if she was willing to throw you into the most dangerous part of that battle. How could she do that unless she saw you only as a resource to be used?"

That didn't help; of course she was a resource. She looked to Lancer Tal for clarification.

"I told Lanaril that nothing could be further from the truth. Yes, you were an asset. But not just any asset, and not one I risked lightly. Vellmar, you're more valuable to me than any warrior other than Micah."

This was straight out of her fantasies and therefore suspect. She glanced at the bottle, wondering if those spirits had a little something extra.

"Have you noticed that I've been mentoring you? Spending more time teaching you to think tactically and plan long-term strategies?"

"Yes." It came out as a croak. "Are you going to tell me you didn't do that with Gehrain when he was your Lead Guard?"

"Micah taught Gehrain, not me. If I'm going to train a warrior to that degree, it won't be for the position of Head or Chief Guardian. I would only invest that kind of time for a higher post."

What was higher than Chief Guardian of the Lancer? That was the ultimate fantasy of most warriors in the protective services, equivalent to a base commander but at the heart of government. The only positions higher than that were caste Prime or—

Her brain froze.

Lancer Tal smiled. "I did warn you that it was a heavy truth."

"You—I—but that's—you're not joking," she finished weakly.

"No, I'm not. I want you to be Lancer after I retire."

"Fahla on a shekking funstick!" She clapped a hand over her mouth.

Amusement curled around her senses as Lanaril rubbed her thigh. "Don't ever change."

"I'm sorry, it just came out."

"I think, in this instance, it might be justified."

Vellmar covered her hand, taking comfort from her presence while the world tilted on its axis. "Why me?"

"Oh, so many reasons. I chose you after you helped me kill my monster. No, that's not quite right. It was after our talk in Lanaril's garden, when I realized what you had done. You learned quickly, you adapted under combat pressure, you made a hard choice with hard consequences, and you were willing to pay the price for it. You were loyal, courageous, and honorable beyond reproach. I've seen all those traits displayed repeatedly since then, not least when you seized control of the *Vengeance*."

"But I'm not qualified!" she blurted, dazzled by the shower of compliments. With her front down, it was clear that Lancer Tal meant every one of them.

"Not yet. That's why I'm training you. I could teach anyone the art of politics, but to *govern*—that requires characteristics that cannot be taught. You have them all. Given time, you'll be more qualified than anyone on Alsea."

"Except you."

"I won't be Lancer forever."

That was a terrifying thought. "I don't want you to retire."

The moment it left her mouth, she heard how childish it sounded. Fortunately, Lancer Tal understood.

"I know. That's why I didn't want to tell you."

"You can say no," Lanaril offered.

Vellmar caught Lancer Tal's eye and saw the knowledge there. "No, I can't. Not now that I know she's chosen me. It's my duty."

"It's your *life*, Fianna."

"My highest duty is to Alsea." If Lancer Tal thought she was the best person to succeed her, then that was her path. To step off would be a cowardly betrayal of not just the Lancer's belief, but also her oath as a warrior.

She closed her eyes, absorbing the sun's warmth and the faint sounds of the swimmers. A heavy truth? This was the weight of the world. Yes, she would have to win an election someday, but with Lancer Tal behind her, she did not doubt the outcome. Someday, she would be responsible for everything and everyone around her.

In that moment, she understood the gift Lancer Tal had tried to give her.

"You spoke truth about the burden," she said. "But I think it might be better this way. I'd rather know what I'm preparing for."

"It does make it easier to train you," Lancer Tal agreed.

"What would you have done if I'd chosen not to know?"

"I'd have begun the search for a better candidate."

Lanaril looked between them, confusion blurring the edges of her emotional signature. "Why?"

"Because I would have put my comfort before yours," Vellmar answered. "It was a test."

"A test?!"

Lancer Tal held up a placating hand. "Not like that, Lanaril. I truly did want to lift the weight I laid on you. If I've learned anything over the past cycle, it's that living openly is the greatest freedom we have."

"But if I chose selfishly, I wouldn't be the kind of Lancer Alsea needs. I'd be the kind we've had too often before now."

"You validate my choice more with every word." Pride washed across the table as Lancer Tal lifted her glass. "To the State Chair. May it go to the deserving and not the desiring."

That was a toast Vellmar could drink to. "I'll have to start thinking about my own Chief Guardian," she said, reaching for the bottle to refill their glasses. "Since I won't be one myself. I'd want Rahel, but she's too happy in space."

"One of the most difficult duties of a Lancer is to make decisions for the sake of Alsea, not individuals. If you truly believe Rahel would serve

Alsea better as your Chief Guardian than on one of our ships, you should ask her. She would not refuse."

Not too long ago, that post would have been Rahel's dream. No, she would not refuse. She would even make the best of it, serving as ably in the State House as she did on the *Phoenix*. Vellmar would love nothing more than to have her friend so close, both a companion and a warrior she could trust with her life.

But would that be the best use of her skills?

"We need her up there more than I need her down here," she concluded. "We have too few trained people for the crews we need to fill. Ronlin would be a better choice."

The warmth of approval confirmed her decision. "I agree." Lancer Tal tilted her glass toward the waterfall. "But even if I didn't, you still couldn't have her. I'm not the only one who has chosen a successor."

44

THE GIFT

Shortly after dawn, Rahel left the pleasure house and took a magtran to the central park, where she walked among the great caste houses and fretted.

That joyous rush last night had been from Micah, a product of instinctive knowledge that the sperm packet and egg had met. Contact was only the first step, however. The packet had to dissolve and release its sperm, and fertilization took several hanticks. They had all gone to sleep last night not knowing the outcome, and Dr. Wells and Micah were still asleep this morning.

She didn't know.

Our child, they had agreed, and she didn't know if it existed.

The uncertainty drove her hardest workout since the battle. After showering, she unrolled a mat in the centering room and attempted to calm herself. Such ridiculous agitation over a small issue, a matter that affected just three people and endangered no one, was not worthy of a warrior.

Twenty ticks later, she rerolled her mat in disgust. She had no more command over her mind than a first-cycle trainee; there was no point in further effort. She would return to the pleasure house and face whatever truth Fahla decided to give them.

The magtran skimmed through its transparent tube above the city and beneath a foreboding sky, where thick clouds blocked all but a tiny fraction of light. Wildwind Bay churned with waves from the earlier storm, only a few ships daring to sail its waters. It felt like late afternoon, though the temple had yet to ring its midmorning bells.

Upon disembarking, she stood outside the magtran station and contemplated the elegant stone walls of the pleasure house directly across the street. Dr. Wells and Micah had surely woken and run the test by now. Her answer was there, waiting.

"Be kind to us," she entreated the dark sky. "Or at least to them."

The familiar arched entry welcomed her to the lobby, where she greeted the clerk on her way to the courtyard. Though it would have been faster to cut across the garden, she turned left and strolled around the protected interior walkway, a small cheat that added half a tick to her time. The ringing of her boot heels on flagstones was too loud in the quiet space.

Halfway around, she climbed the outside stairs to the third level and reentered the building, now in a richly decorated corridor. Thick rugs silenced her steps, a change that seemed ominous when she arrived at the door to their suite.

Only one set of emotions was present within. Micah still slept, but Dr. Wells was awake and broadcasting a quiet sadness that went straight through her heart.

She set a hand against the carved wood and rested her forehead beside it, heavy with sorrow.

No, she told herself. *This is her grief, not yours. Go in there and help.*

Squaring her shoulders, she opened the door and stepped inside.

Dr. Wells stood at the floor-to-ceiling windows in the living area, arms crossed as she gazed into the courtyard. She was fully dressed, her hair up in its usual twist, and appeared more professional than she had in the last five days.

At the sound of the door, she turned and unleashed a blinding smile. "There you are!"

Her elation nearly flattened Rahel, who stood blinking at the sudden shift.

"It—it worked?"

"It did. He's pregnant." The smile dimmed, then crumpled. "We made a child," she choked out.

Rahel met her halfway and held on tight. "Fahla's farts, it worked!"

"Fahla's blessings, you mean." She laughed once, a short huff of air that turned into a gasp. "And yours. You made this happen. I will never, *never*—"

She could not finish the sentence, instead allowing her tightened grip to speak for her.

Rahel rocked her, overcome by the shift in their dynamic. She doubted it would last longer than a few ticks, but in this moment, she was honored to support the person who had done so much to support her.

"Thank you," Dr. Wells whispered.

"It was my pleasure. Literally," Rahel added, smiling at the laugh that brought out. "You worried me. You weren't happy a tick ago."

"Oh, I've been up and down like a wallball, as Micah would say. Flying without a ship one moment, terrified of losing it the next, feeling sad about Josue." Dr. Wells pulled away, wiping her cheeks. "He won't be my only child anymore. He'll be my first child. I don't know why that's suddenly so hard, but it is."

"He's still your only child in your first life."

"Birth and rebirth, hm? You'd know about that." She was back in control, smiling with wet eyes. "I don't think I dared believe it until now. All this time I've been focused on hormone levels and taking care of you and Micah—I never let myself think past the details. Now it's all I *can* think about. If everything goes well, I'll be a mother again." Wryly, she added, "The sleepless nights have already begun. Micah and I woke up and ran the test at night two. I have no idea how he managed to fall asleep after that, but I was up for another hantick, watching him."

Rahel grinned at the vision. "The great protector is now the one under guard?"

"Hm, not quite." Dr. Wells led her to the sofa. "But it might come to that. I make no promises that I won't be the most unrelenting expectant parent in Alsean history. No, I was watching him and thinking about cell division."

Already reeling under the wild swings of emotion and profound relief, Rahel collapsed onto the cushion and burst into laughter.

"Cell division," she wheezed. "Only you would say that. You are a healer down to the soles of your feet."

Dr. Wells shrugged, the careless gesture belied by her sparkling eyes.

"I was remembering the first time I saw fertilization under a microscope. The egg divided into two cells, then four, then eight, right before my eyes. It was magical. Life creating itself in real time. I watched Micah last night and thought, 'It's happening in him right now.' A miracle in every way. How can I sleep through a miracle?"

"You were asleep when I left for the caste house," Rahel pointed out.

"Well, it turns out that creating a miracle is exhausting." She leaned back against the sofa, comfortable and loose in a way Rahel had rarely seen before this ceremony. "I did want to be awake when you woke, so I could tell you. I'm sorry I missed the chance and left you to wonder."

"I didn't give it a second thought."

"Liar."

"I couldn't center at all," she admitted. "But it was worth it to come here and sense you."

Silently, Dr. Wells held out a hand. Rahel took it, accepting the gift for what it was: emotions shared freely.

There was gratitude, of course, alongside worry, relief, and ebullient joy. But strongest of all, as Dr. Wells looked unflinchingly into her eyes, was a fierce, glorious love. Rahel had only sensed this intensity from three others in her life: Mouse, Sharro, and her mother. That Dr. Wells not only felt this way about her but was intentionally sharing it . . .

Breathing was suddenly difficult.

Dr. Wells smiled in understanding, squeezing her hand before letting go. "Micah and I have been discussing parenting," she said, as if nothing had happened. "He plans to step down as Chief Guardian shortly before the birth."

"That's a loss to Lancer Tal," Rahel managed.

"He's been training Gehrain for almost two cycles."

"It's still a loss. Micah knows all the players." As she had for Shantu.

"Gehrain is learning them. Micah wants to cut back his workload and devote it to Salomen. One of us needs to be the consistent one, the parent who can always be there. I was that for Josue, but . . ." She shook her head.

"But you'll be training Alsean healers on the *Phoenix* and setting up the new healing center in Blacksun," Rahel concluded. "You can't be that parent this time."

"Not for the first few cycles, at least. Which brings us to you." Amusement rose from her skin. "You look worried. What do you think we're expecting?"

"I don't know," she said honestly. "I want to be part of this, but I don't know my role. And I can't leave the *Phoenix*, especially now."

"No, you can't and you shouldn't. Rahel, there's a reason Micah told you about his history with Tal. What he was and is for her, that's what we'd like you to be for our child. With one difference," she added. "Our child will know who you are."

She meant to say *Yes, I'd be delighted.* She wanted to say *Thank you for not hiding me in the shadows.* She pictured herself saying *I'll do my best to be a good role model. I'll be there for this child, whenever she or he needs me.*

What she did, embarrassingly, was dissolve into tears.

Dr. Wells pulled her into a warmron, rubbing her back and making comforting sounds. "It's a bit much to take in, isn't it?"

"Fahla, yes. I didn't expect—I didn't think—" She clenched her jaw, trying to stave off a mortifying sob.

"You didn't think you were doing anything more than giving us a gift." Dr. Wells held her more tightly. "You thought you'd walk away today and that would be the end of it, except for occasional visits from Aunt Rahel. That's why I love you so much, you idiot warrior. Because you did this with no thought for yourself. You did it for me, for him." She pulled away and held Rahel's shoulders, her eyes wet again but bright with joy. "I can't think of anyone I'd rather have teach my child what it means to love. You're so damned good at it."

She choked on her response. Not in a thousand cycles would she have thought of herself that way. "I don't know how—"

"Yes, you do. You showed *me* how, don't you realize that? I learned with you. I forgot, all those cycles ago. I made myself forget. You brought me back from that. I have a family now. A family!" She shook Rahel by the shoulders, her smile radiant. "But it won't be complete without you."

A chuckle made its way through the blockage in her throat. "We'll be a unique family."

"I wouldn't have it any other way. Ordinary is boring."

The eye contact was too much. Rahel settled back into a warmron, absorbing the indescribable comfort of being known with all her flaws and loved in spite of them.

She was going to have a child—and a family.

45

VISITOR

To Rahel's gleeful surprise, they extended their stay in the pleasure house.

"I spent five days stressing over this," Dr. Wells said. "I barely got to enjoy any of it. I want to *relax*."

"Besides," Micah added, "relaxing is good for the baby."

"Which is good for my mental health." She kissed him on the tip of the nose. "Which means it's good for yours."

"Words for Fahla." He tried to look innocent. "What? I was agreeing with you."

"A little too fervently. Pay attention, Rahel. He's showing you how *not* to behave in a relationship."

"I'm not getting in the middle of that."

"Wise woman," Micah said with a nod.

And yet, she was in the middle of it—or if not quite in the middle, then just off to the side. Their inclusion of her had not ended with the ceremony, a truth they demonstrated at every opportunity. That they did so unconsciously, as if nothing could be more natural, made it all the more precious to her.

Since Micah had spent little time in Whitesun and Dr. Wells next to none, she showed them the most famous sights of her city. When they had their fill of crowds, she took them to her favorite haunts and the places with personal meaning. At the request of her mother and Sharro, she even took them to the house on the hill, where they marveled at the expansive view of Wildwind Bay, chatted about everything from parenting to winter storms, and fell helplessly under Little Mouse's spell.

Sharro insisted that they stay for evenmeal. It was while helping her serve that Rahel stopped in the kitchen doorway, overcome by a moment of disbelief as she watched the people around the table.

"You make a beautiful family," Sharro said from behind her. "Unique, as any family of yours would have to be."

"I never imagined anything like this. I just thought that maybe, someday, I could have what other people had."

"Why would you limit yourself? Surely your mother and I taught you better than that." Her single dimple twinkled as she slid past. "But you do need to make one change."

"What is that?"

"Call her Alejandra."

"Oh. No, you don't understand—"

"She has rewritten the rules of her culture to create this family. You can rewrite your personal rule"—she tapped Rahel over the heart—"and give the gift of her name. Without it, you hold her at a distance. There was a time when that was appropriate, but that time has passed."

Rahel spent the rest of evenmeal avoiding calling Dr. Wells by any name at all. Sharro was right, of course. But putting that wisdom into practice made surrogacy look simple.

Two days later, they were crossing the courtyard on their way back from mornmeal when Dr. Wells broke into a trot, radiating happy recognition.

"Where is she going?" Micah asked, looking after her as she turned down the next side path.

"I have no—" Rahel stopped when a figure rose from the bench at the end of the path. The distinctive emotional signature was so incongruous in this place that she couldn't credit her senses.

"You look ten cycles younger!" Dr. Wells called.

"I feel like it." Captain Serrado held out her arms, laughing as Dr. Wells barreled into them. They embraced as if they hadn't seen each other in a cycle.

313

"Congratulations, Alejandra." Rahel heard the murmur as she and Micah drew near. "I'm so happy for you. So happy."

"Thank you. It still hasn't sunk in yet. It might not until he gives birth."

"I think you'll get there sooner than that." Captain Serrado looked up and beamed at them, gracefully stepping away to offer both palms. "Well met, Micah. And congratulations."

"Ekatya, well met. This is a surprise! Though not to all of us, I note."

Dr. Wells was unrepentant. "A healer has to have some secrets."

"Don't blame her. I didn't tell her I was coming until this morning." Serrado turned to Rahel, her smile undimmed. "I don't know how to greet you now. I'm not your captain."

"As family," Micah said firmly. "She's part of our family."

"Good, that makes it easier." And before Rahel quite knew what was happening, Captain Serrado was giving her a warmron. "Congratulations to you, too. That's quite a feat you pulled off."

"I had a lot of help." Rahel straightened with the realization. "You only told her this morning that you were coming? You didn't take a regular transport." And without her command, she had no access to the *Phoenix*'s shuttles.

"I'm getting certified on our new shuttles. It wouldn't look good for the first admiral to need pilots to take her around."

"The first admiral could crook her little finger and bring any pilot on the planet running, eager for the honor of serving." Micah crossed his arms disapprovingly. "You're inventing expectations."

"And Lhyn said she and Salomen were making sure you took a moon to relax," Rahel added. "It hasn't even been two ninedays. I can't believe they'd let you start work already."

"Look at that." Dr. Wells nudged Serrado. "Do you see it?"

"That they're in exactly the same pose? Yes."

"They're even jutting out the same hip. Do you think they learn that in training?"

Realizing that her arms were crossed as well, Rahel set her hands on her hips. "You're also not in uniform," she observed.

"Is she telling the truth about getting certified?" Micah asked in a conspiratorial tone.

"Yes, but the rest is excuses. She's doing it for fun."

"Hm."

Serrado laughed. "Alejandra, they're not going to let you get away with anything."

"I know. Right now I'm enjoying it. I'm sure that at some point, I'll want to throw one or both of them out the window."

"Or the airlock, depending on your location. Yes, you're right. I wanted some flight time, but I'm in limbo. Not a captain and not yet an admiral. Fortunately, I know someone who can pull levers. They started me on the certification a bit early, so I came down here."

Micah was unconvinced. "And you chose Whitesun for its balmy weather?"

Rahel glanced up at the clouds scudding across the wintry sky. It was a far cry from summer in Blacksun Basin.

"I chose Whitesun because I wanted to congratulate you. And because I need to speak with Rahel."

Her head snapped around. "With me?"

"Let them talk," Dr. Wells said, tugging Micah by the elbow. "They'll join us for a rajalta after. Won't you?"

"We'll be up when we're done," Serrado promised. She watched them go, then turned to the sculpture given pride of place in this corner of the courtyard. "You mentioned that your mother donated a sculpture. I never imagined anything like this."

The half-scale woman leaned back on her heels with both arms extended, holding the ends of a long, narrow piece of cloth. She was off balance and would have fallen backward but for the large sphere pulling in the opposite direction, trapped in the cloth's loop a body length away. While she and her cloth were dark, the sphere shone brightly, shredding the cloth as it tore free. The woman's arm muscles were corded with the effort, yet she wore a resigned expression.

At the base of the sculpture, a plaque bore two words and a name:

"LET GO"

Ravenel Sayana

"It's incredible artistry." Serrado walked around to the sphere, suspended at eye level. "I'd swear this cloth was fabric. How she made metal look so soft is beyond me. I had to touch it to be sure."

"I've never liked this one," Rahel said flatly.

"Really? Why not? It's a marvel of captured motion. There's so much kinetic energy. I can *feel* her effort."

"Because I'm the sphere." Rahel ran her fingertips over the shining metal. "It was Mother's penance. She's telling the world that she tried to hold me back." She dropped her hand. "When I was eighteen, I thought this was justice. A public apology for the wrong she did me, what more could I want?"

"And now?"

"Now I don't look at the sphere. I look at her." She indicated the woman, straining with every bit of her strength and knowing she had already lost. "I don't want her to keep apologizing, but this sculpture has been here for twenty cycles. It'll be here after we're both gone. It's famous now. People come to the pleasure house just to see it." She scowled. "I wish Sharro would let the house sell it to a private collector."

"That would be a tremendous loss." Captain Serrado circled around to stand beside the woman, looking along the length of straining cloth to Rahel. "Great art has more than one interpretation. It speaks to the viewer, not just the artist. I don't see this as an apology."

That was new. "How do you see it?"

"As wisdom. She could be me." She rested a palm on the woman's bicep. "Trying desperately to stop things from changing because I'm afraid. But they're going to change anyway. If I'd let go, I could relax and watch the sphere instead of fighting it. I wasted so much energy fighting."

Rahel looked at her more closely, noting the lack of sharp edges in her emotional signature. In fact, she glowed with contentment.

"You let go."

"I did. It took the combined efforts of three people, but I got there. Now I wonder why I waited so long."

"Is this about, um . . . ?"

"Andira? Yes. It's not a secret any longer." Dropping her head back, Serrado cried, "*Shek* that feels good to say!" She laughed as a group walking toward the administrative wing stopped to stare. "Hope I didn't disturb anyone in the middle of a creation ceremony."

It was impossible not to laugh with her. This was a version of Serrado she had neither seen nor imagined, but it was a joy to sense.

"These walls are made of stone two paces thick," Rahel said. "The windows are soundproofed. You're not disturbing anyone, but if you do that again, I want to record it."

"Stand by. It's likely to happen without warning." She inhaled deeply, delight sparking off her fingertips. "Technically it's still a secret, but only for two more days. If all goes well tomorrow, we'll be making a public announcement the day after."

Rahel had not expected that. Then again, Serrado and Lancer Tal both had the biggest horns in the galaxy, so perhaps she should have. "What happens tomorrow?"

"Andira is sponsoring me into the warrior caste."

"And you think it might not go well?" She scoffed. "You have as much chance of being rejected as our moons do of falling out of the sky. They might as well reject Fahla herself."

"Despite some confusion, I'm not actually Fahla, so yes, there *is* a chance. I still have to pass the tests."

"Ah. You want to be a caste member in good standing before the announcement."

"If I'm to be presented as worthy of Lancer Tal, I need to be as Alsean as possible." She tilted her head toward the path and began walking. "That's not what I came to discuss with you."

Rahel kept pace beside her. They passed two hand-holding couples and reached the central fountain before Serrado spoke again.

"We expect a media storm after the announcement. We'll give it half a moon to run its course, then I'll accept my new post on the floor of the Council chamber. The day after that, I'll fly up to take command of the *Phoenix*."

"What will her new name be?"

"*Phoenix*. No one wanted to change it, least of all me. But I'll only stay in command for the next cycle, until the *Caphenon* is raised. It's not the admiral's place to go gallivanting out of the system. My place is here. The *Caphenon* will be my flagship."

"Who will command the *Phoenix*, then?"

"Funny you should ask." Serrado stopped and looked her in the eye, alight with expectation.

Rahel gaped. "No. That doesn't even make sense!"

"Why not?"

"I don't know, twelve or fifteen reasons? I don't have any experience, for one!"

"Give me the name of an Alsean with more starship experience than you."

That shut her down.

"You can't. No one comes close for time in space, knowledge of the ship and its systems, or understanding of its strengths and limitations. No one else has mentored with every single section chief, learning what they do and how the sections work together. No one else can walk those chases and brace shafts blindfolded."

"There are hundreds of Alseans who have worked on the *Caphenon* for longer than I've been on the *Phoenix*."

Serrado shook her head. "They worked on a dead ship sitting on the ground. Ask Dr. Wells if there's any difference between dissecting a cadaver and working with a living, breathing patient."

"Captain," she pleaded. "Don't put this on me. I don't know how to lead a city in space!"

"The numbers are just a matter of scale. The issue is whether you have leadership qualities and experience. We focused on teaching you to work as part of a team because that was the experience you lacked, but you certainly didn't lack the ability to *lead* a team. Hedron Periso spent fifteen cycles infiltrating existing networks and earning people's trust."

Rahel faced the fountain, seeking solace in the gentle movement of the water as it flowed over the stones. "Criminals," she corrected. "I earned the trust of criminals."

"And you think that makes you less of a leader? I think it makes you more. They had no obligation to trust or follow you."

"Except the last ones. I bought their service. Then I left them to die."

"How long do you plan to punish yourself for that?" Serrado shifted position, inserting herself in Rahel's line of sight. "You obeyed orders, despite your misgivings, because you trusted your oath holder. I did the same thing. You left your mercenaries to die; I left every Alsean on this planet. I've been making up for that decision every day since." She nodded as Rahel met her eyes. "It has made me a better leader. Let me teach you. I'm still in command for the next cycle. More, if it takes longer to raise the *Caphenon*. Commander Lokomorra has agreed to stay on as my exec for the duration of the Protectorate training. You'll shadow both him and me. Your sole responsibility for the next cycle will be to learn everything you can about taking command."

Rahel sat abruptly on the fountain's edge. "A cycle won't be enough!"

"I know this is a shock." Serrado sat next to her. "I wish I'd had more time to ease you into it."

"The heat death of the universe wouldn't be enough time."

"Spoken like one who walks in space." The air buzzed with an odd combination of amusement and sympathy as Serrado rested a hand on her shoulder. "Sometimes, we're fortunate enough to get the jobs we need. Other times, we get the jobs that need us. The *Phoenix* needs you, Rahel. You're the best choice. I wouldn't be here otherwise."

With a reassuring squeeze, she sat back, her emotional signature confident and serene.

Rahel thought serenity was something she might never achieve again. Her thoughts raced in a hundred directions, but what came out of her mouth was the last thing she planned to say.

"I don't want to be alone again. All that time you spent teaching me to work as part of a team—what a waste, when you want me to be the one person on that ship who isn't a part of any team."

"Rahel—"

"I've *felt* you, Captain. I know how isolated you've been."

Serrado winced. "I wasn't the best role model in that department. In my defense, not all of that was my own doing. At any rate, that's not how I plan to lead the fleet." She shifted to face her. "It's not how I'd recommend you lead your crew. Alseans are not Gaians. You don't have to pretend to be someone you're not for the sake of those looking up to you."

"Hoi, that's all right, then. I can act like I don't know what I'm doing. That should inspire trust."

"You're upset and justifiably so," Serrado said evenly. "But I'm still your oath holder and I deserve your respect. Drop the sarcasm."

"I'm sorry," she mumbled, mortified by the chastisement.

With a sigh, Serrado swept a hand through her loose hair. "Rahel, it's not going to happen tomorrow. You have at least a cycle to learn everything Lokomorra and I can teach you. Think about where you were a cycle ago. Could you have imagined that you'd be one of the best gunners on the ship when you'd never flown in a fighter before? Or that you'd teach *me* how to be an oath holder? You're my most trusted warrior. You kept me in command when Alsea depended on it. Could you have envisioned that?"

She shook her head, embarrassment evaporating under the heat of such sincere regard.

"Then trust me when I say you'll be prepared a cycle from now. Trust me to do my job. I *will* train you." She held Rahel's gaze with an intensity that made it impossible to look away. "A team leader is still a team member. You won't be alone. You'll have people you can depend on, just as I depend on my officers. You'll have me, even when I take command of the *Caphenon*. Don't think I'm going to give you my ship and let you just walk off with it. Captains still answer to admirals." Intensity shifted to amusement as she leaned in with a conspiratorial smile. "Unless the admiral's name is Greve."

Rahel found herself smiling in response. Somehow, in the space of a few ticks, Captain Serrado had reduced a terrifying idea to one that was merely frightening.

"Do you really think people will follow me?" she asked. "I've never served in a normal Guard unit. I don't have any of the usual experience."

"That's part of what makes you such a good choice. We're creating something new. We need new ideas and the flexibility to recognize when something doesn't work. A leader with preconceived ideas of what *should* work is probably the worst person we could put up there."

"Or what shouldn't work," Rahel said as a memory surfaced. "When Candini dove after that missile, I thought she was insane. I told her the grappler wasn't designed for that. Good thing she didn't listen."

Warm approval washed over her senses. "Excellent illustration. First rule of good leadership: don't dismiss ideas just because they sound insane. I think you've already learned that one."

In the silence that followed, the distinctive scream of a spearbill sounded overhead. Rahel looked up in time to see it sail over the courtyard, sleek silver wings spread wide to capture the wind off the bay.

She never heard that cry in landlocked Blacksun. Funny, the things that came to mean home.

"I'm going to tell you something," Captain Serrado said. "First, I need your word of honor that it won't go beyond us. You can speak of it to Alejandra and Micah, because they already know. No one else, not even your mother or Sharro."

Though confused, she didn't hesitate. "I swear on my honor as a warrior."

"Thank you." Serrado shifted into a cross-legged position. "If Andira and I could change one thing about our lives, it would be the length of time it took us to find each other. Not as tyrees, but as friends. We understood each other in a way no one else could, because we were both leading alone."

Rahel nodded. That much she had guessed long ago.

"Our successors have an advantage we didn't. You're already friends. You'll have each other from the beginning."

Realization curled around her spine. She wanted to ask, but the words wouldn't come.

"You've guessed it already. If Andira gets her way, and I can't imagine she won't, Fianna Vellmar will be the next Lancer of Alsea."

"Huh," Rahel said after a moment of thought. "I should have seen that coming."

Serrado stared at her in delight, then slapped her hand against the stone. "Thank you! You just won me a hundred cinteks."

"What?"

"Andira thought you'd be shocked. I said you're only surprised when it's your potential being recognized. You wouldn't blink an eye that she recognized Vellmar's."

She was annoyed by her own transparency before the humor hit. "I'm glad I could help you beat the Lancer. It's probably the only way I'll ever do it."

"I think you'll have more opportunities. Do you know what Vellmar's first thought was as a Lancer in training? That she wanted you for her Chief Guardian."

What an irony. Once, that dream had been in her grasp, until Shantu's betrayal yanked it away. Now . . .

"Her first thought," Rahel said. "What was her second?"

"That you're happier in space, and Alsea is better served with you on the *Phoenix*. She said that before she knew I chose you. But our choices aren't the only ones on the game board. You have one, too. If you truly want to be her Chief Guardian, we'll make it happen. You'd be an enormous asset to her in the role." She waved a hand. "It'll be a wait, though. Andira is in no hurry to retire, and Vellmar needs much more time."

"Lucky her, to get it," Rahel muttered. Yet her own compressed time-line weighed less now that she had a choice. This wasn't being forced on her, as so many things had been.

Chief Guardian in a tencycle, perhaps, and service aboard the *Phoenix* until then? Or captain of the *Phoenix* next cycle?

A winged shadow flashed across the garden, trailed by a scream.

"What *is* that?" Serrado craned her neck, trying to locate it.

"A spearbill. They hunt in the southern waters in summer and come up here in winter." They were explorers, her mother had once said. Creatures of the air who came and went, unafraid of the worst tempests the wild ocean could throw at them.

Rahel put a hand to her chest, atop the wing of her phoenix.

In the end, the choice was easy.

46

WARRIOR

Dazzling in full dress uniform, Andira stood before the door of her quarters. "Ready?"

"Ready." Ekatya rolled her shoulders, testing the fit of her new tunic.

"You can unbend your spine. Your acceptance is a foregone conclusion. They've probably set up a fireworks display."

"There are tests," Ekatya reminded her. "I haven't passed yet."

"You'll pass with all flags flying."

"Don't jinx me."

"Do you always worry so much about little things?"

"It's not a little thing," she snapped. "It's my life."

Andira's cheerful expression fell.

"Oh, no, don't look like that. It's like I've run my shuttle over a litter of vallcat kittens." That earned her a hearty laugh, as she had known it would. "I'm nervous, all right? Let me worry. You can tease me later."

Andira stepped into her space and smoothed the fabric across her shoulders. "You *will* pass," she said, tugging the collar upright. "You've studied the material. You know it back and forth."

"Backward and forward," Ekatya said automatically.

"You Gaians and your idioms. Isn't that the same thing?"

Overwhelmed by a surge of affection, she wrapped her arms around

Andira's waist and rested their foreheads together. "I want to live up to your expectations. I couldn't stand it if I embarrassed you."

"I cannot believe you think that's a possibility." Andira leaned back to look in her eyes. "I'm proud to be your sponsor. If I did nothing else in my life, I'd be content knowing that history will record me as the warrior who brought Ekatya Serrado into our caste."

"Was that supposed to make me less nervous?" She stepped away, running a distracted hand through her hair. "It would be easier if I knew what to expect."

"I've told you—"

"But I haven't *experienced* it. I'm like a damned cadet, tripping over my feet while trying to find my first classroom."

"You don't have to find the classroom. I'm walking you there."

"Lovely. Now I feel like I'm six and Grams is walking me to my first day of school. Don't you dare ask if I need you to hold my hand."

Andira lifted both hands in surrender, then opened the door and stood aside. "After you, Admiral."

"I'm not an admiral yet. Don't jinx me."

She smiled at the chuckle behind her. Despite her dismissal of any hand-holding, she could not imagine doing this alone.

"Lift or stairs?" Andira asked when they reached the main corridor.

"Stairs. I need to move." As she trotted down the steps, the familiar physicality began to calm her nerves. "I have more respect for Rahel these days. She came aboard the *Phoenix* and it was a whole new world for her. Every interaction, every room, every expectation. I thought I knew how hard that must have been, but really, I had no idea. I have a better idea now."

"She truly is an explorer," Andira agreed. "And continuing a long tradition. Warriors have been flagging trails since Ikaren set sail and found a second continent."

"That wasn't Ikaren. It was Isen."

"Ah, that's right. I always get them confused."

Ekatya reached the next landing and stopped at the realization. "You little shit. You're manipulating me. I'll eat my boots if you ever got them confused."

Andira burst into laughter. "I would only manipulate you with the greatest love. You know the material back and forth, Ekatya."

"Backward and forward." But it had worked; her nervousness receded. While she couldn't shake it entirely, it was no longer tying her stomach in knots. "Come on, I have tests to take."

Andira reached the ground floor first and made a flamboyant gesture as she opened the door. Shaking her head, Ekatya walked into the grand lobby and stopped. It was full of Lancer's Guards.

"You need your entire unit to escort you across the State Park?" she asked suspiciously.

"No, she only needs five." Micah moved out from behind Gehrain and surveyed his Guards, hands on hips. "The rest are coming along for the exercise. Isn't that right?"

"Yes, Colonel!" they responded smartly.

"You're supposed to be relaxing in Whitesun," Ekatya accused.

"I got cold. It's winter there."

"We need the exercise, too."

Hearing Lhyn's voice, Ekatya turned to find her in a doorway that had been closed a piptick ago. Beside her was Salomen, who nodded sagely and added, "Morning walks are the best. The air smells so clean."

So much for Lhyn's assurance that she and Salomen would take the opportunity to sleep in. After all, the tests would last half the morning. They would be there in time for the results, she had promised, and like an idiot, Ekatya had taken that at face value.

"Form up!" Vellmar called from the main doors.

With a rumble of boot heels on tiles, the Guards formed two precise lines facing each other, starting at the doors and extending halfway across the lobby.

Andira linked arms with a flabbergasted Ekatya and led her forward. "Let's go to school," she whispered.

"Good luck," Gehrain said as they passed him.

His well-wishes were echoed repeatedly as Ekatya was escorted between the lines. She was too dazed to respond, a situation that worsened when Vellmar opened the outer door.

"Good luck, Captain Serrado," said Lead Guard Ronlin. He stood at the top of the stone steps, heading a second dual line of Bondlancer's Guards. Across from him was another unexpected face, though less so after Micah's appearance.

"You ran away from the Whitesun winter, too?" Ekatya said. "I thought you'd be immune to it."

"I couldn't miss this, could I?" Rahel leaned in and spoke quietly. "Tell the truth and be yourself. That's all they expect."

"At this point in my life, I'm not sure I can be anyone else."

"A truth for which we are all grateful." Andira tugged her onward, and Ekatya passed through another honor guard of warriors who wished her well.

At the bottom of the steps, Vellmar and Ronlin strode past to take the point position, while Salomen and Lhyn moved up to walk beside Andira and Ekatya. Behind them came forty Guards. A few were focused, clearly on duty, but the rest strolled along, laughing and chattering.

It seemed that Ekatya's challenge was a holiday of sorts.

It was also a vivid preview of how her life was about to change. Once the public announcement was made tomorrow, she and Lhyn would both have their own Guards. They had been handpicked by Micah and Gehrain, with additional input from Salomen for choosing Lhyn's. The High Council had authorized funds to expand both the Lancer's and Bondlancer's units, a far simpler solution than the creation of two new state-funded units, which would have required full Council approval. Vellmar and Ronlin had just finished training the new warriors and awarded them their distinguishing armbands: black with silver triangles for Ekatya's Guards, dark scholar blue for Lhyn's.

Ekatya wasn't looking forward to this aspect of life as the Lancer's tyree, but at least she was already experienced in having her own sworn warrior. Lhyn wanted nothing to do with it and had strenuously objected. But there were some things even an accomplished linguist could not talk her way out of, especially when she came up against an expert debater. Despite Salomen's initial distaste for her own Guards, she understood their necessity very well and had impressed it upon Lhyn in sharp and devastating detail.

Sometimes, Ekatya reflected, it was rather nice to sit back and watch someone else do the convincing.

Their route took them along the back side of Blacksun Temple, where Lanaril waited in her open garden gate. "Good morning!" she said brightly. "How inspiring to see so many people enjoying a bit of exercise. Might I join you?"

Alejandra appeared beside her. "Did someone mention exercise? I could use some after the last nineday of doing practically nothing."

"Nothing?" Micah asked incredulously.

"I said *practically* nothing."

When her grandparents stepped out from behind the garden wall, Ekatya gave up. "Is anyone *not* coming along for this?"

"Stars and Shippers, Katya, did you think we would let you go alone?" Nikolay pulled her into a firm hug. "Now go in there and show them what you're made of," he ordered. "Show them why they'll be lucky to have you."

"I think I'm the lucky one, Gramps."

Elanor was waiting as soon as he let go. "I won't tell you to make us proud," she said. "You already have."

Ekatya closed her eyes and held on, swallowing the tightness in her throat. "Thanks, Grams. Wish me luck."

"Good luck, dear heart."

And that, thought Ekatya as their parade wound across the park, was what made Grams so special. Everyone, even Lhyn and Andira, believed this was a foregone conclusion. Perhaps it was, but Grams understood why she couldn't accept that. Blind trust in an outcome had never served her well. Preparation made the difference.

The examiners would test her on morals and ethics, intelligence, and aptitude for a number of areas the caste valued. In addition, they would administer her civics test, a requirement the Council had added to citizenship applications.

The last test was in the dance of combat.

Excluding the civics test, which was scored separately, each caste exam was worth nine points. Out of a possible thirty-six points, she needed twenty-five to pass—and she would lose points in the combat. Had she any real skill with a sword, stave, or knife, she would have been better able to compete against an Alsean opponent. Unfortunately, her skill was hand-to-hand, where her light Gaian bones and less dense musculature put her at a significant disadvantage. Then there was her empathic ability, which would earn her a big, fat zero.

She would need to perform extremely well to make up for those deficiencies.

"You're overthinking it," Lhyn said from beside her. "I did the same thing at the start of my challenge. I haven't given you any advice, because I knew you didn't want to hear it. Will you hear it now?"

The red domed roof of the warrior caste house gleamed in the sunlight, its impressive bulk dwarfing the trees below. Ekatya could not look away as they approached. "Now is all the time I have left," she said.

"They're not just testing what you know. They're testing who you are. They don't want to know about Captain Serrado, just like my testers didn't want to know about Dr. Rivers. They already knew that part of me. They're looking under your skin."

"Lovely," Ekatya muttered. "How is anyone supposed to prepare for that?"

"You don't. That's the point. The other point"—she caught Ekatya's hand—"is that under this skin, you're a warrior down to the marrow of your bones. They'll see that. They'll *want* that."

Ekatya squeezed her hand. "From your lips to Fahla's ears."

She did not let go, not as they turned into the long, grassy promenade that led to the grand entrance, not as they climbed the stone steps, not even when they went through the doors. But inside the lobby, Lhyn gave her a kiss and slipped away.

She took in few details after that, too overwhelmed with the grandeur of the space and the requirements of her initial inscription. Andira took her to a massive desk of wood and stone, where she recited her full name and those of her parents and grandparents, submitted her thumbprints, and gave the equivalent of her service record to the clerks busily recording every word. Andira made a formal statement of sponsorship, signed by her own thumbprint.

The clerks vanished through an archway into what Ekatya vaguely remembered were the archives. Five ticks later, a door opened beside the semicircular desk. Two new warriors emerged, introduced themselves as her testers, and led her away.

She cast a final look back at Andira, who smiled and held a hand over her heart before the heavy door closed between them.

"This way." The taller warrior led her down the silent corridor and through another door. "Please sit, Captain."

"I'm not a captain any longer." She walked to the chair on the far side of the round table while the two warriors sat side by side.

"Not to your Fleet," said the other. "But we don't see your rank as dependent on whether or not the Protectorate continues to hold your oath."

"In truth," said the first, "we've long thought that the Protectorate did not deserve your service. Would you agree?"

They're looking under your skin. Lhyn's advice was suddenly crystal clear: though disguised as a conversational opener, the testing had already begun.

"I served more than the Protectorate," Ekatya said. "I served those who needed me. My crew. The officers whose training I was entrusted with. Protectorate citizens who depended on us. The *Resilere*. Alsea. Yes, there were individuals who did not hold my respect—" She paused, remembering Rahel's advice to tell the truth. "And who didn't deserve my service. But I didn't serve individuals. I served the Protectorate Fleet and its ideals, and I'm proud of my record."

"Even though your record includes abandoning Alsea to the Voloth?" asked the second.

It took every bit of her training to keep a neutral expression. "If my record ended there, no, I wouldn't be proud of it. I obeyed orders because at the time I thought it was my duty, even when the orders felt wrong. Lancer Tal taught me a different way of thinking."

"But not before you challenged her honor." The first warrior glanced at her reader card. "Colonel Micah recorded it, as was his duty. You challenged the Lancer out of anger."

Was this a test or a trial?

"I assume Colonel Micah also recorded the outcome. Lancer Tal ripped my head off my neck and handed it to me."

She wasn't certain, but she thought the second warrior might have let a tiny bit of amusement slip through.

"Yes," he said gravely. "He did record that outcome. Why did you swear an oath of service to her after that?"

For personal reasons that she would not divulge here, test or no test.

"The Voloth were coming and I couldn't get off this planet," she said truthfully. "As a Protectorate Fleet captain, death was preferable to Voloth capture. If I was going to die, then I wanted to go out fighting. There was no better person on Alsea to fight for than Lancer Tal. She had earned my respect."

They nodded again, their faces blank. She had no idea whether or not she was saying the right things, then or for the next hantick as they continued to pick apart her decisions. Belatedly, she realized that this was the ethics and morals test. She had never envisioned it taking this form.

At last, they gave her a cup of shannel and a tentick break. She sipped gratefully, trying to loosen the painful knot that had taken up residence between her shoulder blades. Not even her last hearing back at Command Dome had been this difficult. Then, she had been defending herself against spurious accusations and ridiculous suspicions. She had respected neither the process nor the individuals putting her through it.

These warriors had made no accusations and shown no suspicions. They had spoken no words that were not factual. Yet they had made her painfully aware that her choices were not always good ones.

"Are you ready, Captain?"

She set down her empty cup. "Yes."

"Tell us about the formation of the castes and Unification."

Thank the stars, it was the civics test. Her trial was over.

She spoke for half a hantick without stopping, eager to show what she knew. They gave no indication of any errors she might have made, interrupting only to ask additional questions or steer her toward related topics. Once again, her realization was late: many of these questions were testing her intelligence and aptitudes. She had expected tests with specific, quantitative objectives, but Alsean testing seemed far more qualitative, achieving its objectives in a more diffuse manner.

She wondered, in a brief lull as the warriors consulted over their reader cards, how the point assignments worked in a system like this. Then they asked another question, and she had no time to think of anything but how best to answer.

By the end of the second hantick, she had downed two more cups of shannel and was desperate for a bathroom break. When the warriors set down their reader cards, she was sure they had sensed her need and were discreetly assisting.

"Congratulations, Captain Serrado," the first said.

"Welcome to our caste, warrior." The second stood from his chair and leaned across the table, offering his forearm.

Ekatya rose and clasped it automatically, her brain scrambling to catch up. "You mean I passed? But I haven't done the dance of combat."

The first chuckled, a shocking sound given her blank demeanor of the past two hanticks. "You don't need to. You've already scored a twenty-six point five." She offered her own forearm. "That's nearly a record."

"It certainly puts you in the top one percent," the man added. "Not that we were surprised."

Twenty-six point five? That meant she had lost a mere half point in all three exams.

"But . . . how? I'm sonsales. And what about the ethics and morals test?"

"Empathic ability isn't required," the woman answered. "Though it can be used to make up for lower scores in other areas. Not ethics and morals," she added. "Those stand alone. But we don't judge by who you've been. We judge by who you are."

The man pushed in his chair and rolled up his reader card. "You've been a loyal warrior to two oath holders simultaneously. That's a difficult set of obligations to balance. Your choices and actions have done you great credit."

"Of course we'll want to see your dance of combat as well." The woman slid her own reader card into its belt pouch. "If you'll come with us, we'll take you downstairs."

The changing room would not have been out of place in a luxury spa. Despite its underground location, natural light was somehow brought in from outside, enhancing the warm tones of the wooden lockers and cushioned benches. It buzzed with activity, full of warriors in various states of dress, nearly all of whom looked up and smiled at her entrance. She was the first Gaian to set foot in this room, yet no one said a word. Alsean courtesy beat curiosity.

They stopped in front of a locker that held a comfortable set of her workout clothing. Andira had sent it over yesterday, "so you can wear something that fits." Now, holding the only familiar thing in this entire building, Ekatya wondered if it was also an intentional psychological boost.

"Toilets and showers are through there." The man pointed to an archway at the end of the room, then turned to indicate a closed door on the opposite wall. "That's the door to the training room. We'll wait for you there."

As she passed by the sumptuous showers on her way to the toilets, she thought she would surely be needing one by the time this last test was finished. She had not sparred with an Alsean since her ill-fated challenge fight with Andira, but she hadn't forgotten how completely outmatched she had been—or how much it had hurt.

Nothing worth doing is easy, Grams always said.

Grams would birth a brick when she saw the bruises Ekatya was about to acquire.

A wave of excitement rippled through the room while she changed clothes, manifesting in whispers, the rustles of hurried dressing, and an occasional audible word.

"She is?"

"I have to see . . ."

She found her testers standing by the door with identical expressions of annoyance.

"Have you nothing better to do?" the man asked.

Ekatya stopped, confused, but he was looking past her.

"Not really," said a voice behind her.

"We heard who's out there," said another. "I'm not missing this!"

Ekatya turned to find every warrior who had been changing now dressed and crowded at her back. She looked at her testers questioningly.

"Unlike the others, the physical test isn't private," the man explained. Glaring at the crowd, he added, "But it doesn't usually attract this much attention."

No one moved.

With a sigh, he opened the door. "Come along, then."

Ekatya followed them into a training room with the same natural light and warm tones as the changing room. Padded mats lay flush with the wooden floor, set in a geometric pattern that allowed for multiple activities while looking like an art installation.

Every mat but one was empty, though the walls were lined with warriors wearing workout clothes and eager expressions. She saw several familiar faces interspersed among them.

In the center of the room, her test opponent stood waiting on a dark blue mat.

"As your sponsor, I claim the right to administer this exam," Andira said. "Do you accept?"

It was a smoothly laid trap, one she hadn't seen coming. Andira had repeatedly tried to spar with her, but Ekatya could not bring herself to do it. Her memories of their first and only match were still etched on her conscience: the rage, the ferocious need to *hurt*, the fact that only Andira's exceptional skill had kept them both from serious harm.

In the time it took to reach the mat, she considered and dismissed the option of refusal. It would not affect her caste right, but it would certainly affect her caste standing.

Andira had counted on that, damn her.

"I accept," she said, stepping onto the cushioned surface. As their audience cheered, she stopped in front of Andira and dropped her voice to a furious whisper. "Do you realize how manipulative this is?"

"A good warrior faces her fears. I've asked you ten times to spar with me. You were never ready."

"I'm not ready now!"

"You don't want to do it now. But you're ready."

"You arrogant—how dare you force me into this? Did you think I'd be grateful?"

"I thought you'd be exactly this angry. Do you want to hurt me? This is your chance."

That brought her up short. "No, I don't want to hurt you!"

"Even though you're angry?" Andira's smile held no triumph. It was the soft smile Ekatya saw in their home, the one she gave only to those she loved. "Good. Then spar with me, and we'll show them what the first Alsean Fleet admiral can do."

"I'm not an admiral yet."

"You earned a score of twenty-six point five. You're already in the caste. The only thing between you and your new rank is the official announcement."

"And this," Ekatya said tightly. "Laying hands on you. I can't. I can't do this."

"You've laid hands on me already." Leaning in, Andira whispered, "I've enjoyed every piptick of it."

She stepped back—or at least, Ekatya thought she was stepping back. The leg sweep caught her unawares and sent her to the mat before she knew what was happening. She let out an *oof* as the breath was forced from her lungs, then saw movement above and instinctively rolled away.

Andira landed on her knees and bounced up again, her intended pin foiled. "Well done," she said, grinning as Ekatya scrambled to her feet.

"You're an ass," Ekatya spat, torn between irritation and pride at the compliment.

"So you've said. Don't you want to teach me a lesson?" Andira swung at her, forcing her to block.

One strike after another rained down, pushing Ekatya to her limits as she strove to defend without going on the offensive. It was an enormous handicap, made worse when her brain unhelpfully pointed out that this was the position Andira had been in all those cycles ago, defending against a murderous Ekatya while trying not to hurt her.

The thought made her drop her guard. She caught herself immediately and raised her hands, but it was too late. Andira's fist smashed into her jaw, sending her reeling.

As the approving shouts rang off the walls, she dropped into a familiar mental space. She was on trial once again, defending herself against allies turned enemies.

She was sick of it.

Andira looked startled when Ekatya bore down on her, but rallied quickly enough to deflect the blow. Ekatya went with her momentum, smashing bodily into her and sending them both to the mat. She used the impact to drive an elbow into Andira's stomach, but managed nothing else before a thigh between her legs launched her off balance. Rolling swiftly to her feet, she turned to find Andira upright as well, crouched in a ready position.

The grin was obnoxious enough. The *come and get me* gesture was worse. Ekatya let out a frustrated growl and took a step forward before her training kicked in. No, she would not be goaded like a first-year cadet.

They circled each other, feinting and testing defenses. Andira tried to trip her, but Ekatya saw it coming and hopped over the trap.

The murmur of approval surprised her.

"They're not cheering me," Andira said. "They're cheering any good move."

She dismissed the obvious lie. But as their bout wore on, the evidence became harder to ignore. Then came the moment when she sent Andira to the mat with a well-placed kick to the back of the knee—and the warriors cheered.

In the space of a heartbeat, her mental fog cleared.

She was not the untrustworthy captain on trial for her tyree bond. Neither was she the outsider Gaian trying to fit where she didn't belong.

She had already passed her tests. She was a warrior, and this was the equivalent of an exhibition match.

Andira beamed at her. "Welcome back! Care to take it up a notch?"

"Sometimes I really do want to push you off the top of the waterfall," Ekatya said, exasperated and full of affection. "One of these days, I will."

"I know." Andira launched into a spin-kick that Ekatya barely managed to dodge. She didn't expect the touchdown and instant reverse spin, having never seen that move performed so quickly. The second kick caught her in the chest and sent her flying, but she turned the landing into a reverse somersault and was on her feet to the sound of raucous cheers.

"Nice try," she called.

"I suppose I'll have to try something else." Andira rushed her, then dropped at the last second and rolled into a ball, knocking Ekatya's legs right out from under her.

There was no easy recovery from that. She barely managed to get one knee up before Andira landed on top of her, setting off a flurry of moves and countermoves as Andira went for the pin and Ekatya did everything she could to prevent it.

A twist of the hips and simultaneous knee jab finally put Andira off balance. With a rush of exhilaration, Ekatya rolled them around and smirked down at her. "I like you on the bottom."

"Don't get used to it."

In the next second, she was airborne.

She crashed to the mat on her side, with no idea of Andira's location except that she wasn't directly in front. Her forward roll was stopped instantly by a leg that hadn't been there a second before.

Rebounding onto her back, she saw Andira dropping. A frantic attempt to avert the pin ended when Andira landed astride her chest, knees trapping her arms. The bout was over.

"Do you yield?"

Ekatya looked up at her, captivated by the view. A few strands of blonde hair had escaped the braid to frame her narrow face, softening her appearance. She was breathing hard, her skin flushed with exertion and her light eyes blazing with joy.

In that moment, Ekatya understood what she had denied Andira until now. Sparring was an escape for her, a culturally approved release valve. Sparring with someone she loved—well, she'd never had that option, had she?

Impatiently, Andira pushed on her shoulders. "Do you yield?"

The demanding tone sent a shiver down her spine, as did the realization of her physical response to their position.

She slapped the mat twice, signaling her surrender to the room, and spoke in a low voice.

"Only to you."

Andira's pupils dilated as her breath caught. She stared at Ekatya with undisguised lust, then shook her head. "We're discussing this later," she promised, rolling back on her heels.

"I'm counting on it." Ekatya accepted her hand and rose to the sound of enthusiastic applause, with a few whistles tossed in.

Her testers approached with wide smiles.

"Not quite what we expected," said the woman.

"But highly entertaining," the man added.

Ekatya tugged down her shirt. "What's my final score?"

"Taking into account your physical disadvantage, the number of times you sent Lancer Tal to the mat, and the length of time you avoided the pin . . ." The woman held up her reader card.

Andira took one look and whooped. "Yes!"

Thirty-five points. They had deducted just half a point from the combat test. She had completed her challenge with a nearly perfect score.

"Congratulations, warrior. Your performance does great honor to your sponsor."

"Yes, it does!" Andira held up both palms, laughing as Ekatya met them. "One warrior in five hundred gets a score like that! If Alsea didn't already have plans for you, you'd be wading through the job offers with boots and a pole."

"We'll leave you with your sponsor. Once you've showered, you can return to the lobby for your inscription ceremony." The testers saluted her in unison, then turned and brought up both fists for Andira.

"Come on." Andira tugged her off the mat and toward the changing room.

They showered separately, maintaining appearances for one more day.

Ekatya wondered why they bothered when every warrior in a twenty-meter radius surely felt her desire.

Then again, she reminded herself, that couldn't be unusual. Andira was gorgeous, brilliant, and the most powerful warrior on the planet. Half the caste probably wanted to pounce on her.

She turned her face into the water and grinned. Half the caste wanted to, but she was the only warrior who had the right.

Clean and dry, they walked back to her locker, where Vellmar waited with Andira's clothing and Dewar was opening a small medkit.

"Get dressed," Dewar ordered in the no-nonsense tone of all medics. "Then we'll take care of that bruise."

Ekatya touched her jaw and winced. "I forgot about it."

"Not surprising; battle joy is an excellent analgesic. A pity it doesn't last. Lancer?"

"It's not bad." Andira stood still in all her naked glory, waiting patiently while Dewar rubbed salve into the red circle on her stomach.

Ekatya paused in the act of fastening her trousers, her eyes riveted to the mark.

"Oh, no." Andira held up a finger. "Don't you dare feel guilty. This was a good hit and probably earned you half a point. Another half for the takedown."

"But I was furious. I could have—"

"You were not a threat," Vellmar interrupted calmly. "We all felt your anger after Lancer Tal landed the strike to your jaw. We also felt your control."

"You never came anywhere near what you feared." Andira reached out to rest a gentle finger on Ekatya's jaw. "I'm sorry about this, though. I didn't expect you to simply drop your guard. Please don't let Elanor kill me."

The plaintive tone evaporated her dismay. "She might kill us both. At least Gramps will understand. Mostly."

"It's the 'mostly' I'm afraid of," Andira grumbled, reaching for her own trousers.

Ekatya watched her dress while submitting to Dewar's soothing ministrations. The ointment would dramatically reduce but not erase the bruise on her jaw, a limitation she secretly applauded. This mark was a badge of honor.

Andira fastened her jacket, then unwound her braid and accepted a brush from Vellmar. In a few swift strokes, her hair gleamed once more.

"Thank you," Ekatya said when she offered the brush. "I didn't think to bring one."

Her own tidying was less efficient, distracted as she was by the sight of Andira clipping her hair back into a professional style. Blindly, she held out the brush for Vellmar and only looked around when it was not taken from her grasp.

Both Vellmar and Dewar stood a few steps away, arms crossed and matching smirks on their faces.

"We thought we'd give you space," Vellmar said.

Dewar nodded. "Our blocks aren't strong enough for that."

"If your blocks can't handle a little sensual appreciation, I'll have to rethink my security," Andira said.

"A little?" Dewar's smirk grew.

"Don't embarrass her," Andira warned, all playfulness gone.

Before Ekatya could protest her lack of embarrassment—really, she'd had to give that up long ago—Vellmar closed the distance and spoke quietly.

"It's not the appreciation. It's the partnership. You two move like bondmates. If you don't want this to blow open before you can control the narrative, I'd advise you to focus more on the necessity and less on each other."

Ekatya watched Andira's nod of acceptance and wondered how long it would be before Rahel spoke to her in that tone. Then she remembered the advice she had already received.

"It doesn't take long for them to turn on us, does it?" she asked.

"Fahla, no. Give them a little acknowledgment and before you know it, they're trying to run the show."

"But she's right," Ekatya added.

"That's what makes it so annoying." Andira withdrew a folded stack of crimson cloth from the nearest locker and looked up at Vellmar with a raised brow. "I assume you have no objection to this?"

Vellmar's cheeks flushed a light pink. "No, Lancer."

"Good." Turning to Ekatya, she shook out the cloth to reveal a full-length cape. "I loaned this to you twice before. Once for a day of mourning, once for a day of joy. As your sponsor—and a very proud one, given your score—tradition demands that I offer a gift upon your successful challenge."

Ekatya touched the thick cloth, remembering. "A memorial and a bonding ceremony. It was the same cape? You didn't tell me."

"I also didn't tell you how I managed to get a cape like this in your size on such short notice." She indicated the rich embroidery taking up half the back. "Most formal capes use outlined caste shields. A fully embroidered shield takes ninedays to produce."

Silver metallic thread edged the black pentagon, giving it a three-dimensional appearance. The effect was enhanced by the crossed silver swords, so densely embroidered that they stood out in relief from the dark shield. Protected beneath their blades, five silver stars shone against the black, their glow enhanced by additional metallic threads radiating outward.

Of course such fine artistry took ninedays to create. It was obvious, yet Ekatya hadn't considered it at the time of her first loan—which, she realized with a start, was just three days after she crashed the *Caphenon*.

Her fingers dropped from the material. "Stars and Shippers. Andira . . ."

"My father gave it to me when I made Lead Guard. It is with great joy that I pass it to you now."

"Your *father*." She blinked back tears, overcome by the magnitude of this gesture.

"He would have loved you," Andira said hoarsely. "He would have been as proud as I am."

No words could do justice to the pressure in her heart. Not for the first time, Ekatya was grateful that she didn't need them.

"This is—it's so much more than a gift. It's an heirloom. I'll take good care of it, I swear. On my honor as a warrior," she added, smiling at how easily those words came. "Perhaps someday I can pass it to one of your children."

Andira's answering smile was brilliant. "My children will have Salomen's genes. If any of them become warriors, they'll probably outgrow this cape long before their Rite of Ascension." She swung it around Ekatya's shoulders, settling it in place with practiced hands. "The chain is a placeholder," she said, closing the clasp. "You'll want something more personal eventually. Or you can wear different chains for different events."

She stepped back, never taking her eyes from Ekatya's as Vellmar shook out a second cape, draped it over her shoulders, and fastened the ornate clasp bearing the Seal of the Lancer. She seemed to stand taller, her expression closing off as she slipped into her public persona.

"Ekatya Lucia Serrado," she said formally, "allow me to escort you to your inscription ceremony."

"It would be my pleasure." Ekatya fell into step beside her, keenly aware of the physical and emotional distance now lodged between them.

One more day, she reminded herself, and touched the sides of her cape. Distance be damned, this gift said it all.

She wore Andira's love.

47

ADMIRAL

Tal stood on the floor of the packed Council chamber and watched a dream come true.

It had been half a moon since their public announcement. She had left nothing to chance in her preparations, guaranteeing success in every way she and her communications advisor could think of—including giving full, unfronted access to the four senior Lead Templars. They had come from Whitesun, Redmoon, and Whitemoon to join Lanaril in a test of "the claimed double bonds," as the Lead Templar of Whitesun initially termed them. His skepticism vanished when Tal and Salomen dropped their fronts.

"This is indeed a case of dual tyree bonds, two divine and two normal," he said at the end of the examination, "and therefore a gift from Fahla."

By the time of the announcement, Tal had the Lead Templars and all six caste Primes lined up in support. While a united front of both government and religious leaders knocked down most of the foreseeable objections, she took it one step further by inviting journalists from every major and several minor news outlets to the announcement. These, too, were given unfronted access.

The resulting media storm had yet to die down. Some of the journalists described their experience as a religious epiphany, others as a philosophical conundrum to be resolved. None doubted what they had sensed. Alsea had never before been confronted with the visible reality of bonds that did not fit the cultural standard, but it was making up for that now. From every corner of the world, people were coming forward with their own stories. As long-held secrets were released and the debates continued, the spotlight moved away from Tal and her family. Though they had started the conversation, it was no longer about them. They were already an accepted fact.

Now she waited while Ekatya walked the length of the Council chamber floor, her newly gifted cape swaying around her calves. Relieved of the need for subterfuge, released from her fear of being used as a weapon against Tal, she had blossomed in these last two ninedays.

She was Alsea's weapon now.

Tal brushed a hand against her jacket pocket. The familiar shape hidden within reassured her that this was indeed real and not a daydream. Ekatya had given up her captain's bars and offered her loyalty. Today, she was making it official.

Salomen stood at Tal's right hand, shining in her Bondlancer regalia, while Prime Warrior Ehron was on her left. Only Lhyn had no place in this ceremony, but she was certainly present: two vidcams hovered constantly near her seat in the guest gallery, transmitting her delighted reactions for all the world to see. Beside her, Nikolay and Elanor looked on with palpable pride.

Ekatya came to a stop and brought a fist to her chest, saluting Ehron first. Then she turned to offer the same salute to Salomen—unnecessary according to caste protocol, but a gesture of respect that brought approving murmurs from the watching Councilors.

Finally, she met Tal's eyes before bowing her head and holding both fists to her sternum. "Lancer Tal. It's an honor to be here."

"Well met, Captain Serrado," Tal said. "And that is the last time I will use that rank for you. For the benefit of the historical record, do you confirm that you have accepted the post of Admiral of the Alsean Fleet?"

"Yes, I have."

"Do you fully understand and accept the responsibilities inherent in this post?"

"I do."

"Captain Serrado." Salomen's eyes crinkled in a welcome she could not hide. "As Bondlancer, I stand in representation of the people of Alsea. The Admiral of the Alsean Fleet has many duties, but the highest of all is to protect Alsea, her people, and the ideals for which we strive. Do you freely assume this duty?"

"I do. With a joyous heart."

It was not the scripted answer, but Ekatya's happiness made everyone in sensory range smile in response. Even Ehron needed a moment to look properly serious.

"You will swear your oath to no individual, nor to a government, which may change in time," he said. "You will swear to Alsea herself, for it is she you must protect. But you will report to both myself and Lancer Tal, as the two government representatives best positioned to aid in your duties and assess your progress in carrying them out. Do you acknowledge our authority and accept these conditions?"

"I do."

"Then swear your oath, warrior," Tal said. "As Lancer, I stand in representation of Alsea." She drew her sword grip from her belt and held it out.

An audible gasp rose from Ehron, the thirty warrior Councilors in attendance, and many in the visitor and guest galleries. To swear with the Lancer's sword was an immense honor, one Tal had never before offered for a public oath.

Ekatya accepted the grip with a steady hand. Half a moon of daily practice paid off when she flicked her wrist to the side, extending the blade level with the floor, then executed a precise maneuver to bring the sword up and in. Holding it aligned with the center of her body, she spoke in a voice that penetrated every corner of the chamber.

"I stand before Alsea with a clear heart and an honorable name. I wish to serve her in any capacity I am able. I place my strength between Alsea and harm, my sword between her and her enemies, and my last breath between her and death. This I swear in Fahla's name. I am Ekatya Lucia Serrado, and I ask this gift of Alsea: Will she accept my service?"

She let the blade fall, catching the flat of it in her other hand, and held it out as she dropped gracefully to one knee.

For a moment, Tal could not speak. After all their practice, the sight of Ekatya kneeling before her was no longer startling. But the sight of her doing it here in the chamber, in full warrior regalia and as part of a formal oath, had stolen her breath and her voice along with it.

343

An empathic nudge from Salomen aided her swift recovery. She plucked the sword from Ekatya's hands and retracted it, hoping her hesitation would not be noticeable on the vids.

"Please stand, Ekatya Lucia Serrado."

No amount of emotional control could keep the smile from her face as Ekatya rose. Reaching for her hand, Tal placed the worn grip across her palm.

"You offer a sword extended, and I return it to you sheathed. Alsea accepts the gift of your service with a glad heart, and trusts that you will stand between her and harm. Should your last breath be expended in her defense, I swear to you that your name will be honored to the utmost power of the state, and the flames from your pyre will reach the stars themselves."

She stepped back, leaving her sword grip in Ekatya's hand, and said the words she had long thought a fantasy.

"Welcome to the Alsean Fleet, Admiral Serrado."

48

AFS PHOENIX

Despite having a front-row seat at a ceremony that would surely be remembered for the next five hundred cycles, Lanaril could not keep her mind on the proceedings.

Officially, she had come to the *Phoenix* as Andira's guest. Unofficially, she was here as a hero of the battle, even if classification of details meant very few would ever know it. Andira had met her protestation that she was no hero with a simple question: Would Ekatya have succeeded without her words?

Words, Lanaril thought. Such a tiny contribution compared to those who had risked or lost their lives.

She had always viewed the spiritual world as a system in equilibrium, where tragic events were balanced by positive events elsewhere. At an individual level, it was rarely fair, but on a systemic level, it evened out.

The first true challenge to her faith came when Lhyn was tortured. How could anything be positive enough to balance such an egregious wrong? How could Fahla allow such suffering to be inflicted on one she favored?

Yet Lhyn's trauma was the reason Ekatya had discovered the true strength of their bond. That strength had then bound Andira and Salomen, enabling the four of them to save Alsea and topple an empire.

Throughout that test, Lanaril had kept her faith. It was justified in one glorious, explosive burst of light and power. She had even been gifted with her own part in the miracle.

And in a small, separate miracle, Fianna had come home to her, a moment she would forever remember as a voice in her earcuff: *Lanaril. She's all right. Successful and not even a stain on her uniform.*

Andira had taken time out from directing the most intricate and critical battle in Alsean history to give her that assurance. Not until afterward did Lanaril understand that in order to do so, she had temporarily muted her com call with all those involved in the battle effort and opened a connection just to her. It was a stunning act of thoughtfulness, leaving shame in its wake. How could she have lost trust in such a friend?

She was ashamed a second time when Fianna arrived at the temple the following day, exhausted yet glowing. After a mutual shower and a joining that never made it to the bed, Fianna related her tale. Proudly, she added that she had brought her entire team home whole and unharmed, "except for Senshalon, the grainbird."

Before that moment, Lanaril had not even remembered the thirteen warriors who flew with Fianna into that ship. She had been so focused on her own fear, and then her private miracle, that she had given no thought to the many loved ones who had lived through an equally terrifying day.

Nor had she thought of those whose fear did not end with a miracle. While the fatality list was exceptionally short, limited to a handful of fighter losses, that was no consolation to those lighting pyres at the state funeral.

She had attended, as was her duty. It was not her duty to offer personal counseling services to the mourners, nor could she have found the time had all of them accepted. Four did, and they were the most difficult sessions she had ever undertaken. The grief crushing these patients felt like a living entity that watched her with a knowing smile. *I missed you by the width of a fingernail,* that smile said, *and you did nothing to deserve your good fortune.*

Systemic balance was more difficult to accept when she was a participant in its fundamental unfairness.

"Please stand for the raising of the shields."

Prime Warrior Ehron's voice interrupted her thoughts. She stood automatically, turning toward the wall opposite the exit tunnel.

Now facing Andira's back, she saw Salomen a head above, her dark hair twisted up into an elegant formal style. Lhyn's height topped even Salomen's, blocking Ekatya from view.

When appearing in public together, the four of them invariably arranged themselves in this order. Lanaril had thought it was dictated by their divine and normal tyree bonds, but Fianna argued differently. If that was the case, she asked, why didn't they ever see the two warriors in the middle?

That was when Lanaril learned that warriors positioned themselves on the outside to protect their bondmates. It was also when she noticed that Fianna did the same with her.

She leaned to the side to see around Salomen and Lhyn, revealing Ekatya in the position closest to the center aisle. Across the aisle stood five of the six Primes, each having already had their part in the ceremony. Ehron was on the temporary stage, leading this final piece.

Well above the heads of the crowd, the shuttle bay office took up two decks, its transparent wall crowded with guests who had not qualified for the seating here on the deck or in the risers. They had enjoyed an excellent view for most of the ceremony, albeit with the sound piped in. For the culminating moment about to take place, they would have to watch the vidscreen behind the stage.

The rustling of people standing and turning faded, leaving an expectant silence in the vast bay.

Lanaril shivered at the pensive opening notes of the Ballad of Blacksun. Though her throat grew tight, she dared not clear it. When the voices around her lifted in song, hers was not the only one made unsteady by emotion.

On the second verse, the wind instruments swooped in, swelling the music. Her voice swelled with it, and the banners began to rise up the wall.

It was a brilliant display of Alsean colors and tradition in this alien place: the builder, crafter, and scholar caste shields on the left, the Shield of Alsea heading for its higher position above the shuttle bay office, and the warrior, producer, and merchant caste shields on the right. Together, the seven banners took up the entire width of the bay.

The percussion roared to life on the fourth verse, and now Lanaril sang with abandon. Behind her, Fianna sang slightly off-key but with no less emotion, her hand warm against Lanaril's hip.

The banners arrived at their destinations in a triumphant crescendo of music and song, the culmination of moons of planning, preparation, sacrifice, and at least one miracle. Lanaril poured her heart into the final note and took a shuddering breath, her throat closing once again.

The *Phoenix* was now officially commissioned into service in the new Alsean Fleet.

As the wild applause and shouts of "For Fahla and Alsea!" rang through the bay, Fianna leaned over to speak in her ear.

"I never dreamed of seeing this. Not even when I took the bridge of the *Vengeance*. It hardly seems real."

Lanaril turned to drink in the sight of her, whole and happy and a vision of unearned grace. Though her front was up, something must have shown on her face, for Fianna's euphoric grin shifted to a curious smile.

"What are you thinking?"

"I'm thinking that someone writing a manuscript titled *The Book of Verity* should be open to her own truths."

"What truths?"

"I'll tell you after."

Andira was mounting the steps to the stage, her cape swaying with the movement. She acknowledged Ehron's salute and turned to the crowd as he strode back to his seat.

"How does it feel to be standing in the middle of history?" she asked.

The cheers and applause, which had begun to die down, immediately leaped to their prior level.

Andira laughed. "I feel the same." She allowed the noise to continue for half a tick before holding out her hands, palms down. "We have one more piece of business to conclude. Please be seated."

The applause gave way to rustling and murmurs as the audience retook their seats.

"Those of you who shuttled in today may have noticed the new identity code on this ship's hull. For those who were here before that change, or who didn't see it, here it is."

Behind her, the enormous vidscreen switched from a view of the newly raised banners to one of the ship's bow.

"AFS *Phoenix*, identity code SC zero zero two," Andira said. "The second ship of this class in the Alsean Fleet. I'm sure you can guess what the number one is reserved for."

"The *Caphenon*!" several voices shouted.

"Yes, the *Caphenon*. We'll have another party when we bring her into space."

That set off a new round of cheers.

"The discussion on what to name this class of ship was surprisingly short. I don't believe I've ever seen the war council agree on anything so quickly."

Laughter rippled across the crowd, Ehron's being among the loudest.

"There will only be two ships of this class in our fleet. We will build our own warships, and take this design as a guide, but we will not copy it. That makes the *Phoenix* and the *Caphenon* unique. We needed a class name that fit this unique nature." She looked down at Ekatya. "We couldn't name it Serrado class, since we're already using your family name for our two-seater fighters. Fortunately, you have another name. SC zero zero two means this is the second ship of the Savior class."

Though Ekatya strove to keep the emotion off her face, everyone in the first ten rows surely felt it as the shuttle bay rang with enthusiastic applause.

"Now, we have a commissioned ship in our newly established class." Andira spoke over the cheers, quieting them. "We're missing one thing. A commanding officer. Admiral Serrado, please come to the stage."

Ekatya stood up, resplendent in her one-of-a-kind uniform. It bore the hallmarks of the Alsean Fleet design, with its light blue and black colors representing both sky and space. But where the uniforms normally featured a swirl of small blue triangles on the black torso, Ekatya's triangles were silver. The band encircling her collar was also silver, as were the chevrons on her sleeves and the braid at her left shoulder. Combined with her crimson cape and its fully embroidered black-and-silver warrior caste shield, she was an impressive sight.

More impressive still, Lanaril thought, was the sight of her and Andira together on the stage. Andira's dress uniform was crimson and gold, presenting a striking contrast of colors between them.

"So much better than Protectorate Fleet uniforms," Fianna whispered.

"They are rather subdued, aren't they?" Lanaril carefully did not look at the Gaian officers sitting in the second row.

Fianna gave a quiet huff. "I think you mean dull. She's far better served by Alsean style."

"She's better served by Alsea."

Lanaril watched Andira accept Ekatya's salute and wondered how that was working between the two of them. Having a built-in power disparity was a challenge for any relationship, but theirs had just acquired the additional weight of formality and caste expectation.

Then again, who had more practice at separating public and private than these two women? They even surpassed her.

"In the Protectorate Fleet," Andira said, "tradition holds that an admiral does not command her own ship, though she may claim one as a flagship. That is not our tradition. The Mariners believe that a ship's commander is a ship's commander, regardless of rank. Thus there will be no captain of the *Phoenix* for as long as Admiral Serrado remains in command."

She faced Ekatya. "Admiral Serrado, at your oath ceremony yesterday, you swore to protect Alsea, her people, and the ideals for which we strive. Today we ask a different oath from you: that you will look upon the crew of this ship as your highest responsibility, second only to your oath as an admiral. That you will protect this ship and crew as you would your family, for in many ways, they are. That you will lead with honor. And finally, that you will treat all members of this crew equally, be they Alsean, Protectorate, or former members of the Voloth Empire. Do you accept these duties?"

"I do," Ekatya said firmly.

"Do you agree that service is a gift to be earned, not an obligation to be abused?"

"I do."

Lanaril sensed the ferocity of that agreement as strongly if she were in skin contact. Though it had been two moons since Ekatya was freed from Greve, his influence remained clear in her emotions. She would be relentless in rooting out abuse, not only in her own crew but also in those of the four destroyers. According to Fianna, with the number of former hangers and slaves serving on all five ships, such abuse was virtually certain. Ekatya had her work cut out for her.

"When the Protectorate Fleet conducted its ceremonies last moon," Andira said, "we paid close attention. One tradition in particular struck the war council, and indeed the High Council itself, as one we wished to keep." She turned toward the audience. "First Guard Rahel Sayana, report to the stage."

Boot heels sounded at the back of the bay, and every head turned to look. Dressed in an Alsean Fleet uniform with a producer-green band on each arm, Rahel strode down the central aisle. She held the grip of a sheathed sword in one hand while its tip rested on the palm of the other, a visual reflection of the oath-taking pose.

From the stage came a wave of shock that spun Lanaril back in her seat. Ekatya was watching with wide eyes, one hand covering her mouth. "Is that—?"

Andira smiled at her. "Under normal conditions," she said for the audience, "this ship's sword of command would have gone back to Tashar with the historical conservation shipment. The Alsean government asked to keep it as part of our negotiation for the *Phoenix*. Dr. Lhyn Rivers, will you join us on stage to narrate this tradition?"

"Ha," Lhyn said as she rose from her seat. "She never even guessed." Beaming, she waited for Rahel to pass and followed her up the steps. While Rahel circled around to stand behind Andira and Ekatya, Lhyn moved to the side.

"Alsean crafters no longer produce non-collapsible swords for working use," she began. "They're viewed as artifacts of a more primitive time. But this sword is special, crafted for the *Phoenix* by a master swordsmith on a distant planet. Its sister sword was recently discovered aboard the *Caphenon*, safely in storage but unrecognized until now. There will only be two Savior-class ships, thus there will only be two of these swords in the Alsean Fleet."

"First Guard, present the sword of command," Andira said.

Rahel moved forward and offered the sword, still in a horizontal position. Andira accepted it in a two-handed hold, flipping it upright as she turned to face Ekatya.

"This sword represents the commanding officer's responsibility to her ship and crew, to protect them, guide them, and lead with honor," Lhyn said. "Lancer Tal will now inspect the sword."

"She's using the same motions Admiral Serrado used last moon," Fianna whispered while Andira performed the first inspection. "Precisely the same. She must have watched the vids and practiced."

Of course she did, Lanaril thought. What an irony, that Ekatya would spend half a moon practicing with an Alsean sword while Andira secretly practiced with a Gaian one.

"Before it can be entrusted to its holder, the sword must be in perfect condition. This symbolizes the Alsean Fleet's commitment to both ship and crew."

With crisp movements, Andira rotated the sword and inspected its opposite face, then straightened and sheathed it with an audible *snap*.

"The passing of the sword from Lancer Tal to Admiral Serrado represents the handover of command, with all the duties and responsibilities that entails."

Andira stepped forward. Needing no guidance, Ekatya met her halfway.

"Notice how Lancer Tal and Admiral Serrado are keeping the sword midway between them while holding it firmly with both hands. At no point in this ceremony are there fewer than two hands touching it, but now there are four. This emphasizes the importance of command and the value of both ship and crew. They can never be treated lightly or left unsupported."

Lanaril wondered whether that interpretation came from the Protectorate Fleet or if Lhyn had introduced an Alsean flavor. She would have to ask at the reception.

"The transfer of command is complete only when Lancer Tal releases it into the care of Admiral Serrado. When two hands remain on the sword, this ceremony has ended."

"Admiral Serrado," Andira said clearly, "do you stand ready to accept command of the AFS *Phoenix*?"

"Lancer Tal, I stand ready to accept command."

"Admiral Serrado, you are now commander of the AFS *Phoenix*. Lead her well and with honor. May Fahla fly with you." Andira stepped back, leaving the sword in Ekatya's hands.

Ekatya stared at it, seemingly oblivious to the applause and roars of approval. Then she nodded and looked out at the audience, waiting as it gradually quieted.

"What Dr. Rivers hasn't explained," she said when she could be heard, "is that the crew member bearing this sword to and from the ceremony also bears a great honor. That individual is chosen by the commanding officer as a reward for meritorious service." Her gaze dropped back to the sword as she added, "You may have guessed this part of the ceremony was a surprise to me."

Chuckles rippled through the crowd.

"I had no say in the selection of First Guard Sayana." She turned to face Rahel and held out the sword. "But if I had, it would still have been you. First Guard, I entrust this sword to you for safekeeping. Return it to my office, where it will remain for the duration of my command."

Rahel held a fist to her chest and bowed her head, then accepted the sword. As she marched off the stage, Andira addressed the crowd.

"This concludes our ceremonies today, and just in time. I'm told the food and spirits are ready for a proper celebration!" She swept both arms upward, urging the applauding crowd to stand, and the band struck up a sprightly tune.

"This should be an improvement over the last one," Fianna said. "No Protectorate Fleet dokkers stuffed into uniforms and weighed down with medals."

Lanaril remembered those all too well. "And better food, I hear."

Salomen stepped over, her eyes sparkling with happiness. "Better spirits, too. Fahla, it felt good to see Ekatya reclaim that sword. As if some part of me has been tense ever since she gave it up last moon, and now I can finally relax."

"Now you can all relax," Lanaril said. "It's been a long, difficult path, but you've reached the end of it."

"The end of this one, yes." Without looking, Salomen held out a hand, smiling when Andira walked up behind her and clasped it. "The brighter path is just beginning."

49

TRUTHS

"What are the truths you should be open to?"

Lanaril seemed startled by the question before understanding dawned. "Ah. After the raising of the banners." She sipped her Synobian Sparkler and hummed in appreciation. "This is quite good."

"If I didn't know better," Vellmar teased, "I'd say you were stalling. You said you'd tell me later."

"We're at a reception."

"You *are* stalling." She tilted her head toward the crowd milling about the luxurious conference room. "We've made our rounds. Everyone is occupied with their own conversations. What better time than now?"

"Later tonight, in the privacy of my quarters?"

"You're hoping I'll forget."

"Little chance of that," Lanaril muttered.

Vellmar had just decided not to press further when Lanaril set her glass beside the yellow Filessian orchid in a nearby niche.

"You've spent most of our relationship thinking you had to work to deserve me," she said, taking one of Vellmar's hands in her own. "The truth is, I've allowed it. I've let you carry the burden of proving that we can work. I'm the one who needed convincing. You're the one who always knew."

This was not at all what she had expected. "Lanaril—"

"You asked. Let me finish. The second truth is that I've realized it's not a matter of deserving. If it were, you would not have come back to me after the battle. That was a gift I did not earn." She held up her free hand, stopping Vellmar's protest. "The third is that you are a *gift*. Unlooked for, unearned, yet here regardless, and I love you."

She waited, a slow smile curving her lips while Vellmar tried to get her brain cells coordinated.

"I, ah . . . Goddess above, you do know how to take my legs out from under me." With their hands clasped, Lanaril's honesty had come through in a molten rush, leaving no room for doubt. Vellmar threw her earlier plans out the window and decided, for once in her life, to act on impulse. "May I share a truth I've recently realized? Fair trade?"

Intrigue lit Lanaril's face. "No trade necessary, but I very much want to hear it."

Vellmar caught her other hand. "Lancer Tal thinks she burdened me. In truth, she gave me a gift. You're wrong about one thing—I didn't always know we would work. I worried that I didn't have enough to offer, and someday you'd stop telling me that I did. That's no longer a concern. I have a future. Even if I don't rise to the State Chair, I know I'll go far enough to hold my head high next to you. That was all I needed. Lanaril, will you go into that future with me? Will you kneel with me before your fathers and ask for my inclusion?"

She had certainly tipped the balance back. Lanaril was so surprised that a sonsales could see it. The tumbling emotions flowed through their skin contact, a symphony of sentiment whose instruments fell away one by one until only the soloist remained.

"When I severed my bond, I swore I'd never believe those promises again," she said. "I decided that no Alsean could be held responsible for promises the future would not allow them to keep. I lost my faith. Not in Fahla, but in the strength of our hearts."

Vellmar tightened her grip, needing the contact. Lanaril's answer was in her touch, and she was desperate not to lose even a fraction of it.

"You gave my faith back to me. I trust your heart." Her smile was glorious. "A future with you sounds like the greatest gift I'll never earn, but I'll be glad to spend my life trying. Will you kneel with me before your mothers and ask for my inclusion?"

"My mothers are going to have *kittens*," Vellmar blurted. "A whole litter of vallcat kittens!" She pulled a laughing Lanaril into her arms and wondered why the entire room didn't light up with the joy that poured from both of them.

Then Lanaril kissed her, and she forgot the room, the people in it, and the ship that carried them.

50

UNINVITED

"Would you look at that!"

Boundless delight sang through their link, interrupting the story Tal was telling Ekatya. She turned to follow Salomen's line of sight.

In the far corner of the room, Vellmar and Lanaril were making a public display the likes of which she had not seen since the march in Blacksun. Then, Lanaril had announced their relationship to the world by giving Vellmar a warmron and a kiss on a global broadcast.

This kiss was in danger of melting the bulkheads. Though they were tucked away from the crowd, awareness of their display was radiating outward, quieting conversations and bringing smiles to nearly every face.

"That's a little unusual for Lanaril, isn't it?" Ekatya asked.

"Oh, yes." Salomen bounced up on her toes, too gleeful to stay still. "And for Fianna, too. She's in uniform. At a reception. There's only one reason why she would forget that."

"I need a cultural hint."

"I wondered if promoting her would push her in that direction," Tal said.

Salomen slipped an arm around her waist, happiness pouring off her in a dazzling wave. "I don't think it was the promotion. I think it was the truth."

"Could someone spell it out for the Gaian?" Ekatya demanded.

She had made such progress over the last moon that Tal sometimes forgot about her weak point. Ekatya was no outsider, but it would take many more moons before she fully believed it—and much more cultural immersion, as Lhyn called it.

"One of those two asked the other to bond with her," she explained. "That's the only time a kiss like that would be appropriate in a setting like this."

"Betting both sides?" Salomen joked. "You know it wasn't Lanaril. Fianna is the one who takes risks."

Ekatya watched with renewed interest. "Great galaxies. I'll have to rethink my impressions of Lanaril. Look at where her hands are."

Lhyn appeared next to them, breathless and grinning. "I take two ticks to visit the toilet and look what happens. Can you believe it? Tell me someone recorded this."

The couple finally managed to separate their lips but made it no further than that. They leaned their foreheads together, twin smiles gracing their features.

Well, if Vellmar decided to do this in public, she deserved what she got.

"Now that's what I like to see in my Guards," Tal called out, silencing the few remaining conversations. "Healthy ambition!"

Vellmar jumped back, her entire body telegraphing surprise, while Lanaril lifted her chin with a smug expression.

"I'm the one who just landed the Emissary," she said. "Which of us has more ambition?"

Their audience laughed, and Tal began the applause that spread to every corner of the room. Vellmar looked briefly embarrassed before giving Lanaril another scorching kiss.

Whoops and whistles filled the air, including one shockingly shrill whistle from Lhyn. Tal turned to see her taking two fingers out of her mouth.

"Allendohan technique," she said with a shrug. "It's how mothers call home their broods."

"You're teaching me that," Tal informed her.

"If you think you can learn."

She would have responded to the blatant challenge, but Lhyn headed straight to Lanaril, Rahel pushed her way through the crowd to give

Vellmar a double palm touch, and everyone was suddenly talking at once.

"There's something in the air at these receptions," Ekatya said. "First Alejandra's news, now this." She gave her drink a suspicious look. "Maybe it isn't the air. Maybe I need to have Zeppy check the matter printers."

"Why would you do that when the results are so marvelous?" Salomen set off to offer her own congratulations.

"She makes a fair point," Tal said.

"Still, I should know if—" Ekatya stopped, her head tilting as she listened to something on her internal com. The shift in her emotional signature was unnerving. "Thank you, Ensign. I'll take it in the small conference room. It's Sholokhov," she said in a low voice. "Why would he be calling now?"

"Why is he *able* to call you is the more pertinent question. I issued orders the day of your retirement. Any calls from him go to me or Ambassador Solvassen. We fenced you off."

"He's using the priority blue channel. The protocols are still active, and those calls don't come with an ID code until I put in mine. It wouldn't be anyone else."

"You're not doing this alone." Tal kept pace with her as she strode for the door.

"He won't talk to me if you're there. We need to know what he has to say."

"I'll stay out of sight."

Ekatya did not reply, her emotional signature rigid with apprehension. They left the cheerful, noisy party behind and crossed the corridor to a much smaller room, where the wall display already showed a blue emblem.

The door closed, plunging them into silence.

"Stand over there." Ekatya pointed to a corner on the same wall as the display.

Tal complied, wishing circumstances were different so she could joke about obeying orders.

At the oval table taking up the center of the room, Ekatya activated a control pad and entered a code. Though Tal could not make out details, she saw the emblem shrink to nothing before it was replaced by a string of Common characters.

"It's him," Ekatya confirmed, tapping the pad once more. "Here we go."

The uniform color of the display shifted to a moving image, blurry from this angle but definitely a head and upper body.

"Director Sholokhov," Ekatya said, adding a short phrase that Tal's earcuff translated as "What a surprise."

"A good one, I hope." He sounded jovial. "I wanted to congratulate you, Admiral. You finally have the rank you deserve."

"Thank you. It's certainly good to be out of the cage."

Ekatya said nothing more, the silence growing until he broke it.

"How things have changed. I suppose the days are long gone when you asked what you could do for me."

"Why are you calling?"

"I already gave you my reason."

"Merely to congratulate me?" she asked with a skeptical lift of her brows.

"Perhaps to congratulate us both. And your other tyree. It's not often an opponent deceives me. She had me convinced she would throw you out the airlock if circumstances called for it."

He didn't sound offended, though Tal couldn't be certain without seeing him.

"I'm . . . surprised," Ekatya said. "I thought—"

"That I'd be angry? No, I believe it was more of a disappointment. All that insistence on your vaunted honesty, yet you're no different from the rest of us."

"You forget I learned from the best," she said evenly. "I never lied to you. I simply didn't tell you everything."

"You said you couldn't influence her decisions."

"That was and still is true. Loving Andira doesn't give me any power over her professional choices. She keeps that separate from her personal life."

"Do you expect me to believe that?"

"I don't care if you do." Realization broke across her face. "I really don't," she marveled.

Tal would have given anything to see Sholokhov's face in the ensuing silence. Not being able to sense him over the quantum com had been a serious handicap during their negotiations; only now did she realize how much she had relied on her sight.

"Interesting," he said at last. "But it doesn't change the outcome. We all got what we wanted. I have the empaths and the heavy cruiser, Lancer Tal has her ship, and I put you in charge of the new Alsean Fleet."

Tal frowned at the phrasing.

"That's why you're calling," Ekatya said. "You had another reason to want me in charge. I knew it was more than my inducement to leave Fleet quietly."

"This is what I'll miss. Watching you catch up to me. I'm sure you'll yank the priority blue protocols as soon as I end this call, though I'd advise you to give me a way to contact you. I have my fingers in pots all over the galaxy. You never know when I might be able to pass on something useful."

"You already have a direct line to Ambassador Solvassen and Lancer Tal."

"Ah, but they're not you. Though I admit I have new respect for your Lancer."

Don't do it, Tal thought. She didn't want him to have continued access for this kind of game playing, but she could sense it. Ekatya had already concluded that—

"I'll think about it."

She silently swore. Ekatya was strategizing as an admiral should. That didn't mean she had to like it.

"Excellent. I knew I could depend on your common sense. And your ethical sense, which is why you are where you are. You assumed that I saved your command to gain a conduit to Lancer Tal. I didn't correct you then."

"I'm waiting with bated breath," Ekatya said flatly.

"To repeat your words, I never lied to you. I simply didn't tell you the whole truth."

Tal heard a creaking sound, probably the material of his chair as he leaned back. It appeared he had a story to tell.

"The Protectorate did agree with the Voloth Empire on one thing," he began. "The Alseans are an unknown and possibly unlimited power. That makes them a potential threat. The Voloth unfortunately responded with their usual lack of imagination. Brute force acquired their territory and held it, thus brute force would surely remove this threat. That error cost them an empire."

"But you had more imagination."

"I had more *subtlety*. The Alseans can't be stopped. Holding them back was never the solution. But they're a brand new power, just stepping into the stars. They can be molded."

"You are something else. You're expecting me to mold the Alsean Fleet to your specifications?"

"Oh, no, Admiral. I'm expecting you to mold them to yours. The ever-righteous Admiral Serrado, always standing up for her definition of what is principled and correct. You'll shape that fleet from birth, imposing your limitations on it. I didn't know what to expect from the Alseans, but I know what to expect from you."

"Honor?" she asked in a dry tone. "The same ideals as the Protectorate Fleet?"

"Ideals are for when circumstances allow. You've never learned that and you never will. Lancer Tal knows better, but she's bound by an interplanetary agreement. Even if she weren't, she can't afford to remove you after the fanfare of your promotion, that touching oath, and taking command. You'll stay right where I need you to be."

"I'm right where *I* need to be. I'm where Lancer Tal needs me to be. If that works to your benefit, so be it. Perhaps the Protectorate will finally stop seeing us as an unknown power and realize that we're exactly what we've said all along."

"We," he echoed. "That didn't take long."

"A foreseeable consequence to being hounded out of the organization I devoted my life to. The Alseans value me for the same thing the Protectorate feared in me. I'm home, Director. As you said, we all got what we wanted. Although I got a bit more," she added. "I know you didn't bust Greve down to ensign for me, but it made my day."

"Only one day? I'm disappointed."

She lifted her hands. "Figure of speech. Suffice to say it was extremely enjoyable."

The chair creaked again.

"Some gasbags need to be popped," he said. "That one was overdue. I didn't appreciate his handling of one of my best resources. I didn't appreciate Lancer Tal's handling of you, either, but I've had to reassess that reading."

"Lancer Tal handles me to my complete satisfaction," Ekatya said with a straight face.

Tal pressed her knuckles against her mouth and exhaled slowly, trying not to laugh.

After a brief silence, a low chuckle issued from the com. "You might not be quite as upright as I thought. Congratulations, Admiral. Farewell and good hunting."

The display went blank.

Ekatya's eyes met hers. Her lips twitched, her cheeks reddened—and then a snort escaped. Leaning against the table, she dropped her head back and let out a bellow of laughter.

"Did you hear it?" she gasped. "I finally got him!"

Tal crossed over and leaned next to her. At this proximity, it was like being bathed in glee. "If I hadn't watched you do it, I would never have believed you'd say that to him."

"I couldn't resist." She was winding down, sporadic chortles shaking her body. "I think Alsean honesty is rubbing off on me."

"To the betterment of all," Tal teased. "Is it my imagination, or did he give you the equivalent of a blessing?"

"It's not your imagination. That was quite a finish, considering that he started out ready to tear me apart for lying. And he claims he gamed the whole thing? Dokshin! An Alsean fleet was cycles away when he saved my command. He couldn't possibly have known we'd end up with five captured ships."

Tal thought back to Sholokhov's first offer and shook her head. "No, but I don't think he was lying. He wanted to promote you to rear admiral and keep you on the *Phoenix* until you retired. That would have guaranteed your influence here while we built our fleet. He made a calculated guess that by the time we had two or three smaller ships plus the *Caphenon*—"

"You'd poach me for the position." The cloud of mirth had dissipated.

"I tried to poach you three cycles ago. His assumption was well-founded."

"And Lhyn lives here, so I'd never go anywhere else. If I'm tied to Alsea anyway, why wouldn't I work for you rather than the Protectorate once it became an option? Hades, he *did* plan this. I took a different route than he expected, but I ended up in the same place." Merriment sparkled around her again.

"What are you thinking?"

She spread her hands. "All that planning and manipulation, just to put me here. What I am going to do? Make you more honorable than you already are?"

"Well, if anyone could . . ."

"He outsmarted himself." Grinning, Ekatya pushed off the table and turned to face her. "Director I Know More Than You gave me everything I ever wanted and got *nothing* out of it. But he doesn't know that. He'll never realize that he could have gotten the same results without losing me to Alsea."

"Let's not tell him," Tal suggested.

"Oh, no. Never. For once in my life, I know more than he does." She glowed with satisfaction.

"You're a holcat in the curing shed windowsill," Tal said with a laugh. "I believe we left a celebration in progress across the hall. Shall we give our congratulations to Lanaril and Vellmar?"

Ekatya started for the door. "Twenty cinteks says Lhyn and Salomen are giving advice on where they should go for their bonding break."

"No bet."

"Still stinging from losing the last one?"

"It was one hundred cinteks!"

"So much for warrior courage."

Tal stopped, an appropriate response on the tip of her tongue, but forgot it when Ekatya turned and held out a hand.

She was breathtaking in her new uniform and full cape, yet even those paled next to the beauty of her easy, free smile.

"Are you coming?" she asked.

Tal clasped her hand. "Lead the way."

EPILOGUE

Sixteen moons later

"I'm glad the forecast was right." Tal gestured toward her office windows, dry for the first time in nearly a moon. She had prepared herself for disappointment, knowing the ship launch could be delayed, but the sky was blue with billowing white clouds and no sign of the relentless autumn rains.

"Me too. I wasn't looking forward to walking across the park while trying to keep Little Chunk dry." Micah tenderly rearranged the blanket around his daughter, who slept in her basket next to the sofa.

Alejandra thwacked his leg. "You'd better stop calling her that before she starts learning words."

"It's a compliment! She's in the ninety-fifth percentile for her age. You're going to grow up to be a big, strong warrior," he crooned to the sleeping infant. "Just like two-thirds of your parents."

At four moons past weaning, Micah's body had completed its reversion. The broadened hips enabling birth were slim once more, and he had rebuilt the masculine musculature sacrificed to the energy demands of gestation and lactation. Best of all, to Tal's thinking, his breasts were fully reabsorbed. She had threatened to push him out the nearest window if he made one more smug comment about his being larger than hers.

365

Beside her, Salomen set down her shannel and reached for the plate of pastries on the low table. "Alejandra, correct me if I'm wrong, but doesn't your daughter also have the option of being a scholar?"

"Yes, but it's astonishing how a certain member of the household discounts that. Not to mention any other caste she might challenge."

"She threw a block hard enough to bruise me where it hit." Micah proudly pointed to his forehead, where a minuscule red mark remained. "That's a warrior in the making."

"Or a scholar with a temper," Lhyn added from her chair at the head of their little group.

Alejandra lifted her cup in a salute. "She may not have my genes, but by Fahla, she has my temper."

"Environmental versus genetic influence is *such* a fascinating field of study here." Lhyn leaned over the arm of her chair, bringing their heads closer together. "Did you read the article in *Scholar's Moon* correlating empathic ability with shared character traits between parents, children, and siblings?"

"Yes! The day it came out. What did you think of the methodology?"

"Well, they're gone," Salomen remarked as the two scholars lost themselves in discussion. "I hope you weren't planning to talk to your bondmate for the next hantick."

"Fortunately, I have other things to keep me occupied." Micah captured a pastry. "And others to speak with. Though I do wish Vellmar and Lanaril were here."

"Fianna said her mothers threatened dire consequences unless she brought Lanaril to Pollonius for their thirty-fifth anniversary," Salomen said. "They've hardly seen her since the bonding break."

"How is that working out?"

"There's some cultural adjustment." Tal smiled, remembering Lanaril's exasperation on their last call. "Our Lead Templar is still getting used to the fact that she bonded into a warrior family."

"So am I," Salomen said dryly.

Tal mimed a blade to the heart, making Micah laugh.

"How much longer?" he asked.

She picked up the control for the vidscreen and activated it. "Twenty ticks," she said, watching the countdown scroll in the upper right corner.

"Is Ekatya talking to you now?"

"Corozen," Salomen remonstrated. "Don't make light of it."

Her tyree knew better than anyone how difficult that day had been—the day Tal told Ekatya she could not ride her ship into orbit.

While the builders had included as much redundancy as they could, the margin of error was small. If any calculation turned out to be wrong, or too many boosters or slings failed before the ship reached escape altitude, it would crash back to Alsea with little to no time for pod ejections. The risk was too high, and the need too small, for any crew other than a pilot and backup.

Ekatya's reaction shocked them all. She had unleashed an instant and blazing anger, demanding to know why she couldn't lead from the front like a proper Alsean warrior. The logical explanation only inflamed her more. She accused Tal of hypocrisy and made a vicious comparison to "the last two supervisors who tried to clip my wings" before slamming the front door behind her and vanishing into the woods of Hol-Tyree.

"I didn't know it was that serious," Micah said. "You didn't tell me."

"It was serious," Salomen confirmed. "I sent Lhyn to take care of her while I tracked down Ekatya."

"Did she survive you tracking her down?"

"Barely."

"Salomen was a mountzar in full roar," Tal added. "I was surprised we didn't have a summer windstorm."

"Of course she was. She's more than your divine tyree now. She's your guardian. Alejandra isn't even Alsean, and you should have seen her when someone or something upset me."

"You got upset?" This was news to her.

"Oh, believe me." Alejandra had interrupted her discussion with Lhyn. "He did. But warriors hate to admit that they're subject to hormonal influences like anyone else." She cast a knowing look at Tal. "You're in your second quarter. The fetal growth is putting a greater load on your system, which affects your brain chemistry. Small things can hit you emotionally like big ones. Big things can hit like a star going nova."

"It was a big thing," Tal conceded. Knowing that Micah had felt the same way put her at greater ease.

"Salomen is affected as well," Micah said. "She's under the influence of a chemical directive to protect her mate and the mother of her child. Didn't Healer Wellernal tell you to expect it?"

"He did," Salomen answered for her. "But it's one thing to hear and read about it. It's something else to experience the need to shake someone I love until her teeth rattle."

"In retrospect, we should have done it the other way around," Lhyn said. "I should have talked to Ekatya while Salomen consoled Andira."

"I didn't need *consoling*. I was merely—"

"Understandably distraught," Salomen interrupted. "Tyrina, we're among family. Corozen and Alejandra have been through this."

Tal hesitated. It was not in her nature to admit weakness, but if Micah could . . .

"I don't agree that you should have done it the other way around," she said, nodding toward Lhyn. "You helped me understand Ekatya's reaction. I thought it was a self-evident risk assessment that our only admiral could not be on that ship. Not when she had no skill to lend the launch. She's a warrior and a leader; of course she would agree with that."

"But when it comes to the crash of the *Caphenon*, Ekatya is not rational," Lhyn told Micah and Alejandra. "It's an open wound for her. She's never forgotten the crew members who died in that crash."

"She needed to honor them." Micah understood immediately. "A debt owed to the dead was stronger than a theoretical risk. Being told she could not honor it overwhelmed her rational thinking."

"Right! Deep down, she thought riding her ship up would close the wound. Because it would close the circle. The captain goes down with the ship, the admiral goes up with it."

"I wasn't very rational either," Salomen said. "But perhaps that was necessary. Ekatya was too angry to realize how damaging her words were, but I was ten times angrier."

That might be an understatement, Tal thought. Listening to Lhyn's patient, logical explanation while sensing Salomen's wrath had been an exercise in contrasts. She had felt sorry for Ekatya, knowing what was bearing down on her.

"That alone tells you how deep it went," Alejandra said. "Ekatya is usually very aware of her words."

"I believe it worked out for the best." Salomen reached for Tal's hand. "There's a freedom in knowing that your loved ones have seen you at your worst and still love you just the same. Ekatya has always been a little more careful than the rest of us. Now she knows it's not necessary."

"It made a difference," Lhyn agreed. "And she's content with the compromise. She can accompany her ship back to orbit—"

"And get the best view of all," Tal finished. "I'm envious."

"There's still risk involved. You are not allowed." Salomen rested her free hand on Tal's stomach.

"Guardian is right," Tal told Micah in an aggrieved tone. "I'm not allowed to do *anything* anymore."

"Get used to it," he said sympathetically. "I kicked against it the first moon or so, but it was like kicking a stone wall. Salomen will be even more immovable than Alejandra was."

"You heard Healer Wellernal. I have a biological imperative, and I'm not afraid to use it."

"You're gleeful about using it," Tal muttered, but could not stop her smile. Most of her complaints were for show and Salomen knew it. In truth, having such a ferocious protector settled something deep inside, a primal need for safety while she carried their child.

"Have you chosen a name yet?" Alejandra asked.

Salomen glanced at Tal. "We have. Once we decided in favor of traditional rather than modern, there was no question." She rubbed Tal's stomach, an unconscious gesture that had become commonplace. "He'll know one grandfather and be named after the other."

"You're naming him Andorin." Micah's approval washed over them in a wave of warmth. "Your father would be proud."

"I know." Tal tried to wipe her eye without anyone noticing. Damn these hormones! "He'd be proud of us all, I think."

The next few ticks flew by in a discussion of social changes, until the countdown reached one tick and Tal turned up the volume on the broadcast.

Alejandra leaned into Micah, positioning herself sideways on the sofa. "At last we get to learn what you named your other baby."

Lhyn snickered. "You're not too far off with that."

The program opened with rousing music and the somewhat unnecessary identification of Alsea's two most popular news personalities.

"Good morning and welcome to the big event!" the first said jovially.

"This is a day we've looked forward to for a long time now," added the second. "But we know you don't want to waste time looking at our lovely faces, so without further delay, here is the scene at the launch site."

The view shifted to one from a vidcam flying high above the ship. From the engine cradle forward, it was hidden beneath an immense fabric cover, while a forest of scaffolding surrounded it on all sides. As the announcers explained, the scaffolding had been used first to elevate the ship enough to pass the slings beneath it, then to house the fusion boosters to which the slings were attached.

"Let's talk to someone who knows a bit more about it," the second announcer said. "Admiral Serrado?"

Ekatya's smiling face appeared in a view Tal recognized as coming from her quantum com. "I'm just the shuttle pilot," she said. "You want to speak with Chief Kameha"—she pointed to her right—"or Prime Builder Eroles, standing behind us."

"Just the shuttle pilot?" the announcer repeated in disbelieving tones. "Did you get demoted?"

Tal winced.

"Hardly. I have the best seat in the house. Chief, show them what we're looking at."

The view shifted once again. A vidcam inside the shuttle now showed Ekatya and Kameha sitting in the cockpit while Eroles leaned against Kameha's seat, peering eagerly forward. Beyond them, the scene through their windshield was a close view of the ship's engine cradle as the shuttle hovered above it.

Eroles turned to face the cam. "The vidcams out there aren't allowed within two lengths of the ship," she said. "We can't take the chance of anything interfering with a booster. Admiral Serrado speaks the truth; this is the best view on the planet."

"What is the concern with a vidcam hitting a booster?" asked the first announcer.

"We're lifting a massively heavy object into orbit using one sling every twenty strides. That's forty slings and eighty fusion boosters, each pair carrying a different load. The center of the ship weighs more than the nose or tail," Eroles explained. "The boosters attached to the outer slings can't be operating at the same power level as those attached to the center slings. If they did . . ." She held a hand level to the floor, then tilted it upward, her bracelets sliding down her wrist. "We'd end up with the nose rising faster than the center, or the tail rising faster, or any equally bad combination."

Kameha turned around in his seat. "The calculations involved in establishing power needs made even my brain hurt, and I usually eat those kinds of equations for mornmeal."

"My brain hurts merely imagining it," the announcer joked. "But what I'm hearing is that this is a very delicate operation, and anything could throw it off balance."

"Oh, yes." Eroles nodded. "Every booster needs to provide the correct amount of thrust for that specific point on the ship. Not only that, but the power requirements change as we gain altitude. We had to write a computer program to run the boosters due to the number of adjustments that must be made every piptick." She rested a hand on Kameha's shoulder. "Chief Kameha will be watching the program and making manual adjustments if any of our calculations were wrong. Or if anything untoward occurs, such as a booster or sling failure. We're using more than we need, but any failure will still mean redistributing the weight."

Ekatya looked over her shoulder. "Now do you see why I'm the pilot? The best part of being admiral is delegating the high-stress jobs. I don't need any more silver strands in my hair."

Kameha scoffed. "How many do you have now, three?"

"Five. All from dealing with you when you were my chief engineer."

"They're good," Alejandra remarked as the announcers chuckled and asked another question. "Eroles is competence personified. Ekatya and Kameha make it look like they've worked together forever and nothing is too much for them."

"Ekatya says he was her best chief engineer by far," Lhyn said. "She hated losing him, even though she couldn't blame Andira for poaching him."

"It's a good thing I did, isn't it? He and Eroles are the reason she's getting her ship back."

"I think she's gotten over it." Lhyn smiled at Tal before refocusing on Eroles, who was explaining why the ship couldn't use its own engines.

Tal paid no attention, having memorized these facts long ago. Her thoughts were on Ekatya and the memories flooding in.

When Salomen brought Ekatya back after that fight, Tal could hardly believe she was sensing the same woman who had stormed out half a hantick earlier. The sizzling anger had vanished, replaced by shame and painful regret. The moment their eyes met, Ekatya was stumbling over her apology. Her tentative movements, as if she were afraid she had broken something irrevocably, had hurt Tal nearly as much as the vicious words before.

Wisely, neither Salomen nor Lhyn let it end there. They had conducted a family meeting, based on the tradition Salomen learned from her parents, and made sure nothing was left unsaid or unacknowledged.

While Tal felt vastly better by its end, Ekatya was not convinced of her forgiveness. Words could only do so much. A Sharing was out of the question, given Tal's emotional unsteadiness at the time.

Physical reassurance was the obvious answer, yet when Ekatya hesitantly asked, Tal's *yes* coincided with Salomen's *I'm not leaving you alone with her.*

A guardian's protective anger was too deep an instinct to be assuaged with apologies. Intellectually, Salomen knew Tal was safe. Emotionally, she could not walk away.

Tal had no solution. Neither did Salomen. Ekatya was devastated by the proof that she had broken a trust.

"Then don't leave her," Lhyn suggested. "Stay in the room."

To Tal's surprise, Ekatya agreed to the condition.

Joining with one tyree while the other watched would have sent her through the roof on a normal day. On this day, with pregnancy hormones and a deep need for reconnection enhancing her arousal, she went straight to the stratosphere. Ekatya painted her apology on Tal's skin, love soaking through muscle and tendon to suffuse her bones, while Salomen's silent presence surrounded her with safety, love, and arousal of a different flavor.

At the end, Tal was left a sated puddle in the center of the bed, incapable of reciprocation or even a coherent word. The last thing she remembered before dropping off to sleep was Salomen's lips against her temple.

When she woke some time later, Ekatya was watching her with wet eyes and a tremulous smile.

"She left you in my care," she said.

Six words, Tal thought as Ekatya made an adjustment to her console onscreen. Just six words to describe the most profound change she had ever sensed in an emotional signature, and it happened in the space of one nap.

"What are you thinking?" Salomen asked, caressing her stomach.

Tal caught her hand and lifted it for a kiss.

"Ah. Never mind, I know." Salomen leaned in to kiss her properly. "You were hotter than a black rock on a summer day," she whispered.

"It's the post-battle drive all over again." Lhyn's knowing gaze was on them. "You two can't be apart for longer than ten pipticks."

"And just think, we have three more pregnancies to look forward to." Exuding satisfaction, Salomen settled back against the sofa.

Onscreen, the announcers were leading up to the big reveal.

"We've seen endless speculation about the ship's new name," the first said. "The crafters working on the hull have been notoriously tight-lipped. No one could pull a word from them."

"I heard that bribes were offered," the second added. "The betting has been intense."

"Hope you all have your bets laid down, because we're about to see for ourselves." The first held up his reader card. "This file unlocked forty ticks ago, giving us the name and the background behind it. I have to say, it's a perfect choice."

"I liked the *Caphenon*," said the second. "Once I learned how to pronounce it."

Lhyn laughed. "I've heard that a lot."

"I was career Fleet and even I had to learn to pronounce it," Alejandra said.

The vidscreen was now showing the ship from above. The enormous cover stretching over most of its length had sheltered the crafters from the weather and concealed their work from view. Conjecture over what lay beneath it had consumed Alsea for nearly a moon.

"Here is the statement from the Office of the Lancer," said the first announcer as the cam gradually magnified the view. "Four and one-half cycles ago, the *Caphenon* gave her life for Alsea. In the course of saving our civilization, this valiant ship ended her dance among the stars and crashed to the ground, wounded beyond repair—or so her creators thought. We have always thought differently."

"Words for Fahla," murmured the second.

"The ship we now return to the stars is not the same one that tumbled through our skies on that dark night. She is reborn. She wears a new skin and an Alsean name to celebrate her return to life.

"But what to name a ship with such a storied past and brilliant future? This ship restored our divine tyrees after an absence of one thousand cycles. She saved Blacksun in the Battle of Alsea. She brought us the Savior, chosen by Fahla to end the greatest threat Alsea has ever known. The Templars speak with one voice when they call this ship a vessel of Fahla. And thus, in the end, she named herself."

The view was now so magnified that the ship filled the screen. Silently, the clamps on the port side scaffolding released their grip on the cover. It fluttered to the hull and was drawn away, the starboard rollers tucking it into a neat cylinder to reveal what had been hidden for so long.

"Goddess above," Micah said as the artwork came into view.

Tal sat forward, her fingertips tingling with anticipation. Though she had approved the design and known the name for moons now, this was a moment of pure magic.

"Oh my stars," Lhyn said. "It turned out *beautifully*."

The ship's formerly silver hull was now a gleaming white, reflecting the sun so brightly that it overwhelmed the vidcam's sensor. The broadcast promptly switched to one positioned at a different angle.

Spread across the entire domed section was a great molwyn tree in the circular, stylized form of a Shield of Alsea. Atop its branches, six stars shone in an arc that stretched from port to starboard. But unlike a true Shield, the star representing Fahla was not sheltered beneath the topmost branches. Instead, it was centered above the six smaller stars, dwarfing them as it pointed the way the ship would go. Above it, following the arc of the bow, was the ship's name and identity number.

"SC zero zero one," the announcer said in a reverent voice. "The *Seventh Star*."

Neither announcer spoke again, allowing their silence to mark the import of this event.

On the opposite sofa, Alejandra let out a long breath. "I'd never have believed something like that could bring tears to my eyes," she said, wiping her cheek. "You embedded the truth right into her name."

"I can finally give credit where it's due," Tal said. "Lhyn suggested it. I took her idea to the war council. They had narrowed down the possibilities to a list of five and then argued over them for a solid moon. But when I offered this one, they threw out the shortlist and unanimously agreed. In about six ticks, as I recall."

Micah gave Lhyn an approving smile. "Well done. I cannot imagine a better name."

"Thank you. I have to admit I'm a little proud."

"Be more than just a little proud," Salomen said, her own pride plain to see.

"Great Mother." The second announcer finally spoke. "That was worth the wait. For the record, this is the largest Shield of Alsea ever produced, spanning four hundred and twenty-five strides."

"To put that in a different perspective," the first said, "it's as long as three and a half city stadiums, end to end."

"Or fourteen wallball courts," the second interjected.

"Even more amazing to me is the fact that this is not painted. It's etched and sealed, to make it robust against micro-abrasions from space travel. I can hardly imagine the labor involved or the sheer technical difficulty of it."

"Agreed. This is a magnificent artistic accomplishment and a shining credit to the crafter caste. Admiral Serrado, how does it look from your position?"

The view switched to the inside of the shuttle, where Ekatya was surreptitiously drying a hand on her trousers. She turned in her seat to face the vidcam, the ship's bow filling the window behind her.

"I think it's one of the most gorgeous sights I've ever seen," she said, a telltale hoarseness in her voice. "I have to admit, it hurt to learn that she wouldn't keep her original name. The *Caphenon* will always have a special place in my heart. But it had to be this way. She's not the same ship. A rebirth should bring a new name with it. And oh, look at her." She glanced back over her shoulder, then faced forward again with a brilliant smile. "She'll be the most dazzling ship in the galaxy when we get her in orbit. Prime Crafter Bylwytin," she added in a stronger tone, "I commend you and your team on this work of art. You've created the envy of both the Protectorate and the Confederated Worlds. Prime Builder Eroles? Let's take her up where she belongs."

For the next half hantick, Tal watched enthralled as the final preparations were made. The rolled hull cover was removed from the scaffolding, the tens of builders and scholars in the control room verified the readiness of all boosters, the sling tensions were drawn up, and the announcers checked on the ship's pilot, sitting with her backup on an otherwise empty bridge.

"Not much to do here yet." Candini ran a hand through her spiky hair. "But I'm activating the displays as soon as we get airborne. This is going to be the view of a lifetime."

"We'll be transmitting that view through this broadcast," the first announcer assured the audience. "Everyone will get the view of a lifetime. First Pilot Tesseron, no offense, but I sincerely hope your presence there is superfluous."

"So do I," Tesseron said seriously. "It'll be a new record. The hardest I ever worked and trained, just to sit on my hands and do nothing."

"Not quite the same thing as flying a fighter, is it?" asked the second announcer.

"Fahla, no. But there's a majesty in piloting a Savior-class warship that you won't find anywhere else. My first time in the pilot's chair on the *Phoenix*—whew. Best moment of my life."

"Hoi," Candini said in mock indignation. "I thought that was your first flight with me, right after this ship crashed."

He shrugged. "My standards are higher now."

Tal laughed along with the announcers. Candini had developed into a leader who could be at ease with her subordinates while commanding their respect. Her promotion to Chief Pilot of the Alsean Fleet Fighter Force—or the AF3, as it had come to be known—had raised no objections despite her species. No Alsean could yet match her for either flight or training skills, though Tesseron was getting close. He was her obvious successor and the clear choice for this mission.

The scene shifted back to the shuttle, where Eroles was checking her reader card. "All preparations are complete. We are ready to launch. Admiral Serrado?"

Ekatya turned around with a questioning look.

"As the Prime Builder, it is my right and privilege to give the order for this launch, the culmination of four and a half cycles of work. I hereby cede that right to you."

Tal sat up straight.

"You didn't know she would do that?" Lhyn asked.

"I had no idea."

Ekatya was clearly shocked. "Prime Builder, I—I don't know what to say."

"It was your decision to save Alsea at all costs that resulted in the crash of this ship. It should be your order that sends it back to the stars."

This was restitution on a global and historical stage. Two and a half cycles earlier, Anjuli Eroles had indirectly revealed Ekatya's divine tyree status to the Protectorate. Though the error was inadvertent, Ekatya had paid a high price for it.

"Well done, Anjuli," Tal whispered.

Onscreen, Ekatya lifted a hand. Their palms touched in a private moment viewed by hundreds of millions.

"Thank you, Prime Builder. I accept." She interlaced their fingers and held her gaze for several pipticks, then let go and turned back to her console. "Moving to the safe zone."

The broadcast stayed focused on their cockpit, allowing the audience to see through their windshield as Ekatya flew east, then turned in place and hovered. Ahead, the ship and its scaffolding filled their view.

"Launch team," Ekatya said crisply. "This is Admiral Serrado. Initialize on my mark."

The view changed to one taken by a vidcam mounted beneath the ship, looking down its length at the bases of eighty scaffolds, the fusion boosters they held, and the forty slings stretched between them.

"Three. Two. One. Mark."

Eighty fusion engines burst into life, turning the shadowy scene into one of light and roiling air as hot exhaust filled the airspace. They rose as one, slowly clearing their scaffolds.

For a heart-stopping moment, Tal thought the operation had gone wrong. The ship did not budge. Then she remembered what Eroles had said about the slings being unable to reach maximum tension until they bore the full weight of their load.

"There she goes," one of the announcers breathed.

The broadcast returned to Ekatya's shuttle. From this angle, it was easier to see the change as the ship rose from its bed of scaffolds. It moved so slowly that Tal clenched her fists, willing it upward.

"All slings at optimal tension and holding steady," Kameha reported. "The load is balanced and secure. Boosters at optimal positions. Beginning Phase Two."

Now the ship rose faster, its belly clearing the tops of the scaffolds. At long last, it was fully in the air.

Salomen's hand covered one of Tal's fists, urging her to unclench it. Tal seized her hand instead, too tense not to be gripping something.

Onscreen, they were now on the ship's bridge, where Candini let out an exhilarated whoop. "Look at that!" she cried, pointing down.

The bridge displays were fully active, the central dais appearing to float in the sky. Beneath it, the ground was dropping away.

She and Tesseron grabbed their armrests as the bridge shuddered.

"Booster failure," Kameha's voice said calmly. "Number fifty-three. Compensating."

They were back in the shuttle, where Kameha's fingers danced over a control board in his lap.

"Shutting down boosters fifty-three and fifty-four. Rebalancing."

Through the windshield, they saw two boosters drop toward the ground, their sling rippling between them. Small parachutes erupted, slowing their descent.

"No need for alarm," Eroles said. "We planned for this. There is more than enough redundancy."

"No more vibrations," Candini reported.

"Excellent. Admiral, I'd like a visual."

"Acknowledged." Ekatya moved the shuttle forward and flew a circuit around the ship as it continued to rise. The view from this close was nothing short of spectacular as they passed booster after booster, all straining under the load but working in smooth harmony.

"Seventy-eight boosters at optimal positions and power loads," Kameha said. "Altitude two thousand strides."

"Two thousand!" Tal exclaimed. "Already?"

"Time flies when you're wetting yourself," Micah joked.

"That's the truth and a half," Lhyn said.

The screen filled with a view directly from the bridge display feed. The scaffolding below already looked like a small thicket of twigs, the bare ground where the ship had been no more than an oval of brown against the green fields. Steadily, the oval shrank.

Now the broadcast split the scene, leaving the bridge display on one side while the other showed the view from one of the vidcams at the periphery. Ekatya's shuttle paced the ship upward, tiny in comparison to the behemoth rising through the skies.

Tal's heart thudded against her ribcage. This was the most dangerous part of the launch: high enough to kill Candini and Tesseron should more boosters fail, low enough to preclude any possible measures to save them or the ship's integrity.

"They'll make it," Salomen said quietly. "You heard Alejandra. Eroles is competence personified, and Kameha is the best."

"I know." She forced herself to loosen her grip on Salomen's hand. "It's just difficult to sit here and watch someone else take the risk."

Salomen wrapped her free arm around Tal's shoulders and pulled her in. Nestled together, they watched the ship rise.

At six thousand strides, the broadcast gave up on the local vidcams, which could not fly high enough to show the ship as anything more than a featureless egg shape. Once again, the audience watched through the ship's bridge display and the shuttle's windshield. On the bridge display, Blacksun had come into view in the east.

At ten thousand strides, Blacksun was a toy city, its wheel-and-spoke layout clear to see as it bestrode the junction of two great rivers.

At twenty thousand, Tal began to relax. Should a disaster occur now, Candini had a chance to control the crash, just as she had the first time.

At thirty thousand, she let go of Salomen's hand and snuggled into her side. The measurements changed to lengths, shrinking the numbers while Alsea shrank beneath the ship. The rate of ascent quickened as gravity lost its hold and the ship's weight diminished.

Two hundred lengths up, all of Blacksun Basin could be seen, as well as the white peaks of the Snowmount Range, Fahlinor Bay, and half the east coast of Argolis. The *Seventh Star* was now in low orbit. Should it be necessary, Candini could fire up the engines and take over the ascent with almost zero risk. Still they waited, letting the fusion boosters lift the ship to an altitude that gave them more "wiggle room," as Ekatya had put it. Even if the engines failed to come up to full power, there would be plenty of time to send a team over from the *Phoenix* for repairs.

At three hundred lengths, they could see the southern half of the Argolis continent and the northern coastline of Pallea.

At three hundred and fifty, the *Phoenix* slid into view, watching over its sister ship.

"They're like two-egg twins," Salomen said. "So similar, yet so different."

"I always thought the *Phoenix* was the most beautiful ship I served on," Alejandra said. "But the *Seventh Star* makes her look plain. The white hull, the artwork . . . just glorious."

Onscreen, Ekatya spoke for the first time in several ticks.

"Chief Pilot Candini, initialize engines."

"Acknowledged." Candini was all business now, her expression serious and her hands moving lightly over the console. "Fusion reaction underway. Temperature and pressure rising."

Tal inhaled and let it out slowly. The *Seventh Star* had not brought its engines to full power since the crash. This was the true test.

"No leaks or fractures detected," Candini reported. "All systems nominal. Temperature and pressure rising at acceptable rates."

"From a cold start," Prime Builder Eroles said, "the engines take four point six ticks to reach a sufficient power level for normal operations. We checked and tested every part of these engines on the ground, but for safety reasons, we could never allow the fusion reaction to reach full power."

"So now we wait," Kameha said.

"Now we wait and trust in the skills of our builders and scholars. Stand by."

"As if we could do anything else," Lhyn grumbled. "Ekatya must be ready to chew through a tension bolt right now."

Tal watched the curve of Alsea through the shuttle windshield and marveled that with such a view, she could be worrying about engine pressure.

"Threshold approaching," Candini said after an eternity. "Three, two, one . . . there we are. Engines at full operational power!"

"Is it holding?" Kameha asked. "No surges?"

"Too soon to tell, Chief, keep your shirt on."

"We'd never guess those two have known each other for cycles," the first announcer said dryly.

"True words," said the second. "But I'd rather hear them like this than fully professional, wouldn't you? If they're at ease, we have nothing to worry about."

"I'm not worried. Do I look worried?"

"Stop chewing your thumbnail and ask me again."

Tal chuckled in spite of herself. They were doing a good job of distracting viewers during this tense period of nothing happening on screen.

"Admiral Serrado," Candini said suddenly.

"Serrado here. How does it look?"

"Admiral." Her voice was grave. "I have to report that . . . every single indicator is normal and the *Seventh Star* is ready to roll!"

"Candini—oh, for the love of flight." Ekatya was laughing. "You meant it literally."

All of Alsea saw the *Seventh Star* lift herself away from the boosters and spin gracefully through two complete barrel rolls. On the half of the screen devoted to the ship's bridge, Candini let out a whoop of pure joy.

"She's alive and kicking!" she called out. "Come on over, Admiral, your ship is waiting for you."

"Give me a few ticks," Ekatya responded. "We've got seventy-eight boosters to take care of first."

"Sending 'go home' command," Kameha said.

In perfect synchrony, thirty-nine boosters released their grip on the slings, flipped around, and shot back toward Alsea. The remaining thirty-nine reeled in the slings, tucking them into tight cylinders and housing them in compartments that opened for the purpose. Newly streamlined, they reversed direction and followed their brethren.

"The boosters will be landing back at the launch site," Eroles explained for the viewers. "We'll inspect them, make any necessary repairs, and reuse them for our next launch."

Kameha grinned up at her. "Nice to have proven the technology, isn't it?"

"Oh, yes." Eroles allowed her delight to show for the first time. "The possibilities now are endless!"

"Candini," Ekatya asked, "is the shuttle bay pressurized?"

"Still full of healthy Alsean air, Admiral. The doors are open and force fields are in place. I've even turned on the gravity plating."

"Very well. We're coming in."

The broadcast closed out the view from the bridge, now devoting its full space to the vidcam in the shuttle as Ekatya flew toward her ship. Despite the enormous distance separating them, Tal thought she could sense the merest brush of her emotions.

Fanciful, perhaps, yet stranger things had happened.

She watched raptly as the gleaming ship drew nearer, its white hull reflecting light from the planet beneath. Soon it filled the windshield. A dark square loomed before them, and they passed into the narrow confines of the exit tunnel, familiar green guidance lights flashing down its length. Ekatya emerged into the vast, empty bay and set her shuttle down without so much as a vibration, from what Tal could see.

"We're in and securing the shuttle," she said. "Have a cup of shannel ready for me on the bridge."

The split screen returned, showing Candini looking flummoxed. "Er, we're going to need Kameha to power up those systems, Admiral."

"You mean you didn't bring a flask from home?" Ekatya pulled a thermal flask from a console and held it up for the vidcam. "I never leave without it."

She rose from her seat, the vidcam following as she activated the door release and walked down the ramp, Kameha and Eroles close behind. They crossed the empty space and vanished through a door, while the announcers explained that until all systems were brought online, the maglifts were unpowered. Admiral Serrado, Prime Builder Eroles, and Chief Kameha would be using chases and brace shafts to reach the bridge. The vidcam—which was using the shuttle's quantum com as a relay—could not follow.

In the interim, the scene shifted to the control room, where a party was in progress as the builders and scholars celebrated their success. Footage taken in the room during the launch was now aired, showing utter silence and worried faces when the faulty booster was dropped with its partner, increasing hope as the ship rose, more silent tension while waiting for the engines to reach critical threshold, and finally the moment when Candini announced the successful restart.

Tal's pregnancy hormones leaked from her eyes again as a roomful of focused professionals leaped from their seats, laughing and crying while they touched palms and gestured ecstatically at the scene on the wall display. Tears rolled down many faces when they watched Candini's barrel roll, even as their grins threatened to blind the vidcam's optics.

Salomen handed her a kerchief.

"Thank you," Tal said, drying her eyes. "Maybe by the time it's my turn again, the healers will have found a solution for this hormone problem."

Alejandra laughed loudly. "That's why I like you. You're a dreamer."

"Yes, she is," Micah agreed. "But dreams are what made this day possible."

With the kerchief balled in one hand, Tal placed a call. Onscreen, the control room director waved his arms, quieting the party.

"Hoi, hoi, I've got someone wanting to talk to us!" In a lower voice, he added, "You're on the speaker."

"This is Lancer Tal. I had two speeches prepared for you today. One of them I discarded the moment Chief Pilot Candini rolled the *Seventh Star*."

The project workers burst into applause, accompanied by whoops and cheers.

"The other I'm setting aside as well, because you don't need to hear what a historic moment this is. You know it. You're living it. What I want to say is simply this: congratulations. You have done a spectacular job and made all of us proud. Alsea now has two paths to the stars and a bright future indeed."

More cheers, a few whistles, and many expectant faces. They were waiting for more.

"If I know Admiral Serrado, and I do—" She paused for the laughter. "She'll be on the bridge in another tick. So I won't linger. But before I go, allow me to offer a more physical manifestation of Alsean gratitude for your performance. If you'll open the control room doors, you'll find it sitting outside."

Two builders standing nearest the doors looked at each other in surprise, then raced to open them. The vidcam zoomed in on the stack of crates.

"Glasses are in the two crates on top," she said. "Drink a toast to yourselves first. You deserve it. After that, I leave it up to you. Enjoy!"

She ended the call, savoring the roar of approval as project workers swarmed the crates, unpacking glasses and bottles of Valkinon and handing them out.

"Right, I'll ask," Lhyn said. "How did you manage that? You've been with us the whole time and haven't made a call."

"I had it delivered this morning. Once they closed their doors for the prelaunch, no one was going to open them again."

"But what if it hadn't worked?"

"Ah. I had two deliveries, in truth. If the launch failed, they'd have found grain spirits instead of Valkinon."

"Appropriate for drowning sorrows," Micah said approvingly. "I'm glad it wasn't necessary."

"Words for Fahla," Alejandra agreed.

The view shifted from partying project workers to the bridge of the *Seventh Star*, where the pilots jumped to their feet and saluted. "Admiral on deck!" Candini called.

"Settle." Ekatya strode across the bridge, looking very much at home. Behind her, Kameha and Eroles veered off to the engineering and operations consoles on the lowest tier, while Ekatya walked up to the second level to greet Candini and an awed-looking Tesseron. "Well done, both of you. Let's get this ship operational."

What surprised Tal more than anything else was how quickly the ship's primary systems were brought online. After the fraught lift to orbit and the lengthy wait for the engines, it seemed as if the rest should take considerable time. But as Ekatya had told her earlier, and the announcers explained now, the ship was built for a quick recovery from any interruption in power. In a battle, those resilient systems could be the difference between life and death.

"Prime Builder," Ekatya said, "please call the *Phoenix* and put it on the upper display."

"With pleasure."

Tal found it jarring to see the Prime Builder working an operations console like a junior officer, but it was clear that Eroles was having the time of her life. She entered the final command with a firm tap that made her bracelets chime. "I have the *Phoenix* on the com."

Ekatya looked up at a familiar face on the display. "Captain Sayana. I hope you don't mind a little company up here."

"Mind? I couldn't be more delighted. The *Seventh Star* is a splendid ship with a brilliant name. And a decent temporary pilot."

"Hoi!" Candini protested. "I'd like to see you find a better one!"

One side of Rahel's mouth tilted up. "Admiral, your shakedown team is in our shuttle bay, ready to transfer to their new home and duties. Is the *Seventh Star* prepared to receive?"

"Ready and waiting, Captain."

Rahel ordered the launch, and the coverage switched to a new location: the *Phoenix*'s shuttle bay, where viewers followed a group of excited staff as they boarded the largest shuttle. Though most were Alsean, four stood out for their smooth foreheads: Gaians who had once called themselves hangers or slaves and were now known as members of the Confederated Worlds. The term "Voloth" had shifted its meaning on Alsea, becoming a pejorative not used in polite company.

Ekatya's new crew members settled into their seats, smiling widely and offering greetings to the vidcam as it floated through the shuttle to the cockpit. This part of the program was the result of a suggestion from Rahel, who had pointed out that few Alseans had any idea what their orbital lives were like, so why not take them along for the ride?

Thus viewers were treated to a front-seat vantage point as the shuttle rose from the deck, traversed the exit tunnel, and emerged into space. They were there during the flight, the landing next to Ekatya's shuttle on the *Seventh Star*, and the maglift ride to the bridge. They watched the staff take over various consoles and explain their purposes as, one by one, secondary and tertiary systems were brought online. In a particularly interesting segment, they followed three engineers down to the engine cradle to watch the gigantic surf engines as Candini ran the ship through a series of piloting tests.

For the next hantick, the screen shifted between interior views of the two crews at work, and exterior footage taken by accompanying fighters as the *Seventh Star* engaged in shakedown maneuvers and the *Phoenix* kept pace. The two ships circled, spiraled, dipped into the thermosphere, and danced through space in a ballet that occasionally had Tal in tears. She hid them from the others, but Salomen pulled her close each time.

"She's come a long way, hasn't she?" Salomen asked as they watched Rahel give orders with easy confidence.

Tal nodded. "It's hard to believe that Ekatya had to talk her into accepting."

"She wouldn't have for anyone else. Those two were brought together by Fahla. She once told me that Ekatya knew what it meant to be an outcaste. She said she wouldn't wish that on anyone, but it did mean that Ekatya understood her in a way others couldn't. That made her the perfect instructor."

"I think it worked both ways," Tal said. "Rahel understands her, too. They've taught each other."

Rahel had flourished under Ekatya's tutelage, growing into a commanding officer known for both honor and compassion. She believed in second chances, and the Alsean and Confederated crew of the *Phoenix*, prone to mistakes as they learned their new duties, came to see her as their de facto leader long before she took over the command chair.

She was onscreen now, congratulating Ekatya and her tiny crew on the successful performance of the *Seventh Star*. With the tests concluded, the broadcast was coming to its end.

"Before we turn off these vidcams," Rahel said, "I wonder if you'd like to test those engines one more time? Something different, just to see how good your temp pilot really is."

Ekatya could not hide her amusement. "A race, Captain? To where?"

"Around the sun, six million lengths above the surface, and back to the space elevator. Loser buys a round for both commanding officer and pilot at the winner's favorite bar."

"If I were still in the Protectorate Fleet, I'd have to give you a stern lecture on proper conduct for an officer on duty and appropriate usage of Fleet property." Ekatya let her smile break free. "Since I'm in the Alsean Fleet, my answer can be much shorter. Captain, I believe you've maligned the superior abilities of my pilot. Obviously we'll have to address that. I accept the challenge."

"Get your cinteks ready," Candini called. "You're paying."

"We'll see. Give me one tick, please."

Tal's earcuff alerted her to a call she hadn't expected. The com code was a familiar one, and she answered with no preliminaries.

"Are you calling for a judge?"

Onscreen, Rahel nodded as she spoke quietly. "Will you?"

"Gladly. Put me on."

"Thank you." In a normal tone, Rahel said, "I've procured a neutral judge for the competition. Lancer Tal?"

"I'm happy to oblige. On your return, fly past the elevator dock. I'll tap into the external cam there and watch. Take your starting positions."

As the crews prepared, Tal's attention was drawn to Rahel's uniform jacket, made unique by its two producer-green armbands. Her status as the Bondlancer's sworn warrior had earned the envy of half the population. Salomen's courage and great heart gave her title more meaning than it had carried in generations, and Rahel was nearly as famous for their association as she was in her own right.

Tal lifted Salomen's hand for a kiss, then held it in both of her own.

"What was that for?" Salomen whispered.

She muted the call. "I have one tyree with her hands in the soil and another with her head in the stars. The two of you keep me in perfect balance. Our child will be born into such love, just like Little Chunk."

"For the love of Fahla," Alejandra grumbled. "Not you, too."

Micah's smirk melted into a softer expression as he watched them.

"I feel . . ." She trailed off, searching for the right word.

"Blessed," Salomen said. With her free hand, she reached for Lhyn. "Beyond any of our dreams."

"My stars, yes." Lhyn met her reach. "Not just beyond our dreams. Beyond our fantasies."

"Always the linguist," Salomen teased.

"Lancer Tal," Ekatya said onscreen. "We're ready."

Tal looked up at the vidscreen, showing the bridges of Alsea's two warships. A tap unmuted her earcuff, and she closed her eyes, letting her empathic senses absorb the perfection of this day.

"On my mark," she said, squeezing Salomen's hand once more.

"Begin."

GLOSSARY

UNITS OF TIME

piptick: one hundredth of a tick (about half a second).

tick: about a minute (50 seconds).

tentick: ten ticks.

hantick: ten tenticks, just shy of 1.5 hours (83.33 minutes). One Alsean day is twenty hanticks (27.7 hours) or 1.15 days.

moon: a basic unit of Alsean time, similar to our month but 36 days long. Each moon is divided into four parts called **ninedays**. One Alsean moon equals 41.55 stellar (Earth) days.

cycle: the length of time it takes the Alsean planet to revolve around their sun (thirteen moons or approximately seventeen stellar months).

Alsean days are divided into quarters, each five hanticks long, which reset at the end of the eve quarter. The quarters are: **night, morn, mid, and**

eve. A specific hantick can be expressed in one of two ways: its place in the quarter or its exact number. Thus morn-three would be three hanticks into the morning quarter, which can also be expressed as hantick eight (the five hanticks of the night quarter plus three of the morning). In the summer, the long days result in sunrise around morn-one (hantick six), lunch or midmeal at mid-one (hantick eleven), dinner or evenmeal at eve-one (hantick sixteen), and sunset around eve-five (hantick twenty).

UNITS OF MEASUREMENT

pace: half a stride.

stride: the distance of a normal adult's stride at a fast walk (about a meter).

length: a standard of distance equaling one thousand strides (about a kilometer).

GENERAL TERMS

ADF: Alsean Defense Force.

AIF: Alsean Investigative Force.

bana: an endearment between lovers or bondmates.

block: the emotional equivalent of fingers in the ears; a mental protection that prevents one from sensing another's emotions.

bondmate: a life partner.

cinnoralis: a tree valued for its aromatic leaves (which are dried and burned for relaxation purposes) and the rich, brown color of its wood, used in woodworking and carpentry.

cintek: the Alsean monetary unit.

crateskate: a motorized platform for easily moving large crates or heavy equipment.

dartfly: a small, bloodsucking fly known for its speed and agility.

deme: honorific for a secular scholar.

dokker: a farm animal similar to a cow. Slow moving and rather stupid, but with a hell of a kick when it's angry or frightened.

dokshin: vulgar term for dokker feces.

empath (low, mid, high): the three measured levels of Alsean empathic sensitivity. Low empaths normally detect emotions only through skin contact. Mid empaths can detect emotions without touch, but only at short distances. High empaths can sense emotions at significant distances and are also capable of projecting emotions onto others.

evenmeal: dinner.

Fahla: the goddess of the Alseans, also called Mother.

fairy fly: a pollinating insect famous for its camouflaging ability and gossamer wings.

fanten: a farm animal similar to a pig, used for meat.

front: a mental protection that prevents one's emotions from being sensed by another. Selective emotions can be fronted; a "perfect front" refers to a protection so solid that no emotions can be sensed at all.

gender-locked: an Alsean who is unable to temporarily shift genders for the purposes of reproduction. Considered a grave handicap, denying the individual the full blessing of Fahla.

grainbird: a small, black-and-red bird common in agricultural fields. It is known for singing even at night, leading to an old perception of the birds as lacking in intelligence—hence *grainbird* is also a slang term for an idiot.

grainstem powder: powder derived from the crushed stems of a particular grain, which yields a sweet taste. Commonly used in cooking; also used to sprinkle over fresh bread.

hairgrass: a tall grass covered with soft, silky hairs.

hangers: the middle echelon in the Voloth Empire, higher than slaves but much lower than citizens.

holcat: a small, domesticated feline.

hornstalk: a thorny, fast-growing weed.

horten: an Alsean delicacy, often used in soup. It comes from a plant that, once harvested, stays fresh for a very short time and must be processed immediately.

hyacot: a tree whose twigs, when snapped, provide a pleasant and long-lasting scent. Used in fine restaurants and as a room freshener.

joining: sexual relations. Joining is considered less significant than Sharing between lovers. The two acts can take place simultaneously, though this would only occur in a serious relationship.

leafthrum: a large, arboreal insect known for its nocturnal mating calls, which can be heard at great distances.

losslyn: the Alsean male reproductive organ, which takes five days to produce a sperm packet. The name means "hidden seed," referring to the fact that a losslyn is rarely visible except during a creation ceremony.

magtran: a form of public transport consisting of a chain of cylindrical passenger carriers accelerated by magnetic fields through transparent tubes.

marmello: a sweet, orange fruit.

midmeal: lunch.

molwine: the curved apex of the pelvic ridges on both male and female Alseans. A very sensitive sexual organ.

molwyn: Fahla's sacred tree. It has a black trunk and leaves with silver undersides. A molwyn grows at the center of every temple of decent size.

moonbird: a bird with brilliant courtship feathers that it spreads to impress a mate. Also engages in a graceful courtship dance.

mornmeal: breakfast.

mountzar: a large, carnivorous animal that lives at high elevations and hibernates during the winter.

palm touch: the standard greeting among Alseans in which two people touch their hands together, palm to palm, at eye level. The skin contact allows an exchange of emotions regardless of empathic sensitivity. It is impossible to lie during a palm touch. A **double palm touch** is done only among very close friends or family.

panfruit: a common breakfast or dessert fruit, with an orange skin and blood-red pulp.

Pit (the): Alsea's highest security prison, consisting of five underground levels. It is reserved for empathic offenders; the underground location prevents outside contact and weak points. The worst, most violent offenders are housed in the fifth level.

posthead: heavy wooden mallet used for driving stakes without splintering them.

probe: to push beyond the front and read emotions that are not available for a surface skim. Probing without permission is a violation of Alsean law.

rajalta: a spicy drink made by adding toasted seeds to shannel. A famous Whitesun specialty.

reader card: a portable computing device composed of a flexible material that rolls into a cylinder and tucks into a pouch worn at the belt. Reader cards unroll and stiffen into a sheet for use, then relax and roll back up for storage.

Return: the passage after death, in which an Alsean returns to Fahla and embarks on the next plane of existence.

Rite of Ascension: the formal ceremony in which a child becomes a legal and social adult. The Rite takes place at twenty cycles, after which one's choice of caste cannot be changed.

sallgreen: a tree with prickly, needlelike leaves that have a pungent fragrance when crushed.

sansara: asexual.

shannel: a traditional hot drink, used for energy and freshening one's breath. Made from the dried leaves (and sometimes flowers) of the shannel plant.

skim: to sense any emotions that an Alsean is not specifically holding behind her or his front.

Sharing: the act of physically connecting the emotional centers between two or more Alseans, resulting in unshielded emotions that can be fully accessed by anyone in the Sharing link. It is most frequently done between lovers or bondmates but is also part of a bonding ceremony (in which all guests take part in a one-time Sharing with the two new bondmates). It can also be done between friends and family, or for medical purposes.

shek: vulgar slang for penetrative sex. Usually used as a profanity.

sonsales: one who is empathically blind.

Termegon Fields: the home of the Seeders, according to Voloth belief.

tintinatalus: a tree with silver wood used in woodworking.

torquat: a slimy, swamp-dwelling mammal that has expanded to numerous worlds in the Protectorate due to its ability to thrive in sewer systems. Often used as a pejorative.

tyrees: Alseans whose empathic centers share a rare compatibility, which has physiological consequences. Tyrees can sense each other's emotions at greater distances than normal, have difficulty being physically apart, and are ferociously protective of each other. Tyrees are always bonded, usually for life.

vallcat: a large, solitary feline species, striped for camouflage in the open grasslands they inhabit. Vallcats are known for their strength and ferocity, though they do not attack Alseans unless provoked.

warmron: an embrace. Warmrons are shared only between lovers, or parents and children—and then just until the child reaches the Rite of Ascension. A warmron is too close to a Sharing for it to be used at any other time.

winden: a large six-toed mammal, adapted to an alpine environment. It is wary, able to climb nearly sheer walls, and the fastest animal on Alsea. Winden travel in herds and are rarely seen.

winterbloom: a small, low-growing plant that flowers in the cold seasons. Its leaves have a fresh, invigorating scent.

wristcom: a wrist-mounted communication device, often used in conjunction with an earcuff.

zalren: a venomous snake.

Published by Heartsome Publishing
Staffordshire
United Kingdom

ISBN: 978-1-912684-86-1
First Heartsome edition: July 2020

Book cover design by ebooklaunch.com
Molwyn tree illustration by João T. Tavares/GOBIUS

ABOUT THE AUTHOR

Fletcher DeLancey is an Oregon expatriate who left her beloved state when she met a Portuguese woman and had to choose between home and heart. She chose heart. Now she lives in the beautiful, sunny Algarve and is retraining her green thumb from wet Oregon gardening to survive-a-Mediterranean-summer gardening (and thinks about writing a new book: *How I Learned to Love Succulents*).

She is best known for her science fiction/fantasy series Chronicles of Alsea, which has so far collected an Independent Publisher's Award, a Golden Crown Literary Society Award, a Rainbow Award, and been shortlisted twice for the Lambda Literary Award. She has also been awarded the Alice B. Medal in recognition of career achievement.

Fletcher believes that women need far more representation in science fiction and fantasy, and takes great pleasure in writing complex stories with women heading up the action. Her day is made every time another reader says, "I didn't think I liked science fiction, but then I read yours."

All about Alsea: alseaworld.com

facebook.com/fletcherdelanceyauthor

twitter.com/AlseaAuthor

goodreads.com/FletcherD

amazon.com/author/fletcher

ALSO BY FLETCHER DELANCEY

The Chronicles of Alsea series:

The Caphenon

Without A Front: The Producer's Challenge

Without A Front: The Warrior's Challenge

Catalyst

Vellmar the Blade

Outcaste

Resilience

Uprising

Alsea Rising: Gathering Storm

Alsea Rising: The Seventh Star

Available worldwide in paperback and ebook.

Made in the USA
Monee, IL
28 August 2020

40165067R00239